GREEN LIGHT

LLOYD C. DOUGLAS

UNABRIDGED

PAN BOOKS LTD : LONDON

First published 1935 by Peter Davies Ltd.
This edition published 1966 by Pan Books Ltd.,
33 Tothill Street, London, S.W.1.

ISBN 0 330 20126 3

2nd Printing 1973

Printed in Great Britain by
Hunt Barnard Printing Ltd., Aylesbury,
Buckinghamshire.

Elgin Academy

SIC ITUR AD ASTRA

CLASS _III A_

Russian

PRIZE

AWARDED TO

Lorraine Wilson

Session 19 _74_ - 19 _75_

A. J. GLASHAN, B.Sc.
Rector.

G. MILNE, PRINTER, ELGIN

By the same author in Pan Books

MAGNIFICENT OBSESSION
THE ROBE
THE BIG FISHERMAN

This book is dedicated
with esteem and affection to
A. O. DAWSON
of Montreal

Chapter One

UNCOMMONLY sensitive to her owner's moods – for he had imputed personality to her – Dr Paige's rakish blue coupé noted at a glance that this was one of those eventful mornings when she would be expected to steer her own course to Parkway Hospital.

The signs of Dr Paige's preoccupation were unmistakable. Sylvia, who usually plunged through the street door of the Hermitage Apartments wagging her tawny tail from a hinge located in the lumbar region, was following her broad-shouldered master with an air of gravity absurdly appropriate to the serious concern of his flexed jaw and far-away eyes. Pete, the garage boy, instead of loitering to tell the young surgeon what kind of day it was, had ambled off without venturing the customary amenities valued at a quarter.

Assured that her entire family was safely aboard, the coupé hummed a subdued monody on her twelve well-organized cylinders, and glided into action. Reckless of Sylvia's precarious dignity on the slippery rumble seat, she illegally swung herself around in the middle of the busy block, narrowly missing a ten-ton removal-van, and earning an impolite salutation from the burly driver of a gasoline tank. Dusting apprehensive fenders for a half mile on Elm, she nonchalantly scraped the whole arc of the right kerb at the corner of Euclid, made pretence of colour blindness at One Hundred and Eighty Sixth, where she knew the cop, grazed a hub cap at the narrow entrance gate, forced an empty ambulance into the dogwood bushes as she scudded round the big stone building, and demobilized a small convention of smoke stealing orderlies in the parking ground at the rear.

Pleased with her undamaged arrival, she belatedly made a great show of professional poise, by rolling to a discreet stop on the crunching gravel between Dr Armstrong's sand coloured sedan and the five year old roadster of Dr Lane, who at that moment was noisily tuning up for departure.

Sighting the small car sliding into the stall beside him, the grey haired anæsthetist turned off his cyclone and nodded a greeting without enthusiasm.

'Where to?' queried Paige. 'We're doing that tuberculous kidney at nine.'

'Not till tomorrow,' explained Lane discontentedly.

'What's the trouble?'

'Oh – Endicott has been detained somehow. Just now phoned from Harrisburg or some place. Business conference or something. Back in the morning, or some time. I wish he had given orders for you to go ahead with it.'

Paige, still at the wheel, absently lifted an expressive hand, and with a single flick of the fingers acknowledged the compliment and dismissed the suggestion.

'The lady is Dr Endicott's patient, Lane. Came here especially to have him – and quite properly, too,' he added meaningly, almost militantly, after a frosty pause.

'Of course!' agreed Lane, too fervently to be convincing. 'I said I wished you were doing this Dexter excision because I dislike these postponements. They're too hard on the patient's morale. Once you've got a case all nerved up for an operation, it's—'

The banal platitude perished of its own stupidity under the unfocused steel blue stare. Paige wasn't hearing a word; just sitting there glowering at a distant ghost. What was eating him? Lane guessed – and thought he knew.

Silently curious and more than a little perturbed, he watched the athletic young fellow's abstracted movements as he locked the gears, stepped out of his car, chained the whimpering setter to the steering wheel, and mechanically moved away without another word or a backward glance. It wasn't like Newell Paige to do that.

With narrowed eyes he broodingly followed the tall figure towards the rear entrance, a bit hurt but not offended. He liked young Paige, often wondering why; for, as a passionate

8

social radical, Lane was naturally contemptuous of the well-to-do.

He chuckled a little, Dr Benjamin Montgomery Booth – specialist in radium, with a degree from Edinburgh, one of Paige's most intimate friends – had just been curtly disposed of with the briefest of nods as they encountered each other in the doorway. Bennie Booth's open mouthed expression of bewilderment was amusing. Paige was playing no favourites; he evidently had something important on his mind.

Lane's grin changed to a reflective scowl. Drawing a tiny red book from his ticket pocket, he moistened his thumb and extracted a thin leaf; brought up a small hard package of cheap tobacco, opened it, tilted it, peppered the leaf expertly, tugged the package shut with two fingers and his teeth, rolled a cigarette, ran his tongue along the margin, struck a match, inhaled deeply, all the while reminiscently spinning the reel of Paige's singular relationship to the celebrated Endicott.

It was a dramatic story, the first spectacular episode of which had been witnessed by a very small audience. Lane, himself, knew it only from hearsay, for he had been a mere stripling at the tail of a muddy ambulance in France when Jim Paige died, here at Parkway, of a swift pneumonia, following the malignant flu that had mown a broad swath through the hospitals after the manner of a medieval pestilence.

His old friend Sandy McIntyre, long since a lung specialist in Phoenix, had once recited that initial chapter for Lane in a dusty day coach on the Santa Fe inexpensively *en route* from Chicago to the Coast.

'I understand Jim's boy is working now at Parkway,' McIntyre had remarked in the course of their shop talk. 'Does he still take such good care of his hands?'

'Hadn't noticed,' Lane remembered having replied. 'Why?'

McIntyre had grinned broadly.

'They used to say that when the kid was thirteen or so he would sit on the fence and watch the rest of 'em play ball. Willing to play tennis, sail a boat, ride a horse, dive from high places, and almost anything else requiring speed, skill, and courage, but he wouldn't play baseball for fear of damaging his

9

fingers. Said he was going to be a surgeon. Took up the violin, not because he wanted to be a musician, but to improve the dexterity of his left hand. They tell me that chap could walk right on to a stage and play the fiddle along with the best of 'em if he wanted to. Newell's a chip off the old block. You should have known Jim.'

Sandy had followed with a dreamily reflective monologue. He had been Jim's classmate through their medical training. Knew all about him. He had also known the incomparable Sally Newell.

'As a student,' McIntyre had recounted meditatively, 'I used to think that Jim was the luckiest chap of my acquaintance. Boy! – he had everything! Plenty of money, and mighty generous with it, too. Handsome as a Greek god. Brilliant student. Born surgeon, if there ever was one. Not quite so audacious as Endicott, who was seven years his senior and already making a name for himself, but in a fair way to be as competent when he had had the experience.

'Never knew anybody as serious as he was about his profession,' McIntyre had rumbled on, half to himself. 'They ragged him about it a good deal when we were in school. You remember, Lane, the sort of fooling that goes on among cocky young medicals, as if the whole business was full of hanky-panky. Can't blame 'em much; just sensitive, scared youngsters, trying to build up some kind of defence apparatus against the screams and shocking sights and stupefying stinks of a big hospital. But Jim hated their kidding about it.

'I recall one cruelly hot afternoon when Brute Spangler – best diagnostician we ever had, but hard boiled as the handles o' hell – was leading a flock of us through the open ward of the women's surgical, he growled at Jim, out of the corner of his mouth, "Cheer up, Father Paige. We're not doing the stations of the cross." Jim's heavy black brows drew together into one straight line, and looking down into Spangler's beady little eyes, he said, without a smile, "No – we're not, unfortunately. Perhaps that's what ails us!"

'And then – there was Sally Newell——'

There had been a long pause at this point in McIntyre's

memories. They had made a tedious job of reloading their pipes to account for the delay.

'Paige's wife?' Lane had queried at length, knowing the answer.

'It was an ideal match,' declared McIntyre. 'Most beautiful girl I ever saw. You may be sure it hadn't required old Oliver Newell's money to make her the exact centre of interest wherever she went.'

Lane, who had taken more than a merely inquisitive interest in psychoanalysis, would have liked to ask a few pertinent questions at this point, but had hesitated, knowing that the lean Scot with the prominent pink cheekbones would have closed up like a clam. McIntyre didn't need anybody to inform him – even by tactful indirection – that the heart is located close to the lungs. There was another long wait while McIntyre fondled the things he had laid away in lavender.

'Nothing in my professional experience,' he continued moodily, 'ever stirred me more deeply than the wan and weary little face of their boy on the afternoon of Jim's death. Sally had gone out the same way two days before. God – how helpless we were!

'Naturally, we couldn't let the child into his father's room, for the stuff was deadly. His grandmother, Mrs Newell, waited in the sun-parlour at the end of the hall. The elder Paiges were still on their way in from California. This boy haunted the corridor for hours, his dry, bloodshot eyes fastened on the door. Every time anyone came out, there he was, eager for news and wanting to come in. I'm afraid we weren't very attentive to his questions or his grief. We had all been too worn down to be considerate.

'That was the only time I ever saw Bruce Endicott stampeded. I always maintained he was the greatest surgeon I ever knew, and I don't expect to have any occasion to change my mind about that. Never met anybody with such complete mastery over a situation. . . . Well – I drew the sheet up over Jim's cracked lips and swollen cheeks, and followed Endicott out into the hall. There was this boy – Newell. I told the nurse to go and tell Jim's mother-in-law. Endicott took the lad by the hand and he went back to the library. It was unoccupied. Nobody was patronizing the library much during that frantic period.

' "Well, sonny," began Endicott, closing the door, "we did everything we knew."

'The boy swallowed hard, a couple of times, and asked, "Is my daddy—"

' "Yes," growled Endicott, as if he were reporting some monstrous injustice, "he is; but—" he repeated lamely, "we did everything we knew."

'I fully expected to see the gallant little fellow cave in, for he was nervously exhausted from worry and loss of sleep. But he had a lot of strong stuff packed away that we didn't know about. He stood there tense, his fists clenched until his thin knuckles showed white, his babyish mouth twisted into a hard knot, looking as if he had just been struck a blow in the face. And then, to our amazement, he piped out in a shrill treble, "Now I'll have to be a doctor!"

'Endicott took a turn or two, up and down the room, muttering, "Doctor! . . . My God! . . . He wants to be a doctor!" Then he stood for a long time at the window, looking out. After a while, he came back, reached out his hand to the boy as he might have done had they been contemporaries, and controlling a shaky voice, he said, "Very good, sir. And if I may be of any service to you, I am yours to command." '

In white duck, Newell Paige emerged from the dressing-room on the top floor, where he found Frances Ogilvie. It was not a surprise. He was always meeting her.

By agreement, arrived at many months earlier, they waived the conventional greetings and restricted their talk to necessary business.

'Dr Endicott is not to be here today,' she said crisply.

'I know,' Paige replied. 'I met Dr Lane outside. Has Mrs Dexter been told of the postponement? We were to have had her first.'

Miss Ogilvie's cryptic smile was unpleasant.

'I believe not,' she said. 'The others have been notified,

but' – the carefully pencilled brows arched slightly – 'I thought you might wish to talk to Mrs Dexter yourself.' There was an inquiring pause which Dr Paige might make use of, if he desired, for purpose of explanations, denials, or just plain stammering, but he allowed the opportunity to pass. 'I understand Mrs Dexter has become very fond of you,' finished Miss Ogilvie.

'Thanks.' Paige pushed the button for the elevator.

A bit of a problem – this competent, bronze-haired, physically opulent, chief surgical nurse. Once a warm comradeship between them had been in the making, but they had spoiled it for each other beyond any hope of mending.

One stormy afternoon in March, quite exasperated over Paige's wilful inattentiveness to her rather obvious and slightly disconcerting overtures, she had impetuously tossed herself at him, with awkward results. He had been sitting alone in the laboratory for a half hour, studying an X-ray thoracic which wasn't any too generous with its disclosures. For some minutes she had stood at his elbow looking over his shoulder, before he became aware that she had no errand in the room. Her arm touched his lightly.

'Hello,' he drawled, preoccupied. 'What's the good news with you, Miss Ogilvie?'

She did not respond to the casual inanity as he had expected, and a meaningful silence ensued, of such duration that he had put the plate down on the table and turned his head in her direction, looking squarely and at very close range into a pair of questing blue-green eyes. Had the cloudy pleura been as easy to read, Paige need not have been detained in the laboratory for another moment. The girl's full lips were parted, and there was an entreating little smile on her face, so near to his that the freckles, left over from last summer, were clearly defined on her white cheeks.

'I'm lonesome as the devil – if you really want to know,' she confided, in a low tone of intimacy, adding presently, 'and my name is Frances – I hate "Miss Ogilvie".'

Paige hooked the rung of a neighbouring stool with his toe and dragged it nearer.

13

'Sit down, won't you?'

She complied with some reluctance, her half-impatient gesture and audible sigh implying a wish that she were well out of this unhappy situation.

'I like that name,' said Paige companionably. 'If the hospital regulations encouraged us to have Christian names, it would be easy to call you by yours.'

Her face brightened a little and she murmured, 'I could say yours, I think.'

'For it fits you – exactly,' continued Paige hastily. 'I don't know very many people who have as good a right to it – Saint Francis, you know,' he explained, when it had become apparent she was not following him.

The shapely lips were a little derisive as she replied, 'Rubbish! I have no ambition to be a saint. I'm all fed up with everything; silly rules, stuffy discipline, pompous doctors, jealous nurses, and earnest social welfarers. . . . Tell me something, won't you? Why do you dislike me so? I've got to know!'

'But I don't!' protested Paige sincerely. 'Quite to the contrary. I never knew an operating nurse with a more authentic talent for surgery. If I haven't told you so, it's only because I don't bubble over.'

'Just once – you did,' she muttered, with averted eyes. 'Remember the day we did the little Morton boy's osteo sarcoma?'

Paige winced at the recollection. 'My word! – that was a tough experience.'

'I kept up with you pretty well, you seemed to think, with the forceps and ties. And when it was done, you said – oh, no matter. You've probably forgotten.'

'I hope it was something pleasant.'

'It sounds awfully silly, but it meant a great deal to me. You looked me straight in the face, for the first and last time, and said, "You're a good egg!" I had never thought much about being an egg before.' They both laughed, nervously, and Paige, vastly in need of a little occupational therapy, sharpened a pencil.

'Yes,' he said reminiscently, 'that was the worst one I ever saw. The little fellow didn't have one chance in a thousand, did he?'

She sighed, rose, and moved slowly toward the door, hesitating there for a moment.

'Perhaps it would be better all around if I left Parkway, Dr Paige,' she hazarded.

'I don't see the necessity of that.' He had risen and stood facing her. 'You are needed here,' he continued, in a tone of challenge. 'My God, woman, aren't you big enough to understand that our profession is more important than our personal desires, and gets the right of way over everything – *over everything, I tell you*! Stay – and play the game!'

She studied the floor, tugging at her lip with agitated fingers.

'You saw my cards,' she said morosely. 'It isn't fair.'

'Nonsense!' scoffed Paige. 'I wasn't looking. I don't even know what suit was trump. . . . Look here – you've been working too hard, and the whole business has got on your nerves. I'll tell Dr Endicott you need a week in the country.'

'Thanks,' she said listlessly. 'There's no need of that. And – I'll stay – if you're sure you want me to.'

Paige smiled his satisfaction. 'You're a credit to the hospital,' he declared warmly. 'It's the proper spirit. I knew you had it.'

'And may I still be – an egg?' she queried, with a brave attempt to be playful.

'An uncommonly good one!' He offered her his hand.

When she got to her room that night, Frances Ogilvie found three dozen long-stemmed American Beauty roses bearing Paige's card. It was a mistake, as he discovered next day. If, he reflected afterward, he had wanted to send her some token of his regard for her excellent sportsmanship in a trying position, he should have given her a new clinical thermometer in a gold case, or *The Life of Osler*, or a dated, candied, de luxe egg. Miss Ogilvie was, as Paige had conceded, an exceptionally able operating nurse, but – long before that – she was a woman. She would make a courageous effort to play the game, but she couldn't abandon her belief that hearts were

15

trumps. So the roses, which had been intended to symbolize their friendship on a safer footing, had not cleared the air at all. Newell Paige came to dread the necessity for working in the laboratory, where he was almost sure to be brought to bay. Keenly interested in bacteriology, he had enjoyed nothing better than microscopical research, but no sooner would he be lost in his scientific problem than Frances would saunter in to bend over his shoulder, ruthlessly reckless as she pressed closely against him. He was for ever bumping into her in the corridors. She was at his heels until the whole place buzzed merrily. At length he had been obliged to be almost surly with her, to shut off the insufferable smiles and winks.

'Very well,' she agreed tartly. 'Strictly business, then, from now on. You wouldn't know how to be kind, anyhow – except possibly to your dog.'

Confused and defenceless, Paige had replied, absurdly, 'Well – Sylvia *is* a good dog.'

Mrs Lawrence Dexter's day nurse, Bunny Mather, obediently but unrewardedly studied Dr Paige's face as he entered the room.

Bunny had been given a difficult assignment. It had been suggested to her that she should try to discover the nature of Dr Paige's peculiar interest in her wealthy and prominent patient. She had so much wanted to please Miss Ogilvie, whom she admired to the extent of attempted imitation. Miss Ogilvie's fleeting smile, executed with half-closed eyes and a whimsical little pout, had cost Bunny several long sessions of private smirkings before her diminutive mirror in the nurses' home.

Unfortunately there had been almost nothing to report so far. Dr Paige had been visiting Mrs Dexter at least twice daily ever since her arrival for observation two weeks ago. She was not his patient. Dr Endicott had brought him in, that first day, to present him.

'I want you to become acquainted with my associate, Dr Newell Paige, Mrs Dexter,' he said breezily. 'You two should know each other. It is no secret, Mrs Dexter,' he had added, 'that Dr Paige is in the running to be the chief of staff here when the old fellow retires to the Lido or Waikiki Beach.'

The acquaintance ripened quickly into an unusual comradeship. Sometimes Dr Paige stayed with Mrs Dexter for an hour or more. As her disability was neither painful nor fatiguing, there was no reason why she should not receive callers if she desired. No one of her family was in town. Her husband, an investment broker in a huge Mid-Western city, would come if an operation were decided on. A daughter, Grace, at home with her father, would accompany him. There was another daughter, Phyllis, in Europe for the summer with a party of Vassar classmates. The trip was Phyllis's Commencement gift.

So little had Bunny learned about her interesting patient who, contrary to custom, had been disinclined to discuss her private affairs with her nurse. As for the sudden friendship which had developed between her and the young surgeon, Bunny was regretfully unable to enlighten Miss Ogilvie. No — she hadn't the faintest idea what they talked about, for she was always promptly excused from attendance while these conversations were in progress.

'I mean,' she had explained, under heavy pressure, 'they never have said anything while I was in the room — not anything that really meant anything, if you know what I mean. They have both travelled; maybe they talk about that. Once I heard her saying something about a ship.'

'One they had sailed on?' pursued Miss Ogilvie, alert. 'Perhaps they knew each other before. Maybe she came here for that reason.'

'I don't think so. She quoted something that a dean had said to her about a ship.'

'Dean of a college?'

'I don't know. She was talking in a very low tone. I couldn't hear very well.'

'Did Dr Paige make any reply?'

'Yes — he said he didn't believe it.'

'And then they laughed, I suppose.'

'No.'

'It wasn't just a little joke, then?'

'No – they were pretty serious.'

'But – how do they look at each other?' Miss Ogilvie had persisted, after a thoughtful interval. 'You know what I mean – as if they had something between them?'

'M-maybe,' Bunny had ventured uncertainly. 'I'll try to notice from now on, Miss Ogilvie – honest I will – but' – she added, truthfully – 'I don't think I'm going to be very good at it.'

'Was she nettled,' inquired Miss Ogilvie, unwilling to leave a stone unturned, 'when Dr Paige said he didn't believe whatever it was about the ship?'

'No,' Bunny had replied. 'She patted Dr Paige's hand, and said, 'I hope it doesn't cost you too much.''

'Well – in God's name – what on earth does that mean, Mather?'

'I'm sure I don't know, Miss Ogilvie. You asked me what I heard them say, and I've tried to tell you.'

Anyone should have known at a glance that Bunny Mather was not fitted, by nature, for sleuthing. Life had not been very complicated for Bunny. She had no talent for dramatizing the small episodes which sporadically punctuated her routine. An inordinate appetite for candy, cream, and other fattening refreshments had earned her the cherubic roly-polyness of a Della Robbia medallion. She was not built for the sinister task of crouching at keyholes. Her wide-open, slightly protuberant, bird's-egg-blue eyes lent to her round face an expression of ineffable guilelessness. This ocular phenomenon was due to an incipient exophthalmic goitre, but the fact remained that Bunny was almost, if not quite, as naïve and artless as she looked.

Today she was resolved to stay in the room with them until definitely and firmly invited to leave. No mere hint or inquiring glance in her direction would be sufficient to dislodge her. She had just learned that Mrs Dexter's operation had been put off until tomorrow. After that, there might be a week or more when conversation would be impossible.

One thing seemed sure: it was not a flirtation. Mrs Dexter was nearly old enough to have been Dr Paige's mother. And

18

she certainly wasn't the sort to initiate or encourage a gusty little romance for the sake of passing the time.

Dr Paige always had the manner of a person coming in for advice on some important problem. He was very serious. He never entered with the capable condescension of the physician making his rounds, carolling, 'And how do we find ourselves this morning?' Bunny had thought of saying to Miss Ogilvie that Dr Paige acted as if he were going to school to Mrs Dexter, but had decided against that because it sounded too silly. She didn't care to risk hearing Miss Ogilvie say, as she had once said to her in reply to a remark, 'Don't be an ass, Mather!'

Bunny busied her fat fingers rearranging the books and bottles on the table, glancing up frequently to note Dr Paige's expression and movements. He stood for some moments at the foot of the bed, toying with his platinum watch-chain. Then he slowly nodded his head, and smiled; not a greeting, but an affirmative.

Quickly shifting her search to Mrs Dexter's face, Bunny tried to interpret it, but realized that she had arrived the fraction of a second too late. Mrs Dexter's sensitive lips were parted as if she had just asked an inarticulate question with them – some single-word query that might have been expressed with the lips only. If so – they had a very good understanding between them, these two.

And that would be natural, reflected Bunny, for they were very much alike. They were thoroughbreds. You could always tell. People didn't get to be like that by personal effort or education. If you had it, it was because you were born with it, and nobody could take it from you. You had it whether you were rich or poor, sick or well, happy or wretched. All the money in the world couldn't buy even a cheap imitation of it. Bunny knew very well she didn't have it. She knew Miss Ogilvie didn't have it.

Mrs Dexter had the eyes of a thoroughbred; steady greyish-blue eyes that never widened suddenly in surprise or alarm or curiosity; serene eyes that never gave her thoughts away. There was one little snow-white curl slightly to the left of the parting on the low forehead, definitely outlined from the environing burnished gold. The white lock was not a disfigurement but a distinction. One suspected that in Mrs Dexter's youth her Titian hair had been of a brighter yellow. There were deep dimples in her cheeks. Her hands were long and slender, and she could say things with them. Dr Paige had the same slow-moving eyes and the same speaking hands. He had taken one of Mrs Dexter's expressive hands in both of his and had seated himself at her bedside. These people were somehow related, Bunny felt.

He said something to her in an undertone, and she replied, with a smile, 'What does it matter? – today, tomorrow, the day after. Don't be troubled about this little delay. I shall not be fretting. No, no – it isn't a pose, I assure you. I am quite in earnest. It doesn't matter in the least and I'm content.'

'You are a very fortunate woman,' responded Dr Paige. 'Last night I was thinking over some of the things you had said, and it occurred to me that if somehow it could be reduced to simple terms and communicated, it would practically revolutionize the whole problem of human happiness. But I doubt whether it could ever be made elementary enough for the ordinary intellect. I admit it's too much for mine. I think I get spasmodic little tugs of it – and then it is gone. One would have to be something of a mystic, I presume.'

'No.' Mrs Dexter's negative was accompanied by a slow shake of her head on the pillow. 'No – it isn't a matter of mental capacity or even of temperament. The trouble is that the average individual leaves most of his tasks unfinished, his mental tasks in particular. The world is fairly crowded with truncated minds belonging to people who learned the scales up to three flats and two sharps. If the tune they are interested in happens to be written in any higher signature, they have either to transpose it into one of the keys they have learned or give it up. Most people try to get along with a vocabulary of about six hundred words. This enables them to understand what is going on in the kitchen, the shop, and on the street. Any idea that can't be translated into kitchen-lore or shop-lore or street-lore is dismissed.'

'Did Dean Harcourt ever try to put this into print?'

'No – nor has he more than hinted at it in public addresses. He does it all by the case-method. People in trouble come to him and he tells them. It's really amazing what happens to them. Why – I've known instances—

'You may run along now and have a bit of relaxation, Miss Mather,' Mrs Dexter interrupted herself to say, without detaching her eyes from Dr Paige's face.

Bunny still lingered, tinkering with the magazines and vases, consumed with curiosity to hear what was coming next.

'That will be all for the present,' said Dr Paige, with finality. 'We will ring when you are needed.'

Bunny slowly and reluctantly walked to the door, opened it, and softly closed it behind her.

Chapter Two

BY ADMONITION and example Dr Bruce Endicott – elsewhere genial and talkative – had discouraged all unnecessary conversation in his operating theatres at Parkway Hospital. The sentiment he had built up against superfluous chatter on the part of his associates and assistants was not restricted to the period when surgery was actually in process. He did not like to be distracted even during the preparatory business of scrubbing up. Nothing annoyed him more than some cold bloodedly irrelevant remark, when an operation was impending, 'as if one were making ready to bake a pie or patch a boot.' Daily experience of working together in silence had so harmoniously integrated this particular group of five, that their respective *rôles* in the drama were adroitly enacted without need of prompting or conference.

On this eventful Wednesday the pantomine had been in progress for fifteen minutes, unattended by any noise but the padding of competent rubber-shod feet on the tiled floor, the muffled plunk of the sterilizing machines as they grudgingly disgorged their immaculate contents through belching billows of steam, the intermittent swirl and swish of water rushing into capacious porcelain basins, and the patter and rattle and clink and clank of variously sized, curiously shaped instruments, hot, clean, gleaming.

Gingerly and at arm's length Miss Ogilvie held up the surgical coat, and Dr Paige stretched out his dripping arms toward it, instinctively aware that her eyes were inviting him as they always were in this thrice-a-day experience of a face-to-face contact which lacked only a little of an embrace. The Tweedy girl stood behind him, gowned and masked, waiting to tie the tapes down his back. Dr Endicott was still vigorously polishing his nails. In a moment he, too, would be offering

22

himself to Ogilvie for the same ministrations his associate had just received. By custom everybody was made ready before Endicott.

The anxious face of Lucy Reid, the chief's secretary, appeared in the crack of the corridor door. Miss Ogilvie glanced over her shoulder, visibly annoyed.

'Could Dr Endicott answer the telephone?' inquired the girl nervously, aware that she was taking an unforgivable liberty.

'Certainly not!' snapped Miss Ogilvie, through her gauze. 'You ought to know that much.'

'I told them,' explained Miss Reid defensively, 'but they insisted it was very urgent, and said that Dr Endicott would be at a serious disadvantage if the message was not delivered at once.'

'Who was it?' boomed Endicott, without looking up.

'Riley, Brooks, and Bannister, Doctor. Shall I say you will call them up later?'

He released the faucet-pedal and stood for an instant, head tilted to one side, as if listening for a decision.

'They said it was of immediate importance?'

'Yes, sir.'

'Very well, I'll go. . . . Sorry, Dr Paige. I shall not be long.'

Abstractedly stroking the fingers of his gloves, Paige walked through the alcove, passed the operating table, and entered the adjacent chamber. Mrs Dexter, with the customary modicum of morphine to reduce her active interest in the occasion, spread out her hand apathetically and signed that she was too drowsy to offer it, to which he wordlessly replied, by holding up his own, that he would be unable to touch her, anyway.

Grace Dexter, whom he had met briefly an hour earlier, stood in the doorway at a discreet distance, a bit pale, but entirely self-possessed. Her patrician face had the general contour of her mother's. Had the black hair been straight she could have done an acceptable madonna. Her figure was slight but shapely, as the severely tailored suit, unrelieved by any touch of colour, testified. The brooding grey eyes hinted at a well-developed talent for introspection, an effect augmented by the slightly drooping, sensitive lips. Slim, meditative fingers

23

caressed a silver crucifix depending from a heavy chain about her white throat. Dr Paige smiled, and she answered the recognition.

'Did your father come up?' he asked.

'Yes – and just now went down again. To the telephone, I think. He will be back in a moment. Mother seems quite fit, don't you think?'

'Never better!' said Paige confidently. Then, leaning over Mrs Dexter, he whispered something in her ear which she approved with a contented sigh and several reassuring little nods. She closed her eyes, and the slightly smiling lips relaxed.

'Do I know what that was about?' queried Grace, in the tone of one asking for a password. Paige nodded and retraced his steps into the operating-room, and through the alcove where the white-swathed little company waited.

Presently the door opened and the chief appeared, quite plainly upset about something. Paige watched him anxiously as he resumed his washing with nervous haste. His face was flushed and the muscles of his cheeks twitched. The silence was taut. Endicott seemed to sense it with defenceless irritation. Everybody in the room knew that he had been engaged in an emergency conversation with his brokers, and he knew that they all knew. They knew that he knew they knew. He plunged his arms into the surgical coat with such force that he tore it out of Ogilvie's grip and it fell to the floor. Tweedy came promptly with another. His exasperation was all but out of control. At length, in spite of his haste, he was ready. They filed into the operating-room and gathered about the table.

Lane's thin fingers trembled a little as he readjusted the mask more effectively over Mrs Dexter's face. Endicott noticed it and frowned. He stared glassily straight ahead through the high, bright windows while they waited for the increasingly laboured respiration to signal the moment for action. One more shuddering inhalation would do it. Lane slowly looked up, pursed his lips slightly, and nodded.

A hand-made Swiss watch could have had no better under-standing of itself than this close-knit company of five. Endicott signed his commands to Paige and Ogilvie, Ogilvie signed to the Tweedy and Larimer girls – all the orders given with dexterous gestures. Endicott was working faster than usual.

The hands of the surgeons opened and whatever they required was instantly thrust into them; the others hovering close, alert, lynx-eyed. . . . A scalpel for Endicott, the swift use of a sponge thrust into Paige's fingers by Tweedy, a pair of forceps for Paige, the deft swipe of a sponge by Larimer, more forceps for Paige furnished by Ogilvie, fresh sponges for Tweedy furnished by Larimer, more forceps for Paige; clip, clip, clip, forceps, forceps, forceps for Paige, more gauze for Tweedy, a clamp for Paige, long-handled scissors for Endicott – a tense pause, quiet and stiff as a tableau. Larimer stood ready with the threaded ligator. Ogilvie offered the handles of a secondary clamp. Endicott shook his head. That meant he couldn't use it because there was no room to apply it. There was a quick, barely audible sucking intake of breath by Ogilvie. Endicott frowned.

'I'll hold your clamp, Dr Paige,' he muttered huskily. 'You make the tie, please.'

Paige realized that the pedicle had been cut too short for safe ligation. He adjusted the ligature with difficulty and drew it as tightly as possible. Endicott slowly and with apparent reluctance relaxed the clamp and withdrew it. They waited. The chief breathed as if he had recently been running uphill. He had made two grave mistakes. In his nervous excitement he had neglected to dissect the pedicle – sheath of the renal artery – with sufficient care, and had severed it too short for a secure tie. . . . The pedicle slowly rejected the ligature.

'*My fault!*' gasped Paige, as the flood broke. 'I should have drawn it tighter. *My God!*'

The hæmorrhage was instantly out of control. Sponges would have been equally serviceable at a crumbled dam. The increasing tempo of the splash of big drops falling from the table to the floor quickened to a brisk patter and accelerated to a steady stream.

The chief seemed suddenly to go to pieces – a shocking sight to those who had never seen him panic-driven. He panted for breath and his hands shook. Ogilvie thrust a huge bunch of gauze into the pouring wound. He shouted to her to remove it, and frantically groped in the depths of the geyser with his clamp, hoping to recapture the spouting pedicle by mere blind chance.

'A donor – immediately!' he commanded hoarsely. 'Here, Paige,' handing him the clamp, 'see what you can do.' The frenzied grappling continued.

'How's she holding up, Lane?' mumbled Endicott, half incoherently.

Lane shook his head and closed the valves. Miss Tweedy collapsed on the slippery floor in a dead faint. Larimer dragged her out of the way. Ogilvie sponged the sweat from Paige's white face. The hæmorrhage was subsiding now. It had almost stopped. There was no further energy driving it.

Endicott and Paige washed at adjoining basins without the exchange of a word or a look. The chief was still breathing with an asthmatic wheeze. Paige was so shaken that his tears ran unrestrained.

Two orderlies were mopping the floor. The body had been wheeled into a room across the hall. Tweedy, quite nauseated, slumped over a basin in the corner, supported by Larimer, who was swallowing hard and apparently on the verge of crumpling.

Paige made a quick task of his ablutions, dashed to the dressing-room, and changed into his street clothes. Nothing seemed to matter now but a prompt escape from this place at top speed. His hands shook so violently that he could hardly manage his buttons.

Frances Ogilvie was waiting for him when he came out into the corridor. He pretended not to notice her, and moved quickly to the elevator. She followed, clutching at his sleeve. 'Wait!' she cried. 'I know exactly what happened and I'm going to tell everybody the truth.'

'You're going to mind your own business,' retorted Paige, measuring his words, sternly. 'It was my fault and I've admitted it. And that settles it. You are to stay out of it, and keep your mouth shut.'

The sluggish elevator was in use, its remote rumble threatening a long delay. Unable to bear any more of the tempest that had reduced the Ogilvie girl to a tear-smeared sputter of protestations, Paige suddenly pushed her out of his path and started for the stairway. She pursued him, sobbing aloud. He lost her somewhere between the third and second floors, and ran on. The last he heard of her was an hysterical scream, 'You'll be sorry!'

In the main hall, the superintendent, Watts, called to him, but he did not stop. At the front door he ran into Ted Rayburn, the house physician. He had been closer to Rayburn, for a couple of years, than to any of the others, with the possible exception of Bennie Booth.

'Where are you bolting to?' demanded Rayburn, holding out both arms, semaphore fashion. 'What's happened? You're white!'

'They'll tell you – in there,' Paige replied, over his shoulder, hurrying on.

Walking swiftly to the gate, he hailed a cruising taxi and ordered the driver to take him home. He did not reply when the elevator boy at the Hermitage inquired why he was not using his own car.

The apartment was cool and quiet. Inagaki was out, probably attending to his marketing.

Paige flung his hat on to the table in the small vestibule and walked through the living-room into his library. Although temperate almost to the point of abstinence, he maintained a cabinet of choice liquors for the use of his guests. He went directly to it, poured himself a stiff drink of cognac, and gulped it raw. Unaccustomed to such heroic potations, and having had nothing to eat – it was now twelve-thirty – since his light breakfast at seven, he felt the fiery stuff make his head swim.

Telephoning the garage, he instructed Pete to go out to the hospital for his car.

'No – nothing the matter with it. Drive it back to the garage and bring Sylvia here.'

For a long time he stood at one of the front windows of his

quite luxurious living-room, beating a tattoo on the sash with restless fingers. The thick traffic on the street below was a confused blur of noisy futility. Everything was carrying on down there as if no sudden world-destroying catastrophe had occurred. These people apparently hadn't heard yet that there was no reason for any further effort.

The tragic affair of the forenoon clamoured for appraisal, but it was all too painfully recent for a sensible survey. On the trip home in the taxicab the one blistering fact that mattered most was the wanton destruction of his idol. As they had stood there, side by side, almost touching elbows, scrubbing off the blood that had been so needlessly shed, he had momentarily expected the big, dynamic, generous-hearted fellow to turn to him and say, courageously: 'I was to blame, Newell. We both know that. I shall clear you of any responsibility, you may be sure.' And he had already composed the quick reply, 'Better let the matter rest the way it is.'

But Endicott – damn him! – had buried his hairy arms and pallid face in the square porcelain tub, splashing and spluttering, without a single glance, much less a friendly word. Endicott had crashed, completely cracked up. All that noble talk in his sumptuous library of an evening about professional ethics, good sportsmanship, the inviolability of the Hippocratic (or was it the hypocritic?) oath, the devotion to duty that demanded precedence over any and all personal ambitions – bah! – and to hell with it!

Mentally inspecting him now, toppled from his pedestal, Paige realized that Endicott's moral disaster had not been entirely unpredictable. He had seen the big man slipping, slipping day after day. Too much concern about money. Too much fretting about investments. Too many business conferences downtown. Too much travelling all night and rushing into operations in the morning, for which he had not prepared.

There had been that Baldwin girl, for instance, only last Thursday. Simplest possible appendectomy. Could have done it with his eyes shut. No occasion at all for a fifty-minute exploratory. Hadn't studied the plate, that was the trouble. Was making a speech that night before the PTA on (God help

28

us!) 'The Changing Thought of the Public in Respect to Surgery.' Probably was thinking about that when they showed him the picture of the little stenographer's insides. Or wondering, perhaps, whether steel and rails would be stronger today. No matter if the twenty-dollar-a-week office clerk was kept in bed ten days longer than necessary. That wouldn't discommode the chief.

No – Endicott had not crashed from some dizzy height. He had been sliding for a long time. Paige admitted to himself now that he had been afraid to see the chief operate on Mrs Dexter. Old Lane had been afraid of it too. As much as said so. He regretted that he had been so surly and high-handed with Lane. Lane was an honest fellow, for all his fanatical rot about the soul-destroying effect of easy money. Maybe frowsy old Lane was right. One thing was sure – money hadn't improved Endicott. It had made him puffy, arrogant, bumptious. And now, in an emergency, he had turned out to be a coward and a cad.

Newell's hard-driven pulse pounded in his ears. Unwilling to torture himself any further with thoughts of the execrable Endicott, he went into the library and wrote a brief letter of resignation to Watts, splutteringly addressed an envelope, and rose unsteadily to take another drink of cognac. Briefly cleared, he resumed his stand at the window, and thought of Mrs Dexter.

Subconsciously he had been dreading the moment when his memory would compel a review of her case. To his amazement, the thought of Mrs Dexter calmed him somewhat. He had anticipated that the recollection of her tragedy would haunt him for life. Strangely enough, the painful sight of her on the operating table, rapidly melting away, was driven into complete eclipse by the enduring vision of her in her room. Incomparably steady, she now seemed to stand apart from all the blundering pomposities and blustering incompetence and whimpering anxiety of his madly careering world – an indestructible symbol of self-possession.

Sometimes, seated at ease in her tranquil presence, he had found himself smiling indulgently as she talked of 'the things

29

that make for personal adequacy'. Under ordinary circumstances he would, he knew, have distrusted the phrase. People who chattered glibly of 'the-things-that-make-for' this and that were tiresome, and more often than not turned out to be mentally untidy.

But Mrs Dexter's confident talk about 'personal adequacy' was refreshing. He had enjoyed hearing it because it was so evident that she believed it. He had gone back to her, day after day, just to hear her say it. The very enunciation of the phrase had put her singularly mobile lips through all their pretty paces. And it was a nice theory to toy with, academically; about as practical as a house made of tissue paper; very bright and attractive, so long as it doesn't rain.

He had teasingly said this to her – just about this way – and she had replied, smilingly unruffled, 'But doesn't it look a little like rain – over my house? You don't think I shall go to pieces, do you?'

'No,' he had declared, with sincere conviction, 'you'll not go to pieces, whatever the weather, but that will not be because of your curious philosophy. It's not the philosophy that insures Mrs Dexter: it's Mrs Dexter that insures the philosophy. What difference does it make, after all, what one believes? If your ductless glands are functioning properly, and you're biologically built to be optimistic, your creed will sound attractive. Your Father, Son, and Holy Ghost will allure them. Or your Transmigration of Souls. Or your Iza-Nagi's Magic Wand. Or your Mystic Shrine of the Blue Flame. People with an underdeveloped anterior lobe of the pituitary or an enlarged spleen will come with flowers for your altar, thinking it is the thing you believe that has made you enviably competent to survive the shocks and storms and live beautifully. . . . You might as well expect to get results by screwing a Rolls-Royce nameplate on to a wheelbarrow, and command it to get about under its own power.'

He distinctly remembered her drawling reply, 'Pouf!—You and your glands! You'd better turn your old hospital into a nice new garage.'

It had been very stimulating to talk with Mrs Dexter. There

was nothing wormlike about her serenity. Nothing annoyed her, but she was abundantly able to take care of herself in an argument.

The first time she had hinted at her curious theory, a bit shyly, he had suspected it of being some sort of esoteric religion, and inwardly sighed. Such a charming personality she was, and now she was going to be just another of those boresome, cult-harried women, preparing to unload an incomprehensible mess of sweet and sticky twitter relayed from some soul-surgeon. (Tuesdays at eleven in the Gold Room of the Ritz; a dollar-fifty, or the entire course of twelve for ten, the deep-breathing book gratis to subscribers.)

But it was soon observable that Mrs Dexter, far from being just a gullible neurasthenic, was as remote as he himself from any interest in metaphysical cream-puffs. Indeed, she was his superior in respect to their attitudes toward such fatuities. He was acutely irritated by them; caustically satirical about them. Once he had said to her: 'All religions are opiatic. The old ones stick to straight chloroform. The new ones like a little rose-verbena in their ether, just so it makes them too drowsy to think. One method is good as another.' Mrs Dexter did not deride any of them. She gracefully dismissed them with outspread passionless hands.

Sometimes she had shocked him beyond belief with her bland insistence upon what seemed like an uncompromising fatalism.

'It's an odd thing,' he had said, one day. 'You seem the most gentle of spirits, but this belief you hold is hard as tool-steel. You have the temperament of a mystic, but your philosophy would bite a hole in a battleship!'

Well – she would be an everlasting inspiration. Tomorrow or next day they would carry her out to some shady spot and leave her there to become one with the soil. That grisly aspect of human mortality was made strangely unrepellent as he remembered her self-confessed integration with 'a planned universe' which, in her opinion, was every way sound and worthy.

The doorbell rang. He answered it mechanically. Pete

31

silently handed him the end of the leash and departed unthanked. Sylvia licked his hand as he unfastened the snap from her collar. She followed him closely into the library, and when he slumped into a chair she sniffed his fingers with quivering nostrils, and whined.

'Go lie down!' growled Paige savagely. Then he went to the bathroom and washed his hands, thoroughly, this time. Having finished, he disrobed completely and spent a long time under the shower. Donning a dressing-gown, he sought the liquor cabinet again, telling himself he must not take any more cognac. It should be something light. He was barely able to move about. He poured a copious drink of rye whisky. The telephone was ringing, but he did not answer it. With a whirling head, he staggered into his living-room and sprawled at full length on the sofa, and slept.

Shortly after four he woke. Inagaki stood near, regarding him with concern.

'Dr Rayburn is on the phone, sir,' said the diminutive Nipponese.

'Tell him I'm out,' muttered Paige thickly. 'Tell everybody I'm out.'

'Yes, sir – I told him you were in, sir.'

'Well, you go back and tell him you're a little liar!'

Presently Inagaki was on hand again. He had a tall glass in which ice tinkled. It had a welcome sound. Paige reached for it.

'Did you tell Dr Rayburn what I said, Inagaki?'

'Yes, sir. He also say I am the little liar. He will come.'

'I might have known it. . . . What is this stuff, Inagaki?'

'Limeade, sir.'

'It's pretty flat. Put some gin in it.'

Inagaki found him sound asleep when he returned, and did not molest him. Paige slept fitfully. The room was darker each time he was roused by the telephone bell and the voice of Inagaki reassuringly replying to solicitous inquirers. Once he heard him say, 'No, Miss, Dr Paige is at the hospital. . . . He is not? Then I do not know.'

At length he was aware of talk close beside him. A painfully pungent whiff of ammonia stung him wide awake.

'Hurry that coffee along, Inagaki,' Rayburn was saying, 'and make it strong.'

Raising himself on one elbow, Paige ran his long fingers through his tousled hair and regarded his guests with a feeble grin.

'It's love of humanity brought 'em here,' he intoned, with deep solemnity. 'Spirit of service. Man can't even get quietly inebri – ineber – can't even get quietly drunk in his own house without stirring up a lot of excitement. Did you fellows bring the ambulance?'

Bennie Booth chuckled a little, but Rayburn drew down the corners of his mouth and scowled.

'If you were in the habit of getting quietly drunk in your own house, there would be no occasion to call out the troops.' He settled an ice-bag firmly about Paige's temples. 'Here, drink this!'

'Better mix yourselves something,' suggested their host, his thick head clearing slightly as he sat up and sipped the scalding coffee, 'if you don't like to see me drunk by myself.'

Booth thought it wasn't a bad idea. No use to humiliate Newell unnecessarily. He would feel better if they had something. Assisted by Inagaki, whose bewilderment over his master's plight amused them even in the face of their own anxiety, they returned with ample glasses of Scotch and soda.

'We've got to see this thing through, Bennie,' Rayburn had said, under his breath. 'Newell isn't fit to be left alone. He might do himself some damage. We've had enough of that for one day.'

Seating himself on the couch beside his dishevelled friend, Rayburn studied his glass, and remarked casually, 'Well – tell us all about it, Newell. What happened? Or don't you want to talk about it yet?'

'Not yet – or ever!' mumbled Paige bitterly. 'Inagaki, make me one of those.'

'Mostly soda, Inagaki,' added Bennie over his shoulder.

'But I would like to know one thing,' said Paige, when the

whisky had lifted his fog a little, 'how did the girl – and her father – bear up? I didn't see them afterwards. Wasn't quite man enough to face 'em.'

Booth and Rayburn exchanged glances, each waiting for the other to invent an acceptable lie. Then Bennie shook his head; but Rayburn, noting that Newell had caught them in the act of conference, plunged into the truth.

'It has been a kind of complicated affair,' he began ponderously. 'Of course you've been laid up and haven't seen the evening papers. There was a terrific crash in the stock market today. The whole town is shocked. This man Dexter appears to have been cleaned out, along with a half-million other well-to-do's. Lost his shirt. That, on top of this accident at the hospital – or this on top of that – was a little too much for him. So he pushed off, this afternoon, about five. Not a very neat job. Didn't know his anatomy in the cardiac zone. Lived for a couple of hours.'

'Ted looked after him,' interjected Booth, 'unconscious all the while.'

'He means Dexter was,' Rayburn explained, hopeful of lifting Newell's dejection.

'Damned silly remark,' growled Paige sullenly. 'And what became of the girl? Is she dead, too?'

'Oh, no; we put her to bed, over at Parkway, and sprinkled a little poppy-dust over her worries,' replied Rayburn, pleased to be making an encouraging report. 'But she had herself pretty well in hand, considering everything she'd been through: father and mother both dead and the family stony broke – all in the course of about eight hours. Took it with her chin up. Maybe she was just stunned. Didn't want to go to bed. We thought she'd better. We sent some telegrams for her including a cable to her sister; addressed it to the young woman who is with her sister in London.'

'Dr Endicott about?' inquired Paige thickly.

'Huh!' snorted Bennie. '*That* bird!' Instantly aware of the injudicious slip, he added promptly: 'I dare say he was busy. He had had a hard day. They say he took an awful beating in the market collapse.'

34

Newell shut off this criticism with the surly comment that he didn't care to hear any criticism of Dr Endicott, denouncing Bennie for a drunken fool who ought to have his envy under better control. To clear the air of this slight disharmony, they made another highball. Inagaki offered his employer some advice while this was in progress and was sent scurrying off to bed.

At two, the host having quite definitely passed out, Rayburn and Booth repaired to the kitchen, where they scrambled half a dozen eggs, grilled some bacon, and crowned Inagaki's statuette of Buddha with an inverted gin-jigger. Heartened by their success in giving a jaunty air to so profound a matter, it occurred to them that Newell, on waking in the morning, might appreciate some little memento of their playful mood at the time of taking their departure. Composing his arms and legs, they placed a bunch of celery across his breast, and drawing up two small tables at his head and feet put a pair of candelabra on guard. Bennie was for lighting the candles, but Rayburn, slightly less drunk, vetoed this mad suggestion.

At four-thirty Paige woke, bewilderedly took stock of his position which under any less tragic circumstances would have been ridiculous, dizzily struggled to his feet and muttered, 'Dead, eh? . . . Why not?'

Reviving himself with another glass of cognac, he wrote a brief, businesslike letter to his valued friend, Eugene Corley, junior member of the firm of attorneys who had long since handled his affairs and his father's before him, confident that his secret would be kept and his instructions meticulously obeyed. He rather wished he might have an intimate talk with his bachelor crony, who, although fully ten years his senior, had always been delightfully congenial. A postscript was added to this effect.

He left the letter, sealed and stamped, on the library table, and dressed quickly in a rough suit of tweeds and well-worn walking shoes, the dog following about closely from room to room, sitting on her haunches directly before him while he laced his shoes, studying his face with a somewhat annoying solicitude.

35

'No – you can't go, Sylvia,' he said gruffly, patting her on the head. 'Not where I'm going. You're still alive. Try to make the most of it.'

She followed him to the door, and when he opened it squeezed past him and bounded out into the hall. He tried to coax her back, but Sylvia took advantage of his necessity to depart without raising the house. She made for the stairway, indifferent to her master's low-voiced cajolery and command.

It was still dark in the street and nobody in the vicinity was astir. There was a decided snap in the October breeze from the lake.

Paige turned south on Elm and walked briskly. Sylvia trotted at his heels.

Chapter Three

MISS ARLEN and Phyllis saw them off on the *Berengaria* and took the noon charabanc back to London.

It was pleasant to think that they were to have six weeks of leisurely browsing about together after the seventy-two hot and helter-skelter days on the Continent. Phyllis, especially, had reasons for anticipating this experience with pleasant excitement.

Lined up along the rail on B-deck, as the last hawser splashed, the homeward-bound party looked into the up-turned faces of Phyllis and Miss Arlen with undisguised envy – all but Patty Sumner, who was going home to be married on the sixteenth of October, and Miss Cogswell, who, in spite of her permission to arrive at Poughkeepsie a week later for the opening of the autumn term, was conspicuously restless to be back at her post. At least a normal amount of dispraise had been Miss Cogswell's portion during the twenty-five years of her professional career, but nobody had ever said she was not in earnest.

All things considered, the summer's excursion had been a success. Miss Cogswell, recognized historian and competent art critic, had remained an inflexible pedagogue throughout, marshalling her high-spirited wards with a solicitude that had proved irksome at times, but she had been an able director of the tour, providing handsomely for their comfort.

The managerial technique of Miss Cogswell was canny and irresistible. From the first day out, she had assumed that her young women (she never called them girls, though her discipline – the result of ten years' experience in a prep. school previous to her professorship in college – was better suited to the mood of fifteen than twenty-two) were in Europe on a serious errand, flatteringly imputing to them an ardent desire to devote every minute to the pursuit of culture.

Only one unfortunate episode had briefly interrupted their mutually forbearing display of concord. That had been at Milan. It was too fine a night to be put to bed at nine-thirty. They had just arrived at seven, from a week in Florence of such vast improvement to the mind that an hour of frivolous diversion seemed appropriate.

Miss Cogswell had been bathing her lame heels, when the sixth sense she had evolved through an earlier decade of listening and sniffing at tensely quiet dormitory doors warned her that the peace which rested over their suite in the Metropole was too complete to be real. Tugging on her shapeless dressing-gown, she had paddled about, peering into darkened and disordered rooms. Not a mother's daughter of her flock was to be found.

At eleven she and Miss Arlen located them, rosily merry, huddled close together about a round table in the exact centre of the Café Cova, stowing away tall *parfaits*. Before each culprit reposed an oily plate hinting at a recent *antipasto*, and an empty glass of the size and shape frequently used in the serving of cocktails. It was a humiliating moment, in which the tour-director's young women looked and felt like naughty little kindergarteners.

On the way back to the hotel, Miss Cogswell taciturnly leading on with stiffened spine, determined stride, straight lips, and stony eyes, Phyllis Dexter had lagged a little and fallen into step with Miss Arlen who was dispassionately defending their retreat. Phyllis admired her pretty English professor almost to the extent of adoration, and disliked the thought of having annoyed her. And sometimes she had felt genuinely sorry for her, too, because it was so manifest that she and Miss Cogswell – of necessity paired together – had very little in common.

'I'm awfully sorry and ashamed,' admitted Phyllis, rather shyly.

'You may be sorrier an hour from now,' replied Miss Arlen indifferently. 'It was a shocking mess – sardines and ice cream.'

Phyllis risked a smile but suspecting that the time was hardly

38

propitious for a light-hearted view of their misdemeanour, sobered instantly and said with contrition, 'We were horrid — making you turn out when you were tired and sleepy.'

'I wasn't sleepy,' drawlingly dissented Miss Arlen, 'and it is a lovely night. All the stars on duty.'

'You're a darling!' breathed Phyllis, impetuously hugging Miss Arlen's shapely arm. And then, just as she was withdrawing her hand, abashed over the impulsive liberty she had taken — for Professor Patricia Arlen, Ph.D., was too coolly dignified and remote to be pawed over in this manner — to Phyllis's unbounded delight there was a warm pressure of response to her caress. It brought sudden tears to her eyes. She had distantly worshipped Miss Arlen, often wondering what it might be like to share the confidence of this enigmatic, exquisite woman. She thought she had discovered a little secret. Miss Arlen was human. On the inside, she was a regular fellow.

No attempt was made, next day, to improve upon the comradeship they had tentatively confessed. Miss Arlen was smilingly distant and impartial. But before the week was out, it had been arranged that if Phyllis could secure consent from home, she would remain for a few weeks in London with Miss Arlen, who had contrived a four months' leave to study in the British Museum. She had already won recognition with her two volumes of essays on the Victorian Poets, and now hoped to do another book on a subject she had not bothered to confide to anyone, *The Droller Aspects of the Restoration.*

They followed along the dock as the *Berengaria* was tugged out, waving goodbyes, Phyllis wondering how soon they could decently call it a closed incident and seek the shade. Besides, she was piping impatient to have Miss Arlen all to herself. What would it be like to live in such intimate contact with Miss Arlen; to share the same room with her? Phyllis was on tiptoe with curiosity; just a little frightened, too. She must be restrained, mindful of her teacher's quite justifiable dignity.

At length Miss Arlen turned about, apparently satisfied that the ceremony of farewell had been adequately attended to, and they strolled over to the South Western Hotel where they were to board the charabanc. Presently they were bowling swiftly along High Street, revelling in the welcome shade. As they rattled under the old Bargate Arch, Miss Arlen tugged off her prim little hat with a girlish gesture of independence, as if the boundary of Miss Cogswell's jurisdiction had now been passed, and the significant smile she turned on Phyllis said, as plainly as if she had spoken it, 'There! We are free now to do as we like!'

Phyllis, almost suffocated with pride and happiness over Miss Arlen's comradely informality, again warned herself against the temptation to ignore the considerable difference in their rank and years.

Absorbed in the quaintness of the villages and the ripened serenity of the countryside, they had but little to say to each other until they were within sight of Winchester. Phyllis was eager to talk.

'Are we going back to the Tate Gallery tomorrow?' she asked, remembering Miss Cogswell's parting recommendation, and feeling herself on safe ground here.

Miss Arlen tightened her pretty mouth, gave Phyllis a side-long glance of mock dismay, and grinned! It was not a smile but a lazy grin! Miss Arlen closed one eye in a deliberate, diabolical wink!

'We are going out to Kew Gardens,' she said firmly, 'to lie flat on our backs in the grass and watch the clouds. And the first one who says the word "art" has to buy the lunch.'

Phyllis sighed happily.

'I'm so glad now – about that affair in Milan,' she said reflectively. 'If it hadn't happened, I might have gone home with the others. Then I should have missed all this – being with you, I mean. You were so understanding, that night.'

'It didn't call for much understanding,' drawled Miss Arlen. 'I was sitting in the dark by my window and saw you go. Your dash for liberty was no surprise.'

By the time they reached Basingstoke they were arriving at a least common denominator of mood and manner of talk. Phyllis was ecstatically loving London as they roared and sputtered into increasingly heavy traffic. Miss Arlen had forgotten her professorship.

They had their baggage taken to a little hotel in Bloomsbury, round the corner from the Museum. Phyllis had never stopped at a place so unpretentious; it had been Miss Arlen's suggestion. She had need to economize. Unpacking, they put on their prettiest gowns, Phyllis noting with shy admiration that Miss Arlen, so consistently conservative on the outside, was almost startlingly modern while in the act of hanging her travel togs in the closet. At that moment she didn't look at all like an authority on Tennyson. It had been agreed that they would go to the Trocadero for dinner, Phyllis begging the right to play hostess on this festive occasion. With the assurance of excellent experience she ordered with discrimination, finding Miss Arlen in full approval of her choices.

'I wonder if we shouldn't have a glass of sherry first?' suggested Phyllis, a bit uncertainly. 'It has been a busy day; you're tired.'

'Please,' replied Miss Arlen. 'But not because I'm tired. I never felt better in my life.'

'It seems an awfully long time since you were my teacher,' mused Phyllis, as they sipped their wine, smiling into each other's eyes, to which Miss Arlen responded, casually, 'That occurred during one of our earlier incarnations. We will try to live it down.'

After dinner they saw *Bitter Sweet*, and returned to Bloomsbury in a musty little cab at midnight – Miss Arlen rather pensive and quiet. Without much further talk they went to their beds, Phyllis instinctively sensing that *Bitter Sweet* hadn't been just the thing.

'Goodnight, Phyllis, dear,' called Miss Arlen, from the depth of her pillow.

'Goodnight,' responded Phyllis, her eyes misty, adding, in a reckless whisper, 'Patricia.' Her heart pounded as the silence piled up. She had made the very blunder she had been trying so valiantly to avoid, spoiling everything for them on the first day.

After five long hot minutes of acute misery, she murmured contritely, 'Please forgive me, Miss Arlen. I hadn't the right to do that.'

41

'They never called me Patricia,' said Miss Arlen drowsily, 'except when they disapproved of me. When they like me it was always Pat.'

'Would it be just terribly rude — and presumptuous?' asked Phyllis, her voice trembling a little.

'I think it would be very sweet of you, dear,' replied Miss Arlen tenderly.

Phyllis drifted out, wishing her mother knew how supremely happy she was. She could see her mother's smile when, at home again, she would tell her all about it. And she distinctly heard Sally Welker saying, 'You didn't call Miss Arlen "Pat" — not to her face — not really!'

Had it occurred to either of them, through those enchanted days, to compute in terms of years their respective contributions to the diminishing of the distance which naturally lay between them, it would have been incorrect to think that they had settled upon a relationship midway in mood between twenty-two and thirty-five.

Miss Arlen had, indeed, recovered something of her youth, but to a marked degree had Phyllis achieved maturity. The attractive girl had had her little problems, but they had been of cartilaginous structure. She had bruised easily and painfully, but repair was prompt and complete. She had never seen a compound fracture of lime-hardened bones. Not until now. Miss Arlen had not uncovered her scars with a morbid wish to shock, or a self-piteous bid for commiseration. With cool unconcern she had exposed her irreparable injuries, and Phyllis had grown almost to full stature at the sight. She had even ventured to offer a possible remedy.

The disclosure had come about naturally enough. They had been strolling through the Cathedral grounds at Salisbury on a brown-and-gold mid-October afternoon. Amused by antique epitaphs on the grass-ruffed, eroded stones, blandly certifying to the towering superiority of long-departed husbands as compared with the mousiness of their wives, the talk drifted from mere whimsical satire to a serious discussion of this indefensible relationship and the inevitable problems of matrimony.

42

'Funny you never married, Pat,' remarked Phyllis. 'I wonder how you escaped it.'

'I'm not unwilling to tell you. It is quite a long story, though.' Pat deliberated a suitable beginning. After a moment's reflection with averted eyes she said calmly, 'He fell in love with my sister.'

Phyllis winced and gave a quick little breath of pained surprise, but offered no comment, for it was to be quite a long story and she must not interrupt. She waited, with startled eyes.

'That's all,' said Pat, in the same tone Phyllis had often heard her use when dismissing a class. 'That's all – except that the invitations were out and the presents were coming in – and I found them in each other's arms when I came down to the library to show him my new travelling suit – and my favourite brother fought him and was hurt – and I ran away where they couldn't find me for ever so long – and they were married, and there are children I have never seen – and my mother lives with them – and all my people are in the same town – and I can't go home.'

'Oh – my dear!' sympathized Phyllis. 'How can you bear it?'

'I can't,' replied Pat woodenly. 'That's the trouble. The effort to bear it has frozen me.'

'But you aren't, Pat!' Phyllis brightened hopefully. 'I never felt so close to anyone, outside my own family.'

Pat sighed, smiled wistfully, and nodded.

'I know, dear. I have been very selfish, warming myself at your bright fire. I'm surprised it hasn't chilled you. It really has been a Godsend to me – much more than you realize.'

Phyllis murmured an inarticulate little protest and laid her hand on Pat's affectionately.

'I do wish you could talk with my mother,' she said, searching the heavy eyes with loyal concern. 'She has helped so many people. You'd be surprised.'

Pat's involuntary shrug doubted it. For a silent moment she reproved herself for having bared her wounds, fearing that she was about to learn of some metaphysical patent-medicine –

43

some echo of a psychological wizardry, perhaps, that would dismiss cold fact with an amiable grin and a careless, 'There, there; you'll be all right now.' She closed her eyes, tightened her lips, and shook her head decisively.

'Nothing would help me, Phyllis, but utter forgetfulness of it all. Your mother couldn't help me to that, however kindly she might try.'

'But that's just it!' exulted Phyllis. 'She does it! It's something our Dean taught her when my little brother was drowned. I was only a baby then, so my mother has always had it, ever since I can remember.'

'Your Dean?' repeated Pat, mildly inquisitive.

'Dean Harcourt – of our Cathedral – at home.'

'I'm not religious – not the least bit.'

'Oh – but neither is he!'

'Don't be silly!' laughed Pat.

'I mean – this thing that I'm thinking about isn't religion; heaps bigger and more important than that. I'll try to tell you. But it won't be easy. You see – I've never been hurt. You have to be, I think, before it means very much. I guess it's a good deal like planting a tree. You have to dig the hole first.'

'Perhaps I could qualify,' said Pat dryly. 'Let's have it.'

For more than two hours they sat on the grey stone bench at the entrance to the cloister, the fallen leaves eddying about their feet, Pat slowly tracing meaningless patterns on the dusty flagging with the tip of her umbrella. Phyllis, falteringly at first but with mounting confidence, pointing to the mere mirage of an oasis she had had no occasion to seek personally. She was conscious, all the time, that she was making a very poor job of it; and when, at last, her vague ideas were exhausted, an extended silence meant nothing other than that Pat had remained unconvinced and unstirred.

'I think you get just a flash of it,' pursued Phyllis, unwilling to surrender – 'not the real essence of it, of course, but just a faint glimpse, among these old things we've been seeing lately. I've thought about it, a lot.

'Remember the other day when we were down at Saint Olave's, sitting there in the dusky gloom, looking up at the

44

bust of Elizabeth Pepys? And you had just been talking about all she and Sam had been through; the London fire, the plague, the smash-up of two governments, the frights, the flights, the shocks, the sorrows; and there she was, so calm, so secure; and – outside in the street – you could hear it pouring in through the open doors – the dull mutter and rumble of traffic mumbling, "On, on, on, on" – and you could hear the measured plop-plop of the big shaggy hoofs on the cobblestones. The same old loads were still moving. Same kind of straining horses, bracing their lathery shoulders against the same hot collars, lashed and yelled at by the same cloddish drivers; and Elizabeth, up there, not listening, but hearing; not gladly approving, but accepting. . . .

'So – what? Well – I'm afraid I don't know. I can't quite define it. Maybe it has no bearing at all on the thing I've been trying to talk about . . . I just know that for an instant, down at Saint Olave's, there came over me an almost stifling wave of – of comprehension. And I said to myself, "If ever I get into trouble, I should like to be able to come to some place like this, where today's struggle and pain is being hammered down hard on top of yesterday's – and let mine be pounded into dust and silence, along with Elizabeth's." '

She laid her warm hand, trembling a little with emotion, around Pat's slumped shoulders.

'Do you follow my mood, my dear? Or am I just talking nonsense? I mean – about the – the foreverness of the mumble-rumble, "On, on, on, on!" . . . Three hundred years ago it was fragile, foolish, sensitive, little Elizabeth Pepys, all milled up in the traffic, swept along with it, bruised by it, afraid of it, allured by it, but in it and of it – and now it's Patricia Arlen and Phyllis Dexter.

'But the thing of it is that it's going on, and it has been going on, and it is going to keep on going on – as it was in the beginning, is now, and ever shall be – and my troubles, in the face of it all, aren't really worth worrying about. . . . Do you see what I mean, Pat?'

'Phyllis, child,' said Pat moodily, 'it explains nothing, but it's a sedative. I think it helps – a little. . . . You mean' – she

45

continued, gropingly – 'you mean that we're all caught in the grip of something that's bigger and stronger than we are – something planned from the beginning – something inevitable – and we've simply got to keep coming along with it, whether we like it or not? . . . That's *Fatalism* – in case you don't know the exact name of it!'

Phyllis shook her head vigorously.

'Not at all, Pat. Fatalism is a treadmill. This movement I'm talking about is a *procession*. Fatalism says, "I'm caught in the machinery of destiny and am being whirled around by it. I can't understand what it's all about, and I hereby give it up, and just let it grind me to bits." That's Fatalism . . . The thing I believe in admits the existence of the machinery, but sees it *going forward* instead of merely *going round*. And instead of asking you, as Fatalism does, to *submit*, this better theory invites you to *understand*! It says, "Come along – but come with your eyes open!"'

'It's quite worth thinking about,' conceded Pat.

'I wish my mother could tell you,' said Phyllis wistfully. 'It is so very beautiful, the way she explains it and lives it.'

Phyllis had dashed over to a little shop on Southampton Row to load her camera. They were going out to the old Caledonian Market today. There had been a fog when they woke at seven, but it seemed to be clearing now. Doubtless by the time they had done the tube trip the sun would be shining. Phyllis hoped so, for three consecutive days of murky sky and chilly rains had kept them under roofs.

While she was gone, Pat received the cable. She sat down weakly, buried her face in her hands, and dizzily considered how with the least cruelty she might break the shocking news. Phyllis would be back at any moment, eyes alight, eager to be off for the day's excursion. The door swung open.

'Well – are we ready? It's going to be lovely in an hour or two; you'll see . . . What is it, dear? Don't you feel well?'

'Phyllis, would you mind very much if we didn't go out there today, I'm not quite in the mood for it. Maybe the fog has been dampening me. How about going down to Saint Olave's

– to talk to Elizabeth? I believe I'd like to. We'll try out your little theory on me. Agreed?'

'Of course,' consented Phyllis cheerfully, a little disturbed by Pat's sudden depression. 'We can go to the Caledonian thing any time. . . . I think I would be glad to have another session with Elizabeth.'

Most of the trip was done by buses, and little was said on the way. Pat was so obviously in low spirits this morning that Phyllis decided on silence as her own best contribution to her friend's search for tranquillity. But she must try to do something for Pat today while they were at Saint Olave's. Perhaps she could make her understand what she herself had felt in that steadying environment.

It was only ten when they arrived, and they had the little church all to themselves. Walking slowly forward through the central aisle, they seated themselves in the right front pew where they could look up into the apse at the marble bust of Elizabeth. For ten minutes they sat together in silence.

Stirred by the sound of a suppressed sob and the sight of Pat's face wet with tears, Phyllis interlaced their fingers, and whispered, hopefully, 'Can't you hear it, my dear?'

'That doesn't matter so much,' said Pat thickly. 'Just so *you* hear it.'

'I do!' Phyllis's tone was confident. 'It thrills me! "On, on, on, on" – not just going round and round – but pressing on! Headed toward something that has to be worked out – not alone by Elizabeth, or you, or me – or on some particular day in 1669 or 1929—'

Pat suddenly clutched Phyllis's hand in both of hers, and whispered, brokenly: 'Darling – I must tell you now. Something quite dreadful has happened . . . I wish it had happened to *me*, instead of you. One more tragedy wouldn't—'

Phyllis paled a little and her eyes widened, bewilderedly, as she searched Pat's distressed face. She swallowed convulsively and asked, with a nervous catch in her voice, 'Pat! – what are you trying to tell me?'

With agitated hands Pat opened her handbag, took out the folded and refolded yellow message, tucked it into Phyllis's

47

palm and closed her fingers upon it. Then she slipped to her knees on the worn and faded hassock, bowing her head over her tightly folded arms. . . .

The steady rumble of the ancient city, symbolic of the everlasting procession, throbbed dully in their ears.

Phyllis stared at Grace's cable. It was addressed to Pat.

FATHER AND MOTHER DIED THIS AFTERNOON
ACCIDENT TELL PHYLLIS GENTLY

The message slowly slipped from her relaxed fingers and drifted to the floor.

Too stunned to concentrate, she was conscious only of a pang of such loneliness as she had never experienced. The harsh, strident racket of this foreign city assailed her, its rasp and rattle stinging her to full awareness that she was far from home. There wasn't a sound, in all this tumultuous, metallic, unconscionable din that could be associated with anything she had ever known or believed or cherished. Even the dejected shoulders of the woman kneeling there seemed strangely unfamiliar. She was alone.

Presently the tears came welling to her relief, great, scalding tears that freed the suffocating tightness of her throat a little. She blindly groped with her knees for a hassock and snuggled her trembling body close to Pat, who put an arm tenderly about her.

For a long time they knelt together, Phyllis utterly devastated with grief and sobbing heart-breakingly. The old verger's wife sympathetically brought a glass of water. Pat wanly smiled their gratitude, but did not allow Phyllis to be disturbed. The sobbing gradually subsided. Phyllis was very quiet now. Pat waited. The minutes dragged out into the third quarter struck from a neighbouring clock tower.

Suddenly Phyllis stirred and stiffened to attention. Pat was ruthlessly snatched out of a painful reverie by the clutch of the girl's strong fingers on her arm.

'What is it, dear?' asked Pat.

'Listen!' whispered Phyllis, wide-eyed. 'Pat!' she called, with an exultant little smile, *'I can hear it!'*

48

Chapter Four

IT is presumable that among the more thoughtful of those who sought the counsel of Dean Harcourt, some were impressed by the fact that, although he was a unique personality, not too easily evaluable, his mind and mood were essentially the product of the Cathedral.

For more than three-quarters of a century, Trinity Cathedral had been one of the most highly respected institutions of the entire Middle West. This distinction may have been due partly to her imposing architecture, a stately Gothic strongly reminiscent of York Minster. It may have been accounted for also by her commanding location, for the Cathedral close was bounded by four spacious streets, one of them Lake Boulevard, the most prominent avenue in the city. Moreover, the great edifice faced beautiful Madison Park, to the considerable advantage of her massive towers and old-worldish buttresses.

But Trinity's influential position rested upon something more consequential than these fortunate external phenomena. There had grown up a general public sentiment to the effect that you always knew where to find her. She was not subject to the sudden chills and fevers which wobbled the erratic pulse of many another institution displaying similar symbols in the windows. Trinity had been singularly immune to widespread emotional epidemics. Sometimes neighbouring churches of clamorous importance were exasperated over her reluctance or downright refusal to participate in their tempestuous crusades of reform, and many an ardent front-paged apostle of despair had eloquently rated her for cold-blooded indifference to society's imminent collapse. A devastating crisis was on, shouted the gloomsters, and Trinity merely sat there and mumbled: 'In all time of our tribulation; in all time of our prosperity, Good Lord, deliver us.'

49

She had even kept her poise throughout the war, remaining discreetly neutral until the Government had officially declared itself otherwise, a difficult position which had drawn the fire of several prophets who were eager to be early on the field of battle and hotly impatient of these lackadaisical delays.

Then she had loyally advocated patriotic sacrifice, but without the prevalent hysteria, which had been interpreted by many as another proof of her habitual unconcern. One zealot preached a widely quoted sermon on the Laodiceans, who were neither hot nor cold, and pointed in the direction of the well-known Yorkish towers as a deplorable case of such apathy.

But Trinity did not allow herself to be disconcerted. When most of the other churches were hanging the Kaiser, Sunday after Sunday, she continued to intone, with a dispassionateness that infuriated the swashbucklers, 'Save and deliver us, we humbly beseech thee, from the hands of our enemies.' That was all you could expect, rasped the militants, of prayers that had to be read from a book! They had no capacity to arouse moral indignation!

When peace arrived and it was again prudent for Christian pacifism to put forth foliage and blossoms, Trinity's neighbours had given themselves to an orgy of increasingly bold resolutions that they would never, under any circumstance whatsoever, take up arms in an aggressive movement. Heartened by response to this endeavour, they took the next step fearlessly, declaring that they would never fight even in the defence of their country. Trinity did not go on record with convictions on this subject, and when heavily pressed for a declaration, announced that so far as she was concerned all such matters would have to be dealt with on their own merits when and if they called for a decision. The younger fry among the clergy pointed a disapproving finger toward her, asserting that Trinity was dead on her feet and didn't realize that she was stricken of a disease that would presently carry her off. But she continued to carry on as if quite unaware of the supposed lethal nature of the infirmity.

In the north-east tower a carillon of great value and wide repute played on weekdays, from four to five, the historic hymns of the Anglican faith, and it was traditional that this daily programme always began and ended with *O God Our Help in Ages Past*, which seemed to be Trinity's theme song. On certain occasions of national grief or gratification, when the emotional tide ran high, these serenely confident measures may have stirred many people who ordinarily did not think much about their own spiritual reliances, and it is not inconceivable that some of the more discriminating, who had been bullied and badgered from one extreme opinion to another by institutions given to noisy tantrums of ecstasy or woe, were at least momentarily stabilized.

A high wrought-iron fence enveloped on three sides the Cathedral close. This gave the whole establishment an air of sequestration from the raucous hurly-burly of secular affairs, a redundant precaution, perhaps, for it was hardly necessary that Trinity should thus emphasize her insular aloofness from the contemporary fret.

At the back of the main edifice and facing on to Marlborough, were the Bishop's Mansion, the Parish House, and the residence of the Dean.

It was rumoured that there were telephones, typewriters, an adding machine, a few clerks, and the inevitable paraphernalia of business covertly tucked away in a remote corner of the Parish House, but the casual visitor who had occasion to call there was not assaulted at the front door by the metallic racket of modern machinery.

Latterly there had been a fad, originated by city churches and amusingly imitated by the less busy elsewhere, to give the impression that the operation of 'The Kingdom' should be pursued by up-to-date techniques consonant with the methods of great factories engaged in the fabrication and distribution of commercial commodities. In such enterprising strongholds the prophet's desk was cluttered with telephones dangling from adjustable brackets. A row of buttons served his urgency in buzzing the various members of his staff into his presence to report on the success of last night's "banquet" of the Carpenter's Apprentices, to present printer's proofs of the weekly bulletin and the newspaper advertising for Sunday, the programme for the Advance Club, and what had been ascertained about the leak in the roof. His stenographer sat with her pad on her knee, licking the point of her pencil, poised for action. The Millennium was about to be delivered, FOB, as per yours of the thirteenth which, if you have further occasion to advert to it in future negotiations, should be keyed MBX 13579.

Trinity had never railed at this nonsense, considering it none of her business, but she had not gone in for it herself. The people who entered her quiet precincts were asked the nature of their errands by unflustered employees trained to understand that the less professional they were, the more ably they would discharge their duties.

George Harcourt was a product of Trinity Cathedral. Her mind and his were in complete accord. Perhaps they may have influenced one another somewhat during the twenty years of his deanship. His serenity had become so potent that persons of every conceivable type came to him for advice, consolation, and encouragement. It was a heavy load to carry, but he never complained of it.

Every weekday but Saturday a procession of men tarried in the reception room of his residence, taking turns in conference with him, keeping him at his desk from ten to one. In the afternoon, from three to six, women of all ages and ranks appeared there for the same purpose. He never referred to it or thought of it as a "clinic". He compiled no statistics, posted no records, permitted no clerical fussiness in the handling of this strange business. An unassuming volunteer for the day welcomed the callers and seated them. In due time they would have their turn.

Every morning at eight two young curates placed strong hands under the Dean's elbows and led him – for he was a cripple – into the dimly lighted chancel of the Cathedral, where, whatever storms might be blowing outside, whatever tumultuous issues might be agitating the city or the nation or the world, his resonant voice intoned a petition 'for all sorts and conditions of men; that Thou wouldst be pleased to make Thy ways known unto them.'

When the early morning service was ended, the curates

52

would assist the Dean to a chair placed for him in the centre of the chancel, facing the high altar, and leave him alone for a half hour.

And thus it was that when broken people came to Dean Harcourt for reconditioning, most of them, it was said, went out of his presence with the feeling that they had been very close to Headquarters.

She entered the Dean's office-library and crossed it with the agile, elastic, assured stride of complete physical fitness under superb control, seated herself gracefully in the chair he indicated, directly facing him, laid an expensive handbag on the spacious mahogany desk which separated them and loosened the collar of an exquisite Persian-lamb coat.

'Sonia Duquesne,' she said, in response to his low voiced query.

The interview did not proceed any further than that for a long moment.

Bearing most of his weight on the broad arms of his tall-backed churchly chair, the Dean leaned forward, pursed his lips thoughtfully, and took friendly stock of her. The rather hard, sophisticated smile she had brought along was gradually replaced by an almost entreating expression of self-defence, of meekness, of tenderness too, for it was now apparent to her that his deep-lined face bore unmistakable evidence of suffering.

They studied each other silently, with candid concern, Sonia so impressed and stilled by the spiritual majesty of the man that she accepted his scrutiny of her without the slightest sensation of self-consciousness.

It was a singularly interesting face. The upper lip was extraordinarily long, giving the firm but generous mouth an appearance of being securely locked. Perhaps, reflected Sonia, it was his mouth that encouraged strangers to confide in him. A friend had told her that people found it easy to tell him all about themselves without embarrassment or restraint. Doubtless it was the mouth that made them confident. It seemed to have been built especially for the safe keeping of secrets. And

53

there was something uncannily prescient in his eyes. They were dark, almost cavernous. A veritable sunburst of crow's-feet at the outer corners gave the effect of a residual smile of compassion, which softened the penetrating search and interpreted it as a comradely quest. His thick white hair shone silver in the single light suspended above his head, a light that intensified, by strong shadows, the ruggedness of his face.

'That is your real name?' asked the Dean.

'Yes. I know it is a bit fantastic. But it is mine. My father's people were of French descent and my mother thought Sonia a pretty name. She saw it in a story.'

'It is a pretty name, and I had not thought it incongruous, but you do not look foreign. When was it and where – that your mother read the story?'

'In 1901 – Cedar Rapids.'

'You are unmarried?'

'Yes,' replied Sonia, her eyes occupied with the gloves which she had unbuttoned and was tugging off, finger by finger. Glancing up, she met his gaze, and added, 'No – I was never married.'

'Am I right in surmising that you are engaged in something theatrical?'

'Again I must answer – yes and no—'.

The Dean acknowledged her honest candour with a slight inclination of the head. Sonia saw that she had said the right thing.

'I am the proprietor of a little shop, dealing in gowns. My clients – my customers prefer to think I am Parisian. I make no effort to counteract that belief. The place does have a foreign atmosphere. Perhaps I am theatrical – to the extent of playing a part in the course of my daily business.'

'Do you attend the services of the Cathedral?' asked the Dean, still smiling a little over her frank confession.

'No, sir; I have no religion.'

'Very well, then. Let us begin. Tell me all about it. What brought you here? – and remember that the more directly you come to it, the more time we will have to talk – profitably. What has he done to you?'

She sat for a while with a perplexed expression, her lips parted, slightly baring pretty teeth, tensely locked.

'No – I am not a mind-reader,' explained the Dean gently, 'but I have had much experience in listening.'

'I believe that,' said Sonia. 'Well – he has decided to go back to his wife. She is not very well, and thinks she wants him. She has treated him very shabbily. It was her fault that he lost interest in their home. Now she begs him to return. I urged him to go. And I intend never to see him again. . . . That was yesterday.' Sonia finished pulling off her gloves, and laid them on the desk beside the handbag with a little gesture of finality. Her hands were white and well cared for.

'So – I really did not come to you for advice,' she continued. 'For there is nothing to decide. They told me you were able to help people who had trouble. That's why I came. I'm glad I did . . . this is a very restful place. You will not scold me. I've had all the punishment I can take.'

'You love him – I think.'

'Devotedly! And he loves me. He needs me, too, for he has been very unfortunate recently – since the crash.'

'Did he contribute to your support?'

'Never! It wasn't on that basis, at all. In fact, for the past few weeks—'

Dean Harcourt's lips tightened, and he slowly raised a hand.

'Don't you want me to tell you?' asked Sonia, wide-eyed, shaking her head girlishly.

'Not that. . . . I think you will feel better afterwards if you do not confide that part of it.'

Sonia looked puzzled; then nodded approval.

'I take it that you bear his wife no ill-will?'

'Oh, no, not at all,' she replied quickly. 'In fact, lately, since he has been so hard-pressed, and I knew she was ill, I have—'

'Don't!' commanded the Dean, so sternly that she winced under his unexpected rebuke. 'You mustn't tell that to anybody – not even to me!' His voice grew gentle. 'And may I add that I consider you a very fortunate woman to be possessed of such a soul. . . . If you were my daughter I would be proud of you.'

55

Her lips trembled as she replied, 'Soul? I hardly knew I had one.'

'Yes,' sighed the Dean, running his long fingers through the shaggy hair at his temples. 'Yes – that's the trouble. People collide with circumstances that push them off the commonly accepted moral reservation – and then they assume that they have lost their souls. . . . See here! Do you know anything about football?'

'A little. I often go. I did – last Saturday.'

'Very good. You will have noticed then that a player some-times runs out of bounds. Often it's his own fault, though frequently he is *forced* over the chalk line. But, however it may have happened, he isn't sent home in disgrace. The game officials mark the spot where he went out, and carry the ball back into the field from that point.'

'And then,' said Sonia, 'he loses his right to it.'

'Only temporarily,' corrected the Dean, pleased with this feature of his allegory. 'He may quickly regain his right to pick up the ball. There is no telling but the next time he lays hands on it, he will go through for a touchdown.'

'You don't think I've lost my soul, then?'

'I should be more disposed to think,' declared the Dean warmly, 'that you have just now come to the place in your life where the essential fineness of you is about to have its great chance.'

'What would you have me do?' asked Sonia sincerely.

'You must find somebody or something to absorb your love – a child, perhaps, or a worthy charity in which you may invest yourself personally. Your case is not so difficult as you think. You came to grief through love. It is the people who get into trouble through hate – they're the ones I worry over. Some-times it is very hard to help them. Love is a gift – abused, overlooked, misdirected, quite frequently – but a gift, never-theless. Hate is a disease. And you, obviously, are not a hater.

'This encourages me to believe that you may be able to understand to what an extent the happiness of the world depends upon the clear vision of people who have a natural talent for love – to neutralize the bad influence of the people who are diseased by hate. Let me show you what I mean. . . .'

The Dean edged himself far forward in his chair, rested his elbows on the desk, and looked Sonia steadily in the eyes, urging her earnest concentration.

'You see – not many people take time to consider how they are related to the Long Parade. They snatch their little pleasures; they bemoan their little disappointments; they smile and smirk and sigh and sulk, reacting variously to events affecting them as individuals. But they do not think of themselves as component parts of *an era*. They fail to understand that we are all trudging along, elbow to elbow, in an endless, tightly integrated procession, in which our most important interests are held in common.

'Sometimes they sense it a little when some large catastrophe frightened them into a huddle. It is often reported of groups that they have felt it keenly in time of shipwreck, battle, or mass tragedy. Then they live, for an hour, in a previously experienced state of nobility, discovering themselves to be one, and suddenly impressed by the fact that human beings all related.

People with an extraordinary talent for love should be able understand this in the ordinary process of living, and get same thrill out of uneventful daily life that the ship-ked experience when tugged together by sudden mis-ne.

Now – this brings us up to your case – your love has been urgent that it has led you to defy the social canons. You ld like to atone for it, or at least try to justify your posses-n of a love so reckless. Very well – I say! – you can do it! ou *must* do it! Try to begin your thinking about this by ieving that the successful onward push of the human pro-sion is the important thing, after all; far more important n any of the trifling ups and downs of the individuals. . . . etimes I like to think of civilization as a ship. That ship, friend, is more important than any member of the crew! ou want to pay for the privilege of your love – and the akes of your love – believe that!'

hey sat for a little while in silence. The Dean had made

a platitude sound vital, dynamic. Sonia distinctly felt the strong tug of it. Her eyes were contemplative.

'That's all,' said the Dean, rousing from the reverie into which he had momentarily drifted. 'I shall be thinking of you. We will try to find something specific for you to do. Are you agreed?'

She rose to go, apparently reluctant to leave.

'I hope I can hold this feeling when I am outside again – in the street,' she said meditatively. 'There is something about this place – and you – that has made my worries seem very small. . . . Forgive my asking – if this isn't the thing to say – but shouldn't I pay somebody for this interview – pay it to the Cathedral, maybe?'

'Yes,' replied the Dean, 'I was just coming to that. Yo[u] are to go through that door at the right. You will find a sm[all] dressing-room. Take off your hat and coat, and return [to] me.'

She stood for a moment, mystified; then smiled, and obe[yed.] Presently she was back, waiting orders, her face ful[l of] inquiry.

'Now I want you to go out to the reception-room w[here] you waited when you came here, and inquire who is next. [You] will take that woman, whoever she is, into the small adj[acent] room: you know the one I mean.'

'Where your secretary took me,' said Sonia. 'Really – [she] was the sweetest person I ever met, Dean Harcourt. She [was] so tender – and understanding.'

'I am glad you found her so. . . . Well – you take your la[dy] into that little room and let her tell you all she wants to ab[out] her reasons for coming here, asking her the same general que[s]-tions you were asked. And then you come back and tell [me.] After that, you may bring her to my door. Then you wil[l be] free to recover your belongings and go your way. There [is] another exit from the dressing-room, leading into the hall[.]'

Sonia hesitated.

'But, Dean Harcourt' – she protested – 'it seems such a [thing] to ask *me* to do this when I have had no experience – [there] there is your secretary, outside, who knows exactly what to [do.]'

58

to people. I never met anyone so – so thoroughly fitted to deal with a person in trouble.'

The Dean smiled enigmatically.

'That woman is not my secretary,' he said quietly. 'She was my last caller – just before you came.'

Sonia's amazement parted her lips and narrowed her eyes.

'Do you always make them do that?' she asked.

'No – just the ones I think I can trust to do it well.'

'I'll try,' she said.

She was gone for about five minutes and returned with a distressed face. It was quite evident that she had been crying.

'Well?'

'Oh – Dean Harcourt – it's about her little girl. The doctors told her this morning that the little thing isn't ever going to be right, mentally; a brain tumour, or something. She's simply heart-broken. . . . And there wasn't a thing I could say that would have been of any comfort to her. . . . I just held her – and couldn't talk. I'm afraid you made a mistake in sending me out there.'

'It was very well done, I think,' said the Dean. 'Now go and bring her in. And then you go round to the dressing-room and powder your nose – and run along. It has been a good day's work.'

Sonia impulsively clasped his hand.

'I think you're wonderful!' she exclaimed, smiling pensively through her tears.

'No, Sonia,' he replied, measuring his words slowly, 'I'm not wonderful. . . . But you have made connexion with something, this afternoon, that is *wonderful – wonderful*!' Drawing himself out of the introspective mood in which he seemed to have been speaking more to himself than to her, he added: 'When you leave the dressing-room, if you turn to the right the hallway will lead you directly into the nave of the Cathedral. . . . Go out that way. And when you are there, tarry a moment, sit down, face the altar, and say a little prayer for me. . . . I am not very strong, you know, and I need the co-operation of people like you.'

The clock in the great bell-tower was striking four. Trinity's theme song vibrated in the air.

Sonia sank to her knees beside the Dean's chair and murmured, brokenly. 'People like *me*! . . . *Oh, my God!*'

He laid a firm hand on her quivering shoulder.

'Come,' he said gently, 'your friend is waiting.'

She rose to her feet and walked unsteadily to the door, stood for a moment with her hand on the knob, wiping her eyes and striving valiantly to regain her self-control. Then she glanced back at the Dean, who sat with his elbows on the desk, his seamed face cupped in his hand, and a rapt expression in ' s eyes, listening to the bells.

Sonia smiled bravely, and turned the knob.

'I think I'll be all right now,' she said.

'Yes – child,' replied the Dean, as one answering from a ream, 'you'll be – all right – now.'

Chapter Five

'SOMETHING tells me, Dr Norwood, that you came here to please our mutual friend Sinclair rather than in pursuit of a personal wish.'

Dean Harcourt significantly tapped the typed note with his gold pince-nez and regarded his taciturn guest with an interrogatory smile.

Andrew Norwood, who with suppressed impatience had been dourly torturing a closely clipped, fair moustache, stole a quick glance from under his contracted brows, reluctantly met the Dean's inquiring eyes, recrossed the lengthy legs of a former all-American tackler, and drew his normally pleasant mouth into something halfway between a scowl and a grin.

'Sometimes,' amplified the Dean, with the barest suggestion of a bantering twinkle, 'a letter of introduction is a white elephant.'

The interview was not taking off as Norwood had expected. This Dean Harcourt was anything but the benignly naïve old gentleman he had pictured. His infrequent glimpses of the distinguished churchman had been at a long range. He had seen him, a time or two, on the platform at large civic assemblies; had heard him read a formal prayer at a Commencement; had indifferently assumed him to be the typical stage-jeered clergyman, medieval, other-worldly, unctuous, and sweetly suave. Doubtless he would be so flattered by an unsolicited call from a university professor, bearing a letter from a prominent bank president, that his surprised delight would make him annoyingly agreeable. Norwood knew now that he had been mistaken, and felt himself at an absurd disadvantage in the presence of this man who had the eyes of a fluoroscope.

'It is quite true, sir,' he confessed stiffly, 'that I might not have asked for this conference but for the suggestion of Mr Sinclair.'

Dean Harcourt received this frankness with a cordial bow. Bombarded all day long with the emotional onslaughts of people who hurled their troubles at him through a drizzle of tears, it was refreshing to face this sullen but handsome fellow whose every gesture said that he hadn't wanted to come.

'Robert Sinclair,' remarked the Dean casually, 'is a trustee of Trinity Cathedral and a personal friend of mine. May I inquire how he is related to you?'

'He did not tell you?'

'No.'

Norwood stroked his strong jaw moodily, and considered an explanation.

'I had hoped you might not ask me that,' he said, at length, with a trace of asperity. 'I had occasion yesterday to negotiate a modest loan. As a small depositor with no collateral, I was referred to Mr Sinclair. In the course of our conversation, which involved an intimate account of my personal affairs from the cradle to the grave, he advised me to talk to you.'

'And granted you the loan on that condition?'

'Well,' admitted Norwood, flushing slightly, 'he did not demand it, in so many words; but he made it quite clear that he expected me to comply.'

Dean Harcourt adjusted his glasses and dipped his pen in the ink.

'Now that you have discharged this part of your obligation to Mr Sinclair,' he said dryly, 'I shall sign my name to his letter and restore it to you so that you may be able to prove—'

'Oh, I say, sir,' growled Norwood, hitching his chair a little closer to the big mahogany desk, 'I haven't meant to be so testy and impolite. I have been in trouble. But it isn't the sort of thing I want to confide. If I did, I wouldn't go – off my own bat – to a member of your profession. Whatever feeling I have toward the Church is antagonistic. My presence here is an impertinence. And – anyway – I dislike to air my private perplexities.'

'I can understand that attitude.' The Dean leaned back at ease in his tall chair, as if the business of their conference had been concluded. 'Your disinclination to talk about your troubles puts me on your side, I think. You are fortunate in that you do not want to be pitied. In most cases, pity is ruinous. All one needs to say to many an unhappy person is, "You poor thing!" and the victim immediately sets about to demonstrate how poor a thing he is.'

Norwood pulled a crooked smile which said that he was not going to be taken into camp easily.

'So – we don't have to discuss your affairs,' continued Dean Harcourt. 'I observe that you are a professor of modern history. Perhaps you would prefer to talk about that. Who, for instance, did more for England – Gladstone or Disraeli?'

'Yes – I am a professor of history,' snapped Norwood, suddenly aflame. 'My trouble is located at that spot,' he went on impetuously. 'I came to the university as an associate professor in 1923. Two years later I was given a full professorship. It was no secret in the faculty that when Professor Denton reached retirement age, I was expected to succeed him as head of the department. It was his wish. As you are undoubtedly aware, Dr Denton, after many months of illness – during which time I assumed his duties – died in September. Our new president, Dr Markham, has just announced that he is bringing in Ware of Oxford to take the position.

'This has been a serious disappointment to me, sir. For one thing, I have need of the increased salary; had already liberalized my budget in anticipation of it. But – far more importantly – this has been a blow to my career.'

He paused, and for the first time looked Dean Harcourt squarely in the eyes with a man-to-man request for sympathetic understanding, meeting encouragement in the deep-lined face. Norwood was suddenly struck with the ineradicable marks of long-borne pain which furrowed the tense lips.

'Since the death of my wife,' Norwood surprised himself by confiding, 'there has been little to absorb my time and thought but my profession. That was four years ago. We were very good companions. I have a small child. I am trying to keep her with me. She is a comfort, of course, but the care of her limits my outside interests. My profession, therefore, constitutes my present life. I have thrown myself into it with complete abandonment of everything else. And now it appears that I have gone about as far in it as I am likely to go. At sixty I shall be exactly where I am – at thirty-eight.'

'Do your students appear to have any opinions on this subject?' interjected Dean Harcourt.

'They do!' declared Norwood promptly. 'I am told there was a well-attended indignation meeting, the night before last.'

'Rather unfortunate,' remarked the Dean. 'However, you will be able to correct that before it has done any damage.'

'Damage! What damage? Shouldn't they have the right to express themselves on this injustice?'

Dean Harcourt sat silently toying with a paper-knife, broodingly searching his visitor's troubled face. Presently his eyes drifted slowly to a beautiful etching on the southern wall, at his left – a superb reproduction of Holman Hunt's *The Light of the World*. Norwood's gaze, instinctively following along, rested briefly on the picture. He was annoyed. The Dean was staging a rebuke.

'Of course,' he muttered, nodding his head toward the etching, 'that is the ideal attitude to take – crown of thorns – meek submission – gentle tapping on the door that has been slammed in one's face. Not much of that on display at the university, I can assure you! – and it's supposedly a Christian institution. *He* may have been the light of the world; but, so far as I can see, organized Christianity has done more to keep the world in darkness than any other influence in human history! Even the Buddhists never burned a scientist at the stake!'

'They never had any to burn,' said Dean Harcourt quietly. 'But – be all that as it may, Dr Norwood,' he continued, waiving the irascible comments of his gloomy guest, 'it seems to me that this apparent misfortune of yours is an important event in your career. You have now been offered – left-handedly, I admit – an unusual opportunity. Here are the facts in the case. You have been badly treated and the university knows it. A position to which you were entitled has been given to a stranger. Your students are loyally incensed. They will be prejudiced against the new man when he arrives. This will make it difficult for the history department to function properly.

64

'You, I take it, would be the last man to desire that unhappy state of things, for you are sincerely interested in the welfare of your department – so much so, indeed, that you should have been put in command of it. Why don't you call a meeting of your indignant students and request them to accept the situation exactly as it stands? The ship is more important than any member of the crew – including the captain and the first mate. When this Oxford professor turns up, be his friend.'

Norwood, slightly mollified, was listening attentively now.

'You will discover,' predicted the Dean, 'that your faculty friends will be glad that an episode threatening disruption and bad feeling has been handled with diplomacy. And as for your students . . . man! – what a chance! If you are looking for a brilliant career as a teacher, step into it. It is ready and waiting for you. The average college youngster is much more interested in sportsmanship than scholarship. This disappointment of yours, if properly interpreted, is going to add importance to every word you say in your classroom.

'History must be rather difficult to teach, these days,' pursued the Dean, soliloquizing. 'So much of it has been shown to be merely nationalistic propaganda; monumental falsehoods, spread on a large canvas; unjustifiable mass martyrdoms demanded by the greed and egotism of selfish and pompous men. . . . And that's a pity, for there has been no influence so far-reaching and ennobling as these epics of gallant hazards. To preserve the essential values of that stirring saga, it must be interpreted to this new generation by men who, themselves, are morally equipped to recognize bravery when they see it. If this task of evaluating history is delegated to muck-rakers, idol-smashers, and grave-robbers, the moral losses will be incalculable, and a great deal of the damage will be irreparable. The oncoming crop of young men have had it explained to them that war is a racket. And perhaps it is just as well, for the sake of the world's peace, that this sentiment should be developed. But it should also be taught that *courage is not a racket*! And the man best qualified to point out that distinction is one who can talk about heroism with the authority of personal experience.

'You see, my friend,' persisted Dean Harcourt earnestly, 'we are at our best when serving as time-binders. Heaven help the era that scornfully repudiates its past! The normal human spirit has an instinctive talent for the building of monuments and a reverent regard for the sanctity of tombs. The average man, whether he realizes it or not, has been more directly guided into whatever nobility he possesses by the silent inspiration of the valiant dead than the clarion challenges of his own time. Would it not be a vast misfortune if, by the ruthless destruction of that guidance, we and those who come after us should be doomed to live in a world of pillaged sepulchres and desecrated shrines?

'Now it happens that the very large majority of all these inspiring *memorabilia* are reminiscent of wars. Most of the heroes who sit on iron horses in the public parks of all nations were celebrated soldiers; most of the marble busts of eminent statesmen in the world's cherished halls of fame perpetuate the glory of diplomatists who came by their distinction during period of strife. . . . You historians are very properly teaching the potential leaders of the new day to despise and discountenance war. So be it. You are on the right track, I think. But the thing that worries me is the utter absence of a programme for the monuments to be erected now and henceforth. What kind of people are going to bestride the iron horses of the future? What symbols of valour do you suggest? Perhaps you will advocate the type of courage exemplified in personal sacrifice and self-renunciation for the sake of the general good. Do you think you could ever stir a youngster's pulse with that manner of appeal? Could you make the call of self-abandoning duty alluring enough to compete with the rattle of a drum? I firmly believe you could! But – to do it with any hope of success, you yourself would have to come into your lecture-hall armed with the credentials certifying that *you had tried it*!' . . .

'I do see your point,' agreed Norwood, 'and I admit the soundness of your argument. But – even so – to have been completely thwarted in one's rightful expectation of professional advancement is a nasty dose to take. Perhaps' – he went on, feeling his way – 'perhaps you do not realize just what that means, Dean Harcourt. You yourself have been a very successful man in your profession. You are well at the top of it. I dare say you never experienced what I am going through.'

Dean Harcourt slowly raised his dark, cavernous eyes, and gave Norwood a long, searching look that made him wonder to what length of inexcusable impudence he had committed himself. It was so very plainly written on this man's face that he had suffered.

He waited, flushed with chagrin, for the Dean to defend himself against the charge that he had counselled a sacrifice of personal ambition without a first-hand knowledge of its cost. A whole minute passed. Dean Harcourt ventured no reply to the challenge; sat now with bowed head. It left Norwood defencelessly despising himself.

After a while the Dean glanced up from the reflective mood into which he had fallen, and smiled. It was exactly as if he were tolerantly ignoring the awkward, blustering arrogance of a ten-year-old boy. Norwood disliked to have the interview close on this diminished seventh chord, but it was now quite obvious that Dean Harcourt had no intention of ending it otherwise.

'I meant no offence, sir,' ventured Norwood uneasily.

'Then there is none,' replied the Dean.

Norwood rose to go.

'Thank you,' he said deferentially, extending his hand.

'I wish there was some way for me to repay you for the time you have given me.'

The Dean's eyes suddenly lighted.

'I think you mean that,' he said cordially, 'and I am going to accept your tentative offer. Of late, I have been seriously disturbed about this very matter we have been discussing – the menaced value of history. I want some light on the subject. I have need to consult an expert in this field. There are many questions of a technical nature that I should like to ask you, for my personal benefit. This is, of course, quite unrelated to your own dilemma. . . . I wonder how you would like to come here to my house – it is difficult for me to go to yours – and spend an evening with me, sometime in the very near future. I need your counsel, Norwood.'

'It would be a great pleasure, sir.'

'You would come to dinner, I hope, and afterwards we will talk. It is a custom with us here to have a few guests at dinner on Thursday evenings. Quite informal. A visitor or two; men, usually, though not always. My curates – both of them accomplished and interesting men; Talbot, with an MA in English Literature from Cambridge, and Simpson of Harvard: perhaps you recall his record mile. . . . How about this coming Thursday?'

'Just at the moment,' replied Norwood regretfully, 'I am kept close in the evening. My little girl. I hope to make better arrangements soon. She was at a good boarding-school, but she became homesick. . . . Sorry, sir.'

'You couldn't bring your little girl along, could you? How old is she?'

'Only eight. I fear it would be an imposition.'

'If you only knew,' declared the Dean, 'how we bachelors grab at the chance to entertain small children in this lonely house, you would realize that you are conferring a great favour. . . . May we expect you?'

'I hope it won't be a burden,' said Norwood, offering his hand.

Shortly after five that afternoon Sonia came in, a pleasing picture of radiant vitality, self-confidence, and urbanity.

She paused a moment inside the door, considering Dean Harcourt with such a look of filial tenderness that he raised his hand to her in a welcoming salute, and regarded her with smiling interest as she approached his chair.

'Sonia – nobody has any business to be as happy as you are. What has happened to you?'

'I had a message from Dean Harcourt, asking me to come and see him. Isn't that enough?' She unpinned a bunch of violets from her coat, laid them on the desk beside his hand, and seated herself in the chair opposite him. 'Do tell me what it's all about!'

'It is something you can do for me. On Thursday evening we are to have a few guests here. It is a custom of the house –

these Thursday evening affairs. Most of the people who come here are in need of companionship. Usually they are strangers to one another. And it is not always too easy to – to—'

'No,' assisted Sonia, laughing. 'I shouldn't think it would be.'

'And I need you – this Thursday evening.'

'Thanks! I'll be delighted!'

'Well – don't be too sure about that. Sometimes we contrive to gather up an oddly assorted lot. This time, as it happens, we are to have a motherless child of eight. I particularly want to devote most of my attention to this little girl's father. And I wondered if—'

'So *that's* why I'm asked to your dinner!' commented Sonia, pretending a pout. 'Just as I was having visions of myself at the Dean's right hand, maybe, in my new black velvet, comes an order to eat my porridge in the nursery along with another little girl.'

'I have not seen this child,' said the Dean, amused. 'She may be the most engaging little angel you ever met. It is quite possible, on the other hand, that she may defy your best efforts to entertain her. If she is anything like her father, she will probably resent baby talk.'

'You mean,' said Sonia, impishly wide-eyed with surprise, 'her father doesn't talk any baby talk at all?'

'Not to me, he didn't,' replied the Dean, enjoying her drollery. 'There was a gold football on his watch-chain and I doubt if he ever painted a picture. Well – how about this party? Will you come?'

'You know perfectly well, Dean Harcourt,' she said, suddenly serious, 'that I should be happy doing anything for you.'

'Very good, my friend. I must let you go now. There are many waiting, and I dare not detain them while I talk with a woman as little in need of assistance as you are. Get along with you!'

She tarried at the door, seeming to have something on her mind; turned toward him, smiled, waited.

'Sonia!' called the Dean, 'would you oblige me by showing the next caller in?'

She swiftly recrossed the room, taking off her modish little black toque as she came, and patting her rumpled hair.

'Do you always read people's thoughts?' she asked, at the door of the dressing-room.

'Just their better ones,' the Dean replied gently.

An uncommonly attractive girl, in her early twenties, arose when Sonia, appearing in the doorway of the reception room, asked which of those waiting was next in turn.

'Will you come with me?' asked Sonia graciously, leading the way into the adjoining room. 'Sit down, please.' She pointed to the sofa in the farther corner, and they seated themselves together there.

Sonia, to whom the slightest detail of apparel was important, noted that the caller's clothing, expensively elegant, was not quite of the current mode, instantly surmising that the fair-haired girl, whose manner spoke of special privilege, belonged to the increasing ranks of the poor rich.

'I want to talk to you for a moment,' began Sonia kindly, 'before you see Dean Harcourt. Perhaps you do not know that the Dean is very hard-pressed all day long by people who come to him for advice. We try to shield him all we can. Sometimes it seems that callers have problems on their minds which could be dealt with by one of the curates. So – we make an effort to find out at least a little about it before—'

'I'm glad you do,' said the girl, in a low voice. 'That's quite right.'

'I knew you would understand. Is there anything you would like me to tell the Dean about you?'

'Tell him Phyllis is here.'

Sonia, arriving early as she had promised, learned from Mrs Crandall, the housekeeper, who showed her to an upstairs sitting-room, that there were to be no other women present.

Conscious of her specific errand there to extend hospitality to the Norwood child, she considered herself a member of the Dean's *ménage* rather than his guest, and found the sensation decidedly pleasant. The whole place stood for her as a refuge

70

and sanctuary. To be housed here even as a servant, she thought, would b an honour.

Gifted with a natural flair of easy adjustment to circumstances – she enjoyed nothing so much as playing an improvised *rôle* in some impromptu drama – Sonia quite mystified the gentle-spirited old lady with the confident assurance of her movements as she put away her hat and coat and gave brief but competent attention to herself in the cheval glass. Mrs Crandall, as they had entered the room, was on the point of saying that Miss Duquesne should make herself entirely at home. On further thought, this suggestion seemed superfluous. Indeed, Mrs Crandall would not have been surprised had Miss Duquesne said as much to her.

Mr Talbot appeared in the doorway and was presented. Mr Talbot was stocky, florid, round of face and sparse of hair, genial but not effusive. He hoped Miss Duquesne would not be so absorbed by her duty that the rest of them would have no chance to talk to her. It was jolly good of her to come, and the Dean would appreciate it mightily.

Sonia liked him, liked the tender note that crept into his voice when he spoke of the Dean. It instantly made them kin. She envied Mr Talbot, and said so with a disarming directness that lighted his pale blue eyes. It was evident that Mr Talbot was accepting Sonia as 'one of us', however little she appeared to belong in this ecclesiastical atmosphere.

There was a pleasant confusion in the hall downstairs as of arriving guests. Mr Talbot excused himself. Mrs Crandall told Sonia she might wait where she was, returning presently with the anticipated child, a slim, serious, dark-eyed little creature who, upon interrogation, unshyly replied that her name was Celeste, that her toes were not cold, and that the wooden box she had put down on the table while her coat was being tugged off contained playthings.

'Oh – do let me see!' exclaimed Sonia. 'I wonder if they're dolls . . . why, they're tin soldiers!'

'No,' corrected Celeste indulgently, pouring the contents of the box out on the rug and kneeling before them. 'Kings and queens and – such things. I expect you know them all.' She

71

began setting them up on their feet in a row.

'Well, not intimately,' confessed Sonia, adopting the child's serious attitude, 'but it would be interesting to meet them.'

'You know her, of course,' said Celeste, beginning with an easy one. 'Queen Elizabeth, with the tiara on her head.'

'And the tyre around her neck,' assisted Sonia, straight-faced, exploring her small guest's capacity for humour.

'That's a ruff,' Celeste explained, politely repressing a grin.

'I'll wager it was,' said Sonia sympathetically. 'It looks very uncomfortable.'

Celeste laughed merrily.

'You're funny,' she said, without looking up. 'This is Charles I. His hat comes off.'

'I thought his head came off, too.' Sonia had joined Celeste on the rug. They looked into each other's eyes, and smiled.

'What's your name?' inquired Celeste irrelevantly, stroking the velvet sleeve softly with her finger tips.

'Sonia.'

'Miss Sonia?'

'No – just Sonia.'

'Is Mrs – the lady – your mother?'

'No, dear. I don't live here. I am a guest, same as you.'

'May I sit by you at dinner?'

Sonia picked up the cool little hand and rubbed the back of it against her cheek. 'Yes, dear.'

'And will you play with me – afterwards? Or do you have to talk?'

'Dean Harcourt will be joining us in a few minutes,' Talbot was explaining cordially. 'He asked me to keep you company until he comes down. You are aware, I presume, that the Dean does not get about easily. The lift was an afterthought in this house, and the only place it could be installed on this level was in the dining-room, so we always meet the Dean there when he comes down from his living-quarters.'

'I knew Dean Harcourt was crippled,' said Norwood. 'I never learned the extent of it, or how he came by it. An accident?'

'It is an interesting story,' replied the curate. 'For a full appreciation of the Dean, one ought to know it. When Dean Harcourt was thirty-three, he was stricken down with infantile paralysis. For three years he had been the curate in a suburban parish, and had just been appointed its rector. He was already winning considerable attention as a brilliant speaker, and it was expected that he might become in time one of the great pulpit prophets. Aware of his gifts in that field, he was earnestly ambitious to develop. Life held out welcoming hands to him. He was very successful. His engagement had been announced to a beautiful young woman of distinguished social standing.

'Then – like a storm out of a clear blue sky, came this tragic thing that struck him down. He spent ten months in bed, utterly helpless from his hips.'

Norwood winced, and coloured slightly.

'I have been with him now for more than six years,' continued Talbot, 'and in that time he has spoken to me but once of that period he spent on his back. That was in reference to the joy he had felt when he discovered that he could wiggle his big toe. What he must have gone through, in mental torture, nobody has ever been informed, so far as I know. He may have told the Bishop.'

'I wish I had known that,' said Norwood, 'when I talked with him the other day. I went to him very much upset over a little predicament of mine, and—'

'Oh, the Dean doesn't want any sympathy – if that's what worries you. But I can assure you there isn't anything you are likely to tell him about yourself that can match the troubles he experienced through those days. . . . His fiancée decided, quite naturally, I presume, that matrimony was out of the question, and he cheerfully released her without any bitterness. His church was obliged to call another priest to take his place when it had become obvious that he could not carry on with his work. In short, his career collapsed.

'After an almost endless convalescence, he was able to sit at a desk. Eager to give him some little thing to do, the Bishop had him brought down, two days a week, to assist with his office interviews. After a while it became apparent that he was singularly equipped to deal with a wide variety of difficult cases requiring an understanding sympathy. The word began to spread. He sat there, day after day, building up a reputation probably unlike that of any other man in our profession, and when it was suggested that he be made the Dean of the Cathedral, everybody hailed the choice with enthusiasm. He carries a heavy load. We often wonder how he does it. It would probably have killed a normal man long since.'

Norwood was spared the necessity of comment by the announcement that dinner was served. The Dean was already in his chair at the head of the table when they arrived in the dining-room. The others were there. Celeste detached herself from her new friend, at the sight of her father, and drew him by the hand while he was receiving an introduction to Simpson.

'Sonia,' she said, indifferent to the interested group that had been brought to attention by her childish treble, 'this is my daddy.' And then added, with ice-breaking *naïveté*, 'Daddy – she's wonderful!'

'So you found that out, too!' called the Dean. 'I want you to sit by me, little fellow.'

'And Sonia next?' insisted Celeste. 'And Daddy there?'

'That will be a very good arrangement,' said Mrs Crandall, amused.

Dean Harcourt spoke a brief grace, Celeste regarding the unfamiliar rite with baffled eyes.

'What did you say?' she inquired confidentially, but quite audibly, in the momentary hush that followed the Dean's words.

'I thanked God for our food,' he replied, making a greater effort to be sober than either of his curates could recall of him.

Celeste glanced over the table appraisingly and returned her eyes to his.

'There'll be some here, presently,' he assured her.

'Do you always do that?' pressed Celeste respectfully.

'Always.'

Sonia had begun to feel that somebody had better declare it a closed incident pretty soon, but disliked to take the risk of offending the child. Norwood's dress collar was fitting too

74

snugly. Simpson and Talbot, he observed, were enjoying the episode with shining eyes.

'Even when there's nothing,' persevered Celeste, 'but a glass of milk and a cooky?'

This proved too much for everybody, including the Dean, and Celeste, suddenly suspecting that she was stealing the show, remembered a recent parental injunction strongly bearing on this matter, and blinkingly consulted her father's glowing face for counsel.

'Mushroom soup,' whispered Sonia, 'just as we had hoped.'

Norwood, relieved, addressed himself to Mrs Crandall, but remained quite conscious of Sonia, who with tender tact had caught up his own flesh and blood on the brink of a social disaster. He warmed toward her, and wondered what manner of person she was. Sonia instinctively sensed his interest. The party was too small to encourage group conversations, and they had almost nothing to say directly to each other, but on the few occasions when Sonia ventured a remark to him, she found Norwood quickly attentive and apparently eager to draw her out.

'Celeste has been showing me her gallery of immortals,' remarked Sonia. 'I wondered if this wouldn't be a good way to teach history in college.'

'A novelty, at least,' replied Norwood, interested in her eyes.

'You could have a stage, and move them about.'

'Like chessmen,' he assisted.

'Why not? One often hears of the chessboard of history,' reflected Sonia, hoping the stream she had ventured into was safe for wading.

Catching Dean Harcourt's questing eye, Norwood drew him in by explaining briefly, Sonia illumining the talk with a fragment of the discussion she had had with Celeste about the unfortunate Charles Stuart.

'It's a useful idea, Dr Norwood,' observed the Dean. 'You could rig up a working model of a dynastic machine shop operating during the reign of Charles, for example, showing George Villiers in the jaws of a lathe being turned into the Duke of Buckingham, and—'

'And Wentworth being turned into the Earl of Strafford,'

supplied Norwood, pleased with the game. 'Not a bad idea, at all.'

Sonia, mindful of her trust, smilingly retreated from this cryptic conversation to assist Celeste with her lamb chop, Norwood wondering how closely she had been able to follow. To his delight, she returned to say, 'And the whole Cromwell outfit being turned from tavern-keepers into puffy land-holders.'

'Excellent!' approved the Dean. 'Now we really are getting somewhere. You could show the Cromwells leaving their pubs for mansions. Ah, but what a boon the Reformation was for the brand-new lords who divided among themselves the land stolen from the monasteries. But it was hard on the nation. The machine made a great many nobodies, like the Cromwells, suddenly dangerous.'

Norwood was so happily surprised at this self-disclosure of the old churchman's unprejudiced breadth that his amazement showed in his face.

'Oh, yes – I'm a Protestant,' the Dean hastened to add, 'but that does not blind me to the facts. Had there been no property involved in the Reformation in England, it would have been a far different affair. But the same thing is true of all the religious wars, don't you think, Dr Norwood? The common people were always informed that their holy war was led by men of consecration to a righteous cause; most of them never lived long enough to find out that they had been led by men bent on the confiscation of property.'

'Will there be room in the historical machine shop for all that?' inquired Sonia, dividing her question between Norwood and their host.

'I'll undertake to answer for him,' said the Dean. 'There's always more room in the modern history class for an elucidation of that sickening fact than the picture of honestly brave men throwing their lives away under the impression that they were obeying the divine will of the Lord.'

'Logically, then,' put in Talbot, 'it probably wasn't the will of the Lord that there should have been a Reformation, at all, and in that case Protestantism is a mistake – and Trinity Cathedral is a mistake!'

'There you are,' said the Dean, directing himself toward the professor, almost as if they were alone. 'That brings us back to the thing we were talking about the other day, Norwood. You and I know exactly how we got our Protestantism. But however we came by it, here it is! And whatever is – in the long run – is right! You can depend on that! Here, too, is Catholicism – stronger than ever. By the same token, it, too, is right!'

'Perhaps,' suggested Sonia, when the Dean's eyes had drifted to her, 'perhaps these common men who sincerely fought for their respective creeds weren't so very far wrong, then, in the light of history, when they thought they were doing God's will. Maybe it *was* God's will!'

'Wouldn't that be funny!' chuckled Celeste, feeling that she had been left beached long enough. Simpson, also an innocent bystander, led the laughter in which Celeste tardily but hilariously joined when the general appreciation of her witticism had moved her to regard it a better thing than she had suspected.

Mrs Crandall observed that it was a pity the great and solemn ecclesiastical conventions couldn't be attended by a few little folks like Celeste who might clear the fog with an occasional comment; then the party adjourned, Talbot and Simpson excusing themselves, the ladies returning to the upstairs sitting-room, Norwood wheeling the Dean into a quiet corner of the living-room. It gave him a feeling of tenderness.

Dean Harcourt plunged at once into a series of questions. Did Dr Norwood believe in a "planned universe"?

'It certainly seems so, sometimes,' Dr Norwood heard himself saying, not quite sure whether his reply had been dictated by courtesy, conviction, or confusion.

Well – if it was planned at all, what proportion of its phenomenal activity, in the opinion of Dr Norwood, was directed, and how much of it was "on the loose"? Take a devastating pestilence, for example: was that put on for the purpose of pruning a superabundant or undesirable population; or was it just the natural recompense of filthy living?

'The latter, more likely,' guessed Dr Norwood, adding, 'though I make no pretence to be an authority on sociology – or pathology, either.'

77

'How about a costly forest fire, touched off by lightning: would you consider that accidental or ordained?'

'I am not a theologian, sir,' parried Norwood, pleased that he had found temporary shelter.

'Granted. You are not a sociologist, biologist, or theologian. You are an historian. Now – when the monarchies began to cave in, was that attributable to a widespread epidemic of democracy, or did it indicate that the monarchical system had, for the time at least, served its purpose? And now that the democracies are giving it up, in favour of dictatorships, does that mean that the monarchical system was right, all the while, and that the effort to democratize was a mistake?'

'But it hasn't been proved that we ever had any democracies. What we have called democracies were oligarchies.'

'But the private citizen has had the right to vote for the kind of government he prefers. Isn't that true?'

'Not quite,' objected Norwood. 'He has been permitted to choose which of two or three oligarchies he would consider the least insufferable.'

'Then democracy hasn't really failed, seeing that we've never tried it.'

'No – it's the oligarchy that has failed,' said Norwood.

'Would you call it a failure,' queried the Dean thoughtfully, 'or might it be more correct to say that the oligarchy had been brought on to dispose of the abuses of despotism? If the latter, it was not a failure but a phase of political progress. Does the present clamour for dictators indicate that the social order is at its best under absolute monarchies? Dr Norwood, do you believe that "whatever is, is right" – in the long run? ... *I* do!'

'I'm not so sure about that.'

'Then you'll have to give up your idea of "a planned universe."'

'Well – that won't be hard to do. I'm not sure of that, either.'

'Yes, but what becomes of history, then? Doesn't it lose all its significance?'

'Do you mean to say, sir,' asked Norwood seriously, 'that

78

you interpret every social, political, and economic movement as a response to a predestined arrangement? The bloody revolutions, for example: not a very happy arrangement for the people who experience them, surely.'

'No,' said the Dean, 'but they were a phase of human progress; and, as I said to you the other day, "the ship is more important than the crew." You and I both know that this is true, in our own experience; don't we?' His voice had lowered to a note of comradeship.

Norwood, with the story of the Dean's vicissitudes fresh in his mind, felt a bond of mutual interest between them. At the moment, his own problems seemed of negligible concern. Was it Dean Harcourt's philosophy that had done it, or had his own difficulties been driven into the shadow by a new interest? . . . Who was this Sonia Duquesne?

They left shortly before ten, for Celeste must be put to bed. Sonia, attractively attired for the street, brought the child down, and asked Mrs Crandall if she might telephone for a taxi.

'Can't we take Sonia home, Daddy?' entreated Celeste.

Sonia mildly protested, but consented when Norwood's invitation was pressed.

After the hall door had been closed on them, Mrs Crandall returned to the living-room where the Dean sat, alone, lost in his thoughts.

'Odd little elf, that Celeste,' remarked Mrs Crandall.

'Yes; isn't she?' smiled the Dean absently.

'And you're an old matchmaker.'

'Not this time.'

'He was very much charmed.'

'It takes two. And Sonia wasn't intended for the faculty of a university. Perhaps Celeste will attend to it, but I doubt it. However — Norwood needs something new to worry about. A good cure for trouble is a little more. It's on the principle of a serum.'

'Nonsense!' said Mrs Crandall. 'And it's your bedtime.'

Chapter Six

WHEN Colonel Livingstone Brock was ceremoniously laid away, one dripping April afternoon in 1911, with his militant grey imperial stiffly waxed and the bluish-white fingers of his renowned right hand thrust between the first and second buttons of his worn Prince Albert, it was editorially observed by the *Courier-Journal* that the regrettable departure of this beloved citizen of Leeds marked the close of a picturesque era in forensic oratory.

For sixteen consecutive years no debatable measure had been acted by the State Legislature without the benefit of Colonel Brock's expressed opinion. Not always were his views or his vote predictable. Although by disposition and training a conservative, it not infrequently occurred that a passionately eloquent plea from some gallant old spell-binder of his own political faith would bring the Colonel to his feet; whereupon, to the surprise of nobody more than its beleaguered defenders, this tall, straight-backed senator from Leeds would come valiantly to the rescue of the embattled cause, for sheer love of skilful argument, the felicitous phrase, and the rounded period.

'No matter what was the nature of the resolution,' continued Mr Trumbull, who had been reciting this story for the delectation of a newly arrived guest at the Mansion, as they smoked after supper on the spacious veranda, 'it made no difference how insignificant it was, the Colonel's peroration always called upon high heaven to witness and hallow his imperishable hope that the fair name of the great State of Kentucky might remain for ever unsullied as the driven snow on inaccessible Alpine crags, sacred as the love of a mother for the sleeping babe at her breast, and dependable as the everlasting stars.'

'And then,' suggested the urbane stranger, whom the local attorney was beginning to like immensely, 'the Colonel probably retired to cool himself off with a mint julep.'

'Precisely!' agreed Mr Trumbull, delighted that Providence had sent him someone capable of appreciating his ponderous drollery. 'Precisely! – accompanied by the spokesman for the opposition.'

'Who no doubt paid for the drinks,' added the handsome visitor encouragingly.

'Precisely! I see you're getting an accurate picture of the old Colonel, which is necessary to an understanding of this house and our landlord – and the town, too, for that matter.'

The lean-faced, middle-aged bachelor pounded out his pipe on the rail of the veranda, filled it with fine-cut, draped a long, shabby leg over the squeaking arm of the disintegrating wicker chair, munched reminiscently, and grinned. It had been a great while since he had reviewed the Brock saga, and never had he told it to anyone so prompt to savour the piquant flavour of his ironical wit and to view with quick understanding the pastel nuances of straight-faced pleasantries. Mr Trumbull was at peace with the world. This quiet-voiced Yankee in the adjoining chair was one of the most charming personalities he had ever met. Moreover, the supper had been unusually good, befitting the arrival of a new guest whom the Mansion hoped to impress favourably. The low afternoon sun, unseasonably warm for late November, comforted his spirit.

'And generally,' he went on, chuckling dryly, 'the Colonel's speech would put it over too. . . . The first time I ever heard him make it, I was just a young smart aleck, fresh from law school. It was on a bill to reimburse some poor devil of a farmer four dollars and fifty cents for a couple of shoats that had drowned in a pond on state property. I knew it was funny, but I didn't laugh – not while it was going on.'

'Was there snow in the Alps that time, too?' wondered the good-natured stranger.

'Precisely – and the Morning Stars sang together.'

'How about the shoats?'

'You'd make a good lawyer, Mr – your name is Parker,

81

isn't it? I noticed it on the register. Mine is Trumbull – Jefferson D. Trumbull.' They rose and shook hands, reseated themselves, and Mr Trumbull continued. 'The shoats were paid for by the great State of Kentucky, and if the Colonel had gone on for another five minutes, there would have been a really fine bronze tablet put up in their memory.'

'And our Mr Brock,' queried the interested stranger, 'was he the Colonel's sole heir?'

'Well,' hesitated Mr Trumbull, screwing up his face judicially, 'perhaps "heir" isn't just the word we're looking for. Clay was the Colonel's sole survivor – if that's what you mean. And he did inherit the old man's childlike indifference to the practical things of this world, such as monthly bills and notes payable. Clay's other legacy was this fine old house, which has been gradually falling to pieces for many years.

'I dare say it is a fine thing,' he rumbled on, taking elaborate pains to be serious, 'for a municipality to be distinguished for something unique. Take Leadville, Colorado. Highest altitude. People like to go there so they can write a postcard to the folks from the highest town in the land. And there is a little place over here in Indiana that claims to be the exact centre of US population. You take New York: they've got something that sets them apart. The lions out in front of the Public Library have longer tails than any other lions in this country. . . . Now I want to tell you something distinctive about Leeds. Maybe you don't know that this old house – right where we're sitting – has, in proportion to its assessed value, the biggest mortgage on it of any hotel property in the whole world!'

'I fancy there's quite a brisk competition, too,' commented Mr Parker. 'Is that why they don't paint it?'

'Precisely! The mortgage covers it from the shingles to the ground. This happens to be fresh in my mind just now, because' – Mr Trumbull glanced over his shoulder, took stock of the open windows, and lowered his voice confidentially – 'because I am Clay Brock's attorney and the interest will be due again a week from tomorrow. I don't know of any stated event that comes around faster than these dates for Brock's mortgage interest. It's a good deal like Mr Rockefeller's birthday; seems to have one every few weeks.'

'Hard up, is he? Mr Brock – I mean.'

'Hard *up*! . . . I don't know the exact value of that phrase up North where you come from, but down here in this country when we say a man's hard up, we merely mean that he's broke. Clay's dropped out of that class. The Colonel had dropped out of it before Clay was born – forty-five years ago. . . . By the way – though I reckon it's none of my business – are you planning to stop off here at the Mansion for a spell? I hope you are, if you don't mind my saying so.'

'It is quite possible – thank you. I rather like the old place.'

'In that case, I want to tell you something. Clay Brock – God bless him – is a great hand to borrow ten dollars until Saturday. I'm sure I don't know what bright promise Saturday holds out to him above the other days of the week. I reckon he just selected Saturday as a day when he would pay his debts if he had the money; and he *would, too*!' Mr Trumbull's loyalty to his landlord-client was almost belligerent. 'He's a fine fellow! No, *sir*! There's nothing wrong with Clay Brock except that he was brought up in this expensive house to believe that he would be looked after by the Lord God of Hosts.'

'Maybe that's why he went into the hotel business,' ventured the amiable Parker, gravely.

The seedy lawyer permitted himself to laugh aloud, disclosing the need of much dental attention; then, suddenly sobering, he looked about, furtively, and in a subdued tone advised, 'You want to be careful with remarks like that in Leeds. We take the Lord mighty serious down here.'

'Don't you suppose He has a sense of humour?'

'Umm – perhaps. But I don't think the local brethren play it up much. Be that as it may, I've often wondered if Clay Brock isn't being cared for by the angels. For seven years I have lived under this leaky roof. The Brocks managed to get along somehow. There's always enough to eat. And you'll find Clara Brock to be one of the finest women you ever saw! Now, I wouldn't leave you under the impression that Clay isn't respected. Why, he has been the mayor of Leeds for years. . . . See that traffic light out there on the corner? He had that put up – just to give Leeds an air.'

'I'm rather glad he did,' declared the whimsical Parker. 'It really accounts for our being here. We were headed in the general direction of New Orleans, but in no great hurry. Sort of a vacation trip. The St Louis-to-Nashville bus came to a stop at that light, and while it waited—'

'And it waits a long time,' interposed Mr Trumbull, grinning. 'That's to let the heavy cross-town traffic through. I reckon you noticed the congestion.'

Mr Parker, with half-closed eyes, took a long, deep inhalation from his cigarette before offering the playful rejoinder which he knew was expected. In that brief, painful pause, his thoughts were running riot. How transparently clear it was that this shabby, disappointed country lawyer, whom Life had shunted on to this grass-grown siding, hoped to win an hour of friendly attention with his droll persiflage. Destiny hadn't even been decent enough to Jefferson D. Trumbull to hand him a tragedy loaded with agony. Once – when he was that young 'smart-aleck just out of law school' – Trumbull had hugged the idea of a brilliant career; had sat in the gallery of the State Legislature looking down on the shining bald heads and leonine shocks of white hair, saying to himself, 'I shall sit there, some day!' And Life had elbowed him out to little Leeds.

It suddenly occurred to Parker that the world must be fairly well stocked with brittle old chaps like Trumbull who sat on unpainted country hotel verandas of an evening, ironically spoofing their defeat to the tune of the frogs and the crickets. Once, doubtless, Trumbull had been in a grand state of impatience; then the impatience had mounted to desperation; then the desperation had burned out, leaving the grey ashes of resignation. Now he had reached the point where – lacking even a great tragedy to remember in the afternoon of his life – he was willing to call his pitiful little show a comedy!

'God!' thought Parker, closing his eyes against the smarting

84

smoke, 'will I ever sink to the point where I can joke about it to a stranger?'

Pulling himself together with an effort, he grinned and met Jefferson D. Trumbull on the ground he had staked off.

'No; my attention was too absorbed by this beautiful old house; these tall white columns, the rambling second-floor veranda, the shady lawn. I thought it might be pleasant if we got off here for a few days. We're not travelling on a very rigid schedule.'

'We?' repeated Mr Trumbull curiously. 'Somebody with you? I saw only one name in the book.'

'I never register for her,' explained Parker, motioning with his head towards his companion, who, suspecting an introduction was impending, rose from her contented sprawl in the corner and sauntered toward them.

'Is that *your* dog? I was meaning to ask somebody how she got here. Didn't recognize her, and I know most of the really good dogs in this town. . . . Come here, sister; what's your name?' The shaggy-haired lawyer glanced up inquiringly, and her owner supplied the information.

'What? . . . Well, if that isn't a hell of a name for a dog,' drawled Mr Trumbull, stroking the long, silky ears. 'We'll have to take you out into the country and show you some partridge – Sylvia.'

A week had passed – with surprising swiftness, too, for an idle man who had been long accustomed to a crowded programme of exacting duties. Leeds accepted him for what he seemed to be – a quiet, genteel, young man of leisure. Sylvia, for ever at his heels, disarmed whatever suspicion might have disturbed the mind of the dog-loving public in respect to the stranger.

He had written 'Nathan Parker' on a blank page at the Mansion with an unhesitating hand, for it was not the first time he had registered that way. The name had been adopted a month ago without much premeditation beyond a feeling that it would be convenient if the initials of his alias agreed with the monogram on a silver cigarette-case which was about all he

85

had left now, besides Sylvia, to remind him of the life he had abandoned.

Sometimes he had been amazed at the ease and rapidity of his self-adjustment to his new identity, responding automatically when addressed as 'Mr Parker'. He wondered whether it would come as a shock if someone ever ventured to call him 'Nathan', but that was unlikely. Pains would be taken to see that nobody entered quite that fully into his confidence.

It pleased Nathan Parker that the Mansion Hotel had shown no signs of being actively inquisitive about him. Mr Brock, who had not been about when he arrived, had come up to his huge, shabby, high-ceilinged, second-floor room at nine that first night, to inquire whether he was comfortable. He had tarried for a half-hour, seated on the bed – what time he was not journeying dignifiedly to and from an impressive brass cuspidor, hard-by the antique walnut desk – genially offering comments on his town of Leeds, of which he spoke with proprietorial pride and an affection implied by his tone rather than his words. Mr Brock seemed to feel that the visitor from afar should be much interested in the fact that you could drive from here into Illinois or Missouri or Tennessee 'in two hours; an hour and a half – if you step on it.' Mr Brock, himself, had nothing to 'step on' but his own two feet.

As for Mr Parker's relation to other natural phenomena, the improvident, lovable son of the famed Colonel Brock exhibited no outward concern. Perhaps this attitude did not guarantee a total want of interest. Indeed, reflected the vagabond, it might indicate a conviction on Brock's part that his guest had something to conceal, and therefore might be disconcerted by cordial questions which under any other circumstances would have been considered in good taste.

Young Clay, obviously unhappy and restless at twenty-two, had been for two or three days teetering on the edge of a decision to scrape acquaintance, Parker observed with considerable gratification. The boy was tall, slim, serious, almost sullen; though whether his gloomy reticence was temperamental, or explained by the fact that his clothing was shabby and his menial tasks distasteful, was difficult for a stranger to determine. He would let the youth attend to the overtures of whatever friendship they might have when he got around to it.

Mrs Brock, supervising the whole establishment, was by instinct clearly a lady; by background too, no doubt, for her father, the venerable Dr Graham, who lived three blocks down the shady street, was, according to Mr Trumbull, one of the most important men in the community. Willing to talk – for she had begun to manifest something like solicitude for the lonesome fellow who strolled all day with his dog and retired early to bed – Clara Brock had spoken of her father and of Elise, his granddaughter, who lived with him. It was apparent that she took a great deal of pride in the girl.

'Elise has a voice,' she confided, one evening, as they sat on the veranda. ' I don't mean she just sings a little better than the other girls in the church choir. She has a great voice, and it's a pity she can't do anything about it. Father sent her to Louisville for three winters, but times are going to be too bad this season. And Father isn't so strong any more. Seventy-three. He'll have to stop some day soon. We all think it is a shame that he has to make those long trips; all kinds of weather and terrible roads off the main highways in the winter. But I reckon you understand how it is: when a man's been doctoring in one place for forty-two years, it's impossible for anybody either to come into the world or go out of it unless Father's present. So – he's breaking, and mustn't try to do any more for Elise. It's hard on poor Clay, too, for his grandpa had hoped he would be able to help him when the time came.'

Parker murmured his polite regret that the young lady was unable to finish her voice training.

'The trouble is, Elise hasn't anyone to give her an introduction to the sort of people she ought to know if she's ever to make anything out of her music. It takes money to put on a recital in such a way that she could get a little attention. Of course – I reckon it's natural for a mother – I'm even more worried about Clay. How that poor child has worked, these past four years, putting himself through the State University—'

'Is that true?' Parker queried with surprise. 'I had no idea

87

he was a university graduate; seems so young for that,' he added quickly.

'Oh, I know he doesn't look much like it, around here, helping in the kitchen and doing all manner of odd jobs. He had so wanted to follow in his grandpa's footsteps. I'm sure I don't know what we're ever going to do with him. It's just breaking his spirit. I can see it – a little more every day.'

Mrs Brock rocked gently, thoughtfully, for a moment, and returned to Elise.

'She's kept pretty busy now, what with that big house on her hands, and the telephone, and the dispensary patients – Father had his dispensary right there where you can't get away from it, day or night – and meals at all hours. You wouldn't believe what a trial it is to have a busy doctor in your family. Can't plan anything an hour ahead – not even your supper. So – we don't see Elise very often, unless we go over there. I don't believe she has been here for a month. . . . Well – I must see what's going on in the kitchen. Excuse me for bothering you with our family worries. I don't often talk to people about them.'

Parker said he appreciated her confidence.

'But I reckon,' she observed, with a pensive little smile, as she took her leave, 'everybody has his trouble.'

'I dare say,' agreed Parker, resuming his book.

The next afternoon Elise had come to see her Aunt Clara. Parker had been out for a ramble that had taken him through the town, past the little huddle of shops – Brinkley's Harness and Saddles, with the not unpleasant tang of good leather in the air about the open door; a chain grocery store, whose gaudy front made its neighbours drab; a men's clothing store, with the wax dummy of a wide-eyed, pink-cheeked, stiffly smirking boulevardier dressed in a tight, fawn-coloured suit ticketed at sixteen dollars seventy-five, and a large pile of rough overalls which the saunterer thought he would prefer to the suit in case he was required to fit himself out there; Tanner's Drug Store, a versatile institution with an uncommonly sloppy soda fountain just inside the entrance and a battered lending library at the rear. On the corner was Vaughn's more impressive estab-

88

lishment – a shining plough in one window and assorted tools in the other. Across the street, Sizer's Department Store, a rubbish clutter of cheap merchandise, and the First National Bank, resembling a mausoleum, held down the corners.

Then there was the Post Office with a worn and splintered doorsill, oiled floor, and dingy rows of boxes; Miller's Feed Store with a tin incubator and some meal bags in the window; Hawkins's Meat Shop, a pair of gilded horns over the entrance; a ridiculous little millinery establishment with a display of a dozen hopeless hats priced from a dollar to two-ninety.

This brought you to a petrol station, occupying a great deal of room on the corner, and beyond that was the High School, after which you came to some very good residences. The brown house, with diamond-shaped panes in what were probably the library windows, was Dr Graham's. A small office jutted from the south wing. The little car, out in front had seen better days. Perhaps it belonged to the doctor. It sat there with an air of accustomedness.

The stroller had turned, at that point, to retrace his steps, Sylvia, as usual, winning many a pleasant smile. Parker was glad now that Sylvia had insisted on coming along out of that other life, realizing that his present unstable relation to the normal scheme of things would be unsupportable without the company of his dog.

Frequently men bade Parker the time of day as he passed them, remembering that they had seen him in the street before. He assumed that they remembered Sylvia, and, as an after-thought, recalled that there had been a tall man, of thirty or thereabouts, striding along in her company.

It set him browsing on the subject of the animal's relation to the so-called social order. Not that Sylvia was an animal, of course. The English language was distinguished by a few blind spots. Things had to be either mineral, vegetable, or animal. In this purely academic respect Sylvia was an animal because she was not a mineral or a vegetable. So was he himself, for that matter. He and Sylvia belonged to the same 'kingdom'. And men in the street said 'Howdy' to him because Sylvia apparently admitted herself to be his property. All that being true, wasn't it more correct to say that he was Sylvia's property? In the opinion of the universe, at present, Sylvia was the more important of the two.

He stopped in at Tanner's Drug Store and purchased a tin of flea powder. Mr Tanner himself made the sale.

'Even good dogs have fleas,' observed Mr Tanner, pleasantly making talk with the newcomer.

Parker thought diligently about that for the remainder of the stroll back to the Mansion. Somehow Sylvia's importance seemed to dignify fleas.

Mrs Brock and Elise were talking earnestly in the hall when he entered the hotel. Elise's Aunt Clara could easily have presented him, but she had merely acknowledged his presence with a polite smile. He interpreted it to mean that Clara Brock, while cheerfully willing as his hostess to extend the amenities due a guest in her house – even to the point of impulsively discussing her own anxieties – felt under no compulsion to back him socially. This, thought Parker, showed her good breeding and common sense.

Nevertheless, the little episode was disquieting. He was forced to admit to himself that his equivocal position in this house would presently demand clarification. He must either be on his way or give a satisfactory reason for remaining. A depressing sensation of loneliness swept him as he ascended to his room. For a long time he sat before the window revolving the problem that had been troubling him for a month. Perhaps if he ordered some books and pretended to be pursuing a specific course of study, his occupation would be considered valid. But – what kind of books? He had picked up a little volume, *en route*, on *The Choice of a Vocation*. Doubtless there was plenty of literature to be had on that. He would write to Chicago for information. The decision cheered him.

Elise was walking down the street now, on her way home. Doubtless, he reflected, his undeniable interest in her could be accounted for mostly by the fact that he had not been permitted to make her acquaintance. Had Clara Brock introduced them to each other, his curiosity about the girl would probably have been satisfied. As the matter stood, he found himself possessed of a desire to meet her.

In his one brief glance at close range, he had noted that Elise was a comely brunette, a little better dressed than most of the young women he had seen in the street; had observed also that her impersonal survey of him, without the slightest trace of shyness, hinted a wider social experience than Leeds would be likely to afford. He wondered how much she fretted here, imagining he had read discontent in the moody brown eyes.

Next day Elise again had some occasion to visit her Aunt Clara. Parker had passed her on the front steps as she was arriving. Their eyes admitted, this time, the existence of each other, at least; but she did not speak, nor, of course, did he.

That evening, young Clay tapped on the door. Upon being invited in, he said, with some embarrassment, 'I was putting in a new light bulb, this morning, and noticed that book.' He pointed to the little volume on vocational problems. 'When you are through with it, sir, would you let me read it?'

'Sit down, won't you?' said Parker cordially. 'You may have the book at once, if you like. I have finished it. And I am rather glad you are interested, for I am making a little study of the question. There will be quite a sizeable library on this subject shipped to me within a few days. You will be welcome to read these books when they come. You're casting about for something to do, I suppose. Want to talk about it?'

'I mustn't pester you with my problems, Mr Parker. And there's nothing unusual or interesting about my case. I finished college in June. Worked my way through, with a little help from my grandfather.'

'What was your major?'

'Pre-medic, sir. That's all I've ever had any interest in. But I can't make a go of it in a medical school and work for my living; do you think?'

Parker shook his head and replied that he had always understood a medical course demanded very close application to one's studies.

'So,' continued Clay, with a hopeless little shrug, 'I reckon

I'll have to give that up. But – I don't see how I can stay here – not much longer.'

'No, I suppose not,' Parker reluctantly admitted after a considerable pause during which he sat preoccupiedly stroking the backs of his fingers after the manner of one rubbing on a pair of snug-fitting gloves, an odd little trick he was apt to fall into when thinking with complete absorption. 'There wouldn't be much chance for you here, I'm afraid. . . . It is sometimes very difficult to decide just what one ought to do with one's life.'

As he glanced up to meet Clay's eyes, Parker was conscious of the boy's intense interest in this platitude, and wondered whether he was suspecting the nature of the need that had inspired it. The silence lengthened as each speculated on the other's thoughts.

'Thank you, sir,' said Clay, rising.

'We'll be talking about it again, I hope.' Parker tried to sound optimistic. 'Something will open up. Meantime – don't be discouraged, and – I wish you the very best of good luck.'

'Yes, sir,' replied Clay respectfully, retreating toward the door. 'Same to you, sir.'

Now exactly what did this young cub mean by that? Probably nothing, at all. He had said, 'Same to you, sir,' perfunctorily, routinishly, as he might have mouthed it had one wished him a Happy New Year.

For a little while he sat very still and envied this gloomy, threadbare Clay Brock. 'Don't be discouraged,' he had counselled the boy. He chuckled deep in his throat, bitterly, remembering the old wheeze, 'Here is an excellent hair tonic, sir,' purred the bald-headed barber. . . . 'Don't be discouraged . . . don't be discouraged' . . . *God!*

The arrival of his books by express on Saturday afternoon so immediately and definitely changed Parker's status at the Mansion that he hardly knew himself for the same person within an hour following their delivery. Mrs Brock, who seemed to have got wind of it, though she had not been present when they came, appeared at his door to say that she had found a small bookcase for him, and wondered if the table in his room would be large enough.

Her previous solicitude, which had clearly been tinctured with anxiety, if not downright pity, now moved up a peg. The uneasy concern he had begun to notice in her eyes had been replaced by an almost obsequious respect.

Brock himself dropped in, late that afternoon, reckoning that Mr Parker would probably remain with them for some time, and hoping so with a friendly sincerity out of all proportion to his former attitude of civility.

Next morning, as he sat on the sunny veranda with a Sunday paper strewn about him, Parker looked up to see Clara Brock standing before him, gravely arrayed in an outmoded black silk into which she was so tightly squeezed that she fairly bubbled through the little round interstices between her heroic hooks and eyes.

'Church?' he ventured, noting her hesitation to say whatever it was she had on her mind.

'I reckon you wouldn't care to go,' she said, rather wistfully.

Somewhat to his own surprise, he promptly consented, warning her playfully that he was but little short of being a pagan and would have to be coached when to sit, kneel, and stand.

'Oh – we don't have much of that,' assured Mrs Brock. 'We stand up for the hymns, and sit through all the rest of it. You'll hear Elise. She's singing a solo. It will be good too! I want you to listen, whether you're musical or not. Maybe you are.'

'I used to fiddle a little,' confessed Parker, as they strolled down the quiet street. 'But I was never very good at it.'

'Well,' Mrs Brock observed philosophically, 'when strangers say things like that about themselves you never can tell just what they mean, can you? . . . There's our Elise – going in now. The young man with her is Randy Vaughn. His father is Vaughn's Hardware and Implement Store. They generally come to the hotel for dinner on Sundays.'

The little church was ugly without and dingy within, smelling of varnish, though there was no evidence that any had been applied recently. The pews were severely straight-backed and bare, pitched at an angle demanding a posture which made the scattered company of worshippers appear of formidable character, as if their religion was something that required them to come to attention. It was not a very good place to relax into a leisurely contemplation of the everlasting quest for more information about Deity. Parker ventured a little excursion into the mass-psychology of the company. It was not expectant, as it would have been with the same number of people sitting in a railroad station. It was not fidgety, as it would have been in the receiving-room of a free clinic. It did not evince the eager anticipation of a theatre audience pulling off its hat as the lights dimmed. It was stolid, stiff, and a bit grim – not unlike the daguerreotypes of his great-grandparents.

Presently the principals came in, by doors leading to the choir and the pulpit; a dozen young women and four men edging deferentially into the pews facing the little cabinet organ; and the minister, a youngish man of sober mien, taking his seat in a tall chair, where, it was evident, he sat with a discomfort befitting an occasion whose serious purpose had already been implied by the gravity of the congregation. The organ, at the behest of a plump lady with a large hat, embarked uncertainly on a prelude which at least one member of the audience recalled – not without a pang of nostalgia – as an exercise he had been required to learn when he began his piano lessons. He had been seven, then. The piece was entitled 'Evening'. Quite pretty, too. Elise was not listening to it.

'Evening' quickly passed, swooning at the end as the organist permitted the wind to play out before removing her hands from the keys. The minister rose, and everybody stood with him. He closed his eyes and said, 'Shall we pray?' It occurred to Parker that the psychology of this query was unfortunate. Surely, if other people were as indifferent to the exercise as he himself, they should be urged – if not positively commanded – to make the adventure. He was still thinking about this as he held one side of the frowsy hymn-book from which Mrs Brock sang with fervour. The Bible, a sad book, was read with a becoming gloom. And our Elise arose to sing.

Her selection was a simple little thing, probably chosen with

94

a consideration for the organist's inexperience, but our Elise could sing! She was a pure contralto. In the lower register there was a peculiar haunting diapason quality, and when the score carried her up to the point of a slight voice replacement you saw where she was bound for and, remembering how far down she had been, you wondered whether she would arrive taut and anxious at her destination, but it was accomplished on perfect pitch and effortlessly. Parker was amazed and delighted.

There were three stanzas of the little poem which provided the text, and while she was singing the last one, he changed her badly made brown dress into a modish white chiffon, led her out of the stuffy little choir-box on to a lighted stage, admiring the poise with which she waited for the black-haired man at the grand piano to introduce her first, throbbing, soul-gripping tone.

It was not a large audience, for Elise was of no reputation, but it was an exclusive and discriminating company of persons likely to recognize talent when they saw it.

The song, he felt, would have to be something unpretentious, appropriate to the occasion of presenting an unknown artist whose way must be made on the strength of native ability rather than the finish achieved by much training. 'Calm as the Night' – that, he thought, would be about the right thing. They would go mad about her and she would have the good sense, when she came back, to give them Schubert's 'Serenade.' No – it mustn't be anything showy.

He pursued these reflections throughout the sermon, which was based on something that Moses had said to Pharaoh quite a long time ago. Moses, it appeared, was putting on some sort of revolution in which there was a confused jumble of threats, imprecations, flies, frogs, and a bad epidemic among the cattle. 'Let my people go!' Moses kept shouting. 'Let my people go!'

'A-*men*!' ejaculated a quavering old voice from one of the front rows. Nobody smiled. Parker glanced up at Elise and was distressed to note that even she gave no evidence of suppressed amusement. Perhaps she had not heard the fervent response. Perhaps she was not hearing anything. Her brown eyes were cloudy and the corners of her pretty mouth drooped a little, contemplatively. He wondered where she was.

Moved, doubtless, by the same cerebral activity manifested by the behaviour of those who, as raconteurs, inevitably repeat the point of a joke that had won a little – but not enough – applause, the earnest parson lowered his voice impressively and muttered, yet again, 'Let my people go!'

It was, thought Parker, a good, sound epigram. Why didn't the town of Leeds let Elise go? Why didn't they help her go; insist on her going? Here they were, pretending to agonize over the predicament of certain primitive captives on the other side of the globe, thirty-five centuries ago, utterly indifferent to the quite obvious fact that they, themselves, were keeping their eagle in a chicken pen. Apparently it hadn't occurred to anybody that they should set Elise free to realize the splendour of her great gift. Clara Brock sensed it a little, but even she was not fully aware of what Elise possessed.

Yes – little Leeds, he thought impatiently, would continue to shake itself down for dimes and quarters to send to the mission station in Ting-a-ling, and their own golden-throated Elise would stay here and shrivel. They would never know that they had committed the unpardonable sin of watching a great talent die of starvation.

'Perhaps she will be over this afternoon,' remarked Mrs Brock, as they walked slowly back to the Mansion, Parker having warmly expressed his admiration for her niece's voice. 'Would you like to meet her, if she comes?'

Chapter Seven

RANDY had said he would let himself out and she had listlessly permitted him to do so, smiling an apathetic goodnight without rising from the piano stool.

For the past hour or more their conversation had been difficult for Randy to support unassisted; and when, the hall clock having struck ten, Elise had inquired if that was eleven, he had decided to call it a day.

Towards the last of it, Randy's monotonous monologue had settled into a sort of chanty; rhythmic melodious, sedative, with a well-ordered refrain at the end of each stanza. Vaughn's – all things considered – hadn't done so badly this season. Nine hay tedders, four manure spreaders; *tedders, spreaders, tedders, spreaders*. They had disposed of much binder-twine and dynamite, and had done good business in fertilizers and cultivators; *fertilizers, cultivators, binder-twine and dynamite*. They had done very well with hoes and weeders. There had been a large sale of ploughs and seeders; *hoes, and weeders, ploughs and seeders*. Randy's face had blurred, but Elise could still see his mouth going.

He had paused once to inquire solicitously if she wasn't uncomfortable on the piano stool, his eyes drifting toward the sofa, but she had shaken her head and maintained her irksome posture, believing the strain of it would help her keep awake and feeling also that she needed to do penance for the thoughts which crowded her mind.

After the front door had closed and the purr of the Vaughn motor had faded out down the road, Elise meditatively ran through the album of Chopin Preludes on the desk of her cherished baby grand until she came to Number 20. Tilting up her chin and closing her eyes, she gathered up into her strong, slim fingers a dozen resounding measures of the most potently heart-stirring chords she knew.

Thus cleansed and reinvigorated, she rose, carried the tall glass vase out to the kitchen, changed the water she had poured in at six, carefully snipped off an inch from the long stem of the white chrysanthemum, and restored it to its place on the piano. Cupping the beautiful flower in both hands, she bent over it and inhaled deeply. It was a stimulating fragrance.

Resuming her seat, she sang 'He Shall Feed His Flock', realizing that she was doing it uncommonly well. There were tears in her eyes when she finished. After that, she sat very still for a long time, looking at the white chrysanthemum with the steady concentration of a crystal-gazer until it grew very large and the graceful blades of the petals shimmered with a pale opalescence. She drew a deep sigh and her fingers softly stroked the ends of the white keys. Now slippered footsteps and the familiar reek of iodoform brought her back to say, gently, 'Through for today, Grandpa?'

Elise had not turned her face toward him, but her mental picture of the kindly-spirited old man was, she knew, entirely accurate. An affectionate smile softened the white-bearded lips. The great mop of silver hair was tousled. The knowing eyes were so black you couldn't define the pupil from the iris. He was wearing the tattered, quilted, maroon dressing-gown that Grandma had made for him years ago – the last product of her patient and competent needle. Elise could feel the worn texture against her bare elbow as he fondled the lobes of her ears, one of his favourite expressions of endearment since her early childhood. She reached up and caressed his leathery hands.

'Sure you don't want anything more to eat?'

'I should say not! The Pipers had everything they'd ever raised on the table, including a tough old gander. And I was ready for it, you'd better believe. Big job of carpenter work I had to do out there.'

'Bad break, was it?' Elise had heard the details twice, but knew he wanted to talk about it.

'Nastiest fracture I ever saw, I think. Young Jud – maybe

I told you this – had been up in an old hickory shaking a limb when it broke with him. All of fifteen feet. It was a nasty one . . . right there. "Potts fracture", we call it. Look.' He put up a foot on the piano stool, rolled down his woollen sock, and diagrammed the accident. Elise winced a little when she saw how white and sharp his shin was. 'Very nasty,' he repeated, recovering his balance. 'He'll do well if he's off his crutches by Groundhog Day.'

Elise was appropriately sympathetic and presumed that the Piper tribe was badly upset about it.

'Well,' sighed the old man wheezily, sinking into the deep chair that was still warm with farm machinery, 'it can't be helped. How did you find the folks over at Clara's?'

Suddenly brightening, Elise swung herself around on the stool, and having casually dismissed the perfunctory query about Clara's folks, remarked, 'And I met the Mr Parker who has come here to – to get away from everything while he does some special study. Perhaps he's writing a book about it, though he didn't say so. He wouldn't, of course. Very modest. Doesn't talk about himself, at all.'

'Oh, yes; he's the tall, city-looking fellow with the white sweater and the bird-dog. Where does he hail from?'

'I didn't ask him. Up North, somewhere.' Elise's hasty dismissal of this question proved its unimportance. 'But he is a gentleman; perfect manners. I know you would like him, Grandpa. He's your kind of a man.'

Elise's grandfather stroked his short white whiskers and grinned. His black eyes twinkled. His lips puckered, teasingly. He imitated her own childish gesture of whittling one index finger with the other, her favourite method of discrediting a tall remark.

'Certainly *not*!' denied Elise, colouring charmingly, and exasperatingly conscious of it. 'Nothing of the *sort*! Mr Parker is cultured, knows a lot about music, talks of things I'm interested in. Naturally – I like him. We speak the same language. And I can tell you it's a relief' – she continued with increasing warmth – 'to find a person in this vicinity who is able to talk about something else besides—'

'Monkey-wrenches and post-augers?' suggested her grand-father, noting her hesitancy to make an immediate selection from stock so comprehensive. 'I agree with you, dear. But you'd better go slow with this man Parker until we find out a little more about him. And be careful you don't get Ran-dolph sore at you. I see he left early.'

'He wanted to go,' explained Elise glumly.

'That's what I mean. We'll have to be careful about that.'

For some time Elise, her knees crossed, sat swinging one foot negligently, to prove that her meditation was guileless. Then, with a half-wheedling accent she said softly, 'Grandpa.'

'Yes, dear,' answered the old man, kindly but not without suspicion.

'Grandpa — would you object if I asked Mr Parker here for supper some evening? He's awfully lonesome, and it seems to me it's almost up to some of us to extend a little of the hos-pitality we've bragged about so much.'

'Asking Randolph, too?' challenged her grandfather seri-ously.

'Well — if you think we must. But — don't you see? Randy isn't interested in music or — or anything else that we would want to talk about. And Mr Parker is too much of a gentle-man to discuss things in Randy's presence that he knows noth-ing of. We would just have to keep to hardware . . . and I don't think it's fair,' she finished dismally.

Resolving to let the matter simmer for the present, the old gentleman nodded a few times and cast about for a diverting topic.

'That's an unusually fine chrysanthemum,' he observed. 'It doesn't look like a local product.'

'Isn't it simply wonderful?' Elise offered it to him for close inspection. 'He gave Aunt Clara some because she had asked him to have dinner with the family today. She doesn't know how in the world he got them here so soon from St Louis unless he telephoned for them. They came — special delivery — while I was there. And when I thought they were lovely, he asked Aunt Clara if he might give me one. Gorgeous, isn't it?'

'Elise, dear,' muttered her grandfather ominously, 'let me

100

repeat that we must not offend the Vaughns. I never bothered you with this, for I feared you might be sensitive about it, but Henry Vaughn lent me six hundred dollars, in all, while you were in Louisville taking your vocal lessons. I had hoped to have it paid back long before now.' His face was penitent.

'Oh! . . . Grandpa!' moaned Elise. 'Does that mean that I mustn't ever talk to anyone but Randy until this money is returned to his father?'

'No – it isn't quite that bad. But, as I have just said, we shouldn't go out of our way to annoy them. . . . You needn't worry about it, but be discreet.' He yawned, to encourage her to think that the problem wasn't really disastrous, and said he reckoned it was time for him to go to bed. 'I've been a bit short of breath all day. Had to crank the old machine this morning. Battery's worn out.'

'You ought to get a new one,' replied Elise. 'Vaughn's have them, don't they?'

'I expect so,' he said wearily, 'but collections are slow, and I don't like to ask Henry for any more credit. . . . You invite your Mr Parker here, if you want to, but better ask Randolph too, and maybe one of the girls – Sue Sizer, or somebody. That would make it all right, I reckon.'

Elise went to bed with what she thought must be the sensations of a slave held for debt. She turned her hot pillow over and over. What a mess her life was going to be!

Perhaps Randy would have to go down to Nashville for a couple of days' business before long. He had spoken of it. If she waited until he had made definite arrangements, she could ask Mr Parker over while Randy was out of town. No – that wouldn't do at all. Randy would have even more cause to feel offended.

Maybe she could have Mr Parker here and keep it a secret from Randy, though that would be difficult, with everybody knowing everybody else's business. . . . Her heart pounded. Maybe she could have him on short notice when Grandpa was away on a long trip – a baby case, perhaps. That took all day, generally.

There never had been such expressive hands. And how

101

devoted Clay was! Surely that proved how attractive he was, for Clay was always so reserved with strangers. He had honestly liked her voice, too. He wasn't saying it just to be polite. You can tell. 'Distinguished talent.' He didn't have to do that if he was merely wanting to be pleasant. 'You could go far.' And his face was so serious when he said it.

Funny how some people seemed to be a part of their clothes. Even his blue polka-dotted four-in-hand looked as if it had been made specially for him. His shoes, too. It was probably stamped on the inner sole – 'Handmade for Mr Parker.' No, it wouldn't say that. It would be 'Handmade for Nathan Parker.' She wondered if his people called him Nathan. Nat, more likely. It would be fun to ask him when they were better acquainted. She heard herself doing it; heard herself saying that his name somehow fitted him exactly. Funny about that: everything Mr Parker had – eyes, hands, collar, shoes – fitted together. And his name, too. Names were such queer things, anyhow; seemed to have personality; seemed to be as much a part of you as your hands or your voice. Elise – for instance. That was as it should be. Elise. She couldn't think of herself being anything else but Elise. She had always felt like an Elise. Elise Graham. . . . She snuggled her face into the pillow . . . Elise Parker . . . Elise Graham Parker.

She was making a lovely monogram of this when she heard Grandpa slowly padding down the stairs in his felt slippers; a step, a long pause, a siege of coughing, another step, a longer pause. The banister creaked as if he might be leaning on it heavily. Perhaps he was going to the dispensary for some medicine. It always annoyed him if she seemed anxious about his health; disliked to have her fluttering about him when he had these little spells with shortness of breath. She lay quite still and listened. He had reached the bottom now. Doubtless he would be coming up again presently.

When the clock struck twelve, Elise decided to go down. He was sitting very straight at the desk in his pungent little room, rather pitiful in the absurd old flannelette nightgown, unbuttoned over his bony chest. He had his fingers on his pulse and his blue lips were counting. Each wheezy exhalation of his gasps gave him a spasmodic kick in the stomach. His eyes were straining as if they, too, were sucking for air.

'Can I do anything, Grandpa?' inquired Elise, trying to keep her alarm out of her voice.

He shook his head and remained intent on his pulse.

'I'll do a morphine injection,' he said huskily, 'if I don't get relief – pretty soon. I've had my quota of digitalis.' He pointed to the hypodermic syringe to let her know he had been doing something for himself. 'It's these damned stairs,' he explained, 'and that cranking I did today.'

'Shall I make up the sofa for you?'

He nodded and tried to smile.

Elise was glad to be doing something. She hurried upstairs and collected the necessary bedding. After a while he came, walking very slowly, and eased himself down on to the couch. She patted the pillow, but he shook his head.

'Not yet,' he said. 'Must sit up. I've been neglecting – my digitalis lately. . . . Great thing – digitalis. . . . Couldn't live – without it.' He grinned feebly. 'We both have – favourite posies – Elise. . . . White chrysanthemum – and purple foxglove. . . . You better – go to bed now.'

For an hour she sat on the floor, her feet drawn up under her, nestling her cheek against his knee. It was a great relief to her when he said he thought he might lie down. He seemed very sleepy.

They met in the post office at nine, Elise rather flustered and rosy; for, half a block away, she had seen Mr Parker entering and knew that an encounter would be unavoidable.

It was not that she didn't want to meet him. Her accelerated pulse testified to that. But she wasn't certain that their contact on the street or in the post office, which at this hour of the morning was well patronized, would be a very happy one.

If she greeted him with anything like the personal interest she felt, someone would be sure to notice it and perhaps comment on it. If, on the other hand, she protected herself against the possibility of being chattered about, Mr Parker might be hurt by her attitude of cool unconcern.

Her steps lagged while she debated the respective disadvantages of either course, but quickened when she decided that it would be better to meet him in the post office than outside. He was stowing stamps in his wallet as she approached the little window. His casual greeting gave their slight acquaintance the exact value it deserved, suddenly restoring her self-confidence. Surely nothing would be thought of it if she showed some friendly attention to the dog. Sylvia, however, seemed a bit remote. Observing that she was about to have her ears tousled, she side-stepped the caress, Mr Parker apologizing for her frosty indifference. Sylvia, he said, was a man's dog. A hunter, you know. Elise accepted the explanation, wondering whether Sylvia's attitude toward women was shared by her master.

They walked out of the post office together, Elise completely forgetting the apprehensions that had bothered her a few minutes earlier. It seemed the most natural thing in the world to be walking down the street talking to Mr Parker, and the fact that Leeds could see him accompanying her home did not disturb her in the least.

Grandpa's indisposition being uppermost in her mind, she confided her anxiety, her tall companion manifesting a sympathetic interest which, thought Elise, was just what one might expect of him. She had never met anyone so responsive. He was inquiring now whether they had called a doctor.

'Oh, no,' she replied. 'Grandpa always knows what to do when he has these attacks. I don't know what causes them. He always coughs very hard when he has them, whether he has a cold or not. And he has a lot of trouble with his feet; shoes too tight. I wanted him to stay in bed today, but he says he positively must go out into the country to see a boy who broke his leg yesterday.'

'I don't suppose there is anyone he could send in his place,' suggested Mr Parker. 'It sounds as if he should be quiet for a few days.'

'Perhaps he'll be all right,' hoped Elise. 'He always takes a medicine that helps. I've forgotten the name of it. He said last night that he had been neglecting it and had let himself down to about eighteen grains, whatever that may mean.'

'How much does he weigh?' asked Mr Parker, to Elise's surprise, for the question was so decidedly irrelevant.

'Oh – about a hundred and fifty pounds. Why?'

'I just wondered,' drawled Mr Parker. 'It *was* rather off the subject, wasn't it?'

'Grandpa says this boy has the worst break he ever saw. That's why he's so insistent on going to see him. He said it was "a Potts fracture", whatever that is,' explained Elise, smiling companionably over their mutual ignorance. 'Now you know all about it, *don't* you?'

He nodded his head, profoundly, seeming to pretend wisdom.

'Think your grandfather would object to giving me a ride with him out into the hinterland?' he inquired.

'I don't know about that,' replied Elise, mentally attempting a picture of Grandpa's reaction to such a proposal. 'You might hint. Look! He's just leaving now.' She waved a hand, and the old man waited for them to approach. An introduction was effected, her grandfather delighted her with his cordiality.

'Mr Parker has just been saying that he envied you your drive out into the hills,' said Elise, secretly hoping, for Grandpa's sake, that he would invite Mr Parker to come along, and reproaching herself for wishing, too, that it might turn out some other way. It would be pleasant to ask Mr Parker in.

After a long moment, during which the old doctor looked the newcomer over with an amusingly frank interest, he told Parker to hop in, if he didn't have anything better to do.

'I'll let you drive, too, if you like. Dog going along? Very well. Just open that rumble. . . . Back about noon, Elise.'

It had all happened very quickly. Mr Parker gave her a canny wink as he started the little car. She wondered if he realized what that brief gesture of comradeship meant to her.

'Ever see a broken leg?' shrilled Dr Graham, above the racket, after some desultory talk about the glorious weather and various points of local interest along the road.

'A time or two,' Parker admitted ingenuously.

'Make you sick to look at injuries?'

Parker replied that he presumed he had an average stomach.

'I may ask you to lend me a hand out here, if you don't object. I put splints on this leg yesterday, but I wasn't very well satisfied and I may decide to make a cast for it today. If so, I'll need somebody to help hold it in position while I do the bandaging. Was going to ask one of the boys, but members of the family aren't much good. Too squeamish. Think you'd be up to it? Rather nasty business.'

'I can try,' agreed Parker obligingly, 'if you're not afraid I'll be in your way – or do the wrong thing.'

'There won't be any trouble about that. I'll tell you exactly what to do. Simple job of leg-pulling. You will take his foot and pull while I apply the bandages. They will be wet plaster, and when they dry out – there you are! Hard as a rock.'

'Sometimes you X-ray these bad breaks, don't you, Doctor?' asked Parker artlessly.

'S-u-r-e! That's what should be done, by all means, in this case. But these worthless Pipers haven't a dime. They never paid a doctor's bill in their lives. I've attended the arrival of all the children, and the total proceeds were a couple of hams and a few gallons of blackberries. I advised the X-ray, of course, just to be doing my duty, but they were against it. They're as afraid of a hospital as they might be of a pest-house. No – in cases like this, we just do the best we can and trust to luck and Old Lady Nature. It's amazing, the recuperative capacity of the benighted.'

Sylvia consented to be tied in the little car when they drew up under the shade of a big beech in front of the unpainted old house. A half dozen male Pipers, assorted sizes, of a single pattern, viewed the arrival with big, empty eyes, and hands thrust elbow-deep into the pockets of their tattered pants. Mrs Piper, lacking several front teeth, rolled her thin arms in her brown apron and led the way into the bedroom that probably served as a parlour ordinarily. Mr Piper, in patched blue overalls, lounged into the room and leaned against the head of the iron bed, sucking a cold corncob pipe. Herman, eighteen, stood in the doorway, scowling sympathetically. The

106

patient tried to grin, without much success. He admitted having had a bad night.

Parker watched the old doctor with interest as he paternally chaffed his patient while unwrapping the bulky bandages made of torn-up, coarse, household sheets. He found it difficult to keep from smiling as he surveyed the strange array of home-made plaster bandages that came out of the capacious leather bag he had carried into the house.

'Now, here, Mr Parker,' began Dr Graham, 'you see what we have to deal with. See there? Run your fingers gently along there. That bone – you've probably forgotten your physiology – is the tibia. That's the big one. That's the bad one. Feel that? Now this one – the fibula – you can't feel the break there quite so plainly, but it's broken too. Both bones broken above the ankle and the ends spread apart – so. Understand? Now, when you pull the foot, it will have a tendency to straighten these fragments out to their proper position. I shall put on the plaster bandage while this tension is on – after I've manipulated the ends of the bones into place. Got it?'

'Sounds like it might hurt a little,' observed Parker.

'We'll give him a few whiffs of chloroform,' confided the doctor, a private announcement that brought instant relief to the patient's face.

'*Who will?*' Parker inquired, wide-eyed.

'His father,' replied Dr Graham, adding, reassuringly, 'I'll show him how.'

'But—my God!' exclaimed Parker impulsively. 'Isn't that a frightfully risky thing to do?'

Dr Graham shook his head unconcernedly. 'I'll keep an eye on him. This doesn't call for a deep anæsthesia. I mean,' he explained, 'he'll not need very much. It will be safe enough.'

Well, thought Parker, if this doesn't call for a deep anæsthesia, the Piper boy is going to be a cripple for life. He began to feel sorry for everybody connected with the absurd little tragedy. His amusement and amazement kept abreast as he helplessly watched the preparations for this strange surgical phenomenon. Herman, obedient to instructions, came in from

107

the barn with the long leather lines belonging to the buggy harness and anchored his brother's shoulders to the head of the bed. Mrs Piper came with a bread-pan half full of water and the rolled-up plaster-filled bandages were immersed.

'Soon as it stops bubbling,' said Dr Graham, sprinkling the swollen leg with talcum powder, 'we're ready.'

For a moment, Parker was inclined to be indignant. What right had this old man to do such a slipshod piece of work? But, after all, what else was there left him to do under the circumstances?

They were ready now. Father Piper, as sluggish an organism as had ever been sent in motion among the higher primates, was instructed how to hold the wad of gauze into which the doctor had poured an ounce or more of chloroform. Young Jud's apprehensive tension relaxed after a few eager sniffs at it. The air was already so heavy with the potent stuff that Parker wondered which one of them would go out first.

Standing helplessly at the foot of the bed, he found his nails digging savagely into his palms. In a flash there recurred to him the old story of the retired fire-department horse that had kicked the garbage-wagon to pieces when the alarm sounded, and galloped away from her degrading job to race alongside the gleaming apparatus as it went shrieking down the street.

Parker's fingers itched to lay hold on those young bones that throbbed for competent attention. . . . X-ray . . . Parker had a picture of that Potts fracture in his head! Of all the cruel detainments he had experienced since that fateful morning at Parkway Hospital, this moment of supine waiting for a broken old man to finish his feeble pottering, preparatory to sentencing a husky youth to hobble through life, demanded a type of self-restraint that was an offence to his soul.

'Do you reckon it will hurt him bad?' mumbled Mrs Piper, her scrawny knuckles pressed hard against her wrinkled lips.

'The doctor says not,' consoled Parker, feeling that she was at least entitled to whatever relief could be offered at the moment. There would be plenty of time, later, for Mrs Piper to grieve. She would watch him trudging lopsidedly in from the fields, and say, 'My poor boy.' And when he was forty, the neighbours would speak of him as 'Crip' Piper.

There was a code of ethics in the medical profession. It had been Parker's religion. It was a built-in fixture. He would abide by it. But his nails cut his palms.

Dr Graham, with very shaky hands and a million tiny glistening beads of perspiration on his ash-white forehead, was manipulating the fractures.

'Now, Mr Parker,' he said in a frail treble, 'take the foot firmly in both hands and pull steadily – not too hard.' There was a strained look on his face as he turned to the little marble-topped table for the first of the plaster-saturated bandages. Parker saw him stagger and clutch at the table for support.

'Mrs Piper,' commanded Parker. 'Get Dr Graham a chair and a glass of cold water. . . . Herman, come here and hold this foot exactly the way I'm doing it. . . . Mr Piper, you're holding that much higher than Dr Graham told you. Put it down – closer to the face! That's more like it. Don't let it touch his nose, but keep it close.' He took a sheet they had pulled off the bed and threw it over Piper's forearm, and reached into the pan for a bandage. After a long minute of waiting, he muttered into Herman's ear, 'Now, my son, you pull just as hard as ever you can!'

The deft, vice-like compression of Parker's hands as he manipulated the fractures and tightly applied the bandage, together with Herman's strong tug, fetched a yell from under the sheet that flattened a half dozen Piper noses against the window-panes.

'That will do for the present, Mr Piper,' said Parker. 'Put that gauze aside. We will wait now until Dr Graham feels a little better, and he will do the important part of the bandaging.'

In a few minutes the gallant old fellow had staggered back to the bedside.

'That's excellent, Mr Parker!' he approved enthusiastically. 'I believe we've got it now exactly where we want it.' The business of applying the rest of the bandages went forward in a workmanly manner, Dr Graham still breathing hard but in good spirits.

After they had waited for the cast to dry sufficiently for the leg to be comfortably laid on a pillow, the doctor said they would be off now. Parker could hardly resist smiling as he walked out of the ramshackle house, past the tattered, barefooted Pipers, carrying Dr Graham's shabby old leather kit. He knew people who would have been interested in seeing a picture of it.

For the first half mile of execrable road, the old doctor had nothing to say, but when they came to smoother going on the gravel, and the increased speed stirred an invigorating breeze, he seemed inclined to talk.

'Mr Parker,' he said respectfully, 'you were a great help to me out there. More, perhaps, than you realize.' He chuckled to himself a little as if he had a private joke. 'If this affair was written up for a medical journal, none of the city fellows would believe it. How you ever managed to bind up that leg the way you did, I'm sure I don't know. Did Piper go to sleep at his post? I never heard a more blood-curdling howl than you got out of that boy Jud. But I believe we're going to have a fairly good leg there, thanks to your strong hands.'

Parker idly dismissed the commendation with a remark that he had tried only to obey the doctor's orders, playfully insisting that Dr Graham was pleasantly exercising his talent for the traditional courtesy of the Southland. This being the old gentleman's chief pride, he capitulated to the handsome young Mr Parker – horse, foot, and guns – and upon their arrival home, Parker's protestation that he should not accept the pressing invitation to stay for dinner, on such short notice to the hostess, was clamorously overridden.

'My dear,' announced her grandfather to the rosily excited Elise, when they were seated at the table, 'this young fellow missed his calling.' And when she begged for an explanation, he told her, with much merriment, the story of the morning's adventure. Then, with great seriousness, he said, 'All jesting aside – I've seen *doctors* do worse jobs!'

110

Parker allowed a deprecatory grin and remarked in an aside to Elise, who beamed brightly over the little implication of intimacy, 'Dr Graham is having a spot of fun at my expense.' It occurred to him that with more truth he might have said, 'And so am I.'

Chapter Eight

IT would have been quite impossible for Nat – she had attended promptly to this abridgement – not to have observed, from the first, that Elise Graham was warmly interested in him. To a degree he shared this feeling and was comforted by a comradeship which he badly needed.

After his many weeks of aimless wandering, almost as much a fugitive as if he were stealthily creeping from the scene of a major crime, and heartsore over the sudden collapse of a promising career to which he had given himself with full devotion, this charming and talented girl's unrestricted proffer of confidence was – to say the least – soothing. He was hungry for companionship, and here it was to be had without stint.

It was the last night of 1929. He had just returned from the Grahams', leaving at ten thirty for reasons which he considered good. Something warned him against a *tête-à-tête* celebration of the New Year at midnight, their close friendship having reached the stage where it needed only such a flick of the whip to send it galloping in a direction which, he had firmly resolved, it was not to take.

For nearly a month, Nat Parker had been seeing Elise almost daily, cheerfully abetted by her indulgent grandparent who, nonchalantly 'to-helling' his earlier misgivings over the warrantable annoyance of the Vaughns, had welcomed the urbane stranger to his hearth and table with a cordiality that threatened to become more and more perplexing.

Whimsically trading on the lenient consideration due to the elderly by their juniors, the fine old gentleman had been increasingly reckless with his genial innuendoes. Desirous of nothing so much as the happiness of Elise, and observing her avowal of affection in every tone and gesture, he seemed to be viewing with impatience any further effort to conceal something that had now become plain as a pikestaff. Apparently nothing was farther from his conjecture than that Parker might have any further opinion on this matter than his own.

Leaving them alone together after supper on Christmas Eve, Dr Graham had paused in the wide doorway of the living room to gaze significantly at the mistletoe above his head, after which he had departed with an omniscient grin.

'Grandpa's so fond of mistletoe,' Elise had explained. 'He always hangs it there.' And then she had added, in a confidential tone, 'Grandpa is simply impossible sometimes.'

'He's a dear old fellow,' Nat had replied. 'Loves to tease.'

Seriously taking stock of their present relationship, in the final hour of the year, Parker thought he could truthfully say that he had done little to add impetus to its development. From the first day of this acquaintance, Elise had appointed herself curator of their fellowship, administering its affairs with a generosity at once flatteringly trustful and giddily indiscreet.

The situation, he now felt, was beginning to clamour for quite a bit of taking in hand. He knew he was not in love with Elise. Indeed, he had never been really in love with anybody. Young women had briefly stirred his interest, from time to time, but his profession had been so jealous a mistress that there was no chance for any of these budding romances to put forth a flower. After he had been obliged to make half a dozen last minute cancellations of engagements with some attractive girl, she became justifiably indignant or tiresomely petulant.

For Woman – viewed as an institution – he was conscious of a deep respect bordering on veneration. She stirred his protective instinct and appealed to his chivalry. The insoluble mystery of the feminine mind and heart had been of such interest to him that her body seemed mysterious too, even in the face of a scientific knowledge which, one would have thought, had long since made it as prosaic as the multiplication table. But Parker had never loved any one woman, not even Elise. His calmly considered judgement assured him that her undisguised affection for him needed no ampler explanation than the simple fact that at the moment there was nothing better she could do with it. Any other personable man he believed could have had it.

However much or little they might have been mutually congenial under normal conditions the peculiar setting in which Nat and Elise had discovered each other's social isolation was highly inflammable. His own extended period of bitter loneliness and her hopeless frustration in dull little Leeds had given their friendship a necessitous quality almost as urgent as if they had been shipwrecked and cast up together on a desert island.

Parker liked her thoroughly, sincerely admiring her superb talent, her ready wit, her vivacity, and her prompt responses to a given atmosphere. There had been, for instance the inevitable inquisition to be gone through very early in their acquaintance, concerning the exact state of his heart and the degree of his liberty. Experience had taught him to expect this. He could not recall ever having conversed a second time with any girl whose curiosity on this subject was entirely absent. It was not, he honestly believed, that these chance acquaintances had any designs on him as an individual, but rather as if their inquiries – impudently direct or playfully implied – were propelled by some instinct demanding them to ascertain where a man stood in relation to their species.

Driven by this biological urge, Elise had manœuvred their talk into this quarter with all the premeditated cunning of an experienced chess-player until he was left with but one possible move. Tacitly acknowledging the stalemate, he had conceded her a bootless victory, blandly inviting her attention to other conversational activities, a decision she accepted with a smile.

Persevering as a spider, she had, on another occasion shortly afterwards, requested him to jump through the hoop which she had suddenly thrust in his way; and, upon noting his hesitation, had given him the encouragement of a heartening example by jumping through it herself, in the course of which adventure she had confided more than she had any business to concerning her relation to Randy Vaughn who, she observed, had always taken too many things for granted. But the

Vaughns were like that. It was a congenital infirmity with the Vaughns to consider it an act of impiety on anyone's part to deny them a request.

Somewhat restless in the confessional, Parker had politely absolved Elise of any further obligation to the Vaughns, agreeing that her life should be her own to be disposed of as she wished – after which he had lighted a cigarette and irrelevantly asked her if she was acquainted with the full story of Franz Schubert's composition of Symphony Number Eight in B Minor. She had listened to the tale with full attention.

Tonight, as he was leaving, Elise had made quite a long and elaborate ceremony of putting into his coat-lapel one of the violets he had brought her in honour of the occasion. She had had to reach up a little and stood very close, looking up into his face, offering him a temptation which he was glad now he had been able to withstand, however awkward it had made him feel at the moment of ignoring the gift she had so clearly intended him to take.

Nothing was plainer than that their relationship would now have to be repitched in another key, or he would be obliged to leave Leeds at once. It would be a very ungracious thing to run away. The Grahams had taken him into their confidence almost as a member of their household and at a time when he was all but desperate for congenial friends. He felt himself under an obligation to Elise and her gentle-hearted old grandfather. It could not be discharged by his going through the motions of requiting Elise's affection. He wished there was something tangible he might do for her.

A bright idea! He wondered why it hadn't occurred to him before. He would try to give Elise a chance to demonstrate what she could do with her voice! If all that she required was a public appearance, set up under influential auspices, he would provide the necessary funds.

After much thought about the devices he would be obliged to invent in an effort to bring this about, Parker sat at his desk and composed a letter of considerable length to his warm friend and *confident*, Eugene Corley, junior member of the firm of Corley, Corley and Corley, his attorneys. The church-

115

bells rang and the whistle at the Dietz sawmill blew while he was signing his name to it. A new year had arrived. A sudden cold wave of utter dejection swept over him. He pushed the chair back from the desk and bowed his head in his hands. Sylvia strolled over from her corner and nuzzled into the crook of his elbow.

Happy New Year!

Once a sick man at Parkway, recently bereft of his wife, to whom he had been singularly devoted, had confided how – deep in the night – he sometimes reached out a hand, and, waking, was gripped by a loneliness so utterly desolating that he was physically chilled.

The Baptist bell and the Methodist bell and the whistle at the Dietz sawmill clamoured of a new year. Presently the midnight dissonance subsided, and Leeds was quiet again.

Parker had experienced many a dark hour since his renunciation of everything that life held dear. This hour was the darkest.

He felt sure Elise had the letter today, for he had received one from Eugene stating that hers was going forward by the same post. Eugene had said that instructions were being followed in every detail. There was a pen-written postscript chaffing him. 'As if it wasn't enough for you to lose your job and your name, you seem now to have lost your heart. Do you still have your dog?'

At eight, he strolled down to the Grahams'. Elise met him at the door in a grand state of exultation, threw her arms about him and stood on tiptoes to be kissed. He was happy to meet this impetuous display of gratitude, tendered in the presence of her grandfather, who, with beaming eyes, hovered close behind her. Everything now was exactly as it should be, Parker felt. Elise was going to be his sister. Her chance to make something important of herself had driven her infatuation for him into complete eclipse.

She hurried him by the hand into the living-room, pushed him down on the end of the sofa under the reading-lamp, thrust the epoch-making letter at him, and with all the spon-

116

taneous enthusiasm of a delighted child pressed her cheek against his shoulder, following the lines of the impressive document while he read aloud.

The firm of Corley, Corley and Corley was pleased to advise Miss Graham that their client, Mrs Norma Phelps, who frequently made small 'courtesy loans' to promising artists in need of 'an encouraging subsidy', having learned through Mr Nathan Parker of Miss Graham's unusual talent, desired to place at her disposal sufficient funds to ensure her a deserved recognition.

Unfortunately, Mrs Phelps's immediate departure for Europe would make it impossible for her to manifest a more personal interest, at this time, in Miss Graham's success. Whatever communication Miss Graham might wish to have with Mrs Phelps should be cleared through the office of Corley, Corley and Corley.

The sum of two thousand dollars had been placed in the Fidelity Bank of Louisville, subject to Miss Graham's order. At her convenience, the money could be repaid with or without interest, as she herself might elect. If, for any reason, the contemplated promotion failed to achieve substantial results, Miss Graham need not consider herself obliged to restore the money, Mrs Phelps assuming this risk of her own volition.

'Isn't it simply marvellous?' cried Elise. 'You'll help me, won't you, Nat? I'll need a lot of advice.'

Parker had worried more than a little over the transparency of this singular proposition. He felt greatly relieved to find that Elise did not consider it at all preposterous, probably because she had so great faith in her ability to justify the beneficence of her good angel, Mrs Phelps.

For all of two hours she bubbled with plans for the stupendous event which was to give her her chance, Parker amazed and touched by the evident time and thought she had previously given to this matter. It showed how passionately she had longed for some such thing to come to pass.

'And it wouldn't have been possible but for you, Nat,' she paused once to declare gratefully, to which he replied that it was Mrs Phelps who deserved all the credit.

117

'Do tell me what she's like!' Elise settled herself comfortably to hear a personal sketch of her benefactress. 'Tell me all about her!'

Nat had not prepared for this, and never before having ventured to assume any of the prerogatives of the Creator, this bringing Mrs Norma Phelps into existence with no construction materials at hand except her name, obliged him to do some rapid thinking.

Mrs Phelps, he presumed, was about sixty five. 'In her stocking-feet,' he added, hoping Elise, already in hilarious mood might consider it droll enough to laugh at, thus permitting him a little more time to organize the good lady's biography in such a manner as to reflect no discredit on her. Mrs Phelps, he admitted, had an odd taste in hats. She was an inveterate globe-trotter and an ardent collector; had long since given up maintaining a home; lived in hotels, and liked it. Elise, full of interest, wanted to know what Mrs Phelps collected, and Nat promptly replied, 'Rugs.'

'How funny!' observed Elise. 'What does she do with her rugs, having no home to put them in?'

'I don't know!' replied Nat, with a gesture implying that Mrs Phelps's ways were, after all, inscrutable. 'You'll meet her sometime, doubtless, and you can ask her. I'm sure you're capable of it,' he added. 'I never knew anyone so inquisitive.'

Next day Nat Parker went to the city, at Elise's request, and laid her case before an experienced advertising man. They lunched with a feature writer who was quick to interest himself in the fascinating story of the 'discovery' that had been made in little Leeds.

'Of course, there is no reason why anyone should try to tell *you*, Miss Davidson, who Mrs Norma Phelps is or what she has done to put unknown artists on their feet,' remarked Mr Parker craftily. He had prepared himself to expect that Miss Davidson might be a bit hesitant here and accept the statement – if she accept it at all – on the first bounce. To his happy surprise, she caught it on the fly, running eagerly to meet it.

118

'*Mrs Phelps!* To be sure! Why, the girl will be made!'

There was free discussion of Miss Graham's relation to the late Colonel Brock, a beloved figure still well remembered by the Old Guard. A tender note was sounded concerning her grandfather's long service, largely unrewarded, on behalf of the poor, for whom he had travelled the back roads by day and by night for more than forty years. It was a good story, Miss Davidson said; nor did she change her mind when Mr Parker, taking leave of her, tarried at the little floral shop near the hotel entrance, to present her with a corsage of gardenias. 'With Miss Graham's compliments,' he said. 'She will be wanting to meet you and express her thanks.'

Having given this effective publicity a couple of days to soak into the imagination of the city's musically inclined, Mr Parker made another journey, taking Elise with him. They contrived to secure an interview with Darien Moore, the best-known accompanist in that zone, whose sponsorship of an unfamiliar name would carry great weight. He had seen the story about Miss Graham, and agreed that whoever received the sanction of Mrs Phelps was surely worth attention. Elise sang for him in his studio, and he was delighted. She asked him if he would play for her on the night of her recital, and he consented. Before they left, Parker confided to Mr Moore the fee that Mrs Phelps had suggested if they were able to secure for Miss Graham the services of a widely recognized accompanist. Mr Moore blinked a little. Whatever inquiries may have floated through his mind respecting the identity of Mrs Norma Phelps could now be safely dismissed.

The movement was gathering speed and momentum with such amazing ease that Parker was heartened to unplanned audacities. A drawing-room recital for an exclusive group of potential patronesses was arranged for the coming week. It was a notable success.

Nat Parker had certain qualms about the methods he was pursuing, but he knew he wasn't cheating. He could deliver the goods, however shady was the technique of the propaganda. The point of it was, *Elise could sing!* Any measure that would help her to her rightful chance was pardonable.

119

'You've been a darling!' murmured Elise, on the returning train, when it had become assured that the recital was being backed to the limit by the most influential people in town.

'It has been a lot of fun,' he said, 'and I'm very happy for you. Mrs Phelps will be very pleased.'

That night he wrote to Eugene Corley, telling him that the recital, billed to occur on Tuesday night, the fourth of February, was – from advance reports – not only going to pay for itself, but net a nice little balance.

'This business of serving as an impresario,' he concluded, 'has been full of excitement and adventure. I have met some of the most charming people I have ever known, and I have told more lies in the past forty-eight hours than the sum total of all I ever told in my life. . . . Quite incidentally, your recent kittenish comment implying that I am in love with this girl convinces me that the subject is too much on your mind. I can definitely assure you I am not.'

On Nat's advice, Elise had gone up to the city for two weeks of intensive work with Mr Jaqua, her former vocal instructor. Not only would it serve to give her more confidence, but, they were all agreed, she should be free of home responsibilities.

Mr Jaqua was glad enough to give her this special attention. He was quite ecstatic over his favourite pupil's good fortune, and the fact that he was about to bask in the reflected glory of her talent made him garrulously enthusiastic. Who, indeed, had been chiefly responsible for the proper placement of that golden voice if not Jaqua. He said this in several quarters, and in consequence was interviewed at length concerning his impressions of Miss Graham, thus adding fresh fuel to the bright bonfire of publicity which was lighting her path to glory. The whole event had now been set up in such a manner that Elise would have to do very badly indeed to escape the recognition planned for her.

'Nat,' she said, in the final conference they were having on the night before she left home, 'you think I am to make a little money with this recital. I am very anxious to give it to

Clay, so he can matriculate at the medical school at the beginning of this next term.'

'Excellent!' approved Nat. 'You are a very good girl.'

'But – Grandpa borrowed six hundred dollars from Mr Vaughn when I was studying,' continued Elise with a troubled voice, 'and it really should be paid back to him. I can't do both things.'

'Why not? Mrs Phelps does not expect you to return her loan immediately. Pay back part of it now, and attend to Mr Vaughn and Clay with the balance.'

'Would that be quite fair?'

'Write to Mr Corley,' Nat advised, 'and tell him all about it. As Mrs Phelps's attorney, he will unquestionably approve. I am very glad about your thought for Clay. My dear – there's something fine in you that keeps cropping up.'

'Isn't it natural,' she asked, with a self-deprecatory little gesture, 'that I should want to help my cousin, now that so much has been done for me?'

'No,' said Nat brusquely, 'it isn't. Unfortunately the genius possessed of an outstanding gift is more often than not afflicted with a badly inflamed ego, and a shocking capacity for self-indulgence. The very best thing about you, Elise, is your simplicity – and your ability to keep your head. Have you said anything to Clay?'

'Not yet. I didn't want to take the risk of disappointing him.'

'Good sense again – but now you may tell him. He should be given time to make his plans; the new term will be opening in a few days.'

Elise was thoughtful. How could Nat be so sure that Mrs Phelps, or Mrs Phelps's attorney, would sanction her wish? He must be much closer to Mrs Phelps than he had admitted. The query added mystery to the vasty spaces in Nat Parker's life which, to her, was *terra incognita*. For a moment he seemed almost a stranger.

'And afterwards?' she murmured, half to herself.

'After *what*?' asked Nat absently, for he, too, had been wool gathering.

121

'After the recital. What am I to do then? Come back here and wait for something to turn up? Have you any further plans for me?' Her eyes queried him childishly. 'I can't expect you to stay here in Leeds very long. You don't belong here. We both know that. You've another world. I am not acquainted with it, but I know there is one. I've tried to piece little scraps together and paint a background for you, but there's been very little to work on. Except for your early childhood, and the music, you might as well have lived on Mars, so far as my own information goes.' She was very pensive, her moody eyes accusing him of not being quite fair. 'What am I going to do,' she asked after a little silence, 'when you leave me?'

'It's quite the other way about,' countered Nat, seizing upon her last query. 'You will be leaving *me*. Your liberating chance is plainly in sight. Your career is just arriving. Mine, you see, has just—' He left the sentence unfinished, and when she prodded him with '—Has just *what*?' he replied, jocularly, 'Well – yours is nearly full-blown, and mine is too full-blown; blown up, in fact.' He ventured a little laugh, to prove that it didn't matter; that he was readjusted.

'Nat – did you get into trouble?' Elise's voice was tender.

'Yes – will you be content not to ask me anything more about it? It's a very painful subject.'

She nodded reluctantly and laid her hand on his.

'Will I ever be told?' she asked.

'Probably not.' He rose, and signed that he should be taking his leave. 'As for you,' continued Nat, 'your future is assured. I shall always be keeping track of you, wherever you are, wherever I am.'

'Will there ever be anything I can do for you?' asked Elise, putting both hands on his arms affectionately.

'Yes!' he replied, almost gruffly. '*Succeed!*' He turned away toward the door, altered his mood suddenly and said, with a companionable smile, 'I'll be seeing you – on the triumphant Tuesday!'

'It's almost as if we'd been saying goodbye for ever,' murmured Elise.

Dr Graham and Clara Brock and Clay had proudly put her

on the train, next morning, Clara reporting an hour after-wards that Randy Vaughn had shown up at the station to offer his good wishes.

'Poor Randy,' added Clara, offering Parker a chance to comment, 'he's been feeling rather left out of things lately, I reckon.' She laughed knowingly, as if they had a little secret.

'Good practice for him,' observed Parker dryly, which made Clara laugh quite gaily, for Elise and Nat had not been able to fool her very much. She knew how *that* was going to turn out, and had known it 'from the first day they had set eyes on each other'.

'I think Randy knows his suit is lost,' she said, confidentially muffling her prediction behind her hand.

'Randy never had a case,' agreed Parker, meeting her secret-ive mood. 'He should have known he couldn't harness the Heavenly Maid to a plough.' Clara missed the allusion, con-sidered it an exuberant outburst of devotion, and squeezed his hand, whispering, 'You two!' He had a notion to detain her and attempt to set her right, but she had scurried away, satis-fied that her suspicions had been happily confirmed.

The days dragged abominably, Parker more restless than he had ever been in his life, his sole diversion – except for tedious evening hours with Jeff Trumbull – being Clay's eagerness to be off. The youngster, curiously enough, had determined to go to the one medical school that Parker knew from crypt to spire. It was sometimes difficult, in the face of the boy's almost hysterical enthusiasm, not to offer some detailed information and a few helpful hints.

'Isn't Elise a brick?' he exclaimed fervently, watching Parker's face for tokens; hopeful of learning something.

'It runs in the family, I think,' drawled his non-committal friend. 'Very stout fellows – all of you. You'll probably make a famous doctor, Clay; mostly because you want to. That's the main thing. Some day I might live in your town and want my liver taken out.'

'I'd do it,' said Clay happily, 'for nothing.'

'I wouldn't get the full value of it that way. Anything you get for nothing is no good. I'll pay for it. I'll pay you now!'

123

He drew out his wallet. 'There. Run down to Nashville to-morrow and order a suit of clothes. And remember,' added Parker sternly, 'it's on account!'

Clay tried to protest, but Parker was firm. The next morning, after breakfast, when he went up to his room, Clara was making his bed herself, which was unusual. For a little while she busied herself with her task, paying him no attention, and then she blurted out, explosively, half crying, 'I don't know why you're so good to my boy, but he just loves you – and so do all the rest of us' – after which she bustled out of the room, very much overwrought.

Dr Graham was taking his meals, through these days, at the Mansion. The slight alteration of his mode of living was a bit exciting. He tarried to talk frequently, and in the genial buzz and stir of the little hotel he seemed to find pleasure. It was doubtful, however, whether this distraction from the calm routine of his quiet home was good for him.

They marvelled at the Mansion that he was so spry and told him so, thinking to please him. It was true. He was spry – too spry.

One afternoon Parker accompanied him into the country to make a call, tactfully suggesting in the course of their conversation that physical exercise could easily be overdone. More people in mature life, he thought, were damaged by over-activity than underactivity.

'Any of your relatives doctors?' inquired the old man.

'My father, sir.'

'Ever go with him? – ever see him set a broken leg, for instance?'

'No, sir. My father died when I was a small boy.'

'You would have made a good doctor yourself, I think.'

'Thanks,' said Parker, wondering how much more of this there was going to be.

'Ever consider it?' persisted Dr Graham, measuring his words significantly.

'Oh, perhaps.' Parker tried to be casual. 'Every boy toys with the idea at some time. . . . It's nice that Clay is to have his chance, isn't it?'

124

On the Sunday evening preceding the recital, Dr Graham was quiet and pale. He ate little and tottered feebly out of the dining-room. Parker could hear him in the hall assuring Clara there was nothing the matter except a little shortness of breath.

Shortly after nine, it suddenly occurred to Parker, who had retired to his room early to read, that he should stroll down to the Graham house. It was in darkness except for the little dispensary where a single light glowed through the shutters. He rang the bell, rapped with his knuckles on the door-panel, and after long waiting, turned the knob.

Dr Graham, wide-eyed with agony, was seated astride a chair, his hands clutching the top, desperately struggling for breath. It was evident that he was badly frightened, as he had a right to be. His nails and lips were cyanotic. Parker laid a hand on his shoulder.

'Anything I can do?' he asked sympathetically.

The old man pointed a shaky finger toward the familiar leather bag on the table, and Parker held it open on the back of the chair. After much frantic rummaging, a tarnished hypodermic case was fetched up from the depth of the clutter of tools and bottles, and the doctor tried unsuccessfully to open it with cold, impotent hands.

This was no time, decided Parker, for an attempt to preserve his secret – not at the risk of another man's life! He tossed the worn old bag aside and took the hypodermic case from Dr Graham's hands. Opening it, he laid out the steel syringe and what seemed to be the best of the small assortment of needles. He found a test-tube and heated a small quantity of water over a candle-flame, the old man's anguished eyes following him closely. He looked over the long, slim phials of tablets in the old-fashioned case, and tapped one out of the morphine tube.

'A quarter?' he inquired. Dr Graham nodded.

The tablet was quickly dissolved in the warm water, sucked up into the barrel of the syringe, and the shank of the needle deftly screwed on. The old man was fumbling with his sleeve button. Parker bared the arm, polished a little spot with a wisp

125

of cotton saturated with alcohol, grasped the pathetically flabby skin with experienced fingers; and, tipping up the syringe, pushed the piston gently to expel the air. He caught Dr Graham's searching black eyes, realizing that if nothing he had done, so far, had given him completely away, surely this last tell-tale gesture with the hypodermic instrument would settle the matter. It was quite beyond belief, he knew, that a layman would go about this business with the quick precision which certified to thorough understanding and long practice.

The administration of the drug was adroitly, painlessly accomplished, Parker gently massaging the little bump with his thumb after the needle had been withdrawn. The effect was almost instantaneous. The doctor drew several long sighs and began to relax. Then he looked steadily for a minute into his young friend's eyes, and said, huskily, 'I should have known it – that day – out at Pipers' – when you reduced the Potts. *I did know it when I took off the cast!*'

'Would you mind – keeping this a secret, Dr Graham?' said Parker. 'I have good reasons for asking.'

'It's a pity,' mumbled the old fellow.

'It's a secret?' repeated Parker. 'Not even Elise. Agreed?'

Dr Graham nodded, and clung tightly to Parker's arm as they went into the living-room.

'I'm afraid I shall not be able to go to Elise's recital.'

'No,' said Parker, 'nor shall I unless you are much steadier in the morning. Be at ease now. I'm staying with you tonight.'

'Thank you, Dr Parker.' The tired old voice was very husky. 'Your name is Parker, isn't it?'

'No. . . . Perhaps you'd better give your poppies a chance now.'

'Perhaps so,' came the sleepy drawl. 'Thank you – Doctor.'

It was a great disappointment to miss witnessing Elise's triumph, but Nat felt that his first duty kept him close to the fine old man in Leeds.

Unable to go, he ordered a great armful of roses, wired encouragement before and congratulations after, reassuringly explaining her grandfather's absence on the ground of 'extra pressure of emergency work', which was nearly true, since the old gentleman was at that time putting in twenty-four hours a day trying to keep a worn-out pump going.

Next morning he jubilantly read to Dr Graham – obediently in bed – the abundant and flattering Press reports of the mighty victory. All the rich adjectives of unlimited commendation were sprinkled generously through the chronicles of 'the season's outstanding musical event'.

'It's what she has always dreamed of,' said the old man weakly. 'And she has you to thank for it – Doctor.'

Elise was to arrive home that evening at eight. Her grandfather watched the clock, impatient to hear her story from her own lips. Clara stayed with him while Nat went to the train.

As she descended from the steps of the Pullman to the old wooden platform, it was quite evident that something epochal had happened to Elise. She had realized her possibilities – had glimpsed her destiny. She had gone up to the city a half-frightened girl, and had returned a self-possessed woman, calmly conscious of her new estate. From now on, henceforward – her manner said – she was assured. Parker was delighted.

In the loose-jointed little taxicab she did not let herself splutter a torrent of superlatives, as he had anticipated while waiting for her train. Elise was a confident artist now. She reached for his hand in the dark, but he knew that her thoughts were on more important matters.

'I've been having a very interesting correspondence with Mr Corley,' she said casually. 'Naturally I wrote to Mrs Phelps, thanking her for everything. Mr Corley replied that he was forwarding my letter to her and suggested that she might appreciate a photograph. So I sent him one – you remember, the one with the little black hat.'

'Eugene will like that one, I know,' agreed Parker.

'Yes – he does. So – then – I asked him if he couldn't send me a picture of Mrs Phelps to hang in my studio: the one I'm going to have.'

'And he sent you one?'

'No; he said that unfortunately they had no photograph of

Mrs Phelps, but seeing I was transacting all of my business with her through him, he would, if I desired it, send me one of his photographs. Wasn't that odd?'

'Well – no; not for Eugene. Is it a pretty picture?'

'Marvellous! . . . And Mr Laughton, the booking agent, is coming down to talk over contracts and such things on Saturday.'

'Excellent!' said Nat, still smiling in the dark.

'And I've promised to sing at Trinity Cathedral at Easter. Mrs Robert Sinclair – wife of *the* Robert Sinclair, you know – attended the reception. She was visiting her sister, Mrs Carter. You remember – you met her. Mrs John Fielding Carter. Mrs Sinclair's husband is prominently connected with Trinity Cathedral. Has a lot to say about the music. It's a male choir, of course, but I'm to sing a solo on Easter morning, and I'm to be Mrs Sinclair's guest. Isn't that marvellous, Nat?'

He tried to keep pace with her enthusiasm. Privately he was browsing among the memories he cherished of the most important woman he had ever known and her recurrent allusions to Trinity Cathedral. She had wanted him to go there, some day, and see for himself. She had hoped he would meet her Dean Harcourt. How strangely one's life seemed to proceed on a definite orbit, as if predetermined from without!

For a fleeting moment he toyed with an idea that would have seemed absurd a year ago. Was it possible that all the bother he had given himself these past few weeks on Elise's behalf was for the purpose of driving him – willy-nilly – into the presence of the great Harcourt? . . . Ridiculous!

'You'll go, won't you, Nat?' Elise was insisting.

'Go?' His voice came back from a long distance.

'At Easter – to hear me sing – at Trinity Cathedral. Promise!'

'Yes,' he answered soberly.

Chapter Nine

SPRING had been in no hurry. Indeed, she was so sluggish that many of the temperamentally frail of faith had begun to wonder if the whole universe had not been slowed up by the economic depression. But early in the second week of April, as if suddenly startled wide awake, lethargic spring had developed an amazing energy, arriving in a few hours at full gallop and steaming hot, attended by excited convoys of overdue robins and bluejays.

A noisy and colourful pageant of thunder and lightning had preluded a pelting rain that washed the city as nearly clean as it was ever likely to be. Hyacinths, tulips, and daffodils popped up like mushrooms. On teeming pavements, tops and marbles screamed above the din of the hurdy-gurdy for their ancient rights in the dizzying confusion of roller-skates and skipping-ropes. In the parks, new perambulators and old canes made long slim parallel lines and neat little round holes in the spongy gravel paths. The big buses careered top-heavily as they sputtered along Lake Boulevard with top decks crowded and plenty of room inside. The big aviary in Madison Park was a pandemonium of shrieks and squawks in every key and a-flutter with loose feathers of every hue. And everywhere the hope-reviving, spring-like scent of warm, moist earth, was in the air.

This impetuous advent of belated spring had put the spur to every manner of business affected by the seasons, crowding the streets, the shops, the suburban trains. Harried merchants, who in exasperation had daily watched great splotches of wet snow ironically blurring the windows they had decorated with straw hats, gay ginghams, lawn furniture, and Easter fluffies, now found themselves so busy that some of the more optimistic said, 'We have turned the corner.'

Sonia, happily weary after a long Saturday's profitable toil in her small but elegant Parisian shop, had felt justified in the unaccustomed extravagance of a taxi, telephoning home immediately before taking it. Unlocking her apartment door, she smiled, sniffed appreciatively, and followed the aromatic trail of a sizzling steak.

'Phyllis, dear,' she chided, 'you're much too tired to be doing that. We should have gone out. But now you're at it, I certainly am glad. I'm tired as a carthorse and hungry as a wolf.'

'So am I. It will be ready in five minutes.'

Lingering in the doorway of the snug little kitchen, Sonia carefully lifted off her swagger spring hat and surveyed the impromptu cook with affectionate admiration.

'I believe I'll put in a line of aprons *de luxe*,' she remarked, with professional finesse, 'provided you will consent to act as model and show them off. Of course, no apron could ever hope to look like that on anybody else, but a lot of women might think it would. What an adorable figure you have, Phyllis.'

'Thankee, mum.' Phyllis bobbed a kitchen curtsy. 'Faith an' ye ought to know, mum, a-wearin' a sixteen, and it's many a tear Oi've shed fer ye, what with yer a-drinkin' th' coffee black, and a-rollin' on th' floor ivry blessed morn like an animal to presarve yer a-lookin' like a high school lass . . . but it's a good thought,' she went on, abandoning her foolery – 'about the aprons, I mean. If our customers are to do their own work, they may as well look their best. We'll dignify the kitchen and glorify the apron and make cooking a noble art.'

'You'd have a rough time selling that sublime idea to me,' scoffed Sonia. 'I hate greasy pots and pans – and I thank God I do!'

'That's because you have another job,' argued Phyllis. 'If it had been your destiny to run a house, and circumstances forced you into the kitchen, you'd welcome anything that would make your drudgery less ugly. Perhaps if we sold pretty aprons, we should be contributing that much to the—'

'Oh, yes, I know,' broke in Sonia teasingly, 'to the sum of human happiness. That's what the Dean would say.'

'And he would be right – as usual.'

'Yes, dear. Everything one does should somehow be good for the troops. You still believe that; don't you?'

'And so do you,' retorted Phyllis, 'for all your pretended spoofing.'

'Of course. I just wanted to hear you say your catechism.'

'Get on! . . . Wait! – hand me that platter. Now – scram! – unless you want to eat this cold.'

The intimate friendship of the two had become firmly established almost immediately upon their chance meeting at Trinity Cathedral more than four months ago. Sonia, momentarily serving as Dean Harcourt's 'secretary', had met the charming stranger in the reception room. After a minute's friendly talk, she had returned to the Dean, saying, 'A very lovely girl, cultured, in her early twenties, wants me to tell you that Phyllis is here. Perhaps you will know.'

'Yes – I do,' replied the Dean quietly. 'Bring her in – and after about twenty minutes, come back.'

Phyllis, quite calm and self-possessed, had followed along until they reached the familiar library door which she had so often entered with her mother. Entirely unaware of the tender relationship between the attractive caller and Dean Harcourt, Sonia had opened the door, expecting the girl to enter rather diffidently. So completely taken by surprise that she stood for a moment unable to turn away, Sonia heard a little cry of mingled sorrow and relief, and had a fleeting glimpse of Phyllis – her well-disciplined reserve utterly tossed aside – as she rushed across the room like a frightened child running to her mother's arms.

Obedient to instructions, Sonia returned after a while. Phyllis had drawn up a chair very close beside Dean Harcourt's, and had regained her composure, though it was evident that she had given way to her grief.

'Come here, Sonia,' said the Dean gently. 'My Phyllis Dexter – and yours too, I think – has been very badly hurt. Her father and mother, both warm friends of mine, recently met tragic deaths and her home is consequently broken up. She has just returned from England. Her only sister is in the hos-

131

pital, convalescent from an illness. The other relatives live else-where. There are plenty of friends to whom she might go, people who would welcome her, but—'

'You mean you're going to let me have her?' asked Sonia entreatingly, confidentially, almost as if Phyllis were not present.

'Yes, you are going to take her for a few days – until she decides what next to do. . . . You see, dear,' tightening his clasp on Phyllis's hand, 'I knew what Sonia would say.'

'Thank you – Sonia,' murmured Phyllis, looking up with admiring eyes. 'I want to go with you.'

'It's like this,' explained the Dean meditatively. 'If Phyllis goes out to the Sinclairs or the Duncans or almost anywhere else among the people with whom the Dexter family has been intimate, they will keep her thinking and talking about her trouble and treat her with the well-intended but thoroughly enervating compassion that delays prompt readjustments. . . . Now, run along, and see what you make of each other.'

Phyllis had risen, pensively grateful, laying her hand on Sonia's arm in a little gesture of confidence. Sonia hesitated, and seemed suddenly depressed.

'Did you tell her' – the words came reluctantly, almost inaudibly – 'about – about me?'

'Phyllis,' said the Dean soberly, 'do you believe there is any-thing I could tell you about Sonia that would alter your present estimate of her?'

For an instant the two women looked each other squarely in the eyes. Phyllis's lips parted in a smile, and she slipped her arm through Sonia's, their fingers interlacing.

'Does that answer your question, Sonia?' asked the Dean gently.

'You are very good to me,' she said, barely above a whisper, again as if they were alone.

They left the room, arm in arm, turning at the door to smile a farewell. Without any silly conceit, each was aware that the pair of them offered a startling contrast in feminine pigments – Sonia a striking brunette, hair so black it was blue, skin so white it was almost pallid; Phyllis with yellow-gold bobbed

132

curls, dark brown eyes, and pink cheeks deeply dimpled.

Dean Harcourt held up an outspread hand as the door was closing and they paused – Gaul and Saxon at their fittest, heads close together – to hear his parting injunction, suspecting from the merry twinkle in his eyes that it was not going to be a very solemn utterance.

'If you two highly gifted women,' he said slowly, 'are as different on the inside as you appear on the outside, you should have an interesting friendship.'

'What do you think?' exclaimed Phyllis, as Sonia joined her at the table. 'Pat's coming!'

'For Easter? How awfully jolly! . . . No potatoes, thanks.'

'Gets here Thursday evening; stays through Tuesday. Look – I'll read it you: "I am very anxious to see your Sonia, and I think she is a darling to want me to come—" By the way, doesn't anybody in the whole world know that you have another name besides Sonia?'

'No – but I'd like some of the Worcester sauce. Proceed, please.'

' "But I don't like the idea of crowding you, as is likely if her apartment is as tiny as mine." '

'I'll wire her a night letter to ease her mind. . . . And the pepper. . . . I can sleep comfortably on the sofa. No, little one, you're too long-legged. . . . Does she talk like a university professor? Her subject is English, isn't it? I hope I'll pass. I've just failed in Modern History.'

'Sonia! You don't mean—'

'Of course I do! The man isn't in love with me. He is lonely and Celeste likes me and that's about all there ever was to it. I interest him because I'm not too hard to look at, and know how to wear my clothes, and pick the right spoon, and am amusing to his little girl. But he doesn't love me and I'm not the least tiny mite in love with him. Really – I think Andy was relieved when I told him so. He knows I wouldn't fit into that university picture. I would never feel comfortable. And there's another reason – plenty good, too – that you don't know about.'

On two or three previous occasions when confidences were being exchanged, Sonia had cryptically turned the knob of her closet door with a hint that there was a rattleable skeleton.

'If you ever want to tell me, my dear, I'll listen,' said Phyllis quietly. 'And if it's anything very bad, I won't believe it. . . . I've a letter from Grace,' she continued, when it had become apparent that Sonia had no notion of pursuing the veiled topic.

'How is she liking it by now at Saint Agnes's?'

'Well, for one thing, she has more liberty than I supposed. It's an Anglican institution. I don't think their regulations are quite as severe as the older sisterhoods. . . . I would like to read you part of it.

'She says – "Sooner or later I would have come here in any event. It has been on my mind for some time. The thing that happened to us brought me to a prompt decision. There was nothing I could have done for you. I would have been just one more problem on your hands. I'm utterly unpractical. If I had tried to go through the motions of making my own living, I would have been a mere pensioner on the charity of an employer who might have taken me on for Father's sake." '

'Don't read it to me,' murmured Sonia, when Phyllis had paused for an instant. 'It sounds very private.'

'But I'd like to talk it over with you. Let me go on. . . . "Frankly, I had grown tired of the world. It wasn't the flesh, which I always had fairly well in hand, or the devil, who is just a fantastic old myth; but the world, in my opinion, isn't a natural habitat for a creature of my disposition." '

'What a deliciously droll way to say it!' laughed Sonia. 'She must be awfully funny.'

'Grace inherited her dry humour from our mother.'

'You got quite a generous share of it yourself, Phyllis, besides the gift of her eyes and her mouth. Your resemblance to your mother's picture at your age is the most amazing likeness I ever saw. . . . Well – go on! Grace's letter promises to be good.'

' "I don't feel a bit like a dependant here," ' read Phyllis. ' "Even if Father hadn't made that lavish gift, back in '25, I would have no misgivings about putting in at Saint Agnes's.

The people who support this institution get their money's worth out of us. They know we pray for them, which is of course only common decency on our part; though, personally, I would be willing to do my share of that, anyway. I know some of them very well and I think I can say – without betraying any secret – that they are jolly well in need of it.

'"Sister Cecilia, who is supposed to read all our outgoing mail, may stroke her pretty chin and wonder whether the foregoing paragraph is discreet, but I don't see how she can consistently delete it, for if our benefactors are not in need of supplications, we are wasting a good deal of our time, and we rather pride ourselves here on the worthwhileness of our daily intercession." Evidently,' commented Phyllis, 'Sister Cecilia decided to let this indiscretion pass.'

'Something tells me I'd rather like that censorship job,' drawled Sonia. 'Frightfully entertaining!'

'"You may want to know why I grew tired of the world. I'll tell you. In the first place, it's too noisy, and growing noisier every day. Many of the newer noises are leading to mental decay. The world has now quite passed the point where an individual may decide whether or not to take the risk of listening to the radio. It now intrudes upon him – in the hotel, in the observation car, on the highway. There is no place left where one is protected from the throaty sobs of bad music set to worse grammar. Don't misunderstand me. I have no quarrel with these soloists. Doubtless they are very fine people. Nor am I contending that the general public is to be criticized for liking and wanting this sort of entertainment. The fault is entirely with me. The world loves it: I don't. I am pleased to be insulated against it.

'"There is a high stone wall round this place and it is three miles from the town. No motors, no automatic rivet-hammers, no crash and clatter of tramways; no ambulance sirens shrieking that another pair of people, showing off their recklessness, have met head on and catapulted through their windscreens. And, what is much more important – *no speeches*! You can't realize, until you've experienced it, the ineffable peace that derives from one's knowledge that one is for ever out of ear-

135

shot of the pompous, arrogant, opinionated men who harangue the world from every corner. I believe I could have stood the world if it hadn't been for the loud vulgarity of the people who are trying to save it." '

'I wonder what the Dean would say to that,' speculated Sonia.

'He would probably agree,' thought Phyllis, 'though he might say it differently.'

' "But that wasn't all I wanted to escape from. I was weary of a world of haste, worry, strain, and artificial whoopee; weary of the frantic struggle to say and do the things that happened to be vogue this week in our social set; weary of sour grins across the bridge table and the poor sportsmanship of losers; weary of trying to decide whether I would rather be a fuddled giggler at the country club or refuse the cocktails and be sneered at for a prig and a spoil-sport. And I was tired of being pawed and mussed by men for whom I had no intellectual respect – big, brassy creatures who liked to brag that they didn't know one picture from another, and ridiculed classical music, and hadn't read a book all the way through for two years; hadn't anything but money (and now hadn't even *that* – which made their poverty complete). They couldn't talk to you intelligently; seemed to think you ought to feel yourself flattered if they tousled you . . ."

'Look, Sonia!' Phyllis reversed the page, showing where three lines had been carefully inked out.

'That must have been too thick for our Cecilia,' chuckled Sonia. 'I wonder if she grinned when she read it.'

'Of course,' Phyllis declared. 'She's a woman. There isn't a woman on earth who wouldn't think that was amusing.

' "Here at Saint Agnes's, there is pleasant work to do. We have an excellent library, pianos, orchestral records for our recreation hours. The garden is lovely. Each of us has a little plot of her own. There are looms and workshops where we make pretty and serviceable things of leather, wood, brass, silver, and clay. Some of us specialize in needlework. In the afternoons at five we assemble for a half-hour's organ recital and the vesper service. Nobody preaches about the mistakes of the Government or what would become of us if we had another war. It's all very peaceful.

' "I want you to come here, some day, and see me. You may find it uneventful, for you will be not allowed to stay long enough to cool off. The calmness is just a bit bewildering until your nerves have had a chance to relax their tension. That takes some time, depending of course on how badly diseased they were.

' "Don't worry about me. I am not morbid. I am not moping. I am not fanatical. I am not goofy. We have a good time. We laugh with each other and at each other – not boisterously, but merrily. There is no talk of money – either to prattle of money made, or sulk over money lost. Nobody frets because she can't afford to buy the hat that would make Mary Does's hat look—" ' Phyllis paused to explain. 'Cecilia has scratched out a word here and written "out-moded" above it. What do you suppose it was?'

'*Lousy*,' suggested Sonia. 'That's what the world was calling a bad hat when Grace retired. . . . In fact, it's a good word *yet* – for a bad hat,' she added thoughtfully.

' "Nor am I worrying for fear the lapels on my last season's spring jacket may be three-eighths of an inch too narrow. Saint Agnes's doesn't bring out a new model very often; hasn't, at least, since I've been here. And in that length of time, out in the world, I might have had two complete new outfits and already be looking like something that ought to be under glass in the Smithsonian. . . . Don't pity me. I don't need it." '

'Sounds good, doesn't it?' sighed Sonia. 'Especially when you're tired. . . . And more?'

'Just a few lines. "I haven't many responsibilities here, and am still childishly indulged by my betters. They seem to understand that I came here in response to a push rather than a pull. I'm not yet sure whether or not I have a vocation." '

'Maybe it's a vacation,' observed Sonia. 'Whatever it is, I can't help envying her all that peace and quiet.'

'And not having to try to keep in the fashion,' added Phyllis.

'That reminds me!' Sonia pushed back her chair and beckoned Phyllis to follow her into the modernistic living-room.

Opening a box and tossing aside the tissue-paper, she held up for inspection a sports blouse. 'That,' she declared, with conviction, 'is the best-looking beige we've ever had!'

Monday had been another very active day in the little shop until about four when, as usual, business slacked. Sonia had retired to the tiny cubicle she called her office and was busy totting up her accounts.

'Phyllis,' she called, 'get out! We're through for today except for this desk work and you can't do anything about that. Run along. I'll be home about six-thirty.'

Strolling for a short way down Lake Boulevard, Phyllis boarded a bus, leaving it at the corner of Madison Park, where she sauntered for a while among the formal flowerbeds, inhaling the fragrance of the fresh spring blooms. The massive towers of Trinity Cathedral, across the way, were casting long shadows. The carillon was booming 'Lead, Kindly Light'.

She was not often alone, these days. Perhaps that was just as well. Sonia had been a precious darling, had taken her into the shop and given her a chance to be busy; useful, too, Phyllis believed, reassured by her sales-slips and Sonia's increasing confidence in her ability. And Sonia had taken her into her home, where she had been happier than she had ever expected to be again after the sudden devastation of everything that had constituted her life.

But now that the bewildering novelty of the new scene had rubbed down to something like a settled order, Phyllis was beginning to find herself occasionally inundated by an almost suffocating wave of unrest. Work in the shop had been quite a lark at first; ever so much more pleasant than she had anticipated. Remembering stories she had read about the trying experiences of sales people, she had fortified herself to deal with women whose attitude might range all the way from pitying condescension to insufferable hauteur, deciding in advance that she would probably prefer forthright rudeness to lofty compassion.

To her happy surprise, there had been very little of this, and what little there was had been merely amusing. She had talked about it to Sonia.

138

'Both right,' Sonia had declared laconically, 'you and the stories you used to read. There has come a great change. The customer isn't quite so sure of herself. She doesn't know what minute she'll have to ask for credit. Much better manners on tap now in all the shops. And worse manners in the street.'

Phyllis had asked for further light on this psychology and Sonia had elaborated her theory.

'I figure it this way,' she said judicially. 'Many men whose positions were secure a little while ago are now on tenterhooks for fear they'll lose their jobs, or have to take a cut that will damage their pride and curtail their budget. They go about, all day long, smiling and smirking and yes-sir-ing and after-you-sir-ing; and when they get out in the street they've simply got to compensate for the day's bootlicking. Of course – after they've *had* the big cut, and are doing twice the work for half the salary, then they begin to be a little more considerate. I'm afraid I haven't any formula that will explain this part of it. I just know it's true. But you can depend on it, young woman, when some big, red-faced bruiser tries to run over your toes, with a savage twist of his wheel at a right-hand turn, or runs close to the kerb so he can splash you, he hasn't got his cut yet, but has spent a bad day of crawling about on all fours, hoping to stave it off.'

'Isn't that a pretty low estimate of people's general character?' Phyllis had asked, rather ingenuously.

'Perhaps,' agreed Sonia, adding dryly, 'experience has taught me to practise some restraint in making up that invoice.'

This afternoon, perhaps because of fatigue, Phyllis was gradually slumping into a mood of dejection such as she had not experienced for many weeks. The future looked grey. Her awareness of being utterly bereft swept her all the way through. Impulsively she decided to attempt a few minutes with the Dean. Happily for her, only one caller remained in the reception room, and in a few minutes her case was dispatched. Mr Talbot came in, smiled pleasantly, and said, 'You know the way.'

She entered, slowly crossed the already shadowed room, and, without speaking, raised the hand he offered her and held it tightly in both of hers, pressing it hard against her throat.

'Somebody been hurting you?' he asked gently.

She did not answer for a moment, but stood with downcast eyes slowly rubbing her soft chin against the back of his hand. Then, suddenly brightening, she shook her head and seated herself opposite him.

'Everybody's been good to me,' she said, forcing a smile. 'Sonia especially – Sonia's wonderful. I think these warm spring days make one restless. I can't remember ever having been so – so caged. Does one grow more restless, in springtime, as one grows older?'

'No. It is a physiological phenomenon,' replied the Dean playfully, 'common to later adolescence. By thirty, the attacks are said to be quite harmless. I think the actual figures on sad spring poetry report that the peak of production is reached on the fourteenth of April by persons in their twenty-second year.'

Phyllis pulled a pensive little smile and shook her head. 'Twenty-three,' she corrected. 'Going on for twenty-four. . . . Going on going where, going on doing what, going on being what? . . . Are you ashamed of me?'

'No – not ashamed,' mused the Dean, 'but I suppose you should be quarantined until you get over it. It's contagious.'

'Speaking of quarantine, I've a long letter from Grace.'

'So have I. Good place for her, down there. Valuable institution. There ought to be more of them. Perhaps there will be, some day. We can't afford it now; have to spend all our money making new trinkets and whim-whams for Mars. There has been a great change in Mars. He used to be a brave and burly old ruffian who made his own tools; whittled out his bows and arrows; gathered up his own stones and clubs. But we've indulged him until he isn't content with last year's machinery. We've humoured him with expensive luxuries until I fear he has become somewhat of a coward. Quite a different fellow, shooting ten-thousand dollar cartridges at long range, from what he was when he fought in the open with a long-handled axe. I'm afraid his character is deteriorating. . . . Well – what I meant to say – we'll probably call a halt on this big expense, sometime, and that will leave us a little money to spend on

140

other institutions. I should like to see a number of walled towns built where people may go who can't bear the racket and confusion of the modern world. They could study, meditate, create new art-forms, compose music, verse, plays, literature. And raise their own vegetables.'

'How does one get in?' inquired Phyllis, falling into step with his whimsical mood.

'I was just coming to that. Whenever a man declares that the world is, in his opinion, going to the dickens, and expresses his belief that the times are out of joint, he could be sent there for an indeterminate period, exactly as we put people away who suffer from any other serious hallucination.'

'Wouldn't some people want to go there just because they were lazy?'

'Doubtless – but we should have the lazy to keep, anyway,' observed the Dean. 'It would add nothing to the general expense.'

'But,' queried Phyllis, remembering the Brook Farm experiment and other similar sequestrations, 'do you think these maladjusted people, who can't get along in the world, could be entirely happy penned up at close quarters with one another?'

'Probably not; but that isn't the point. They would not be at large, contaminating persons who are free of the complaint. . . . My thought is,' soliloquized the Dean, 'that all our restless people – particularly those given to expressing their views in public places – should be asked to decide whether they wished to be considered a component part of the social order, believing in it, hopeful for it, sharing its risks, burdens, joys – not as spectators and reporters but participants – understanding its wistfulness, its infirmities, its internal contest of the angel and the tiger – or preferred to withdraw behind some walled enclosure and say, "Go by, mad world."

'I've often thought, Phyllis, that our conventional statements of Christian faith are inadequate at this point. We seem to be doing so little to improve the public's estimate of our civilization. We practise a very faulty psychology, pleading on the one hand for world fellowship, neighbourliness, and faith in the ultimate victory of the good, the true, and the beautiful, but

141

spending the best of our time and energy rating the world for its disabilities. Instead of these flagellations, we should be offering a graphic picture of civilization as it stood a hundred years ago, three hundred, five hundred, and plot the curve. We've had a lot to say in our pulpits and journals of religious opinion about the greed of the so-called capitalistic system, but mighty little about free clinics, day nurseries, hospitals for crippled children, parks and playgrounds, maternity homes for unfortunate girls, and a myriad of rehabilitation schemes which the world hadn't dreamed of so recently as a half-century ago.

'The trouble is, some of us are too impatient. We forget how rapidly we have come from the jungle and observe only how slowly we are approaching the Golden Age. Or, if forced to admit ourselves better off today than men were a hundred years ago, we contend that we are standing still *now*. And, of course, this can't be true. Civilization is an organism – like a tree. If it ever is required to give a final account of itself, the Great Forester who cuts it down will find on its stump hard, narrow rings made by eras of drought and struggle to survive, and broad, pulpy rings left by seasons of nourishing rains and easy living, but there will be *some kind of ring* to testify to every year of that growth! At present, we're making a narrow, hard, tough one! But it's *growth*! . . . Why, can't you see that?'

For some time Dean Harcourt sat silently contemplating the Holman Hunt picture toward which his gaze so frequently wandered when he talked. Phyllis's eyes followed his and lingered on the placid face.

'*He* wasn't impatient,' said the Dean reverentially.

'It's a wonder a person so sensitive as that didn't run away from it all, and live by himself,' ventured Phyllis.

'He did think of it – once. Don't you recall the wilderness?'

'Why – of course! And was tempted to turn stones into bread, so He wouldn't starve to death.'

'It wasn't a matter of starving. A friend of His had lived out there for years – eating locusts and wild honey. . . . No – it wasn't that. He went out alone to consider what it was the world needed to make it a suitable place for people to live in.'

142

'And decided that the big thing was bread?' queried Phyllis, with increasing interest.

'Well, He was tempted to think so,' answered the Dean, 'because He was very hungry. For a little while it seemed to Him that if the world could solve the bread problem, the other questions would solve themselves. It was for bread that nations made war, and neighbours quarrelled, and traders cheated, and robbers stole. If you could find some way to feed the world all it wanted to eat – some magical process such as *Stones – be bread!* – you would dispose of all the world's grief and confusion and enmity in an hour.'

'And I believe it *would*, too!' declared Phyllis.

Again Dean Harcourt was silent for some moments, deep in reflection. Then, as if returning from a long distance, he said softly: '*He* didn't think so. He considered the world's need from every possible angle and decided that *bread wasn't the solution.*'

'But *we* think so,' said Phyllis, '*don't* we?'

'Mostly,' agreed the Dean. 'But fewer people are sure of it today than ever before. . . . Now, I have preached to you quite long enough. Let's talk about *you*.'

'There isn't much to be said about *me* – not after that,' Phyllis replied dreamily. 'It's a funny thing,' she went on, thinking aloud, 'I get so worried over my own problems, and then, when I talk to you, they seem to be so little and insignificant. It's like coming to a fountain when you're very thirsty.'

'I'm glad you feel that way, Phyllis. But – I am not the fountain. I just lend you my cup.'

Chapter Ten

ALTHOUGH he had been warned that one must arrive early for the eleven o'clock Easter service, Nathan Parker was astonished at the density of the crowd in which he found himself wedged at ten-forty on the broad steps of Trinity Cathedral.

He was even more surprised at the personnel of this fan-shaped throng whose apex poured through the huge bronze doors into the enveloping gloom of the Cathedral nave. All about him were interesting and attractive faces of people he felt were worth knowing.

Parker had never given any determined reflection to the matter, but he had gathered from innumerable half-contemptuous quips that churchgoers, as a class, were persons of restricted social interests and dubious mentality, who relied upon religious forms to recompense them for their lack or loss of the material things which furnish a privileged life.

The Church, as an institution, had no place in his inventory of significant concerns. Never in his life had he entered a church entirely on his own initiative or in response to a personal wish. His appearance here today was pursuant to a promise he had made Elise. Honesty compelled him to admit that he hoped also to satisfy his curiosity concerning the man who had provided an inspiration for the most charming personality he had ever known; but that inquisitiveness would not have brought him to Trinity Cathedral today or ever.

That the event, considered as a whole, would be boring Parker had no doubt. He would slip in quietly and share a pew between a straight-lipped, whaleboned spinster of the sort dear to the cartoonist and a smug old gentleman with white whiskers and a black umbrella.

It was now quite evident that the mental picture he had

drawn of this occasion was startlingly incorrect. These people about him, pressing forward by inches toward the Cathedral doors, failed to conform to the type that dutifully drowsed through tedious sermons in the half-empty and wholly stupid church of the 'comics'. In fact, from where Parker stood, the waiting crowd graded somewhat higher intellectually, he thought, than an equivalent number of people congregated at 8.25 pm in the foyer of a fashionable theatre, or clustered about the gate leading down to the Twentieth Century Limited.

A few minutes before, he had sauntered across Madison Park with something like a grin, wondering how it would feel to be an integral part of an audience composed of the queer, the isolated, the other-worldly. It occurred to him now that he might feel a bit more comfortable if he had gone to the bother of providing himself with formal clothes. The paragraphers and comic artists, he felt, had let him down.

The pew to which he was shown was well to the back, but his aisle-seat was favourable to a comprehensive observation. From overhead in the spacious organ gallery drifted music of a quality calculated to build up an atmosphere of serenity and reverence. Every appointment of the place was symbolic of religious history, memorializing the legends of Christianity and the earlier Hebraic culture from which it had derived a considerable amount of its emblems and tokens.

Parker found himself unresistingly relaxing into the hypnosis which, he assumed, this environment promised to induce, but retaining enough active consciousness to analyse rather uncritically the nature of the appeal made by these venerable emblems.

It seemed clear enough that the towering Gothic arches aimed at the dwarfing of the individual. But in what respect would this illusion of his own diminutiveness minister to a man's spirit? Of course, reflected Parker, the smaller I am, the less important are my perplexities. The smaller I am, the lighter my burdens. These tall arches and gigantic pillars invite me to look at myself through the big end of the telescope. Thus viewed, my anxieties are reduced to a minimum. Doubtless if one considered this matter while standing on the pavement in front of the Woolworth Building, one would entertain the same tension; for, after all, was this not a mere illusion produced by comparative heights and weights? Or was it? Parker half-dreamily considered the problem and decided that it would be utterly impossible to think such thoughts while under the influence of the Woolworth Building – or the Rock of Gibraltar.

The organ music continued to pour through the great nave in waves, graduated in length and strength with the quality of an incoming tide on a level shore, the tempo and urgency of one's own reflections measuring to the ebb and flow, now inundating one with the roll and break and futile spray of elemental problems mounting high and dashing themselves into total disintegration by their own weight, now returning quietly to the mystery from whence they were derived.

But, mused Parker, this theory of one's perplexities being diminished by the vastly superior height of these Gothic arches cannot have any foundation in fact, for the same inverted telescope that minifies my burdens also minifies my capacity to carry them, leaving me exactly of the same stature as before. My spirit would be dwarfed commensurately with my anxieties.

Curiously enough, although he was aware of the illusion of diminutiveness in respect of his worries, Parker could not sense a relative diminution of personal power to deal with them. There must be something in the appeal of the Gothic that minifies one group of values leaving other considerations untouched, or actually magnifying them. His burdens were dwarfed in the presence of these lofty arches, but his capacity to carry burdens was undiminished – increased, if anything. How should one account for it?

Parker was suddenly struck with the fact that every detail of the Gothic worked toward the creation of a majestic, harmonious whole. Not a line or a curve or a device had gone into it that distracted from the one inevitable demand *to be lifted up*! The whole task of the arch and every infinitesimal detail composing that arch was in reply to the Gothic's *urge to rise*! Therefore, it called to the Gothic element in every man's soul. It did not actually diminish the importance of the 'un-Gothic' in one's mind – such as secular worries, fears,

146

chagrins. It so strongly attracted and evoked the Gothic properties of a man's life that everything else – including perplexities, terrors, and despairs – remained static, while his aspiration mounted to meet the challenge of this strange art-form.

The windows were crowded with saints who had distinguished themselves for wisdom, courage, and sacrifice. They may have been separated chronologically by a double handful of centuries, but here in the pictorial windows they were nearly enough alike to have been blood-brothers of one undernourished family, with a strong hereditary leaning toward melancholia and a probable tendency to pulmonary tuberculosis.

Taking stock of them by normal standards, Parker decided that none of them would be able to qualify for any vocation requiring genius, strength, or adroitness. He would have been very reluctant to hire this Peter to lay a wall, dig a well, stitch a wound, sing a song, or mow a lawn. But, for all that, these ancients had something; no question about that. Query: had this 'something' been imputed to them by centuries of sacred tradition, or was there an intrinsic value resident in these anæmic figures not one of whom, if set in motion in our contemporary scene, could earn his daily bread? Parker tried to make short work of the whole illusion by accounting for the spiritual superiority of these saints on the ground of their antiquity. They seemed of another category because they had belonged to remote ages. This was sheer nonsense, however, for in that case one would have the same sensations in the presence of a sculptured Hercules.

There wasn't a symbol on the Cathedral dating from a period closer than the Crusades – a thousand years ago. It occurred to Parker that this place was just a museum. But he knew he had never entertained such thoughts in a museum. Now he had it! It was simply an appeal to the æsthetic. But this, too, was nonsense. People didn't feel like this in an art gallery.

The organ had altered its dreamy mood and was introducing the stirring measures of an Easter hymn. The congregation stood. A tall young man in vestments, bearing a crozier, was moving slowly up the aisle. Behind him came the choir in pairs; little boys first, quite angelic in fresh surplices, their childish voices shrill. Now the boys were growing taller. Now they were grown men. Among the tenors Parker found Elise. He wondered how many of the congregation observed that there was a girl in the choir. It was not too easy to discover at a glance, with her black bobbed hair and the same uniform. The basses rumbled ponderously. 'Alleluia! . . . Alleluia!'

After a little space, two clergymen followed, and behind them an ethereal old man of obvious distinction, gorgeously arrayed. Someone in Parker's pew whispered, 'The Bishop!' It was pleasant to know that the Bishop was to be on duty today. Parker had never seen a bishop. He was disappointed, however, for he had hoped to have a glimpse of Dean Harcourt.

The choir was presently swallowed up in the dimness of the distant chancel and the ritualistic service began, the Bishop in charge. The beautifully gowned woman on Parker's right tried hard to steer him through the maze of the prayer book. He felt at a disadvantage. Whenever religion or the Church was mentioned in his presence, he had been in the habit of confessing himself a 'pagan'. In this declaration of paganism, he identified himself as of that genteel company who trust nothing to warm emotions which cannot be accepted by cold intellect. It had pleased him to think that he was too sophisticated to consider the Church seriously. At this moment, however, dumbly bewildered over proceedings which these cultured people understood as thoroughly as the alphabet, his appraisal of himself was anything but complacent. He suspected that the well-groomed lady whose baffling black book he shared was not saying to herself, 'The man is sophisticated.' It was more likely she was thinking, '*Gauche!*' Parker didn't feel a bit superior; just *de trop.* . . . It made him very warm and uncomfortable – and humble.

For a while he was so intent upon his own dilemma that he almost lost sight of the goings-on in the chancel. At length they sat, not as people poised to rise or kneel, but with an air of relative desistance from their duties, and a hush fell over the

148

congregation. The organ – a generous part of whose pipes, Parker had discovered, were located in great alcoves on either side of the chancel – softly modulated into Mendelssohn's 'But the Lord is Mindful of His Own'. He was glad the place was so quiet for the opening notes of the solo. He had thought he knew what Elise could do with the muted 'cello in her throat, but this heart-stirring diapason of hers surpassed anything he had ever heard. Elise had demonstrated, on previous occasions, the quality of her contralto, but this was the first chance she had been given to set it free in an environment that lent it wings. To realize that what Elise had to offer demanded a cathedral!

It was evident that the organist was deeply moved, too, for when the final measure of the solo had been taken, the accompaniment was muted down – and down – and out – until nothing was left of it; and Elise's golden voice, sustaining the retarded tone, finished alone. You hardly knew exactly when the bell-like vibrations ceased. She had stood at the end of the choir stall, facing the audience, and when she sat, there was a long, slow intake of breath, almost as if the people had suspended respiration throughout this impressive event.

Another hush settled over the congregation. The two clergymen Parker had seen in the processional were assisting a crippled man into the pulpit. He grasped the desk firmly with both hands as his aids turned and left him there. 'Nobility' was the only word adequate to describe this man's face. Parker remembered now that Mrs Dexter had said Dean Harcourt was a cripple.

The first words were spoken very quietly, their restraint serving to make them more unusual than they might have seemed had they been uttered with intent to be oratorical.

'The implications of this hour,' began the Dean, 'represent the utmost reach of human audacity. Men's ambitions, throughout the ages, have mounted from their terrains of experience, dearly earned, toward heights of achievement, to be as dearly bought. We have warmed our hearths at the world's internal fires. We have broken white sunlight into healing rays. We have traversed under the water, through the mountains, and in

149

the air. We have found antidotes for every poison, anodynes for every pain. Yesterday's miracle becomes tomorrow's commonplace; yesterday's luxury, tomorrow's necessity. But no aspiration of ours will ever rival the hope we celebrate today – *immortality*!'

Parker no longer attempted to analyse his own thoughts, resigning himself utterly to the appeal of the dynamic, pain-scarred, spiritually majestic prophet. . . . A legendary Adam had been expelled from Eden 'lest he eat of the tree of life and live for ever.' . . . A comprehending Christ, when men marvelled at his capacity for surmounting the pains and perplexities of our flesh, had said, 'Greater works than these shall ye do!' Adam had been condemned for inquisitiveness. Christ had said, 'Seek, and ye shall find!'

It was like a tonic. It was like an injection of strychnia! It was an invigorating breeze rushing through the stuffy darkness of Parker's unexplored soul. . . . 'But if ever you are to be immortal,' declared the Dean, 'you are immortal *now*!'

Never in his lifetime had Parker invested so much mental energy in following a public address. Dean Harcourt's words were not mere words as words are commonly conceived. They walked up and down on Parker! They lifted him out of his lethargy, shook him wide awake, tramped ruthlessly on his sophistications, and companionably held out a hand to his despairs. He had always presumed that sermons were tedious. This one was now finished, leaving him taut as an E string. . . . God! – what wouldn't he give for an hour – alone – with this man!

As for the rest of it, Parker hardly knew what was going on. They took the collection and he tossed in the largest banknote he had. There was a long prayer which he did not follow. The choir was filing out of the stalls and into the aisle, singing the recessional – *Jerusalem, the Golden*. They were out in the spacious vestibule now. The Bishop pronounced a benediction.

Dean Harcourt was being led out of the chancel through a side door, two young men in vestments supporting him. Parker wished he dared go back there and see this man at close range; wanted to take his hand and look into his face. Indeed, the impulse was so strong that he tarried indecisively in the foyer, jostled from all sides, until the current swept him along.

The bright sunlight did not eclipse his meditative mood. He crossed the street and entered the park, still debating whether to return. Deciding that it might be an untimely intrusion, he abandoned the idea with reluctance, sat down on a sunny bench, and studied his own mental upheaval, but vaguely conscious of the stream of strollers on the broad gravel path before him.

Parker felt that he had recovered something that offered compensation for the most serious loss he had ever experienced. To have looked toward one dominant personality for years, focusing one's admiration there, and then to have seen that anchorage slip its moorings, had been a catastrophe that had shaken his life through and through. In certain bitter moments he had said to himself that he would never again risk a similar disillusionment. . . . But today another dynamic personality had captured him. There was a peculiar spiritual magnetism resident in this man Harcourt. Human life, which had recently seemed to Parker a mere matter of reflexes instinctively responding to heat and cold, hunger and thirst – mere motor-replies to the same urges that propelled Sylvia, for example – now appeared as a high adventure directed by forces from without. Human interests were more than mere elaborations and refinements of jungle necessities and atavistic desires. Life had suddenly taken on majestic proportions.

Until now, spiritual concerns, in Parker's opinion, had been a hazy conglomeration of untenable myths and impractical mysticisms. Today, personal power seemed to belong properly among the energies dealt with in textbooks on physics.

Under the dreamy spell of his own reflections Parker became so detached from his environment that the people passing by meant nothing but a succession of shapes and shadows. . . . A man drifted out of the stream and joined him on the iron bench, but Parker, thoroughly absorbed, took no notice of him. Presently the man spoke.

'Beg pardon,' he said, 'but aren't you Mrs Norma Phelps?'

The reunion with Corley was attended by some peculiar

sensations. Not to have seen a familiar face for six months, or to have heard oneself addressed in terms associated with one's true identity, had wrought changes in the lonely man of which he himself had not been fully aware until momentarily tugged back into the life he had surrendered.

For a little while they tried to conduct the conversation in a light bantering atmosphere of persiflage. Eugene admitted, under much hectoring, that his business errand in the city had been fortunately timed to coincide with Elise's appearance at Trinity Cathedral.

'And did you ever hear anything like it, Newell?' exulted Corley. 'She had 'em completely hypnotized!'

Newell agreed that Elise had indeed given a very moving performance, acquitting herself with high credit, and added: 'She would have had to do very poorly not to have impressed *you*. It's easily seen that you were in a hypnoid state, at least, when you decided to come.'

'Yes,' sighed Eugene comfortably. 'She's a great little girl.'

'That settles it,' drawled Newell. 'When a hard-boiled old thing like you calls a grown-up woman "a great little girl", it's time to make out the commitment papers.'

When, after a while, the talk became serious – Corley spluttering impatiently of Paige's aimless vagabonding – the vagrant grew restless and suggested luncheon. He must go and feed Sylvia, he said.

'You don't mean to tell me that you take that dog along everywhere you go?' chaffed Corley.

'It wouldn't seem silly to you,' Paige muttered, 'if the only thing you had left in the world was a dog.' Suddenly it occurred to him that this statement was giving the lie to his real feelings. Brightening, he queried, 'What did you think of Dean Harcourt?'

There was a long silence before Corley answered.

'Well – you see' – he hesitated – 'all that sort of thing is out of my line. I never think about it – one way or the other. So – my opinion really isn't worth a damn. But I'll say this much: if somebody had gone to the trouble of drilling that idea of

152

life into me when I was in my teens—' The sentence was left unfinished.

'Too late now, eh?' queried Newell moodily.

'Certainly. . . . Nobody does any new thinking after he's thirty.'

'Nonsense!'

'I mean,' explained Corley, 'one doesn't do any thinking after thirty that demands a brand-new outfit of hypothesis concerning himself and his place in the scheme of things. You don't believe it possible, do you?'

'I don't know,' answered Paige. 'I would give a good deal to find out. I'm looking for some new ideas about myself – and *my* place in the scheme of things.'

Phyllis turned to Patricia and smiled as the congregation rose to go. Sonia, at the end of the pew, was leading the way.

'Do you think I might see him?' Pat whispered.

'We could try,' said Phyllis, detaining Sonia, who nodded agreement.

They went through a side door from the nave and down a long hall. Mr Talbot was just coming out of the Dean's library.

'Do you think he would see us – for a minute?' asked Sonia.

Mr Talbot said he would inquire, and reappeared presently telling them to go in. The Dean was alone and would be glad to see them, he said. Sonia led the way, turning to wink a stealthy 'I-told-you-so' to Phyllis while Pat's attention was briefly engaged by some little amenity of Talbot's.

They had brought Pat almost by force to the Cathedral.

'Why, how ridiculous!' she had exclaimed at breakfast. 'To spend a glorious morning like this – in a musty old church! What must you be thinking of?'

'But you will hear Dean Harcourt,' Sonia had replied. 'Phyllis and I think no day is quite fine enough to interfere with that.'

After much persuasion, Pat had reluctantly consented to go with them, remarking at the Cathedral doors that she would stroll in the park until the service was over. At this, they had closed in on her, deaf to her protests. Once inside and seated,

153

Pat had resigned herself to the affair rather indifferently, but when Dean Harcourt began to speak, she had gripped Phyllis's hand. Sonia, stealing a sidelong glance at Pat's enraptured face, smiled. The Dean had bowled Pat over completely. It was almost amusing.

Sonia now led the way into the library. Dean Harcourt had shed his surplice and sat at the big mahogany desk robed in his long black cassock. The three of them crossed the room and stood before him.

'We aren't staying long,' said Phyllis. 'We wanted to present Dr Patricia Arlen.'

Patricia was uncomfortable. The use of her title seemed farcical. In this presence she had none of the sensations of a Ph.D., or a college professor. Her state of mind was rather that of a small child shyly approaching an idolized teacher.

Dean Harcourt held out his hand and she walked around the desk to take it. Every well-worn phrase of the conventional prattle employed in receiving an introduction seemed either stiffly affected or trivial and inept. While she was debating what to say to him, he kindly took the situation out of her hands.

'You are Phyllis's Pat, aren't you? And Sonia's too, I see. I'm glad you wanted to come to the Cathedral this morning.'

'But I didn't want to,' Pat was surprised to hear herself saying – wondering whether this man's eyes had the capacity to evoke the unvarnished truth from everybody as they were now demanding it from her. 'I never do. They insisted. . . . But I wouldn't have missed it for anything in the world! You were talking directly to *me*.'

'I always preach to myself,' said the Dean. 'I've found that if I talk about the problems that interest me personally, and the hopes that are of urgent concern to me, I am likely to make other people feel that I am well acquainted with their dilemmas – and their wistfulness, too.'

'You make people feel as if they all belonged to one family,' said Sonia.

'Don't they?' inquired the Dean, artlessly sincere.

'We seemed so today,' agreed Patricia.

Apparently deciding they had had enough serious talk, Dean

Harcourt asked Patricia how long she was remaining in the city, suggesting that the three of them should come to dinner with him on Tuesday evening, an invitation promptly and unanimously accepted in face of their remembrance that tickets had already been bought for a popular musical comedy that night.

'Sonia, your shop should be rather quiet on the day after Easter. My secretary is to have a few days' vacation and I need someone in the reception room tomorrow morning. Could you or Phyllis come?'

'I want to,' announced Phyllis. 'May I, Sonia?'

'Certainly, dear – but you'll not have a very good time. He sees nothing but men in the mornings,' commented Sonia, with a slow wink. 'Are they ever interesting men, Dean Harcourt?'

'All men are interesting, Sonia,' declared the Dean, smiling.

'Perhaps,' she agreed. 'In the same sense that you would say, "All men are mortal."'

'But Dean Harcourt wouldn't say, "All men are mortal,"' objected Patricia.

'Would *you*?' he asked gently, searching her eyes.

'I don't know,' replied Patricia. 'I think I might have said yes if you had asked me two hours ago.'

There was a little pause which nobody seemed disposed to make use of. They said their goodbyes and moved toward the door. Patricia's steps lagged. Returning on impulse to the Dean's desk, she said, rather nervously, 'I must have a talk with you – please.'

'Quite right. At three – tomorrow.'

Eugene Corley had left Paige at the hotel immediately after their luncheon, promising that he would preserve from Elise the secret of Newell's identity. This problem had not seemed of much importance until now that they were all together at close quarters, likely to be thrown into contact at any time.

'I am Parker to you,' demanded Newell. 'See that you don't make any slips!'

'You are expecting to see Elise, aren't you?' asked Eugene.

Newell grinned amiably.

'I think you're better able to answer that question yourself. You have probably planned to monopolize all of her time while she's here. I shall try to content myself with a telephone conversation. Doubtless she will be satisfied with that. . . . And you can tell her I think she was wonderful today. That will be true!'

He had expected to be lonely after Eugene scurried away, intent on his engagement. To his surprise he was serenely contented, and glad to have an opportunity to resume his thoughts. It was strange how this two-hour association with his old friend Corley had reappraised his own personality. He seemed to have divested himself of the Parker concept and to have reverted to Paige, probably assisted by Corley's frequent use of his name.

It was as Newell Paige, therefore, that he strolled along the beautifully landscaped lake front, Sylvia tagging him rather demurely. He had not talked to her very much today.

Had he seemed preoccupied when Corley was with him? It occurred to him that there had been long lapses in their talk. And why wasn't he more eager to meet Elise? He had sent roses and a warm note to her by messenger, but had no desire to talk with her, or with anyone. Except, of course, Dean Harcourt. This idea kept recurring – his need of an interview with this man who now seemed to offer a harbour for his storm-riddled mind.

If any one had told Paige that he could possibly be gripped by a dissertation on 'Immortal Life' he would have grinned. He didn't believe in it; didn't want to believe in it; couldn't think of anything less desirable than immortal life. The very thought of living for ever made his flesh creep.

The Harcourt interpretation of it, however, had made an incision into the problem in an unexpected quarter. The Dean had urged his listeners to be 'Eternity-minded'. *'Eternity-conscious'*.

'Time that is measured in terms of so many sunrises and sunsets per month,' Dean Harcourt had declared, 'is more of an obstacle than a convenience to straight thinking. . . . What happens today – of good or ill – or what promises or

156

threatens to happen tomorrow, is never of enough importance to disturb the ballast of men and women who hold the concept of "the everlasting life".'

'Has it ever struck you queerly,' the Dean had continued, 'that every race and nation, ancient and contemporary, barbaric and civilized, has possessed an inherent desire for and belief in immortality? For the most part – probably because it was so much easier to practise – the people have interpreted this immortality as a continuance of consciousness after death. They have dated it from the grave and speculated on it in terms foreign to human experience. Only a few, comparatively, make use of the immortality concept as a practical measure available *here and now*. Whatever may be the value of it elsewhere, in some other pattern of life, its chief benefit accrues to us in our daily living.

'For Eternity deals with the big issues! They who are Eternity-minded are stabilized. Nothing disastrous can happen to them. Their ups and downs compensate. They expect their ship to pitch and roll, but they know it will not capsize. When some mental, moral, or physical victory is won by a group – for a season – they do not raise the hysterical shout that the Kingdom has come! And when some circumstance has brought on a period of savage selfishness, ruthless fraud, and the various phenomena of retrogression, they do not whine, "Lo – there goes the Kingdom." If you are Eternity-conscious, you are not only insured against transient ecstasies – loaded with the makings of disappointment – but protected against buckling under the strain of some apparent catastrophe.

'The Eternity-minded do not believe in catastrophes. There is no place in their vocabulary for such a word as "crisis". In their opinion, what the day-by-day and hand-to-mouth opportunists would call a "crisis" is but a phase of *the irresistible onward drive*!'

Newell entered his hotel after dark, physically weary but mentally alert, resolved that he would make an attempt to see Dean Harcourt tomorrow. He was not sure what questions he wanted to ask. The main thing was to have a face-to-face contact with this man. He understood now the nature of the influence that the Dean had exercised over Mrs Dexter – one that had given her a mysterious radiance. It amply explained her possession of the gift she had so often referred to as 'personal adequacy'.

Learning after breakfast that Dean Harcourt was available for private interviews between ten and noon, Paige had set out for the Cathedral early, arriving as the clock was striking ten.

He had taken Sylvia with him, knowing that she would wait interminably for him outside a door or wherever she was told to remain. It seemed very strange to be having an errand in a church, and as he rounded the corner and neared the Dean's residence he wished for a better knowledge of the procedure and proprieties incident to such a call.

A small printed card in the glass door panel extended an invitation to enter. This unqualified bid seemed broad enough to admit Sylvia into the vestibule. At Paige's bidding she crouched on the rug obediently while her master proceeded along the hall to an open doorway. He moved slowly, adjusting his eyes from the bright sunshine without to the gloom of the rangy old house. The reception room was apparently unoccupied.

Walking in quietly, Paige saw that he was not alone. A young woman stood in the bay at the far end of the room, looking out through the window. She was without hat or coat, and evidently belonged to the establishment. The sunshine lighted her gold hair. Intent upon what she was seeing or thinking, the girl remained unaware of his presence. He walked slowly toward her, momentarily expecting her to hear his step.

His position was bidding fair to produce an awkward moment. To proceed any farther in her direction was to take the risk of startling her. To be caught beating a retreat would be equally embarrassing. He stood – waiting. At length she seemed to sense that she was not alone and slowly turned her head. Paige caught his breath at the sight of her profile. She faced him directly now.

Reconstructing the baffling moment, later, Paige realized that her expression of perplexed inquiry was a mere reflection of

158

his own. She stood there motionless, unsmiling, with wide eyes and parted lips, while he silently regarded her with an amazement quite undisguised. She was the living image of Mrs Dexter as she might have appeared in the full bloom of her youth!

Just how long they stood there staring at each other neither of them knew. At length, the girl stirred, smiled tentatively, advanced a short step, and said, in a low voice, 'You came to see Dean Harcourt?'

'Yes,' replied Paige, still searching her eyes – the same heavy lashes, the same patrician arch of the brows, the same dark-amber iris. 'My name is Parker,' he added. 'I am a stranger to the Dean. I do not live here.'

'Please sit down, Mr Parker,' she said, with a little indication towards a big leather chair – the same trick of hand that had made Mrs Dexter's brief and restrained gestures so strikingly expressive. 'I will tell Dean Harcourt you are here.' She took a few steps toward the door, his eyes following her graceful movement as she walked. Apparently on impulse, she halted, faced him again, and said, 'I am Miss Dexter.'

Paige bowed and replied, almost inaudibly, 'Yes . . . Miss Dexter.'

Phyllis left the room and started down the hall toward the Dean's library in a state of complete mystification. The peculiar experience had shaken her a little and her heart was beating fast. Suspecting that her cheeks were flushed, she delayed her entrance to the library until she felt herself under better control.

Opening the door and crossing to the Dean's desk, she said, 'There is a Mr Parker here to see you.'

The Dean had been poring over a letter. At the sound of her voice, he raised his eyes slowly and looked steadily into hers for a moment. Then he smiled and beckoned her to come closer. She responded, standing close beside his elbow. He took her hand in both of his, raised it closer to his eyes, bent back her pretty fingers gently, and inspected her palm after the manner of a fortune-teller, pretending to be intently studying the lines. Releasing her hand with affectionate reluctance, he nodded, after the manner of one confirming a guess, glanced

159

up with an expression of kindly concern, and said quietly, 'Show him in.'

Making no comment, Phyllis left the room. Dean Harcourt smiled as he watched her go, fully expecting her to turn at the door and offer some reaction to his playful pantomime, but to his slight surprise she did not do so.

When she returned to the reception room, Mr Parker was standing by the window where he had found her upon his arrival. She hesitated in the doorway, disliking to speak to him from that distance. It would sound too perfunctory. She hesitated, also, to cross the room to where he stood, for she did not feel herself disposed to face another direct encounter with those searching eyes. He glanced in her direction and walked toward her. The barest suggestion of a smile was on his lips. It was Phyllis thought, almost a comradely smile.

'He will see you now,' she said, leading the way.

'Thank you – Miss Dexter,' said Mr Parker, as they halted before the closed door of the library.

Phyllis glanced up into his eyes and seemed about to speak – to ask a question, perhaps; but, deciding otherwise, opened the door, and without accompanying him into the room, closed it softly behind him. Then she walked very slowly through the hall, past the door of the reception room, and toward the front entrance.

Sylvia rose as she approached, and sat on her haunches. Phyllis stroked her silky head, murmuring little phrases of friendly attention. Then, turning, she went back into the reception room and preoccupiedly resumed the position she had earlier maintained at the window. Presently she was stirred from her thoughts by a soft, warm, wet touch on the back of her hand. She sat down on the window-seat, and the dog laid its muzzle on her knee.

'I believe you like me,' whispered Phyllis confidentially. 'You think you know me – don't you? . . . Well – you don't. I never saw you before.' She toyed with the setter's long ears. 'But – no matter,' she murmured softly. 'I like you – just the same. . . . We will be friends – won't we?'

160

Chapter Eleven

DEAN HARCOURT did not extend his hand or offer any word of conventional greeting as his caller approached the desk. Pushing aside the pile of correspondence and slowly removing his gold pince-nez, he indicated the vacant chair near him with a gesture that was hospitable but not effusive.

'And what brings you in out of the sunshine, Mr Parker?' he asked quietly when his guest was seated.

Perhaps under any other circumstances the direct query, phrased and inflected as if acquaintance had already been made, might have helped a stranger to proceed with dispatch to a statement of his errand. As the case stood, this abrogation of the conventional amenities – so useful to the needs of subterfuge – left Mr Parker with an uncomfortably short run for his take-off.

However difficult it had been to look down into the long-lashed, amber-tinted Dexter eyes and lie about his identity, it was even harder to face the analytical gaze levelled at him from beneath the serious brows of Dean Harcourt.

'My name is Paige, sir,' he replied, after a moment's hesitation. 'Newell Paige.'

The Dean slowly raised his head and seemed to be making a more intensive survey of his visitor.

'I beg your pardon,' he said, with deliberation. 'I must have misunderstood.'

For an instant, Newell debated the advisability of letting the matter rest there, but the cavernous eyes insisted on integrity. They did not pry. It was rather as if they entreated.

'There was no misunderstanding,' he found himself confessing. 'I did tell the young lady that my name was Parker. There are reasons why I have—'

'You need not explain,' interposed the Dean, 'unless it comforts you to do so. I dare say your reasons are not dishonour-able, else you would not have confided your real name. . . . Tell me why you wanted to see me.'

There was something peculiarly intimate in the tone of the low-pitched voice, something almost paternal; not the slightest hint of a reserved suspicion or a suppressed curiosity. Paige felt himself in the presence of a powerful personality whose scrutiny of him was not that of a photographer but rather that of a radiologist. The deep-set, pain-circled eyes seemed to ignore such superficial, impermanent phenomena as clothes and names, penetrating through to one's durable inner structure.

'Thank you, sir,' said Paige gratefully, drawing his chair a little closer. 'I came to see you about your – about the address you delivered here yesterday morning.'

'I observe that you are not in the habit of attending religious services,' remarked the Dean dryly.

'That is quite true, sir. I should be interested to learn how you know. Perhaps I look like a heathen.'

'You referred to my sermon as an address,' the Dean ex-plained, with a responsive smile. 'You were on the point of calling it a sermon, but shied off at the word because you dislike to admit that you have any interest in sermons. I can't say that I blame you much. Now, just what was it in my – in the address that brought you back to ask questions?'

'Well, sir – you talked about the terms of a stabilized life. The idea attracts me. I wondered if you might not be willing to pursue the subject a little further for my personal benefit. I am in need of it.'

Dean Harcourt relaxed in his chair, stretched his long arms to full torsion, interlaced his fingers behind his head, and gave himself to a reminiscent monologue that began far afield from the focal point of inquiry.

'I have not driven a car for many years,' he mused com-panionably. 'It used to be my favourite recreation. I distinctly recall that when I learned to drive, my instructor took me out on a quiet country road in the early morning and taught me the rudiments. I think I must have had a natural feel for it from the first. Within an hour I was operating my new car with

162

a good deal of self-assurance. I could start it, stop it, go forward, backward, and shift the gears smoothly. It seemed to me that driving wasn't much more than a trick, after all, and I remarked to the man that I thought the difficulties of managing an automobile had been largely exaggerated.

'He said, "Maybe so," with a mysterious air of mental reservation, and suggested that we drive back to the main highway and see how the new car behaved before company. This pleased me very much, for I knew it would be more interesting. It was after eight o'clock now and the citybound traffic was in full swing.'

Paige smiled his comprehension of the problem that was about to arise, but the Dean carried on with his allegory.

'Immediately upon being hurled into the ruck of all this confusion, I found it difficult to remember what I had just been taught. I became nervously sensitive to the swift scurry of cars overtaking and passing me from behind at dangerously close quarters and appalled by the threatening aspect of reckless monsters bearing down on me from the front. The road seemed so narrow and the drivers so unconscionably inconsiderate that I felt my confidence rapidly oozing, and at the first corner we came to I turned off, slowed my car to a jerky stop, and said, a bit shakily, "If it weren't for the other people! . . ." "Yes," replied the man, with a grin, "that's about all there is to driving a car: the other people."'

The Dean disengaged his hands and made a little gesture implying that the story should now be able to speak for itself without need of further elaboration.

'I quite agree,' nodded Paige, feeling that some response was expected. 'One never knows what the other people are likely to do – even one's trusted friends. . . . I have come to believe that it's just as well to assume, on the road, that the other people are going to do the wrong thing; don't you think so?'

'No,' replied the Dean, 'I don't think so. I did – at first. The man ahead of me was my potential enemy. I believed him entirely capable of enough absent-minded selfishness to nail his wheels to the asphalt almost any time without signalling his intention. And sometimes he did so, obliging me to grind hard on my brakes to avoid a collision. . . . But, after my indignation had cooled, I was usually able to recall that in the excitement of protecting myself I had quite neglected to let the fellow behind me know what was about to happen. And then it would occur to me that perhaps the fellow ahead of me had done the same thing.

'That was a long time ago,' the Dean continued. 'Experience and observation have taught me a few facts in the meantime. I think – if I were able to drive again – I would try to do it in a slightly different state of mind; vigilant, of course, but a little more sympathetic. Instead of glaring suspiciously at the back of the other man's head, and wondering what species of fool he might be, I believe I would be inclined to appraise him now as a person beset by the same conditions which make my own presence on the busy road perplexing to all the other people who follow me.'

'You would give the other fellow the benefit of the doubt?' commented Paige.

'It's practically impossible to live a stabilized life in any other mood, my friend. Sometimes' – the Dean went on, soliloquizingly – 'my cronies drive me about, and it always interests me to observe their respective attitudes toward those with whom they share the highway. One friend of mine, in particular, keeps himself in a steaming stew. "Now *will* you look at *that*!" he growls, when somebody cuts out of line on a hill "People like *that*!" he grumbles. "They ought to have their licences taken away!" . . . Well – perhaps. But the fact remains that all sorts and conditions of men are on the road, and it is decidedly in the interest of one's poise and peace to accept the traffic problem exactly as it is, without too much fretting over other people's bad driving.

'Now – apropos of stability – it would be quite simple, at least for healthy minds, to manage one's own machinery if it were not for the confusion of one's environment and the uncertainty of other men's decisions. . . . But what is more difficult for most of us to remember is that we ourselves are contributing to this general confusion. Even the *good* people.

Sometimes they add to it at the very moments when they are most complacent about their behaviour. They go into the temple to reflect that they are law abiding, generous, just, and fortunately unlike almost everybody else. They feel that some merit attaches to the business of being isolated from the pack. There is almost no limit to the versatility of human error, but *this is the great mistake*! What we most need to drill our-selves is that we are essentially alike, and that – in the main – the problems of each are the problems of all. This is the first requirement of any man who hopes to achieve poise and stability. If you want better information on the matter, I sug-gest a painstaking study of the Sermon on the Mount – and the poems of Walt Whitman.'

Newell Paige was conscious of registering an expression of surprise at hearing these unrelated documents rated in the same category by an accredited ecclesiastic. The Dean, prompt to interpret the query on his visitor's face, defended his attitude.

'Many persons,' he observed reflectively, 'seem to think the only way you may do honour to a hero or his deed is by pro-claiming him and it unique. Thus they try to sublimate the Author of the Sermon on the Mount high apart from the ordinary current of human life. I do not believe the Great Galilean wanted that. He was too deeply touched with a feeling of our infirmities for that. I think He would have liked Whit-man's "Leaves of Grass". He might have regarded it as a fit companion-piece to his own rhapsody, "Consider the Lilies" . . . Yes – shaggy old Walt unquestionably captured the spirit of the Master when he wrote, "Passing Stranger – you do not know how longingly I look upon you. Surely somewhere I have lived a life with you. You grew up with me, were a boy with me or a girl with me. I must see to it that I do not lose you."'

The Dean sat in silence for a while; then, stirring from his reverie, he asked gently, 'Have I been answering your ques-tions – at all?'

'I particularly like the idea about the road, sir,' said Paige.

'It bears acquaintance,' nodded the Dean. 'Indeed, there is no end to its possibilities. Sometimes it is helpful to attempt a mental reconstruction of that highway from the very beginning and trace it forward through human history. Endless procession. On foot, at first – barefoot; then sandal-shod; then on muleback. Clumsy wooden sledges, sledges with rounded runners, sledges on rollers, rude carts on heavy wheels drawn by ropes. Better carts with lighter wheels drawn by horses. Accelerated speed. Reduction of drudgery. Motors! . . . Every little while a radical change in methods, manners, mechanisms – but the same old procession! Ah – but it has passed through a lot of discomfort to come so far! When I review it, I know that nothing could possibly happen to me which hasn't happened to others – thousands of times before – and immeasurably more severe. I'm rather proud to belong to the procession. Mighty sound stuff in that old parade, my friend! It has travelled a long way – up – out of the wilderness.'

'Do you think that we evolved from something pre-human, Dean Harcourt?' asked Paige, not quite sure whether the question would fit into the thoughtful churchman's picture of the valiant pilgrimage.

'We've been a little inclined to impose on that word "human",' replied the Dean. 'It's the arbitrary names we assign to things that fog our thinking. We've always done it; have gone to war, again and again, over words and names. You may recall that in the legend reporting the creation of Adam, the first thing that he did, after surveying his surroundings, was to name everything in sight. That has been our chief occupation ever since – naming things, and getting into trouble with one another over it. . . . It's very difficult to fix the day when the remote cave-ancestors of Pithecanthropus achieved the right to be called "human", according to our present valuation of that word. It's as difficult as to define the exact moment when an unborn child may be properly referred to as a "human" being. Perhaps we might do clearer thinking if we permitted ourselves to speak of degrees of "humanness". In that case we might say that the uncivilized bushman of Central Africa – engaged in a coconut war with the baboons – is slightly less human than we, since he is more at home with the monkeys than he might be in urbane society. . . . But – let us leave the word "human"

166

out of it for the present, and that will dispose of "pre-human" too. Agreed?'

'Quite!' Paige found himself heartily enjoying Dean Harcourt's technique of clearing away the brush before stating his views.

'Let us begin, then, with the hypothesis that from the very dawn of animate life there was a potential man-in-the-making, related to present day man much as an acorn is related to the oak it is to be. At one phase of this creature's upward progress he closely resembled what we know as the harbour seal. Dissatisfied with his ocean, because he was possessed of an instinctive urge to escape his limitations, he climbed up on a rock and at the cost of who knows how much agony – endured by generations of his kind – he achieved a capacity for recovering oxygen from the air instead of the water. It is quite conceivable that of all these creatures who made the experiment, only a comparative few had the fortitude to see it through.

'The next phase in the evolution of the most audacious was to crawl and flop along the ground, inland, nature gradually helping them and their posterity to more suitable means of locomotion than flippers. The new food demanded new teeth, with a differently shaped oral arch to accommodate them, and a larger brain to handle the increasing business of the ambitious creature's sensory and motor plexuses. . . . I feel sure you are familiar with this part of the story, but it is possible you have not considered the sub-plot.

'That sub-plot concerns the creatures who were left behind. Some of them hadn't the courage to climb up on the rock, at all. Some climbed up and stayed a little while, but were glad enough to slip back into their sea. Some went through all the suffering necessary to achieve lungs to replace the old gills, but hadn't the valour to travel inland. They remained sprawling on the rocks, when they were not swimming about with all manner of things more or less like them.

'The most venturesome, then, moved upon the land, leaving the harbour seals behind them. I presume you are acquainted with the story of the next step.'

'Yes, sir,' ventured Paige. 'The foolhardy ex-seal climbed a tree and developed legs. Right?'

'Exactly. And when, after a few hundred thousand years, he decided to climb down and fight it out with the tigers, he left up there in the tree tops a large number of creatures who, like himself, had been brave enough to go through all the pain of escaping from the sea, but weren't up to the job of forsaking the shelter of the forest. They chattered shrilly as they watched this little handful of daredevils build a hut, shape a stone axe, and hollow a log into a boat for more ambitious fishing. . . . Then came the day when a smaller selected group decided on a long trek into the distant mountains, the large majority voting to stay where they were and take no further risks. Those who went forth encountered fresh hardships which taught them things they had never known in the jungle and bound them together socially for mutual defence. After that the development proceeded with rapidity. The primitive and his sons built a habitable house, made a wheel, tamed the cattle, turned the soil, sheared the sheep, fired a forge, raised an altar, elected a mayor – and began to pay taxes.'

'His dull friends, back in the woods, were spared the taxes, anyway,' observed Paige with a grin.

'Yes – they dodged the assessor and occupied themselves with their ancient flea-quest. . . . Now our chief trouble in thinking about evolution is that we fail to understand that it is going on *today*! This creature with the irresistible desire to rise is still evolving. His physical readjustments to meet the imperative demands of new climates, new soils, and radically altered modes of existence, seem to have been completed. But that does not mean that his evolution is finished – any more than it means a baby's development is finished when the teeth he had cut, at the cost of much pain, have turned him from milk to meat. Man's evolution has been operating for some time in the field of his mental progress. He is now about to make long strides *morally*!

'The harbour seal who, at a frightful price, learned to breathe, but who – at the one critical hour of deciding whether to justify this suffering by going on – inland, to possess the

168

earth – is now sadly imitated by the people who have endured the pain and grief and anxiety of their existence, but lack the courage to proceed toward the achievement of that peace and personal power which is their rightful wage. Many people who have fully paid for it have no awareness of their own *personal adequacy*!'

'That phrase stirs me, sir,' muttered Paige. 'I have heard it before.'

'It is very satisfying,' remarked the Dean. 'I often have occasion to use it.'

'Yes – I know.' Paige's voice was husky, and he measured his words. 'The person who offered me that phrase said she had got it from you, sir.'

The Dean leaned forward attentively.

'Would you like to tell me?' he queried searchingly.

'I had it from Mrs Dexter – in Parkway Hospital – a few days before I helped to – to take her life.'

Dean Harcourt folded his arms on the desk and looked Paige squarely in the eyes for a long moment.

'I was never satisfied with the story, Dr Paige,' he declared firmly. 'There was something very mysterious about it – even though the responsibility seemed to rest on you – when you ran away. I have often worried about you, my son, wondering where you were, and if you were still alive. . . . I confess it was a bit of a shock when you told me your name, a while ago.'

'I had not meant to tell you, sir, when I came.'

'Thank you,' acknowledged the Dean. 'I surmised as much.'

'I should like to talk to you about it. Would it be impertinent if I asked you to promise me that you will let me revert to "Parker" when I leave – and keep my secret?'

'Yes, Dr Paige. I shall keep your secret.'

'Forgive me for asking. I didn't want to risk an accident that might tell Miss Dexter of my identity. Of course,' he added, 'she might not recognize my name.' He paused, and, after a considerable silence on the part of the Dean, inquired, 'Would she?'

169

'Yes . . . she would.'

'She thinks I was responsible for the death of her mother?'

'Yes, she does,' replied the Dean reluctantly. 'But *I* don't!' He raised his hand, and pointing a finger directly toward Paige's face, said, almost accusingly, '*You took the blame!* . . . I strongly suspected it – all along! Endicott told me – though he didn't mean to! You were a brave fellow! I'm proud of a chance to talk with you!'

'Well – I don't feel very brave,' muttered Paige. 'It's good of you to take that view of it, sir.'

'Don't misunderstand me, Doctor. I said you were a brave fellow when you shouldered the blame. I'm not so sure you were a brave fellow when you ran off and hid. Surely there must have been some better way out of your predicament than that! What do you intend to do – remain a fugitive for life?'

'I don't know, sir.' Paige bowed his head despondently. 'It's almost killing me. I'm not sure how long I can stand it. . . .' Then, shaking off his mood of despair, he asked, suddenly. 'Is she bitter toward me?'

'Phyllis? . . . Yes, and no. If anyone asked her if she thought of you bitterly, she would probably deny it. She wouldn't like that word. But she thinks you caused her mother's death, through carelessness or ignorance, and naturally any mention of your name would be painful. . . . However – no occasion need arise for any further contacts between you. So that feature of your problem need not be worried over – do you think?'

Paige raised his eyes to meet the Dean's, was on the point of shaking his head, but – after some delay – replied, in a tone that was barely audible: 'I'm not so sure about that. . . . Mrs Dexter was one of the most remarkable personalities I have ever known. I think my – my affection went out to her more than to anyone else I ever met.'

'And Phyllis resembles her so much that you want to be sure she bears you no ill will – is that it?'

'Yes – something like that,' agreed Paige, confused.

Had anyone told Newell, an hour earlier, that he was likely to speak of his tragedy to Dean Harcourt, he would have thought it quite impossible. But now he found himself not only talking about his problem but literally forced – by those demanding eyes – to tell the story straight!

'Do you have any theories – you surely must have some – about Dr Endicott's reasons for – for letting you down?' asked the Dean, when Paige had finished.

Newell shook his head.

'My sympathy is all with you, Dr Paige. Perhaps, if I were in your place, I might find it very difficult to think of any extenuation for your chief. But it seems to me that this case calls for a great deal of calm and impartial understanding. . . . Endicott had been building a reputation for many years; had come to the height of his powers; couldn't afford to have anyone think he was capable of a mistake. A bad state of mind, to be sure, but not unique. It's an old man's disease. I think it quite possible that if you hadn't left town that day his spirit of decency and good sportsmanship would have prodded him into doing the right thing. . . . But you were gone – and he put it off; and the fact that you had run away made it seem so obvious you were to blame. So he never got up the courage to tell the truth. I dare say he is a very unhappy man. In fact – I know he is. When he talked to me, on the occasion of an errand he had in the city a few weeks later, he was too painstaking in his explanation. It was much on his mind – festering, painfully. Endicott's development came to an abrupt halt on the day he lacked the courage necessary to the carrying-on of his evolution. Up to that hour, we may say, he had fulfilled the requirements to be a real man! But at that one moment of testing, he decided to remain behind. Same old story that we recounted of our early ancestors. Endicott, figuratively, had gone through all the pain and fatigue of crawling up out of the ocean. He had walked on the bleeding stubs of his flippers into the forest. He had succeeded in climbing the tree, but—'

'But funked it on the day he should have climbed down?' ventured Paige.

'It would seem so. . . . Now – will you not try to look at it in that way? It will ease your mind. I promise you.'

171

'And I' — muttered Paige — 'funked it on the day I ran away?'

'I wonder.'

There was a long silence. The Cathedral clock tolled noon. Paige became suddenly aware that he was imposing on Dean Harcourt; had monopolized the whole morning. He rose to his feet.

'Just a moment!' The Dean's gesture commanded him to sit down again. 'Before you leave I have something further to say to you. I want you to know that I am not a stranger to the problem of frustration. It has not been my custom to speak of my own dilemmas, but you have a right to benefit by my experience. Whatever I have been able to achieve — in personal poise, stability, adequacy — has come to me by way of the obstacles I have met. . . . This has always been true of men — since the dawn of the world. Emergencies have always been necessary to men's evolution. It was the darkness that produced the lamp. It was the fog that produced the compass. It was winter that clothed us, hunger that drove us to exploration. The aviator can taxi all day on the ground with the wind behind his back, but if he hopes to rise he must drive into the face of it. Doubtless you will find a way to solve your problem; and, when you do, you will discover that your evolution has proceeded faster than could have been possible — but for this heroic test!'

The timbre of the Dean's voice — habitually low and resonant — seemed to have changed markedly. His tone was vibrant as he proceeded:

'For your comfort, my son, let me tell you that I have laid hold upon a truth powerful enough to sustain me until I die! I know that, in spite of all the painful circumstances I have met, *my course is upward*! I know that the universe is on my side! It will not let me down! I have been held up at times — but — eventually *I go on through*!'

Paige stared, almost transfixed, and listened breathlessly to the mounting crescendo of Dean Harcourt's voice as the masterly, pain-battered prophet leaned farther forward over the desk, the deep-set eyes radiant with some inner light. Supporting himself on his elbows and outspread hands, the Dean seemed actually rising from his chair. He was all but on his impotent feet now.

'*I go on through!*' he repeated earnestly. 'I have suffered – but I know that I am right. . . . *You* have suffered – but *you, too, can carry on through*! . . . Take it from me! I know! In spite of all the little detainments, disappointments, disillusionments – *I get the lucky breaks! I get the signal to go forward!* I have been delayed – long – long – long – but – at length – *I get the* GREEN LIGHT!'

It was very quiet in the room for several minutes. Dean Harcourt had sunk back into his chair, quite spent by his exertion. Newell Paige had an awesome feeling that he had witnessed a dramatic episode which very few people would have suspected possible of the calm, self-possessed Dean of Trinity Cathedral. He had heard men and women casually mumble their 'I believes'. Today it had been his high privilege to *see – in active operation – the force that propelled a majestic soul.* Occasionally he had stood in great power houses, almost stupefied and suffocated by the flashing lights and clamorous noise and vibrating floor – watching huge, tortured dynamos hurling forth energy! Today he had seen the Herculean possibilities of a trained human spirit! It stirred him to his depths. His voice sounded very unlike his own when he impulsively broke the silence, exclaiming hoarsely, 'God! – *I wish I had that!*'

Newell had taken his departure through the Cathedral nave, and was seated on a bench in Madison Park, waiting for the clock to strike the second quarter. Then he would go back for Sylvia.

He felt limp. The close of his interview with Dean Harcourt had been quite upsetting to his emotions, and he had behaved in a manner entirely out of accord with his customary management of himself. He had been in the act of going when the Dean had said, very gently, 'Come here, my boy' – and had taken his hand in both of his own. It had been such a long, torturing strain, these past six months. He hadn't quite realized,

173

until now, how painfully tense he had become, or how near to the breaking point. Dean Harcourt's fatherly tenderness had finished him off. He had pinched his eyes tight shut and clenched his teeth – but – damn it! – the tears would come. . . . However, the Dean understood; knew he was neurally fagged. The Dean wouldn't think him a baby. Newell had felt like a little boy – a weary, hurt, bewildered, little boy.

Now that he was pulling himself together and getting steadied up again in the air and sunshine, it occurred to him that he had indeed played a juvenile part, especially when the Dean had said, tactfully, 'You needn't go out the way you came in, Newell. . . . Take this hall to the right, and leave through the Cathedral nave.'

'But I left my dog back there,' he had explained, for all the world like a ten-year-old. It had helped to clear the air a bit for both of them. They had laughed, the Dean wiping his eyes.

'Very well – go and get him.'

'But – I don't believe I can face that girl again, sir.'

'Then leave the dog here,' suggested the Dean. 'Miss Dexter will be going presently. About half past, I should think. You can come back. We will take care of him for you.'

This had sounded sensible. He had made his exit as directed, out through the huge front door into the bright noon, into the green park.

When the bell in the tower had tolled the third quarter, Newell felt that he had waited long enough. He was about to rise, when he saw them entering the park, Sylvia walking so close that she brushed her tawny flank against Phyllis's dress. Very odd of Sylvia and quite out of keeping with her habits. His heart pounded as he watched them approaching. He strolled to meet them. Phyllis smiled – the same slow, rather enigmatic smile he remembered so well when some bit of playful drollery impended.

'Really, Mr Parker, I didn't coax her to come along,' said Phyllis defensively. 'She followed me – just as if—'

'Just as if she knew you were going out to get something to eat,' aided Mr Parker, noting her slight flush when the

174

sentence she had begun seemed to be getting her into difficulties.

They were standing face to face now, Phyllis's eyes studying
his with an almost childish inquiry.

'I waited for you,' she said companionably. 'Did you forget
the dog?'

'No . . . To be quite honest, I wasn't up to seeing anyone –
after I left Dean Harcourt. I was going back, a little later,
for Sylvia.'

'Funny name for a dog,' laughed Phyllis. Then, sobering,
she knitted her pretty brows, and said, half to herself, 'Where
was it? Some place I heard of another dog whose name was
Sylvia. . . .' A little cloud swept her face, and she murmured,
almost inaudibly, 'I remember now,' and apparently dismissing
whatever serious recollection had been stirred, she brightened,
smiled amiably, and seemed about to move on. 'Now that you
and Sylvia are reunited,' she said casually, 'I shall go to my
lunch.'

He bowed, lifted his hat, and thanked her. Phyllis said
goodbye, patted Sylvia on the head, and turned away in the
direction from which she had come. This, too, he thought, was
strange. Had she known, or suspected, that he was in the park?
And had she come here purposely, expecting to find him? He
stared at her graceful retreating figure for a moment and
slowly took a step or two. Sylvia, probably supposing her
master expected to rejoin her new friend, trotted on ahead and
was presently at Phyllis's side, where she turned to make sure
her deductions had been correct. He had stopped now indecisively. Phyllis, finding the dog beside her, glanced back
over her shoulder, smiled, halted. Sylvia, much disturbed,
slowly retraced her steps to half the distance between them,
looking from one to the other. Phyllis laughed merrily.

'Let's all go to lunch, together,' called Parker, 'and afterwards Sylvia can decide what she wants to do.'

For a moment Phyllis remained standing where she was,
obviously debating whether the invitation should be accepted.
Parker walked toward her, Sylvia gleefully wagging herself
almost off her balance.

'I'm not sure that I ought to,' reflected Phyllis, in a tone that all but invited him to counsel her as to the prudence of it. 'After all – leaving the dog out of it – we aren't acquainted, are we?'

'Well – we really can't leave Sylvia out of it,' admonished Parker. 'It's on account of her that we are here together. And – if this doesn't sound too silly – I want to say this is a very discriminating dog, very fussy about her friends, and a little inclined to be a snob. Sylvia's social approval should be sufficient.' He fell into step with Phyllis and they walked slowly toward the park entrance.

'I really shouldn't,' she protested mildly, as they waited on the corner for an empty taxi. 'I promised to meet a couple of friends in town at one.'

'Might we – collect them – and all have lunch together?' suggested Parker, not very enthusiastically.

'Of course not,' murmured Phyllis, with a chiding grin.

'Why? – because we're not acquainted?'

'Don't you think that's a good reason?'

The taxi had drawn up at the kerb, the driver stretching an arm back to open the door.

'Can't you telephone them?' entreated Parker.

She nodded, and, having made her decision, gave herself to the little adventure wholeheartedly. Sylvia, with lolling red tongue, sat on her haunches, looking up into their faces with such an absurd expression of complacency that it made them laugh.

'I never saw so friendly a dog,' remarked Phyllis. 'It's a wonder you can keep her from following people – and getting lost.'

'Sylvia is *not* a friendly dog,' said Parker, turning to look Phyllis soberly in the eyes. 'She never followed anyone before in her life – and has been almost rude to women.'

'How curious!' exclaimed Phyllis. 'She acts as if she had known me.'

Parker was suddenly stirred to remembrance. . . . He had long since forgotten the little episode. One day, in comradely conversation with Mrs Dexter, he had mentioned his dog, and she had expressed a wish to see her. Next morning, he had led Sylvia on her leash to Mrs Dexter's room, where she had been patted and talked to almost as if she were a person, an attitude she had liked, apparently, since it was much the same as his own – for he had never addressed Sylvia with any of the puppy-talk commonly employed by most people in speaking to their dogs. . . . But it was incredible that Sylvia remembered!

'I feel as if *I* had known you, too, somewhere,' confessed Parker, with averted eyes.

'Isn't it odd?' murmured Phyllis. 'I felt that you did – though I knew you were mistaken. And now' – she went on, rather breathlessly reckless – 'somehow – I feel that way about *you*! . . . I can't understand it.' She glanced up, with a puzzled expression, and let her wide eyes ramble over his face, completely unselfconscious. Parker's pulse beat faster under her candid scrutiny and it was quite impossible for him to disguise his tender admiration in the responsive look he gave her. Intent upon her study of his face, in an effort to recover a recollection, Phyllis had not looked squarely into his eyes. She met them now, and was held for an instant, her lips parted. She glanced away quickly, and a slow flush crept up her cheeks.

'Where are we bound for?' she asked, a bit nervously, searching for solid ground on which their conversation might proceed.

Parker had it in mind to say, 'I wish I knew. . . .' Evidently in the anxiety of her deciding whether to accompany him Phyllis had not heard his order to the driver. 'We'll go up to the St Lawrence – my hotel,' he replied, 'and turn Sylvia over to the porter. He knows what to do for her. . . . Then, if you are agreed, we will go to a nice little restaurant I know where there is quite decent music. Would you like that?'

'Please,' said Phyllis, preoccupied.

At the St Lawrence they disposed of the dog, and were presently on their way down Lake Boulevard in the swift current of traffic, Parker trying to be casual in his talk, regardless of his feelings. Phyllis was finding it difficult to share responsibility for their conversation. . . . At length, as they were moving slower in the congestion of the thick traffic area, she said abruptly: 'I have remembered, Mr Parker, where I heard about the other dog – Sylvia. My mother, who died a few months ago, wrote to me about it. I was in London at the time, and did not know that my mother was so ill. And she needn't have died.'

Her voice trembled, and Parker's mouth was dry as he waited apprehensively for her to continue.

'There was a young surgeon, a Dr Paige. She was so fond of him and he came to see her every day. Once he brought his dog. Her name was Sylvia. . . . Then they operated on my mother and Dr Paige helped. He made some frightful mistake that cost her life. Of course' – she went on, brokenly – 'it was just a dreadful accident, and he must have been terribly sorry. He ran away. They never saw him again.'

She lifted her swimming eyes to Parker's face. It was white and haggard. For a long moment, Phyllis stared, frightened. Then, with a slow, audible intake of breath that articulated an agonized little 'Oh!' she buried her face in her hands and shuddered.

They were approaching a corner now, and, when they slowed to a stop in the heavy traffic, she said, in a husky undertone, 'Would you be – just awfully hurt – if I were to get out – here? . . . I don't believe I can – I know I can't possibly go on with it. . . . I'm sorry.'

Newell tried to think of something to say to her, as they stepped out of the cab, but no words seemed adequate to express his feelings. It had all happened so quickly that, before he realized he was losing her, Phyllis had murmured goodbye and sped away.

He stood watching her until the little red feather on the jaunty black hat had disappeared in the milling crowd.

Chapter Twelve

DRIVEN by an almost frantic desire to escape, Phyllis had pushed half-blindly into the dense throng of midday saunterers, grateful for the shelter.

At the next corner she turned to the right and with slowing steps and trembling knees covered the distance westward to Commonwealth, so upset by her unhappy discovery of Mr Parker's real identity that she took no account of her surroundings or the rough jostling she received while passing the exit from the roaring elevated railway at grim and grimy Wallace Street.

On brighter and wider Commonwealth, Phyllis turned again to the right, proceeding north in the direction of the largest of the department stores, where Pat and Sonia would be waiting and wondering what had become of her.

When nearing this destination, a mirrored glimpse of her heavy eyes and drooping mouth discouraged the feeble hope that she might contrive to brave it out. While passing the entrance to the Potter House, she had slipped into the corridor and touched up her pale lips with a cold, shaky finger, but the shock she had suffered was too devastating to be camouflaged with rouge. Never had she felt so forlornly desolate.

Occasionally she paused, pretending interest in an attractive window display, trying to gather courage to face the two pairs of solicitously inquisitive eyes, knowing all the time that it was quite impossible. She practised the smile they would expect, but when she appraised its authenticity in the glass it conveyed about as much genuine light-heartedness as the grinning bravado of a convict on the way to execution.

Perhaps if it were either Sonia or Pat, alone, she might have made the venture, though at the almost assured risk of being called upon to explain what ailed her. . . . On further consideration, she knew that her problem was too complicated, too heavily charged with conflicting emotions, to be confided to anybody – even to Patricia, who knew her through and through, even to dear Sonia, whose sympathetic understanding could always be counted on, even to the Dean, incomparably kind and wise.

Phyllis now decided to go home, directing her uneven steps toward Lake Boulevard again to take a north-bound bus. There was a renewed surge of panic as she contemplated the affrighting possibility of coming face to face with *him*. But it was unlikely. He would be at lunch by now. Unhappy, doubtless, though still able to eat. Men were said to be that way. As for herself, the thought of food was intolerable.

When the traffic changed she crossed with the stream of pedestrians to the east side of the street and took her position at the kerb where the bus would stop. It suddenly occurred to her now that Pat would unquestionably return to the apartment in a little while. She didn't want to see Pat – or anyone.

The famous Art Institute, only a minute's walk, offered sanctuary. She decided impulsively to go there and make an effort to compose herself. Phyllis was not a stranger to this interesting place. Frequently she came here to look at the pictures and other noted art objects. Her favourite room was the big, two-storey hall which housed massive replicas of heroic statuary, medieval tombs, shrines, sculptured façades. An open hallway, after the manner of a viaduct, transversed the great room on the second floor, narrow stairs descending from it. Standing now on this bridge, and about to go down, Phyllis moodily surveyed the huge plaster reproductions which rose impressively from the ground floor below.

Suddenly she started, pressing her white knuckles hard against her agitated lips, for at the south end of the spacious hall, he was slowly and dejectedly pacing back and forth, his head inclined, eyes fixed on the flagging, his soft grey hat crushed under his arm, hands deep in his coat pockets.

Furtively, self-defensively, Phyllis retreated on tiptoe out of range, tarrying for a brief instant in the broad doorway of the corridor to look down with brooding eyes. Safe within the

180

arch, she stopped, tugged off her hat, and nervously swept her forehead with the back of her wrist as if to erase the painful scene on which she had unwittingly intruded, reflecting that she had no right to witness his agony, however desperate her own might be. A wave of something like compassion overwhelmed her.

For so long had the name of Newell Paige been indissolubly associated with her mother's tragic death that it had acquired, in Phyllis's memory, a peculiarly sinister quality, symbolic of an inexcusable and irreparable disaster. She had never tried to visualize him. To have given Newell Paige, in her imagination, a concrete face and form, would have been as unthought-of as to attempt a mental materialization of Nemesis, Mythol, or Karma. Just his name – that was all – a name that served as a sort of arbitrary algebraic symbol for the catastrophe that had destroyed everything she had held dear. Sometimes she had made an attempt to resolve that frightful combination of circumstances into its component parts. Doubtless her indulgent father's self-destruction was to be partly accounted for by his financial losses, perhaps Grace's retirement from normal life was destined to happen, anyway, possibly her mother might have died of her disease in any event – but, after she was all done trying to disentangle the various factors of the problem, the final result was *Newell Paige*.

The fact that her mother's reported interest in him had been but little short of maternal devotion was completely shadowed by the stark calamity in which he served as axis, core, and pivot. Granted that it was an accident – it was one of those accidents whose recollection sears everything it touches.

Phyllis had never harboured the fear that they might meet – it was reasonably sure that he would keep his distance. Now – the whole Paige concept had been radically altered for her. It suddenly occurred to her that her mother – if she could be aware of it – would be deeply grieved over this wretched situation. Suppose it *were* her mother, instead of herself, who had come here and found Newell Paige disconsolately lonely, tortured by the ineradicable memory of his fatal blunder. What would *she* do? Or, suppose her mother – by some means

181

aware of their strangely spontaneous mutual interest, and the unfortunate discovery that had destroyed it in a flash – were to walk in here today and take stock of their misery. Phyllis could hardly imagine her mother doing otherwise than taking each of them by the hand and delivering them to each other.

For an instant she was gripped by an almost uncontrollable urge to run down the stairs and apologize for the pain she had caused him. She even ventured a step in that direction; then clutched at the wall, frightened.

At length she went with spiritless, uncertain steps to the picture galleries. Seating herself in a room temporarily free of visitors, she tried to bring her turbulent mind to order. Sooner or later she must return and account for her strange behaviour, and the longer she remained away, the more explaining she would have to do. She had, she felt, caused enough distress today without adding anything to it unnecessarily. But for a full half hour she sat there dully staring at canals and clouds in the Netherlands, and a Spanish dancer, unsympathetically gay with her fan and castanets, whose derisive, disillusioned mouth seemed about to inquire whether Phyllis hadn't better get to the root of the matter with ruthless honesty.

Searching herself critically, Phyllis was obliged to admit – though this candid analysis made her cheeks burn – that her heavy anxiety to relieve Newell Paige's mental agony was inextricably tangled with the undeniable fact of her personal feeling for him. This sentiment she now tried to assay. It wasn't, she told herself confidently, a mere physical attraction. His being six feet tall and strikingly handsome, really, truthfully, had nothing whatsoever to do with it, she said. It wasn't a matter of his being urbane and distinctly of her own world. Nor was it his slow smile, his curious trick of brief but singularly expressive gestures, his serious, searching eyes that rambled all over your face and came to rest in the exact centre of yours – not impudently, but earnestly in quest of you. No – it was his tenderness. . . . She could account for that now, though it had puzzled her at the time. He knew who she was and wanted to tell her how sorry he felt. . . . But –

182

wasn't it a little more than that? When she talked, he had watched her lips with a queer little smile in his eyes. He had liked her. She knew that.

Phyllis glanced at her wrist watch. It was two-thirty now and high time to go, yet she found it very difficult to venture out into the corridor. The long emotional strain had made her an easy victim to a peculiar hallucination. For the past few minutes she had been increasingly sensitive to the shadows moving across the open doorway. Something inside her had begun to urge an attentive interest in these shadows cast by people strolling through the corridor. A timid little obsession maintained that presently one of these shadows would materialize into a person who would enter by that door.

So strong had this expectation grown that Phyllis knew she would have to take herself severely in hand to move in that direction. She would meet him, she knew, directly in that doorway. It became so real that she vividly experienced it in imagination. Mentally she crossed the room, heart pounding hard. In the doorway she encountered him, face to face. For a long minute they stood staring into each other's eyes, Phyllis trying to wink back the hot tears. He held out both hands to her, and she, trying desperately to breathe through the sob that nearly suffocated her, gave him her hands, and whispered, 'I'm – so awfully sorry.'

The powerfully realistic little drama left her wet eyed, limp, and nerveless. Summoning all her resolution, Phyllis rose unsteadily and walked toward the door, certain that the stirring daydream would actually come true.

But no one met her there. She drew a deep breath, not quite sure whether she was disappointed or relieved. Then, straightening, she achieved the briskly assured stride habitual with her, and proceeded, chin up and eyes clear, down the corridor, her competent heels clicking regularly and determinedly on the marble floor and thus into the outer air.

The incident of her discovery of the real Newell Paige was now definitely closed. It was inconceivable that she would ever see him again. The conditions that would keep them apart were insurmountable, irrevocable. But she had, Phyllis felt,

183

gained something of value by this chance meeting, however painful had been its eventuality. She had been relieved of a self-poisoning aversion. Hereafter, the name of Newell Paige would not be an embittering symbol for the chain of disasters that had made her life difficult. From now on, she told herself, his name would stand for the one enchanting half hour of singularly sweet comradeship – an event to be for ever cherished, though never repeated.

Finding the apartment unoccupied, Phyllis went directly to the telephone and called Sonia at the shop. It comforted her to find that Sonia had not been very much upset by her failure to appear, a complacency probably accounted for by the news with which she was bubbling – Andy Norwood had invited the three of them to have dinner with him.

'Tell Pat to prettify herself,' advised Sonia.

'Where is she?'

'Having a talk with the Dean. Didn't you know?'

Phyllis remembered now, thinking it odd that she had forgotten about Pat's engagement to go, this afternoon, to Trinity Cathedral. For it had been much on her mind, yesterday, and she had wondered what might happen there – reproaching herself for wishing she might be a mouse on that occasion. Today's strange events had swept it all from her memory.

Breathing more freely, now that attention had been diverted from her unusual behaviour, Phyllis became almost light hearted, made herself an egg-nog, and took pleasure in putting the apartment to rights. She carried her mother's photograph to the window and looked at it for a long time. Then she went with it to the mirror of her vanity table and sat down to study her eyes. The likeness had never before seemed so uncannily identical. Perhaps her own experience today had matured her eyes a little, or at least had offered a hilltop glimpse of a destination to be arrived at in due time – something like the feeling of autumn briefly sensed on a crisp early morning in latter August.

Exploring the box of rather pitiful little keepsakes in her trunk, Phyllis re-read her mother's long letter – her last one –

in which there had been so much of Newell Paige, his almost obsessive interest in his profession, the high opinion in which he was held by Dr Endicott who, she understood, had already nominated the talented young surgeon as his successor when the time should come for his own retirement.

'I think it quite beautiful – almost touching,' continued the letter – 'this relationship between these two brilliant men. Whenever Dr Endicott's name is mentioned, Dr Paige reacts to it much as an exceptionally devoted son might speak of an admired and revered father. I gather that he thinks Dr Endicott is working too hard.'

Phyllis lifted her eyes and stared at the wall, her thoughts busy elsewhere. Then she shook her head, reluctantly, and read on.

'It occurs to me also that this charming young fellow lives a very lonely life without quite realizing how completely his duties have cut him off from the interests and associations a man needs, especially at his age. Everybody seems to like him tremendously, but nobody, apparently, gets very close to him. He often talks about his love of music, occasionally dropping remarks which indicate that he is well posted. I asked him once if he had ever considered music as a profession. His eyes widened as if the thought had never before crossed his mind, and he replied, "Oh, dear, no! There's never been anything but this – not for a minute!" Every morning, in fair weather, his dog comes along to the hospital and sits waiting in his car. I told him I wished I might see his dog, not imagining that he would give my casual request another thought. Quite to my surprise he brought her up to my room – a beautiful red setter named (if you will believe it) Sylvia! If he has any other intimate friends I do not know about them.

'You will be wondering why I go on chattering about this lovable boy (for in spite of his professional dignity he is, at heart, very boyish), but I can't help thinking about him. There are so many wide-open gaps in his experience of life. Thoroughly materialistic, and on the surface cold-blooded as the Sphinx, but giving himself away, every little while, as a sensitive, wistful fellow in great need of something to tie up

185

to besides tinkering people's organs into proper running order. I already have a promise from him that he will come to see us some time when we are all at home again. I think you would like him.'

Phyllis folded the letter and replaced it with the others in the box. Her mother seemed very near, today. And her bereavement swept over her almost as if she were fully realizing it for the first time.

Pat was now quietly letting herself in, very deliberate about taking off her things. Phyllis called, but received no answer. Presently Pat appeared in the doorway of the bedroom.

'Hello, darling,' said Phyllis, over her shoulder. 'Did you have a nice visit with the Dean?'

Pat nodded, rather pensively, and turned away, Phyllis following her into the living-room, where they sat down together on the sofa.

'I'm afraid I can't talk about it – not just yet,' said Pat, in a muffled voice. 'I've been up above the snow line – in a strong gale . . . almost *too* refreshing – up there. Air very light – makes you giddy. Makes you feel heavy when you come back to sea level. . . . I'll be all right . . . but don't ask me anything about it.'

'I know, dear,' sympathized Phyllis. 'He does that to people. I'm glad you went. Aren't you?'

Pat's face had been averted, but now she turned slowly to confront Phyllis with cloudy eyes.

'I'm not sure yet,' she replied hesitantly. There was a long pause. 'God! – it's a frightful price!' she suddenly muttered, as if to herself. 'And – if I can't afford it – I'm worse off than I was before I saw him. . . . That man's *hard*!' She pressed her finger tips so deeply into her temples that they left little chalk-white marks.

'You needn't try to tell me, dear.' Phyllis affectionately patted the shapely arm. 'There are plenty of things one can't talk about. Believe me – I know!'

Pat's wan and puckery little smile hinted that an inexperienced young thing like Phyllis was hardly in a position to understand the full significance of her own platitude. A great deal of water, remarked the brief bitterish smile, would have to go over the dam before Phyllis Dexter – dimpled and rosy and twenty-three – could realize what it meant to have a double handful of deep-rooted fixations ripped out of your viscera or wherever they were located, and every dangling, aching, red nerve fibre of them coolly examined under a microscope. . . . Phyllis interpreted the smile, and returned to her room wearing one that looked very much like it. She too – if Pat only knew it – had been pretty thoroughly ploughed up since they had breakfasted together.

'Pat!' she called, after some minutes had passed. 'We're dining with Dr Norwood. Sonia telephoned.'

No answer.

'Even if you don't feel quite up to it, Pat, better make the effort. Sonia will be frightfully disappointed, you know.'

There was a stir in the living-room, but no reply.

'I'd rather be shot, myself,' pursued Phyllis, from the depth of her clothes closet. 'I've had a rough day, too, I'm telling you!'

'Very well,' came Pat's weary voice resignedly. 'But I don't feel very playful.'

'Of course you don't, but we mustn't let Sonia down. She's counting on us. . . . What are you going to wear – so our colours won't fight?' Perhaps this query might prove diverting, Phyllis thought.

'How about sackcloth and ashes? – both of us.'

Phyllis grinned. The sardonic note in Pat's voice was encouraging; sounded more natural. Pat strolled in and sat on the bed.

Sonia now arrived breezily, glanced suspiciously from one to the other, drew a long face, and intoned lugubriously. 'If there are no further remarks concerning the deceased, we will now repair to the cemetery.'

'Sonia!' chided Phyllis. 'Pat's been talking to the Dean.'

'I know it, and I've a notion she feels as if she'd been tugged feet first through a knot-hole. . . . I had that experience, Pat, and damn' near cried my eyes out for three days. But you're a lot steadier person than I am, and you've just got to pull

187

yourself together! You're going to meet my Andy Norwood. And he's quite a dear – if I do have to say it myself.'

'How silly!' chuckled Pat. 'Sounds as if you'd brought him up – from the bottle.'

'Well,' blurted Sonia, 'when I began to take charge of Andy, he was nothing but one of those dry old university professors! Couldn't talk about anything more recent than the French Revolution. Now he can dance – 'n' everything. . . . You go and take a hot bath and a half hour's rest.'

Unable to withstand Sonia's blithe commands, Pat yielded and was presently splashing in the bathroom.

'*You* must have had an exciting day, little one,' began Sonia, when they were alone. 'One o'clock – we were hungry as bears – I called up the Cathedral office to see what had become of you. Mr Simpson answered; said he had seen you going down Marlborough a few minutes earlier accompanied by a red dog. Is Simpson crazy – or am I?'

'A little, I should say – both of you,' replied Phyllis, 'but' – her voice grew confidential – 'there was a red dog. Her name was Sylvia.'

'Sylvia! – a dog . . . Well – go on. But it doesn't sound the way it ought to. You wouldn't try to spoof me; would you?'

'There was a Mr Parker came to see the Dean. He left his dog in the hall. After two hours he escaped by the front entrance. Sylvia remained. About half past twelve I went to the Dean's library – the other man who had come to see him had given it up and gone away – and, finding Mr Parker was not there, I said, "He forgot his dog." "Perhaps he will remember – and come back," the Dean said.'

'Why should *you* have cared?' demanded Sonia meaningly. 'It must have been an uncommonly attractive dog.'

'Yes,' replied Phyllis absently.

'So was Mr Parker – I'll bet you a pair of gloves!'

Under this affectionate but relentless inquisition, Phyllis proceeded to narrate her strange encounter with the absent-minded Mr Parker, the amusing circumstances of his inviting her to go with him to luncheon, their taxi drive to the St Lawrence Hotel with the dog – 'and – and then—'

188

'But this is *most* exciting!' beamed Sonia, as the reel snapped, leaving the story hung up in mid-air. 'And then—'

Phyllis, a bit frightened, busied herself with a rearrangement of the vase of blue irises on the table, Sonia watching with shining eyes.

'So then,' she continued reminiscently, 'we drove to a little French restaurant that he knew of – it was in Hayes Street.'

'How funny!' interposed Sonia. 'In *Hayes* Street – of all places.'

'Yes,' lied Phyllis gallantly, her voice trembling a little, 'and we had – let me think – a caviare canape – and sherry – and an omelet – and—'

'And one of those sweet wooden pancakes on fire, I suppose,' assisted Sonia, eager to push on with it.

'Yes – *crêpes suzette*. . . . And then we danced – there was very nice music.'

'Good dancer?' wondered Sonia, to which Phyllis replied with a nod and a brave though not very convincing smile, still fingering the flowers. 'Did you like him?' persisted Sonia. 'Of course I see you did. You look no end guilty.'

Pat, in her dressing-gown, rejoined them at this juncture, to Phyllis's immeasurable relief, Sonia suggesting that she follow Pat's example. As soon as the door closed on Phyllis, Sonia perched on the arm of Pat's chair and grew suddenly confidential.

'Look! . . . Phyllis met a man today, more or less by accident, and he seems to have put her in some kind of trance. I gather that they fell for each other – hard. For he took her to lunch on short notice, and she was terribly fussed when she tried to tell me about it – leaving big chunks out of the story, and—'

'And probably,' drawled Pat, 'putting big chunks *in*.'

'Doubtless – and I don't blame her, for I had her on the run, and she was doing her best to dodge me. Well, it has just occurred to me: this chap's a gentleman, obviously – and I'm going to ask Andy if he won't try to connect with him and ask him to the dinner tonight. Wouldn't that be fun? We'll say nothing to Phyllis – and there he'll be!'

'I don't know about that,' reflected Pat. 'If everything was in order, I don't believe Phyllis would have found it so hard to tell you. She's been quite upset about something. Maybe she doesn't want to see this man. Better ask her – don't you think?'

Sonia impulsively went to the bathroom door, rapped, opened it an inch, and called, above the racket of the shower, 'Phyllis! Will it be all right if Andy asks your Mr Parker to dinner tonight?'

There was a protracted silence, during which the water was shut off, and much swift thinking could be imagined. . . . Pat closed her eyes, shook her head, and felt that Sonia's well-meant interference in this affair was turning out badly.

'He won't come,' said Phyllis, as from a long distance. 'Thanks, all the same, Sonia. Don't bother, please.' The shower came on again, noisily.

'They've had a tiff,' growled Sonia. 'It's a beastly shame! She had been the loneliest thing, restless, discontented as a fish out of water – and here comes the first man she's had any interest in – and something silly has turned up to make them peeved at each other.'

'If we knew a little more about him——' speculated Pat.

Muttering something unintelligible that began with 'damn,' Sonia walked determinedly to the telephone, called the Cathedral, and got Mr Simpson, who, locating Dean Harcourt in his private rooms, put him on the line.

'Sorry if I'm a nuisance,' she began, 'but our Phyllis met a Mr Parker by mere chance today. He'd been calling on you. Forgot his dog. That's how it came about. I would like to include him in a little dinner party tonight. Is he all right? Know anything about him? Shall I ask him?'

Pat listened attentively to the resonant voice of the Dean, plainly audible from where she sat. Sonia's eyes were brightening.

'Yes – I know him. . . . He is all right; I would have no hesitation about inviting him to *my* house.'

'Wonderful!' exclaimed Sonia. 'Maybe you *will* – tomorrow night!'

'I'll – see,' hesitated the Dean, after a lengthy pause.

After Sonia had put down the receiver, she sat for a while with puzzled eyes, tapping her knuckles against her pretty teeth.

'Pat,' she said seriously, 'we've stumbled into a secret. Parker is all right – fine fellow – good enough to be invited to the Dean's table – *but not tomorrow night.*'

'Better let it go now,' advised Pat, 'before you get yourself in a mess.'

'No, sir,' declared Sonia. 'I'm going to see it through!'

Taking up the telephone again, she found Norwood, explained that Phyllis had made a delightful new acquaintance, and easily secured his consent that Mr Parker should be asked to the party.

'It's a bit late to invite him,' commented Norwood. 'He probably has something else to do; but I'll call him. . . . St Lawrence – did you say?'

Phyllis, emerging from the bathroom, found Sonia at the telephone desk in a tense attitude of expectancy. She glanced from one to the other inquiringly, and Pat, feeling she should be loyal to her hostess's well-intended intrigue, no matter how much she privately doubted the wisdom of it, explained, 'We're going to have a pleasant little surprise for you in about a minute.'

The telephone bell jangled, as if to offer prompt confirmation of this threat, as Phyllis stood wide-eyed and undisguisedly apprehensive of whatever dismaying plot might have been contrived in her behalf.

'He left the hotel about an hour ago,' boomed the friendly voice of Andy Norwood. 'Didn't say where he was going and left no forwarding address. Phyllis must have had a bad effect on him. Perhaps he jumped in the lake.'

Sonia begged his pardon for the trouble she had caused him and clatteringly dropped the receiver into its slot.

'Well,' she said, with an air of finality, 'that's that! . . . Your Mr Parker has left town.'

'I could have told you that,' replied Phyllis quietly, 'and saved you all this bother.'

191

'Oh?' Sonia's inflection hinted at a trace of chagrin over her audacity in trying – with so little co-operation – to accomplish a generous deed. 'So he told you he was leaving – at once?'

Two pairs of affectionate eyes waited, watched, and wondered, Phyllis realizing that she had misled Sonia into an awkward situation. Impetuously deciding that the truth was now demanded, she shook her head.

'No,' she replied. 'He didn't.'

Sonia rose with a little gesture of bafflement and sauntered toward the door. Pausing, she grinned rather sheepishly and facing Pat remarked in the approved manner of litigious dryness, 'You may take the witness. . . . The State rests.'

Phyllis quickly followed her into their bedroom, put an arm around her, and murmured: 'Darling – I didn't mean to hurt you. But I simply couldn't see him any more. Can't you understand? Forgive me for not telling it all quite – quite as it was: I couldn't!'

'It's not your fault at all, Phyllis,' conceded Sonia gently. 'I was a meddlesome Miss Fixit. . . . But I thought you really liked him and I wanted to do you a good turn. You know that; don't you, dear?'

'Oh, Sonia – of course!' Phyllis hugged her close. 'But – please! Let's drop it now – and never speak of him again.'

Shortly before five on Tuesday Phyllis went to the Cathedral, relieved to find that the last caller for the day was just leaving. Dean Harcourt was alone in the library. Crossing to where he sat at his desk, she stood very close to the arm of his chair, almost childishly waiting for him to say something.

'So – you delivered the dog to Mr Parker,' he said, at length, looking up into her moody eyes. 'They told me the dog was in your company when you left, and there has been no report that Mr Parker returned to claim him.'

'Yes,' admitted Phyllis. 'We met in the park.'

'Pleasant fellow.'

'Very.'

'Something tells me you rather liked Mr Parker, Phyllis.'

'I'm afraid he deceived you. His name is not Parker.'

192

'What makes you think that? Did he tell you?'

'No. Not directly. But I have reasons for being quite sure that he is the Dr Paige who ran away after he made that terrible mistake in Mother's operation.'

'Does Mr Parker know that you suspect him of being this Dr Paige?'

'Yes – I'll tell you all about it,' said Phyllis, seating herself opposite him.

It was quite a long story and not an easy one to tell, especially the part in the Art Institute. Several times Phyllis stopped and waited so long that it seemed the story was ended. Then she would compose herself and continue. At length she relaxed in her chair.

'Perhaps,' reflected Dean Harcourt, 'you would have done better to obey your impulse. I agree with you that your mother, under such circumstances, would probably have gone to him and relieved his mind.'

'But I'm a *girl*! I couldn't!' she protested, with swimming eyes.

'I'm not chiding you, my dear,' assured the Dean kindly, 'but it seems to me you might have approached him – seeing how distressed he was – with some little token of your sympathetic feeling for him.'

'That's just *it*!' Phyllis expostulated. 'If it had been only a matter of forgiveness, but—' She dropped her eyes and her voice lowered almost to a whisper. 'I liked him – very much – and I'm afraid he couldn't help knowing it. . . . That put me in an – an awkward position to go to him – about *anything*. . . . If it had been the other way about, and he had come to me – it would have been different.'

There was a little silence, and Phyllis, coming to attention, seemed struggling with a desire to say something more – something that was difficult to express.

'Would you mind if I asked you a question?' she entreated.

'Yes,' replied the Dean. 'If it's the question I think you are going to ask, I would indeed mind – very much. You mustn't.'

'No – I suppose not.' She brightened a little and began tugging on her gloves. 'Forgive me – won't you – for asking?'

'You didn't ask, Phyllis.'

'That's true.' She rose to go.

'We'll be seeing you tonight at our dinner?' said the Dean.

She nodded, patted his hand, and crossed the room. At the door, she paused, smiled, and said softly, 'I'm glad he wanted to tell you all about it.'

Chapter Thirteen

IN her gentle and modest way Mrs Crandall felt that she was an efficient hostess, and enjoyed a secret pride in her accomplishments at the other end of Dean Harcourt's table. But tonight she had occasion to question the infallibility of that sixth sense on which she had long relied for guidance in the suitable seating of his guests.

At five-thirty she had written their ten names on as many slips of white paper, spreading them out on her tidy desk and jockeying them into position with a due regard for their respective superiority, their precedence in relation to this particular affair, and their probable congeniality.

She had always been exceptionally good at this, even when her knowledge of a dinner's personnel was so sketchy that she had little more than instinct to direct her, plus the practical belief – which Mrs Crandall confidently carried into her various undertakings – that all things work together for good to them that love God, including such minor articulations as the one in which she was at that moment engaged.

Because they were interesting out-of-towners, it was clear enough that Professor Patricia Arlen and Miss Elise Graham should be seated at their host's right and left. The distinguished lawyer whom the Sinclairs were bringing – probably a business friend of Mr Sinclair – might find Miss Arlen an enjoyable companion. Sonia Duquesne, whose sparkling small talk could be counted on, should assist in this entertainment of Mr Corley, with Dr Norwood at her right of course, for these two must not be separated. Doubtless their friendship would have flourished amazingly by this time.

The Robert Sinclairs, man and wife, Mrs Crandall proposed to take care of herself, for she wanted to discuss with them the urgent need of a new rug for the large sitting-room in the Parish House. Mr Talbot, at the right of Mr Sinclair, would be primed in advance to assist her in this worthy cause, and since Talbot wouldn't relish the job she would put Phyllis Dexter next to him as a reward of merit. Simpson, on the other side of Phyllis, could amuse this Miss Graham whenever the Dean might be engaged in learned talk with Professor Arlen. . . . So – there you are, said Mrs Crandall to herself, and a very nice arrangement too, she added, quite erroneously.

It was not until they were seated and the grace had been said and the soup had been served that Mrs Crandall began to suspect her hitherto dependable instinct of having fallen asleep while on duty.

Sonia was saying to Dr Norwood, 'You and Patricia must have had a wonderful time this afternoon. She came in simply beaming!'

And Dr Norwood, purringly pleased and self-conscious as a cat caught in the cream, had replied, 'Indeed?' with such unsuccess at casualness that he had hastened to add in a confidential tone, 'It was a great day for *me*, Sonia.'

'I asked her,' Sonia was continuing, teasingly, 'how she liked the new University Library – you were to have taken her there, you remember – and she looked a bit dazed for a minute, and then said, "Oh – *that*. It's quite wonderful, isn't it? I mean – we didn't get there. Drove up to Lake Grove, instead. Everything so beautiful! Marvellous!" Andy, I told you the right woman would show up, some day. . . . *Didn't* I?' she persisted, when his reply had been slightly delayed by a sip of soup. Dr Norwood grinned amiably, nodded an indulgent affirmation, and leaned forward a little to see how Miss Arlen was getting on. But he needn't have been exercised for fear she lacked attention. Mr Eugene Corley was seeing to that – and no mistake! At the moment, Mr Corley was making an audacious pretence of confiding something of an amusing nature into the pretty pink ear of Miss Arlen, during the Dean's temporary occupation with the Kentucky contralto.

Mrs Crandall's brief absorption in this little drama had been made possible by Phyllis's replies across the table to matern-

196

ally solicitous queries from Mrs Sinclair, and Mr Talbot's dissertation to Mr Sinclair on the dry fly as a preferential trout bait. She reluctantly detached herself when Mrs Sinclair, leaning close, mumbled, 'We've been in an odd tangle, this afternoon.'

Mrs Crandall, with the pursed smile and faraway look of one roaming about with an exploratory toe for the elusive bellpush button, said, 'Oh?'

'You know Elise Graham is just as good as engaged to Mr Corley . . . didn't you? Well – they are. That's why he is in town, really. They've been together almost constantly. And they had arranged to see each other this afternoon at three. Mr Corley had a luncheon engagement with some old college friends who kept him so long that Elise – who is rather impulsive – thought he had forgotten. So she was out when he arrived. They haven't seen each other since – not alone, I mean – and I observe that there is—'

'Danger of a slight frost tonight,' cannily assisted Mr Sinclair, as Dr Norwood, at that unpropitious moment, turned to make himself agreeable to his hostess. 'We occasionally have them,' amplified Mr Sinclair, 'late as the middle of May.' He raised his bushy brows to Dr Norwood, who felt obliged to confess he'd never noticed.

So *that* accounted for what was going on at the other end of the table. Mr Corley was proving by his gaiety that so far as he was concerned there was peace on earth and goodwill among men, nor did any constraint exist between himself and a fellow creature.

And Miss Graham, not to be outdone by this geniality, was demonstrating a guileless gladness that would have made a surly cynic of Pollyanna. Elise had, it appeared, been just now receiving much adulation for her singing on Sunday – Simpson, really, was an awful blarney – and the table, gradually drawn into it, was making appreciative little noises in confirmation of this tribute which she well deserved, for she had indeed sung beautifully, and it was no more than fair, Mrs Crandall thought, that Elise should have the entire stage to herself while she took her bow.

She accepted the applause very prettily, and began replying to queries, the Dean's first, who wanted to know something about life in little Leeds; and Simpson's, who hoped she would give them the highlights on her recent spectacular début in Louisville. Perhaps it was the proprietorial complacency of Mr Corley's expression that determined Elise's decision to share her honours with her valued friend, Nathan Parker, who, she gratefully conceded, was responsible for her success, and without whose timely assistance she might have gone on for life unrecognized. She spoke his name softly, caressingly.

'Tell them about him, dear,' urged Mrs Sinclair. 'I think it is *so* interesting,' she added, intimately and with promising little nods to Sonia, whose eyes she had happened to pick up at the moment.

'Well – to make a long story of it—' began Elise, girlishly ingenuous. 'Nathan Parker mysteriously dropped in at Leeds, late last autumn, on no particular errand, accompanied by a lovely red setter.'

'I *say*!' piped Mr Talbot's Oxonian treble. 'Dashed if that isn't odd! Wasn't that the chap's name, sir, you said would return to claim a dog he'd left here yesterday? He must have come back while I was out.'

Dean Harcourt seemed unimpressed by this coincidence, returning his attention immediately to Miss Graham, implying with a nod that her narrative had the right of way. Simpson was observed to be grinningly mumbling something into Phyllis's ear which brought a quick flush to her cheeks and an entreating glance toward Sonia whose alert eyes registered a knowledgeable interest.

'But – by Jove!' went on Mr Talbot, blinkingly suspicious of this by-play of Simpson's, 'you must have seen him, Miss Dexter – and the dog, too. Whatever became of him – the dog, I mean?'

'Better tell him,' growled Simpson, 'so Miss Graham can proceed. It's his British instinct. Once he gets hold of an idea, you might as well help him work it out, for there's no peace until—'

'It's no secret,' said Phyllis evenly. 'The dog insisted on

going along with me when I left, and we met Mr Parker out-side.'

'Then that can't possibly be my Mr Parker,' commented Elise decisively, 'though it is a fact that Nathan Parker is in town; I hope to see him – tomorrow. But I happen to know that Sylvia wouldn't walk away with anyone.'

'Sylvia!' exclaimed several voices in various pitches of incredulity.

'Yes – and a one-man dog if there ever was such an animal. If Sylvia were going to follow a stranger – which she wouldn't – I'm sure it would not be a girl. She hates women. I saw her nearly every day for months and she never thawed – not the least bit.'

Mrs Crandall thought she observed a little smile playing about Phyllis's eyes which were raised to meet Sonia's. And Sonia, looking into them, was replying with a slow sly wink. . . . This whole affair was becoming more complicated every minute.

'That point being cleared up, then,' the Dean was remarking quietly, 'Mr Nathan Parker arrived in Leeds, and—'

'And lived at my Uncle Clay Brock's hotel,' continued Elise dryly, the interruptions seeming to have dampened her enthusiasm. 'Naturally – we met, and – well' – she hesitated, lowered her eyes shyly, and groped her way – 'that's about all there is to it. Nat took an interest in my voice and arranged everything for my recital in Louisville. . . . And my grand-father liked him so much that – that we saw quite a lot of him.' There was another pause, accompanied by a delicious telltale confusion which fetched a high-keyed 'Ah-*ha*!' from the privi-leged Talbot, followed by a brief outburst of merriment. Elise, it seemed, had unwittingly given herself away.

'I wonder what she's up to – the little rascal!' muttered Mrs Sinclair out of the corner of her mouth.

'Punishing Mr Corley, I should say,' reflected Mrs Crandall.

'Well – she mustn't!' decided Mrs Sinclair. Raising her voice, she said sweetly, 'Oh – do tell them, Elise, how Mr Parker helped your grandfather the time he fell ill while put-

199

ting on a cast . . . *such* a droll story, Dean Harcourt.'

Elise, who had recovered now from her embarrassment, told it all and told it well – the interesting case of the Potts fracture – 'Really, the very worst kind of break there is, Grandpa says' – and how, by sheer accident, and not knowing a blessed thing about it, Nat had successfully applied the cast. . . . During this recital, Sonia's eyes never left Phyllis's face, and Phyllis's eyes did not rise from her plate.

'I *say*! – but that *was* odd!' squeaked Mr Talbot. 'Incredible! Maybe the chap *was* a doctor!'

Elise shook her head, smiling tolerantly.

'My grandfather would have known,' she said. 'Wouldn't he, Dean Harcourt?'

'One would think so,' agreed the Dean, politely but rather non-committally. Sonia still intently studied Phyllis's face, and Phyllis, actively interested again, had turned her eyes questingly toward Dean Harcourt, who, briefly encountering them, gave his attention to Miss Arlen, his attitude seeming to say that we could now do nicely with another topic of conversation. Mrs Crandall had definitely decided that there was a great deal going on at this party.

Dr Norwood, in excellent spirits on arrival, was taciturnly tinkering with his fork. Sonia had left off prodding him back to life and was herself preoccupied and demure. Phyllis was seeing ghosts. Talbot, probably still pondering over Mr Parker's lay performance of difficult surgery, was blinking rapidly in that curious way he had when agitated and perplexed, a nervous batting of the eyes that twitched his nose, rabbit fashion. Mr Corley, whose exact relation to other objects was in doubt, smiled glassily as if in a mood to welcome good tidings from almost any quarter.

'And how is our little Celeste?' inquired the Dean jovially, rousing Norwood to attention.

'Quite contented, sir, in Miss Warren's school.'

Patricia leaned forward, smiling interestedly.

'Dr Norwood's little girl,' explained the Dean, 'contributed a valuable thought to a weighty discussion here, some weeks ago.'

200

'It was also the *final* thought on that occasion,' remarked Sonia.

'*Most* amusing!' said Talbot, who was requested to describe the event for the benefit of the party. It wasn't too easy a job, but Talbot managed, general laughter rewarding his tale.

'Unfortunately,' observed Norwood, 'Celeste's droll comment suddenly terminated a stimulating discourse at a point of absorbing interest. As Mr Talbot has said, Dean Harcourt was declaring, or at least strongly implying – if I misquote you, sir, please correct me – that a whole generation may be involved in a violent clash of opinion, apparently of local and transient significance, and never live to realize that their fanatical struggle was of signal importance to the progress of civilization. I remember, sir, that I was eager for this question to be pursued.'

'Why not?' called Mr Sinclair, 'I think we should all like to hear something of the sort from the Dean.'

Attention promptly centred on Dean Harcourt, who sat for a. moment with narrowed eyes apparently debating a suitable point of departure toward the suggested talk.

'It all gets back at last,' he began thoughtfully, 'to the engaging story of the Long Parade. We must break our bad habit of talking about human progress as if it were a gradual upward journey from the jungle to Utopia. It isn't quite as simple as that. We'll have to think of that upward course in terms of planes, as if mankind proceeded on a series of steps up—'

'Like climbing a terrace?' asked Mr Sinclair.

'Exactly! The half dozen generations comprising a certain era will move along rather uneventfully, at times almost apathetically, on an approximately level plane. The upheavals, revolutions, and excitements of climbing up out of the era immediately preceding will already have become legendary. In this particular economic and political system that we are considering, customs crystallize rapidly into laws, the laws take on dignity and resolve themselves into codes, constitutions, charters. Manners beget morals. Traditions become established. After a while, there is a well defined group of reliances: the

State, the Church, hero worship, ceremonials; standards of beauty in art, standards of gallantry in conflict, standards of social conduct, standards of intellectual fitness. Very well. Then – when everything has become neatly integrated and the Parade has had its relatively serene period of recuperation from the now almost forgotten struggle of the climb to the level on which it is travelling, it wants to look out! – for the time has come for the taking of another steep grade!

'Customarily, these sharp ascents have been made within the space of a single generation. Sometimes it has taken a little longer – but not often. The people who are called upon to make the climb up to the next level unquestionably get a more comprehensive view of the great plan for humanity's eventual destiny than is possible for the people who live midway in an era when things are, as we would say, normal. In the course of this rough scrambling up to the next plane of living, practically all of the old reliances are under heavy stress. Long-respected statutes are found to be obsolete and obstructive. Emergency measures of an economic nature inevitably upset the morals which had prevailed – for the ethical imperatives of a given time are, in most cases, the product of economic conditions. Cherished dogmas, vital and useful yesterday but now defunct, are skinned and stuffed for museums. Art – supposedly long lived, in relation to the fleetingness of Time – yields to the clamour for reappraisal, along with everything else. . . . A hectic period that does strange tricks of transformation to the people appointed to go through it . . .'

'Appointed?' asked Patricia.

'I – think so,' declared the Dean, measuring his words. The room was very quiet. 'Yes,' he repeated, after a little silence, 'I think so . . . *appointed* to go through it.'

'Because they're stronger, better, fitter?' wondered Talbot.

'No – not necessarily. And not appointed as individuals. The time had come for another step upward. The era – as an era – had—'

'Had done its stuff,' suggested Corley, as the Dean hesitated momentarily.

'Exactly! If a fair judge were to have analysed its personnel,

202

perhaps it would be seen that if all the people participant in that era were as forward looking as three per cent of them, the era would have been much shorter, and if all had been as sluggish as half of them, it would have been longer. But – taking the era as a whole, it now had – as Mr Corley puts it – "done its stuff" . . . No, Mr Sinclair, the people who happen to be in the line of march when destiny determines that a step up is to be taken may be no better, no stronger than their fathers; no fitter than their sons. They just happen by chance to be members of the Long Parade when it arrives at the foot of the ascending hill.'

'Hard on the old folks,' grinned Mr Sinclair.

'Quite! . . . Whatever sympathy may be felt for bewildered youth on these occasions, the people in the Parade who find the climb most difficult and painful are the mature. For they have learned all they know about living under the more or less stable and predictable regimentation of the long plateau over which they have come. It does strange things to them, as individuals. The same degree of heat required to refine gold will utterly consume a pine forest – and that doesn't mean that a pine forest is of no value. In such periods of transition many individuals who, in a normal time, might have been very useful, crumple into defeat. Many others who, under normal conditions, might have lived mediocre lives, endure the unusual with high distinction.'

'Proving,' reflected Mr Sinclair, 'that the race is not to the swift or the battle to the strong.'

'Under ordinary circumstances,' the Dean observed, 'that old saw is backed by a substantial element of fact. During the period of taking a hill, all the old saws are valueless.'

'And then the good people and the wise people get their innings?' piously inquired Elise, whose conservative religious training inspired her to think it was about time for the Dean to be insisting on something of the sort.

'That's where most of the trouble comes from, my dear, on these difficult ascents. The old standards have been tossed aside. The good people and the wise people who had earned their reputation for goodness and wisdom by steadfastly maintaining that twelve inches make one foot, and a penny saved is a penny earned, and the children should be seen but not heard—'

'And a woman's place is in the home,' aided Sonia.

'Where charity begins,' added Talbot.

'And ends,' remarked Patricia.

'Thanks,' said the Dean, 'all of you. . . . These wise and good are usually persons of ripe age who have become incapable of drastic readjustments.'

'Which gives the youngsters a chance,' declared Simpson brightly.

'Who are too immature,' said the Dean, 'for such a responsibility. So – they all go scrambling up the hill, everybody talking at once, very shrilly. And, at length, they reach the top and come out upon a broad plateau; write off their losses, tie up their bruises, mend their tattered boots, and the Long Parade trudges on. New customs settle into laws. New codes are framed. New constitutions written. New moral standards agreed upon . . . and then—'

'Another half dozen generations of *that*,' assisted Norwood.

'Yes – and when everything has become nicely articulated again in that era, so that the people know practically what to expect of their institutions, their schools, their banks, their parliaments, their methods of transportation, communication, propaganda, social welfare; then you need to look out! It's about time to take another step up!'

'Why – we're taking one *now*!' exclaimed Elise, wide-eyed. '*Aren't* we?'

'And we're having coffee in the drawing-room,' announced Mrs Crandall, who for the past few minutes had been on the edge of her chair waiting for a semicolon to appear. Simpson chuckled merrily. She felt like shaking him sometimes. And he knew it, too!

They all rose, and Simpson stepped to the back of the Dean's wheelchair, prepared to guide it out of the room. Dean Harcourt raised his hand and they came to attention, grouped near the doorway.

'A moment – before we leave this,' he said soberly. 'As Miss

Graham has just observed, we are taking one of these steps now. It isn't asked of us whether or not we would like to be members of the Long Parade during this brief period of hard climbing. We *are* members of it. And the only option extended to us, as individuals, is our privilege to determine whether we prefer to be *dragged up* – in which case we are an obstacle and a liability – *or to go under our own power*. Some of us – like my good Simpson – will have to give others a push, now and again. . . . Very well, beloved,' he finished, giving Simpson's hand an affectionate pat, 'lead on. . . . We will have our coffee now.'

Patricia, standing close to Norwood, who had moved at once in her direction, laid her hand on his arm, and murmured, 'Isn't he superb?'

'If we were all like him,' rumbled Norwood, 'there would be no plateaux. We would climb – directly – on – up!'

Phyllis lagged as the others filed out of the dining-room.

'May I help too?' she asked tenderly.

'Simpson,' said the Dean, over his shoulder, 'think up some little errand for yourself. I want to ask her a question.'

With a companionable wink at Phyllis, Simpson sauntered toward the door and waited. Dean Harcourt's eyes twinkled. Taking Phyllis's hand, he drew her closer and she bent over him, listening.

'Did Sylvia snap at you?' he asked, barely above a whisper.

Phyllis shook her head and pinioned a smiling lip with a row of pretty teeth.

'No,' she answered, flushing a little. 'Why?'

'I just wondered,' said the Dean dryly. 'She hates women. . . . Simpson!' he called, 'we're ready now.'

They saw Pat off on the midnight train for the East – Sonia, Phyllis, and Norwood. At the gate Sonia said, 'We can't all go through. You take her, Andy.' He had smiled his gratitude.

Their steps grew shorter and slower as they walked down the platform toward Pat's carriage.

'I wonder what will come of that?' speculated Phyllis.

'Vacancy on the Vassar faculty,' said Sonia.

Pat and Andy had stopped now and were shaking hands. Then Pat waved a hand to Sonia and Phyllis. Andy followed her into the car. The porters shouted 'All aboard' and tossed their portable steps into the vestibules. Andy stepped down as the train began to move and waited until Pat's car had passed, holding out a hand towards her window; then, with squared shoulders and shining eyes, he came back to the gate.

'We didn't like to say goodbye to Pat, did we, Andy?' teased Sonia gently, slipping her hand through his arm as they moved towards the taxi stand.

'"*Au revoir*,"' corrected Andy. 'That's what we said to Pat.'

Then he rode home with them, a trip distinguished for the long lapses in their conversation. They bade him good night at the door of their apartment house, and the taxi scurried away with him.

Each being busy with her own thoughts, no communication was established between Sonia and Phyllis for the first ten minutes, except the exchange of weary smiles when they collided at the open doors of the clothes closet.

'How did you like Miss Graham?' inquired Sonia, rather indistinctly, with her pretty black velvet half off over her head. 'Unhook me, won't you? I seem to be caught.'

'I thought she had a lovely voice,' said Phyllis, attending to the task of setting Sonia free. 'And she played her own accompaniment beautifully.'

'She knows your Mr Parker very well, it seems.'

'Yes,' replied Phyllis, slipping into her kimono. 'Odd — wasn't it?'

'I gathered that a good deal of that was for Mr Corley's benefit,' pursued Sonia, busy with her hairbrush. 'She was taking him for a ride.'

'I felt a little like a passenger, too,' confessed Phyllis, 'part of the time.'

'Didn't you think that yarn was exaggerated — about Mr Parker's setting that badly broken leg?'

Phyllis, sitting on the edge of her bed, continued patting her face with cold cream, silent so long that Sonia slowly turned towards her inquiringly.

206

'No,' replied Phyllis absently.

'It didn't sound right to me,' declared Sonia. 'I don't believe anyone would have known how to do that – not the way she told it – but a surgeon.'

'He *is* a surgeon,' muttered Phyllis.

'Then she was just stringing us about Mr Parker?'

'I don't think so. . . . I don't believe she knows much about him.'

'You do – apparently.'

'Well – I know that much about her Mr Parker. He is a surgeon.' Phyllis rose and strolled towards the door leading to their living-room. 'And his name is not Parker . . . I think I'm ready to tell you all about it now,' she added unsteadily.

For a half hour they sat facing each other on either end of the sofa, their feet drawn up under them. Phyllis reciting from the beginning all that she knew about Newell Paige, Sonia infrequently venturing a query. Mrs Dexter's final letter lay open between them.

'I know how painful it must be,' said Sonia gently, 'for you to be reminded of the operation, but do you think you could recall the details of it just as Grace gave them to you?'

'I don't think Grace knew very much about it,' replied Phyllis, with a deep sigh. 'She and Father and the nurse went up with Mother to the operating-room – or to a little room connecting. And while they waited, Father was called to the telephone. Mother had been taken in, and was under the operation when he returned. Father seemed very much excited. Grace didn't know at the time what troubled him. Of course they were both anxious and nervous because Mother was in there. They walked to the end of the hall, she said, and waited. Father was white and shaky.'

'You said Grace saw Dr Paige for a moment just before the operation. Did she say whether he was upset or excited?'

'No – she didn't notice anything like that. The nurse said they were being delayed a little because Dr Endicott had been sent for to go to the telephone.'

'Wasn't it queer,' speculated Sonia, 'that he should be doing any business on the telephone at the moment when everything was set for an operation – patient waiting – and all that sort of thing?'

'Emergency call, perhaps,' thought Phyllis.

'Maybe it was the same emergency that took your father to the telephone.'

'It's quite possible,' Phyllis agreed. 'I recall now – Grace told me it was reported that Dr Endicott lost nearly everything he had, that day.'

Sonia shifted her position, leaning forward, her arms folded, her brows contracted studiously.

'Let's try to organize a little picture, Phyllis. Dr Endicott is getting to be an old man. Everything he thinks he owns is tied up in stocks. He is just ready to go into a difficult operation. He is called to the telephone and told that he hasn't a dime left to bless himself with. He is an older man than your father – and you know what that same news did to him. Then – Dr Endicott comes back from the phone – *and operates.*'

Phyllis stared, pressing the back of her hand against her lips.

'Now' – pursued Sonia steadily – 'let's come at it from another angle. Young Dr Paige is the assistant. Dr Paige' – she tapped the letter with her fingertips – 'is devotedly attached to Dr Endicott. The operation proves to be fatal, and—'

'And Dr Paige runs away – and hides,' said Phyllis thickly, 'which he would not have done if he hadn't made a terrible mistake.'

'I've just been wondering,' reflected Sonia, half to herself. 'I've been wondering which of those two men would have been the more likely to make a mistake – on that particular occasion.'

'Yes – but why should he have taken the blame?'

Sonia took up the letter, and slowly read a few lines aloud.

' "I think it beautiful – almost touching – this relationship between these two brilliant men. Whenever Dr Endicott's name is mentioned, Dr Paige reacts to it much as an exceptionally devoted son might speak of an admired and revered father" – listen to *this*, dear – "I gather that he thinks Dr Endicott is working too hard." '

Phyllis shook her head.

'I tried to make something of that, too,' she said dismally.

208

'But it doesn't make sense. Dr Paige had no interests at all, except his profession. I think it very doubtful that he would throw his life away to shield another man.'

'You mean,' queried Sonia seriously, 'that from what little you saw of him, yesterday, you doubt if he is the sort to do such a thing?'

'No – I don't mean that, at all. . . . Perhaps he might.' Phyllis was thoughtfully silent for a little while. 'I think he might,' she added.

'And *I* think he *did*!' said Sonia decisively. 'There are people loyal enough to do that. I fancy he's one of 'em.'

'We'll probably never know.' Phyllis slowly disengaged herself from the steamer rug, and tugged Sonia to her feet. 'Come, dear, it's late. . . . There's nothing we can do about it. I've told you everything there is to tell. Let's forget it now.'

'Meaning – truly' – said Sonia, putting an arm around her – 'that you'd rather not talk about it – any more – ever?'

Phyllis nodded pensively.

'I'm going to put the whole thing out of my mind,' she insisted. 'I never expect to see him again – and no amount of worrying on my part would do him any good.'

'Very well, dear,' agreed Sonia, 'if that's the way you feel about it.'

They went to their beds, snapped off the lights, and there was a full half hour of silence.

Phyllis cautiously rose up on her elbow and listened.

'Sonia!' she whispered. 'You awake?'

'Of course.'

'Wasn't that absurd – what she said about his dog?'

Chapter Fourteen

MOMENTARILY stunned by Phyllis's impulsive decision to leave him, Newell had stood at the open door of the taxi – deaf to the indignant honking of impeded traffic – dazedly watching her until she was lost in the surging crowd.

Jarred now to full consciousness of the driver's rasping demand for further instructions, he clumsily fumbled in his wallet, overpaid the surly fellow, and turned away. It had all come to pass so suddenly that he had not even said goodbye. Her final 'I'm sorry' lingered in his ears. It had been spoken hardly above a whisper, intimate, almost sympathetic, as of a shared disappointment.

With no definite plan except to seek some quieter spot where his painful bewilderment would be less conspicuous, he crossed to the comparative tranquillity of the east side of the boulevard, finding himself in the immediate vicinity of the Art Institute. It suggested a temporary refuge. Mounting the broad steps, he entered and proceeded along the main corridor.

Such vague attention as he paid to his surroundings seemed vested only in a fantastic desire to know how many people annually drifted into this place for the sole purpose of self-recovery from a cruel blow, or privately to take stock of what little still remained after some unanticipated loss. Doubtless – especially now that the tide was exceptionally strong – a considerable quantity of well-gowned flotsam and white-collared jetsam washed up here, dismayed people of the better sort who, finding their burdens too heavy to carry, might put them down for an hour while they made pretence of interest in these various works of art.

Nor need it be a mere pretence. It was not inconceivable, thought Newell, as he strolled down the corridor lined with exquisite statuettes and busts on pedestals, that many a thoughtful person – subconsciously remembering that the greatest of the artists lived in poverty and executed their best work under stress of heartbreak – might find in these things a strange comradeship.

Arriving in a great hall of gigantic reproductions of European church doors, elaborately carved choir stalls, shrines, and the like, Newell sauntered among them with misgivings. For it was quite impossible to appreciate, today, either their historical significance or their artistic value. Under normal circumstances, he knew, they would have stirred him deeply.

He paused before the Colombe tomb-statue wrought in memory of Francis II, last Duke of Brittany, and Marguerite de Foix, his wife, whose recumbent figures surmounted the catafalque. A stringy, high domed lad of fourteen, accompanied by a nearsighted cleric of forty who was obviously his tutor, discreetly palmed a yawn and indifferently asked in a fluty treble, 'What did *he* do?'

'Oh – nothing,' replied the bookish one with equal unconcern, as if this sort of immortality could be had at small cost.

'Then why is he here?' queried the boy, with unexpected wisdom, thought Paige, glad to be diverted for a moment.

'Well – he really isn't,' confided the tutor. 'It's Colombe that's here. This Duke Francis was a nobody. He wasn't even *there*' – he chuckled dryly – 'that is, he wasn't *all* there.'

'Was Colombe so important then?' grinned the boy.

'As a matter of fact – no,' replied the tutor with a shrug. 'Michel Colombe was just a good all-round stone mason. He made this piece from a drawing by Jehan Perreal.'

'So – Colombe isn't here either,' decided the youngster. 'It's *Perreal* who's really here.'

'Mmm,' agreed the tutor, with a forward thrust of his underlip. 'That is, if Perreal actually conceived the idea. There's no telling. He may have stolen it from sketches drawn by some bright pupil.'

'Like me, for instance,' suggested the boy, apparently willing to toss his teacher this cue for some astringent pleasantry.

'Yes – at least that bright.' Pleased with his disciple's reaction to this sally, the tutor sobered and pointed to the foremost of the supporting figures on the west side of the statue. 'This one, you will observe, has two faces, the younger one looking forward, the grim, bearded, old one looking backward. Make a note of that and do me a page or two of your impressions . . .' His further instructions became inaudible to Paige as the pair ambled away.

It occurred to the eavesdropper that he would be much interested himself in seeing what this smooth-cheeked, inexperienced lad might write about the ironic playfulness of Fate in perching the effigy of a ducal nonentity atop this celebrated memorial to a good, all-round stone mason who had copied the drawing of an artist who might have filched the design from a clever student. It was incomprehensible how some men were tossed into the hall of fame accidentally, while others, who had earned a right to be there, lacked even a grave marker in some neglected cemetery. Paige thought it would be interesting to hear a few words on that from Dean Harcourt. And what might the Dean have to say about this gloomy old owl who looked backward over the course that the bent-shouldered bearers of Francis the Unimportant had plodded, these three thousand miles and four hundred years? How much of this bewhiskered old philosopher's dull-eyed apathy was attributable to fatigue, how much to saintly patience, how much to human understanding, and how much to a weary disgust? . . . Oh, well – what the hell! . . . The longer you thought about this sort of thing, the more addled you were.

Newell turned away and walked to the extreme south end of the vast room, where for a long time he paced slowly back and forth. 'I'm sorry,' she was still saying in that low-pitched voice of hers that made everything she said sound almost like a confidence. He sensed her presence as keenly as when she had sat close beside him in the taxi. Doubtless the feeling would pass, presently, and the image would fade, but for the moment Phyllis seemed very near – so near he could see the little gold flecks in the amber of her uplifted eyes. The spot on his wrist, where her bare forearm had rested for an instant when they were fondling Sylvia's silky head, was still aware of that accidental contact.

His longing to have another word with her – to replace the poignant memory of that ultimate 'I'm sorry' – was so strong that Newell tentatively sparred with the idea of writing her a note, but when he ventured in imagination upon the first sentence of it, he rejected the thought. It would only cause them both more unhappiness to reopen this hopeless case.

A strolling guard seemed mildly curious. Newell caught his inquisitive glance and slowly moved away, mounted the narrow stairs to the next level, and sauntered down the long corridor whose succession of open doors led into the picture galleries. He walked aimlessly around the walls of two of them, the paintings blurring into a motley panorama of meaningless irrelevance. In the third room he sat for a while trying to debate what next to do. . . . Elise had called up saying she would be engaged throughout today and tomorrow. He had promised to see her on Wednesday afternoon. But what was the good of it? The very thought of trying to be sprightly and amusing for Elise's entertainment was irksome, even repugnant. He would drop her a line.

So – what? Go back to weedy little Leeds? For what purpose? True, he had told the Brocks and Dr Graham that he would return – but what did it matter? He was under no obligation to do so. If he did, he would probably be trumping up errands to come back here, again and again, in the hope of a reconciliation that could never be effected. No – the farther away the better. Why not to the Coast? Why not *now*? He glanced at his watch. It was half past two. Plenty of time to gather up his light baggage and take a late afternoon train.

He rose, reproaching himself again for his dull indifference to the pictures, and crossed the room, glancing briefly at two or three of the more arresting subjects. With listless steps he continued along the corridor which, forming a huge square, would lead him back to the main entrance. At open doors he halted briefly, wishing he might shake off his lethargy and take advantage of an opportunity he would have welcomed in any other state of mind. Through one doorway he caught a colourful glimpse of the lithe, life-sized figure of a green gowned dancing girl, a mocking, twisted smile on her red lips. He stood,

213

for a moment, half-minded to go in and view her at closer range. After an instant of irresolution, he walked on.

Out in the street again, he hailed a taxi and drove across town, securing accommodation on the 5.45 train, returned to the St Lawrence, and began packing.

Once more the idea of writing Phyllis a brief letter was debated and dismissed. Common civility suggested his cancelling the engagement he had with Elise, but after experimenting with several explanations to account for his sudden departure, he damned all the half-scribbled pages into the waste basket and gave it up. His mind turned toward Dean Harcourt. It would be ungracious to rush away without some expression of gratitude to this wise and kind priest. The note he composed was brief, but the Dean would understand. 'I am leaving this afternoon,' he wrote, 'for the West. You were very good to me . . .' He tapped the barrel of his pen against his teeth, meditating a sentence that might explain his abrupt decision to go so far away, but shook his head. A few moments later, in the lobby floral shop, he ordered a heavily budded rosebush to be sent to the Dean, accompanied by the note.

Sylvia eyed him reproachfully as he led her past the long row of Pullmans to the baggage car. She had become accustomed to travelling in this manner, but it was plain that she did not care for it.

The train rolled out through the yards, gathering speed. A white-capped, white-aproned waiter passed through with a dinner gong under his arm. The elderly lady across the aisle considered the respective merits of the half dozen magazines her relatives had handed her to beguile the time. The heavy cars pounded the rail ends with increasing zeal. Newell stared moodily out the window. 'I'm sorry,' murmured Phyllis. 'I'm sorry.'

The tall, tanned young man with the bronze hair and belted sports clothes had ineffectively snapped his lighter several times and Paige, who also had been among the earliest to emerge for the comfort of a cigarette, offered the appropriate courtesy.

'Thanks,' said the accommodated, after a deep inhalation. 'Pretty fair show – for stock.'

'Not too bad,' agreed Paige. 'It'll do for a time-killer.'

By consent they fell into step, moving slowly through the chattering foyer's increasing crowd, which they conspicuously overtopped, fetching up in a quiet corner well out of the foggy whirlpool.

'You San Franciscans,' Paige was remarking idly, 'have a great lot of fun panning the golden sunshiners farther down the coast, don't you?'

'They really do,' chuckled the other mirthlessly. 'Surefire stage joke. The childish interest these two big towns take in berating each other is quite beyond all sober calculation.'

'You don't belong out here, I take it,' said Paige unnecessarily.

'Nor anywhere.' The grin accompanying the growl was unpleasant. 'Once upon a time' – a little more graciously – 'the south shore of Lake Erie was my habitat.'

'Indeed? Same with me. My name is Paige.' Might as well tell the truth this time, he thought. Not likely ever to see this chap again.

'Mine's Ingram – David Ingram. Glad to have run across you.' They smiled briefly and shook hands. 'Been here long, Mr Paige?'

'Since noon. Spent most of the time since arrival in a Turkish bath, boiling out the sand. Dirty trip. Very tedious.'

'Don't I know?' grumbled Ingram. 'Landed here from Shanghai, two weeks ago yesterday. Round trip to New York since then.'

'Back to China now, eh?' wondered Paige.

'No.' Ingram was curt.

Paige flicked the ashes from his cigarette and gave an involuntary shrug as if to say it was of no momentous consequence to him where sullen Mr Ingram went.

'I didn't mean to be rude,' said Ingram gruffly. 'I'm sorry.'

Paige nodded his acceptance of the apology. When would people stop telling him they were sorry . . . 'I'm sorry' . . . There wasn't a phrase in the language that had caused him more mental torture. He ground out his cigarette butt in a convenient ash tray.

The buzzer sounded a warning that the third act was ready, and they sauntered into the crowd drifting toward the entrances to the aisles.

'Doing anything in particular afterwards?' asked Ingram.

'No,' said Paige brusquely, 'nothing.'

'Meet you – out here, maybe.'

'I don't mind.'

They separated in the dimming light, Paige groping into his seat down in the third row centre. The comedy carried on, noisily overplayed but amusing. The *ingénue* was fairly good, Newell thought, but thinned down cruelly for thirty-two. Women at that age had to be careful. Couldn't stand continued starvation, especially those blondish types. Odd thing about that: brunettes could take more punishment; seemed to be strung up better, neurally. Room for some intensive thinking on that subject: relation of pigmentation to nerve structure. This Clarissa Montrose ought to be carrying at least fifteen pounds more. Knife edged clavicles, ash white elbows, acute pelvic definition, and breathed only from the top.

'And you thought I was Jerry's wife!' twittered Clarissa coyly.

'All the eggs she can hold, a quart of milk a day, and keep her quiet,' Newell heard himself saying to the nurse, outside her door.

'Angel!' cooed the leading man, tipping up her lean chin with his fingers.

'Not yet,' reflected Newell, 'but she's going to be.' He pulled down the sheet, applied the dangling end of his stethoscope to the upper tip of her right lung. 'Say "ninety-nine", Clarissa. . . . Now, take a deep breath. That's good. Hold it!' He moved the bell of the stethoscope across to the pitifully flabby left breast and listened to the regurgitation of a gallant but not indestructible heart.

'We won't tell Jerry yet,' counselled the leading man.

'He might not approve.'

'I know I wouldn't,' meditated Newell, 'if she were my

216

sister. Your kidneys are full of copper, Mr – Mr – er—' He consulted the programme. '—Mr Romaine. . . . I'll want another specimen of that, nurse, to check up on that albumen cast we got yesterday. Might have known what we'd find, of course. Big, spongy ankles, puffy lower lids, cloudy cornea. Drinking too much hard stuff. . . . No more red meat, Mr Romaine, until I tell you. And your highballs for the next six months are going to be made of sauerkraut juice with a little dash of spinach.'

'My mistake!' Jerry was expostulating as he blundered into the scene while Clarissa was being kissed.

'You're making a bigger mistake than that,' mused Newell, eyeing him critically. 'You'd do well to have a dental X-ray. I saw you wince when Clarissa clutched your arm a while ago. If you don't look out these focal infections are going to make one solid arthritical chunk of you, from your neck to your heels, by the time you're fifty-five.'

Newell's entertaining pastime of conducting these imaginary clinics was growing on him of late. Sometimes, as he sat in a hotel lobby or a railroad station, he diagnosed everybody in sight, fervently wishing he might verify the more abstruse by laboratory tests.

On the train coming out, two middle-aged cronies seated next to him in the club car were engaged in desultory talk, and the one with the squint remarked that he'd lately been having hot shooting pains in his legs – 'like rheumatism, only worse' – and couldn't read very long without seeing double. . . . Newell had put down his book and glanced at the speaker out of the tail of his eye. A moment afterward, he resumed his novel disinterestedly, reflecting that it wouldn't be long – a couple of years, perhaps – until the least informed layman could interpret the exact meaning of these two canes this fellow would be stamping hard against the pavement, to steady his shambling gait.

'Funny,' the man was saying. 'Bottoms of my feet feel like I'm walking on wool.'

'It's not a bit funny,' Newell mentally replied, 'locomotor ataxia isn't.'

'Yep,' sighed the man, 'it's difficult getting around, these days.'

'Oh, well,' thought Newell, 'you've been around.'

Sometimes he held extended debates with himself on the ethics of his former profession. This code had constituted the fundamental premises of his loyalty. Its demands were, to him, the most urgent of all the moral imperatives. Lacking a religion, this had served in its stead. Indifferent to political movements and an adherent of no party, this was his politics and this his patriotism.

In his present plight, Newell had occasion to wonder whether some of these recommendations were sound. For instance, there was that old man with whom he had rubbed elbows in the Pullman dressing-room. With elaborate care the fine old fellow had gingerly shaved round the edges of a small sullen sore on his cheekbone. The ethics of the medical profession bade Newell mind his own business and volunteer no counsel. He wanted very much to say, 'My friend, if I had that little spot on my face, I would see a good cancer specialist without delay.' He couldn't and didn't say it. But something told him he had failed of a duty that made a higher bid for his action than the code of ethics which forbade it.

Ingram was waiting for him after the show, and they strolled out into the balmy May-day evening towards the hotel where both were stopping. Prudently casual queries were exchanged and discreetly evasive replies were given, Ingram taking the initiative, for Paige still remembered the fellow's gruffness in the theatre lobby and did not propose to encore it.

Two hours later, lounging with unbuttoned collars and open waistcoats in Ingram's room, they had admitted to each other that they were adrift. Neither had come to the point of disgorging details, but after much careful cat-footing around the rim of their respective predicaments and a few drinks from Ingram's quart bottle, supplemented by ice and ginger ale from below, it became clear enough that however they might have arrived at their present state of uselessness, they were equally useless.

Suddenly candid, Ingram launched upon his story. Most of

218

it was hot and spluttery, for the rank injustice that themed it was fresh in his mind. He had been out in China for five years in the employ of a great American industry. Under no circumstances would he have endured all the discomforts incident to this small paid job but for the promise – at least the reasonable expectation – of frequent advancements in salary and responsibility.

The girl had finally decided, two years ago, after a tedious and nerve destroying correspondence, that she wasn't quite up to spending her life in a foreign land. So that was that, and Ingram had got over it without much damage; with a sense of relief, to have the matter settled. With increased interest in his job – for it was now up to him to demonstrate to himself that textile machinery was more important than Hortense – Ingram became a glutton for work, permitting himself to be shockingly imposed upon by his superiors. Nothing mattered any more but to please the company. He merely grinned when Hortense wrote that she was marrying Bradford, his closest friend back home. It had always been in the back of his head that Bradford would be his best man. He wished them luck and hurried to catch a train to Tientsin on an errand another chap should have done.

Entitled to six months' leave, he had sailed for the States, not hilariously, for there was nothing he cared to come back to, but mildly curious to note the changes in his country. He had gone directly to New York for the customary interview with the people at The Top, and had been informed of reorganization that would degrade him both in pay and prestige, explained of course by the Depression, which Ingram profanely declared would now be offered as an excuse for fraud, ingratitude, extortion, and the evasion of contracted obligations.

During the latter part of his narrative, Ingram paced the floor, gesturing with his glass, just drunk enough to disclose his real feelings, but not so drunk as to convert the story into maudlin melodrama.

Newell's eyes interestedly and sympathetically followed him up and down the room, vicariously relieving his own pent-up sentiments by listening to Ingram's passionate speech. On occasions he, too, could be fairly competent in the use of strong terms, but he was obliged to concede tonight that this man's versatility in all the accepted techniques of vituperation made him feel very humble indeed. Newell learned, during David's peroration, that certain adjectives of damnation could be converted into adverbs, giving them a fresh piquancy. Deeply as he sympathized with his new friend, it was difficult at times for him to keep his face straight when the tempest was in full fury.

He kept wondering whether Ingram's complete purgation of all his bottled up venom was going to require him to turn himself inside out also. Even in the sweat and sacrilege of David's address, Newell found himself concocting an autobiography that might be adequate to account for his own plight. He had no notion of telling Ingram the exact truth.

It soon appeared, however, that the red-faced chronicler was much too obsessed with his own misfortunes to insist on knowing the nature of Paige's calamity.

'Look!' Ingram, winded and perspiring, had become suddenly inspired with a large idea. 'You and I need a long breath of absolutely fresh air. Away up in the mountains. Away up above the fog. We gotta get out of the sight and sound and smell of the whole damned farce. We'll buy a coupla blankets and some beans and lease a burro – and lose ourselves for a month or two. Whaddayuh say?'

Paige grinned and shook his head.

'I wouldn't be any good at that sort of thing. Never went camping in my life.'

'Neither did I. We'll take a guide. Get one for a song.'

'Maybe we'd better wait and talk it over when we're both sober,' suggested Paige indulgently.

'How do you mean – "both sober"!' challenged Ingram truculently.

'When *I'm* sober, then, little one, if you're so sensitive.'

Ingram slumped into a chair, scowled, grinned, mopped his face, and said he needed a bowl of hot onion soup. Paige reflected that a glass of iced buttermilk would be more to the purpose. After a quarrel about the respective merits of these restoratives, they started to go down to the grill.

'You'd make a much better impression there if you wore your shirt,' advised Paige. 'Here it is – and brush your hair.'

'Yeah – that's what comes from living soft!' rumbled Ingram. 'Gotta wear a shirt. Gotta brush your hair. I want a breath o' air. Mountains! Beans! Burro! Open spaces!'

'All right! A-l-l-r-i-g-h-t' drawled Paige. 'We'll do it. Sounds silly – and I'll bet we're back in twenty-four hours. But – we'll try it.'

They had considered themselves lucky to have found a guide at liberty. True, Pete was an ugly, sullen rascal, but – as Ingram said – they weren't taking him along as a social companion, and if he minded his own business and didn't try to be too chummy, so much the better.

It was late afternoon when their train arrived at Bayley's Gulch. Leaving their luggage with the station master, they had sauntered up the shabby street to the General Store which was also the post office. Restrained curiosity dully smouldered in the eyes of the loafers in all the postures of indolence and fatigue on the unpainted wooden steps. Something like a sneer accompanied the unanimous inspection of the strangers' new boots as they came to a stand in front of the ramshackle building.

Ingram inquired pleasantly whether it would be possible to secure a guide to take them up into the mountains on a hiking trip. Two sourly shook their heads, three or four shifted their positions slightly and gazed at one another in silence; then they all spat, in concert.

'Well!' said Ingram testily, and the two of them tramped up the steps and into the store. The postmaster was gruffly responsive, but didn't know of anyone who might want the job.

'How long?' growled a swarthy hulk of a fellow, seated on a nail keg in the far corner.

Ingram and Paige moved in his direction and outlined their plans. Pete – he seemed not to have another name – drove a hard bargain, but they were in no position to haggle in such a tight market. It was agreed that they would start in the morning, shortly after sunrise. The postmaster gave them a room for the night and they slept together on a thin mattress in a bed that squeakingly protested.

They were off at five-thirty, Pete and the burro leading. The day was fine and the adventurers were in excellent form. Sylvia, unused to walking on sharp stones, picked her footing daintily, pausing now and then with elevated nose to sniff the new atmosphere with an amusing attitude of distaste for this unprecedented foolishness.

'Pete,' remarked Paige, as they sat eating their lunch at eleven beside a noisy little mountain stream, 'we're not trying to break any records, you know. This climbing business is not exactly in our line and we'll be needing a day or two before we're as tough as you are. Better take it a little slower this afternoon.'

At six they called it a day and sprawled on the ground, admiring the sunset and nursing their lame feet. Pete stolidly prepared supper. It was delicious – thick sliced greasy bacon, beans – Ingram was especially pleased with the beans – leather flapjacks, and heroically strong coffee.

'No great hurry tomorrow, Pete,' counselled Ingram. 'We've got all the time in the world.'

In spite of the admonition, breakfast was a-sizzle at five and they were scrambling up the difficult trail at six. Pete seemed in slightly lighter spirits when they halted at noon in a comparatively level spot where a waterfall had encouraged some hardy vegetation. He suggested that they might camp here for a day or two, his clients heartily approving.

At one Pete sauntered off with a pick on his shoulder and did not return until dark. They watched him leave the trail a hundred yards up the slope and turn to the left, disappearing among the white crags. When it was suppertime, and he was still absent, they proceeded to do their own cooking, agreeing that it was more tasty than Pete's, and not caring whether the contemptuous fellow ever came back.

'One thing about the Chinks,' continued David, refilling his pipe as they lounged on their elbows before the smouldering fire, 'they're fundamentally honest about their work. A sort of innate respect for their jobs. The Chink's employment is never thought of as a vocation. It is an inheritance. If his honourable parent is a cobbler, he has no itch to be something better or other than a cobbler. His great-great-grandfather was a cobbler and his great-great-grandson will be a cobbler. If he was born on the land, he stays on the land – same land that was tilled by a whole graveyardful of ancestors.'

'Which, I suppose,' reflected Newell, 'accounts for their lack of enterprise.'

'Judged by our Yankee conception of progress – yes.' David tugged energetically on his pipe for a while, and continued: 'A fellow was telling me in New York the other day, that when you have your oil changed at a garage you had better stand right there and watch carefully to see that the chap screws the nut back on tightly, or he's likely to neglect it, and he wouldn't care if all your oil leaked out at the cost of a burned bearing.'

'I don't believe that happens very often,' Newell objected patriotically.

'Well – this fellow thought it did; said he thought the majority of the young fry in this country considered themselves too good for their jobs, ingenious only in devising methods to avoid work, hating the idea of serving anybody, and with no interest whatsoever in sound workmanship for its own sake. No more guild-pride. . . . You don't think that's so?'

'In the main – no. But perhaps I'm not the person to consult. As I remember the conduct of the people who worked with me, I think most of them were very attentive to their business. It might have been a bit different in their case, however. It was rather dangerous to be reckless in that institution.'

'Powder factory?'

Newell delayed his reply, making quite a task of poking the embers into a blaze.

'Hospital,' he answered, at length. 'I think I'll tell you about it.'

It was after ten o'clock when they rolled into their blankets, Ingram indignantly muttering that they'd both had a rotten deal, Paige replying that perhaps they'd better try to forget about it and make use of their excursion, in view of what it had done to their feet.

Pete was gone, the next morning, before they were up.

'I've a notion,' observed Newell, 'that instead of hiring a guide, we're financing a prospector.'

'It's no matter,' chuckled David. 'I'm just as glad he isn't hanging about all the time. So long as he doesn't abscond with the food and leave us marooned up here, I'm willing he should keep out of sight.'

After breakfast they decided on a tramp to the right of the trail. It was rough going and an hour of it was plenty. They sat to rest near what had once been a waterfall.

'Pretty bit of rock that,' remarked Newell, rolling a fist-sized chunk of parti-coloured stone about with the toe of his boot. 'The green is copper, no doubt. What are those bright brassy flecks?'

'Yeah – you'll be finding gold,' yawned David stretching flat on his back, hands behind his head. 'Boy! – if there was any of that stuff lying around loose on the ground, this close to civilization, there'd be a mob up here fighting for it.'

'I'm not sure about that. We're three-quarters of a mile off the trail. This particular spot may never have been visited before.' Newell was idly hammering his discovery with a hefty round stone.

'And it's never going to be visited again, far as I'm concerned,' muttered David sleepily.

'I say, old man,' exclaimed Newell, 'have a look at this stuff!'

It was dusk again when Pete returned to find his employers making the fire. Paige told him he had arrived just in time to be useful, a hint he acted upon reluctantly. It was evident that Pete was in an ugly mood. He had had a bad day, no doubt.

'Might as well push on tomorrow,' he advised gruffly.

'No hurry,' replied Ingram. 'We like it here . . . Eh, Sylvia, old lady?'

'There's nothin' to see,' growled Pete. 'Better view higher up.'

224

'We'll see it when we get there,' said Paige shortly. 'We're staying here for a couple of days. If you want to ramble about, that's your privilege.'

Pete sulkily lumbered off after supper, tethered the burro some fifty yards farther away, and seated himself at some distance from the fire.

'He has thoughts of moving on early in the morning without us,' suspected Ingram. 'I think I'll drag the pack over here where he isn't so likely to be tempted.'

If Pete had been meditating an unannounced getaway, there was no evidence of it next morning. He was surprisingly attentive at breakfast and made no move to leave camp. Ingram grinned and winked.

'I wonder if the chap hasn't smelled a mouse,' he suggested.

'We can easily find out,' thought Newell, outlining a plan.

Lighting their pipes, they strolled off toward the left of the trail, elaborately unconcerned about their course, leaving Pete polishing the pans with amazing diligence. After nearly a half mile of wearisome clambering over tumbled rocks, they agreed they'd had enough and sat down in the lee of a big one to smoke their pipes. Ingram took off his cap, twenty minutes later, and cautiously drew himself up to peer over the top of the ledge.

'Yep – he's a faithful guide,' reported Ingram. 'Coming right along.'

'That kind of devotion should be rewarded. Let's go back and present him with one of our pebbles. If he wants to think we found it over here, that will be his own affair.'

Pete was back in camp when they returned. Paige dug in his pocket and handed him a little stone with the remark that it looked as if there was a bit of gold in it.

' 'Bout five cents a ton,' scoffed Pete disgustedly.

'That all?' Paige threw it away, appearing indifferent to the assay, an episode that seemed to amuse Ingram.

As they had expected, Pete strolled off early in the afternoon on an unnecessarily circuitous route toward the place where he had seen them in the morning. When he was safely out of sight, they retraced their steps to the wash where they had found the gold.

'God – Newell – don't let that dangle!' groaned Ingram. 'It's broken in a dozen places – grinding – ends scratching.'

'I know,' panted Paige, 'but there isn't anything I can do about it – not out here. I'll be as easy as possible.' The one hundred and seventy pounds burden on his back was beginning to make his head swim. Sylvia was excitedly scampering in aimless circles, with high-keyed little whimpers of sympathy as if she regretted her inability to help.

Pete had set off early that morning with his pick on his shoulder, David watching him go. He shook Newell awake.

'Look!' he said, laughing. 'Hot on the gold trail!'

Newell yawned, stretched mightily, and raised up on an elbow, his thick mop of hair tousled.

'That leaves us free for a good day's work,' he said. 'Our Pete isn't as crafty as we thought.'

Arrived at the precipitous slope where long ago the wash had been left on the mountainside by a stream whose course had been deflected, perhaps by an avalanche, they began to climb, admitting to each other that it was very risky business for inexperienced people.

A dwarf pine had snapped with Ingram, dropping him twenty feet – rigid and topside up – on a slanting rock. He had crumpled, clutching his leg. Paige had quickly followed down, slipping, sliding, clawing for handholds. A hasty examination of the injury showed a serious fracture. The torturing trip back to camp was begun.

'Stiff upper lip, old fellow!' encouraged Newell. 'Not very – far – now.' He heartily wished he was telling the truth. At times he feared he was about all in.

After a few eternities, with his head pounding and his lungs on fire from the gruelling strain, he gently eased his burden down, and set about the task of attending to Ingram's hurt.

'Now this is going to be nothing but a makeshift, my lad,' he warned, as he began tearing up their shirts into bandages and drawing nails from the wooden box containing their tinned meats. 'We'll have to wait until we're down before this can be properly set. I shall do the very best I can for you.'

'By the way' – Ingram gritted his teeth – 'how are we going to get down? Think this rapscallion can be trusted to go for help?' He clenched his fists and watched Paige's experienced hands fashioning the splint.

'No,' muttered Paige. 'We are all going down together.'

'Look – he's coming now! He followed us, after all.'

Paige hotly confronted Pete with the charge that he had trailed along behind them, too lazy and indifferent to offer help. Pete grinned sourly and declared it was none of his business if they broke their legs trying to hide a find from him.

Ingram ventured to express his feelings on this subject, but Paige silenced him with a shake of the head. They couldn't afford to make war on Pete – not in this predicament.

'Break camp at once, Pete,' commanded Paige. 'Pack the stuff. We will start down immediately.'

'Not today,' growled Pete. 'I'm staying here over tomorrow. Mean to have another look around – over there where he broke his leg.'

Something in Paige's head snapped. The limit of his forbearance had been reached. His right fist crashed into the fellow's jaw. Pete measured his length and lay very still.

Chapter Fifteen

FOR the first time in his adult life, Newell Paige had slept all the way around the clock. He awoke drenched with perspiration, his eyes blinded by the dazzling sunshine. Dully exploring his stiff lips with the tip of a sluggish tongue, he encountered the longest bristles he had ever acquired.

The severely simple appointments of the room helped him to locate himself. He closed his throbbing eyes for a long moment and shuddered at the recollection. Every sore and swollen muscle of his body protested as he raised up on an elbow to reach for his watch on the white enamel table beside the high narrow bed. It was ten-thirty. He grimacingly eased himself back on the damp pillow and ventured a heavy sigh which was so strongly objected to that he gave it up.

There was a gentle thumping on the floor beneath the bed. Newell grinned, lowered an arm over the edge, snapped his fingers softly, and felt Sylvia's wet tongue on his hand. Then her red head appeared and her forepaws were laid on the mattress close beside his pillow.

'What have you got there?' inquired Newell.

Sylvia opened her jaws and put down on his chest a ragged piece of dusty, hard-textured cloth about the size of a man's two outspread hands. Newell held up the doubtful gift and inspected it closely. Then he chuckled, and Sylvia laid her muzzle against his arm.

The door, which had been left ajar, was now cautiously pushed open. The nurse, with basin and towels, smilingly approached the bed, Sylvia dropping down on all fours to make way for her.

'So – you're awake. How do you feel?' She began washing his face. 'If we didn't have the most awful time with this dog, last night! We tried to keep her out of your room, but she made so much racket that Dr Stafford said we'd better let her in before she roused the whole hospital.'

'I can't remember much about it,' said Paige listlessly. 'She just now handed me this. It looks suspiciously like a fragment of somebody's corduroy trousers.'

'Yes – it's the seat. I know about it. We found you and your friend Mr Ingram lying out in the driveway, the dog barking furiously. You were so thoroughly exhausted that you passed out completely. A big rough-looking fellow was leading a burro away. And while we were carrying you both in, your dog turned and went after the man and—'

'And paid her parting regards,' finished Paige. 'Did she hurt him?'

'Probably not seriously. He got away under his own power.'

A big bushy-haired man in white duck appeared in the doorway.

'This is Dr Stafford,' said the nurse. 'I suppose you don't recall much about being put to bed.'

The doctor entered and stood for a moment grinning amiably, with his arms folded, and his rubber-soled feet wide apart. His expression hinted that he had a joke on his patient. Paige nodded in response to the sly smile and wondered what sort of banter was to follow.

'Well – what can we get you first?' asked Dr Stafford companionably. 'Poached eggs on toast and a cup of coffee?'

'I think I'd like a deep breath,' replied Paige, with a wince.

The doctor stepped forward, unbuttoned the coarse white jacket and gently prodded him in the ribs with inquisitive fingertips. 'Hurt?' he asked.

'It's deeper in, Doctor.'

'Where does it seem to catch you – internal intercostals?'

The doctor gave the nurse a slow wink that tipped up the corner of his friendly mouth. They were sharing a little mystery. Paige thought he knew what it was and decided to be dumb. Perhaps he could bluff it out.

'You'll have to talk English to me, Doctor,' he replied, guileless as a child.

'Now don't you try to kid me, my son.' Dr Stafford pointed

229

a challenging finger close to Paige's innocent eyes. 'When I took off that splintage I found it to be the work of an experienced surgeon. And you put it on because your friend Ingram said so. He denied that you were a doctor, but I know better. I have just seen the plate and the adjustment is perfect. The fracture was slightly comminuted, too, and you know what that means – and I damn' well know you do. . . . *Now!* Just where does it grip you when you inhale. You may tell me "in English" if you don't mean to come clean about yourself. . . . Where? Ribs or belly?'

'Cordiform tendon,' growled Paige.

'Attaboy!' Stafford nodded a triumphant I-told-you-so at the nurse. 'Now, how do you want your eggs, Dr Paige?'

'Promptly. . . . How's Ingram?'

'Fit as a fiddle and asking about you. That must have been a frightful trip. You got your lame diaphragm by heavy lifting. Mr Ingram says you not only had him to look after, but had to keep a vigilant eye on your rascally guide. Never mind – we're going to make it hot for that fellow. I don't see how you managed.'

'My dog helped. She stayed very close to him with her nose wrinkled and all her teeth on display.'

'I see she's got her name in the papers this morning,' said the doctor. 'Miss Adams, go and see if you can find a copy of the *Chronicle*. . . . We had a little accident in the mine, late yesterday afternoon,' he explained. 'Some timbers slipped and produced a couple of cracked heads and a flock of bad contusions. Young fellow here – Johnny Malloy – wires mine news to San Francisco. He dropped in to inquire about our patients just as your party was arriving. We had a lot of excitement. Your dog was racing about in the hall with this piece of pants in her mouth; you were dead to the world; your friend wouldn't talk. Naturally, Johnny was curious.'

'Printed our names, too, I suppose,' muttered Paige, rather testily and revealing a good deal of anxiety.

'No – we did not give him your names. Your friend objected. However, Johnny heard him call to the dog. That's how he got her name. And I think somebody told him that the broken leg had been uncommonly well looked after, which led him to hint – as you will notice – that the whole affair seemed a bit mysterious.'

Paige took up the paper which the nurse had laid on the bed before scurrying away with the announcement that she would be back presently with his breakfast. The brief dispatch had dealt jocularly with Sylvia's revenge on a disobliging guide who had refused to be of assistance to an injured friend of hers. The accident had occurred in the mountains and a serious fracture had been expertly treated. Both the injured man and his extraordinarily competent friend, who knew more about first-aid than most, had seemed to prefer that their names be kept out of the news.

When he had finished reading, Paige glanced up to find Stafford's eyes fixed on him interestedly. He seemed to have something perplexing on his mind.

'I feel forced to say' – he lowered his voice – 'that you two strangers, and this long-nosed Johnny Malloy, have placed me in an awkward position. This hospital is maintained by the Grey Lode Mining Corporation for the exclusive use of its employees. Emergency cases from the immediate neighbourhood are accepted, but the company is very particular about full reports on outsiders. I'm especially sensitive because I really don't belong on this job. I am filling in for my friend Newcomb, who is the chief here, while he is East on a three months' leave. The company will see this paper and ask questions. As for you, a day's rest should put you right, but I'm obliged to report on you just the same. Ingram can't be moved for some time. He will have to make arrangements. We will want to know more about both of you than you have been disposed to tell.'

'I understand your position, Doctor,' conceded Paige. 'Ingram's all right.'

'Well, I hope so.' Stafford's tone was curt. 'We don't want to get ourselves in a scrape. . . . Sure he isn't wanted somewhere – for something?'

Paige pulled a wry grin and shook his head.

'No,' he said dryly. 'That's his trouble. He isn't wanted

anywhere – by anybody. Lost his job. But – he can tell you about himself. Probably will, if you explain your reasons for wanting to know.'

'That's good. How about *you*?' Stafford's voice was more conciliatory.

'It's a bit different with me. I can assure you that no trouble will come to the hospital or you because of my being here. But my little problem isn't the sort of thing that I care to talk about. In short – I don't want anybody to know where I am, and I'd like to keep my name out of circulation.'

His breakfast had arrived now, and Dr Stafford, not wishing to pursue their talk before the nurse, picked up the paper and strolled out of the room, promising to return later in the afternoon.

He wished this affair hadn't turned up. It had been the first annoying situation since he had taken over for Newcomb. The brief assignment had been very pleasant, after his long and dangerous twenty months in the Government's research laboratory in a Montana forest studying the virus of the deadly Rocky Mountain spotted fever. He would be expected to return to that pestilential little workshop three weeks from today to resume a monotonous, repulsive, and extrahazardous occupation – deucedly important, but decidedly unpleasant and risky. Three young bacteriologists had died up there. It would be unfortunate if, during his brief tenure at Grey Lode Hospital, the institution became implicated in some kind of mess. Couldn't take the chance of harbouring a couple of criminals. These chaps might be all right – but he had only their word for it.

Back in his little office Stafford looked again at the copy he had made of the only scrap of writing they had found in Paige's pockets. Having noted Ingram's reluctance to confide, and disturbed by the obvious lie he had told when asked if Paige was a physician, he had felt obliged to go through their clothes. It went against the grain to do it. Both were abundantly supplied with money, but that was no recommendation; it might even be considered a reason for suspicion. The only thing he had found on Paige was an address written on the stationery

232

of the Hotel St Lawrence – 'Harcourt, 9721 Marlborough.'

This Harcourt, whoever he was, might be willing to talk. If young Paige was trying to lose himself out here – which certainly didn't look very well for a highly-trained surgeon, prowling about in the hills, unwilling to give himself a clean bill when queried by a colleague – perhaps this Harcourt, man or woman, might supply a few of the missing links. . . . For a while he meditated a letter of inquiry; then an idea occurred to him. He pursed his lips and nodded. This, he thought, should fetch a query from Harcourt. Opening his pocket-knife, he cut the provocative paragraph from the *Chronicle,* slipped it into an envelope bearing the hospital insignia, wrote his name below the device, addressed it – as bluntly laconic as the memorandum he had found in Paige's pocket – and affixed airmail postage.

The company messenger lounged in with a capacious leather bag slung from his shoulder and Stafford handed him the outgoing mail. It was a hot day, they agreed. . . .

Miss Adams stood in the doorway.

'Dr Paige would like to speak to you,' she said.

Stafford nodded and proceeded down the hall to Number 63. Paige was sitting up in bed. He had shaved, and his lean jaw was flexed determinedly. It was evident that he was in a serious mood.

'Thank you for coming, Dr Stafford. I want to apologize for putting you in an embarrassing position. I am ready to tell you about myself. It would please me if you were to regard it as a confidence – at least as much of it as may not be absolutely necessary to your report.'

Stafford pushed the door shut, straddled a chair, and folded his arms on the back of it.

'Very well,' he said quietly. 'Tell it straight – because I am disposed to believe you.'

Ingram bore his misfortune with easy fortitude, chuckling dryly when sympathy was offered. He was really having the time of his life. What with a half dozen impressionable nurses competing in their efforts to entertain the urbane stranger, and

233

Dr Stafford's leisurely calls, and Newell Paige's whole-afternoon visits, Ingram's sagged morale improved until it was evident that the accident which had detained him was worth all the bother and discomfort it had cost.

Nor had Paige fretted over his unanticipated sojourn at the Grey Lode Mine. Stafford had secured comfortable accommodation for him in the company's clubhouse, where several of the bachelors among the younger executives were quartered and where their married seniors drifted in after dinner for cards and pipe-chat.

He had been very cordially received. Nobody seemed actively curious about him, his presence being amply explained by the fact that his friend was laid up. Only one trifling incident, which occurred during the first week, caused him an anxious moment. Twice he had been invited to join in at the nightly poker game pursued by a few of the junior members in the far corner of the big smoking lounge. He had declined graciously, and when pressed had replied that it wouldn't be quite fair to pit 'beginner's luck' against experienced skill.

One night about ten – Stafford had been over to spend an hour, and had just left – Newell was starting up the open stairs to go to his room when Billy Masters, a callow young chemical engineer, called to him from the card table. Masters had been steadily winning all evening and was in an expansive mood. The stakes had not been large, but he seemed pleased with the little handful of crumpled ones and twos and fives which represented his success.

'Better join up, Mr Paige,' he called, his tone just a bit derisive, 'and contribute something to this worthy cause.'

Not wishing to appear standoffish, Newell turned, came down, and approached the table, inquiring idly how they had all fared. The losers grinned sourly and Masters pointed to his winnings.

'Want a stack of chips?' he inquired. 'The blue ones are a quarter, the red ones are only a dime, and the white ones can be had for a nickel. A few white ones – maybe?'

The smile that Paige had brought to the table was replaced by a dark frown. He rolled his magazine tightly in hands that

234

seemed to need some distracting employment, and replied, 'Thank you. I'm turning in.'

'Spoken like a Scotsman,' drawled Masters, without looking up.

The other four glanced inquisitively at Paige, observing his flush of annoyance and wondering how much of this sort of thing he would be likely to take without active resentment.

'I regret to have conveyed the idea that I am too stingy to risk some small change,' he said frostily. 'I don't care to play – but I wouldn't mind cutting the deck with you, Mr Masters.'

'That's the proper spirit!' Masters handed the cards to Madison, with a gesture inviting him to shuffle the pack. 'How much – ten dollars? Best two out of three?'

'As you like.' Paige's nonchalant rejoinder hinted that it was a very small matter, the outcome of which gave him no concern.

'Let's say twenty,' suggested Masters, attempting to be equally casual.

'Let's say a hundred – and one cut instead of two out of three.' Paige drew out his wallet and laid his bet on the table, the money in one piece.

'Agreed!' snapped Masters, counting his wager in bills of various denominations. It was observed that he held his pocket book rather close to his face as he extracted the bulk of the money, obviously unwilling to reveal the strength – or more likely, the weakness – of his resources.

Madison shoved the deck towards the newcomer, the others leaning forward in their chairs attentively. Paige unconcernedly made a cut and produced the Jack of diamonds. Masters more deliberately drew the eight-spot of spades and gave his money an impatient flick of his fingers.

'Want to cut again – maybe?' asked Paige, making no move to pick up his winnings.

Masters growled his agreement and pushed the deck back to Madison for another shuffle.

'Two hundred?' Paige inquired.

'Sure!' said Masters arrogantly; then, grimly, added, 'provided you'll take my IOU for half of it if I lose. I'm not in the habit of carrying everything I own on my person.'

'It's good with me,' consented Paige indifferently. 'Your first cut this time.'

Masters' hand trembled a little as he slowly exhibited the ten of clubs and swallowed noisily. Paige topped it with the Queen of spades.

'Another?' he asked, with exasperating disinterest.

'No – that will do for me, thanks,' muttered Masters, scribbling a memorandum on the back of his card, the others quietly winking at one another with sly grins.

Paige pocketed the money with no show of pleasure, said goodnight with quiet cordiality, and started upstairs again.

He left his door open, knowing that Masters would pass it presently on the way to his own room. It was almost an hour before he came up.

'Come in here a minute, won't you?'

Masters paused at the summons and strolled in, hands deep in his pockets, an unpleasant grin twisting his mouth.

'Sit down, won't you?' invited Paige pleasantly. 'I hope you're not going to be offended, but I don't want your money. There it is.' He laid it on the table beside Masters' elbow.

'Well – excuse *me*!' snarled Masters, rising. 'I'm no piker, I want you to understand!'

'You sit down there, young fellow!' commanded Paige, crossing the room to close the door. 'And keep your shirt on!'

The sudden outburst, so unexpected, dazed Masters a little and he resumed his seat, scowling darkly.

'You say you're no piker,' continued Paige, towering over him ominously. 'You tried to insult me before your friends down there tonight, feeling pretty sure that as a guest of this club I would ignore it rather than have a row. And I let you get away with it. You're a reckless, cocky young ass, working on a small salary and pretending you're a sport. You probably have spells of wishing you could save up enough money to go back to Colorado and marry that girl . . . I suppose—' His voice suddenly lost its crisp derision, and he resumed his chair, tipping it back against the wall – 'I suppose there is a girl,

236

there or somewhere. . . .' The half finished sentence trailed off in a soliloquizing rumble as if he had completely forgotten his quarrel with the contemptible little Masters, who sat staring, bewildered.

A whole minute passed in silence, Paige dreamily puffing at his pipe, his faraway eyes — mere narrow slits — searching in the milling crowd for a final glimpse of a jaunty little red feather on a snug little black hat aslant on bright gold curls. . . . Her last words came back, words spoken half chokingly, but very tenderly.

'I'm sorry,' he said, rousing to attention. 'As I was saying — you shouldn't be throwing your money away. But if you're bound to throw it away, you'll have to throw it at somebody else besides me. I don't want it and I won't have it.' He pointed again at the crumpled bills on the table and began tearing up the profligate little IOU into small, precise squares.

Masters scowled and grinned.

'*I* would have kept it,' he muttered, 'if I had won it from *you.*'

'Perhaps,' said Paige, after a pause. 'Perhaps not. I've a notion that, if you had reasons to suspect that my impetuous bet had stripped me clean, you would have hunted me up afterwards and given it back to me. I don't like you, Masters, but — well — something tells me you could be depended on to do about the same thing I'm doing, under similar circumstances.'

'Thanks,' said Masters, elaborately dry. 'You flatter me.'

Paige nodded slowly. 'Yes,' he drawled, 'I see that — now.'

There was an extended silence, Masters blinking rapidly as he meditated an appropriate reply. Paige studied his face and gave way to a smile.

'A short time ago,' he said cordially, 'a very fine old chap was telling me about his experience in learning to drive a car. Fellow in front of him would come to a sudden stop without signalling. People all along the line would come to sudden stops, each cursing the man ahead of him for failing to signal and not one of them putting out a hand to let the man behind him know what was going to happen. . . . Tonight you were

237

hectoring me, probably because somebody had been hectoring you. You may not have been conscious of your desire to pass along your grievance to someone else, but I think it likely you've been recently ruffled. That so?'

'I don't see how it's any of your business,' grumbled Masters.

'There you are,' said Paige quietly. 'Just as I thought. It isn't any of my business, but what I've been saying is true. Somebody has been getting your goat, and because you felt bereft without it, you thought you'd get mine. And I'm bound to say you did.'

Masters ventured a chuckle.

'Yeah – I've had a rough day, all right. Old Man Huntington. Tired of licking his boots. He's my boss in the lab. Mean as hell!'

'Had it ever occurred to you that the old man may have been having his tail twisted by some of the Higher Ups?'

'I hope they tie a hard knot in it!'

'Perhaps his immediate superior has an infected tooth – or a kidney stone.'

Masters noisily exhaled a cynical sigh through a cloud of cigarette smoke.

'I suppose it's easy enough for you to dope up some psychology that explains it all very nicely. If somebody had handed you a dirty deal, maybe you wouldn't be quite so damned calm. You're probably sitting on top of the world. You act like it, anyway.'

After Masters had sauntered out – he had refused the money, but was plainly weakening in his resolution not to accept it and would undoubtedly comply by tomorrow – Newell lighted his pipe and gave himself to some rather cheerful reflections. This young cub had felt sure that nobody could be so damned calm if he had experienced a serious injustice.

Sitting on top of the world! That was the impression he had made on Masters. Perhaps Dean Harcourt's philosophy wasn't so fantastically unpractical after all. It couldn't be dismissed with an indulgent grin and a smothered 'Oh – yeah?' Now that Newell had tried to explain it to Masters, it sounded in every way plausible. At all events, he had impressed Masters as a person who had himself well in hand, with nothing to worry about and possessed of a sense of – of what? The haunting phrase, so frequently recurring on Mrs Dexter's pretty lips, came back to him with a fresh vitality. 'Personal adequacy.' That's what young Masters had seen at work in him.

'Come here, Sylvia.'

With a prodigious yawn, she rose, came to his chair, squatted facing him, and looked up inquiringly.

'I observe,' confided Newell, 'that you took no embarrassing interest in the savage remarks I exchanged with Mr Masters. I presume your serenity may be accounted for on the ground that you knew I could have pitched him through the window without your assistance. You showed excellent taste, I think, in remaining quietly seated on your haunches and not giving way to your private sentiments. I thank you. As I have often remarked in your presence, it's a pity you can't talk. I am sure there is something you would like to say.'

Sylvia yawned again, self-consciously, and, assuming that the brief conference was adjourned, went to her favourite corner and sprawled on her cherished steamer rug.

'I've something else to say to you.'

She returned deliberately and, putting her forepaws on his knees, thrust her muzzle so close to Newell's face that he leaned back a little to dodge the caress which Sylvia occasionally bestowed if he was not vigilantly on guard. He gently tapped her on the nose with an impressive fingertip.

'Sylvia,' he declared solemnly, 'perhaps you hadn't noticed it, but we're sitting on top of the world.'

As an interested and competent student of the *genus homo*, not only in respect to the creature's physical structure but its psychological states, Newell Paige was well aware that a superficial view of a casual acquaintance is likely to be misleading.

On meeting a stranger, he often found himself speculating on the probable depth, contents, configuration, and natural history of the subterranean mountain whose exposed summit, painstakingly landscaped, had possessed its comparatively little self of an identity, a name, a tongue, a fleet, and a flag. Sometimes, on further acquaintance, he had made dismaying discoveries just below the sea line, and again, of course, he had been happily surprised.

He presumed that there were two Staffords, but he was totally unprepared for his first glimpse of the sub-Stafford. So much of the Dr Sidney Stafford as had been candidly on display was rather noisily amiable, fussily energetic, and artificially gay with a good humour that seemed to be operated under forced draught.

Newell couldn't help liking him, though he found the man's nervous tension somewhat wearing after an hour with him. More often than not, Stafford came to the clubhouse about nine and, after a breezy round of the loungers, whom he hilariously teased and spoofed without regard for age, rank, or brevity of acquaintance, he would suggest to Paige that they go up to his room for a quiet chat. Paige smiled at the recollection of these quiet chats. Stafford was never still for an instant, for ever lighting his pipe which seemed always to be out, shifting from one chair to another, pacing the floor, tousling Sylvia, fiddling with the magazines on the table.

On a couple of occasions, Newell had tried to sound him concerning his work in the research laboratory in Montana, but his replies were laconic and the conversation was swiftly led into other quarters. When Newell persisted, Stafford waved the subject aside with a dismissing gesture of his pipe. The Government was trying to find out what was the source of spotted fever, that was all. They had been at it long enough to know that the virus was carried by some sort of insect – a wood tick, very likely – and now the job was to find what manner of poison the bug carried, and where he got it, and under what circumstances he made use of it. Then – if they ever discovered these facts – doubtless they could contrive an antitoxin.

'Damned tiresome job,' said Stafford, and waved his pipe to indicate he was ready now to talk about something more interesting, such as travel tales and stories of adventure on the sea and in the jungle. He had seemed almost obsessed by blood-freezing yarns of foolhardy fellows risking their lives in big

240

game hunts, and he had an inexhaustible repertoire of fright-fulness that made one's flesh fairly creep. No matter what you talked about, sooner or later you knew you were going to be plopped down into tall jungle grass for a debate with a nest of cobras, or pitched out of the boat into a flock of crocodiles.

Sometimes it seemed as if Stafford studied your face to see how you liked the idea. He'd let a shark bite your leg off at the knee, and then pause at whatever he had been fussing with – his hands were never in repose – to stare at you for your reactions. Tarantulas in your bed, exotic nettles that pricked your hand and grinned at you while you swelled up and died. Odd mentality – Sidney Stafford's. Funny thing – he never seemed to get going on his pet horrors in any other company but Newell's.

'I should think there would be plenty of danger in your tick business,' Newell had remarked.

'Oh – now and then,' Stafford had replied, off-hand, rum-maging through his pockets for the match box that was always eluding him, 'now and then . . . mostly dull and nasty tinkering with bug juice . . . ever take any special interest in bacteri-ology?'

'Very much. If I hadn't gone in for surgery, I might have moved in that direction, I think.'

'Ever find time since school days,' asked Stafford, 'to squint into a microscope?'

'Yes – quite often. It was a little hobby. I *own* a Green-hough Binocular.'

'My uncle!' shouted Stafford. 'I'll say it was a little hobby!'

On the sultry morning that Newell made his startling dis-covery of the sub-Stafford that was not on public view, he had dropped in at the hospital to take Ingram the papers. On the way out, as he passed the chief's office, he met the Adams girl who had looked after him when he had arrived with Ingram. She seemed upset about something as she closed Stafford's door behind her and stood holding the knob and looking frightened.

'Go in there,' she said huskily, 'and talk to him.'

Stafford was slumped down in his swivel chair with his

241

elbows on the desk and his face in his hands. He looked up, heavy-eyed.

'Hope I'm not intruding,' said Paige. 'Anything I can do?'

'No.' Stafford's voice was thick. 'Look at that wire. Spaulding's dead; my chief, up there, you know. Died of it. Closest friend I ever had. The dirty stuff just melted him down. Sick eight hours. And practically alone, except for old Murray, our orderly. And here I was – safe as a baby in a cradle – spending my time daubing iodine on sore thumbs, while Spaulding was up there by himself risking his life – and losing it. . . . Just been talking to San Francisco. I'm to be relieved here in the morning. So I can go back. I'll be in charge now. Alone, too, until I can find somebody that's as big a damn' fool as I am.'

'Do you think *I* am?' asked Paige quietly.

Stafford slowly drew himself up, leaned heavily against the desk, and looked him squarely in the eyes from under level brows.

'Don't say that, Paige, unless you really mean it!' he growled.

'I mean it, Stafford. I'm going with you.'

'Do you realize that it may cost you your life?'

Paige nodded, and offered Stafford a cigarette.

'Can you be ready to go at noon tomorrow?'

'Quite!' Paige's eyes were shining.

Stafford studied him with frank interest.

'I hope,' he drawled meaningly, 'that you're not thinking of this as some sort of pleasure excursion.'

'No,' said Paige seriously. 'I understand – but I don't mind telling you that I was never so happy in my life. I'll be dying sometime, anyway – and I'd rather burn than rot.'

Chapter Sixteen

Dr Stafford's lengthy letter was, he felt, the most interesting communication he had ever received. And this was saying much, for no small part of Dean Harcourt's daily labour was the handling of correspondence voluminous in bulk and confidential in character.

His incoming mail was of infinite variety. Most of it came from troubled people who had heard him speak in the Cathedral – as if to them individually – and, lacking either the audacity or opportunity to confer with him face-to-face, had, according to their respective tempers, dipped their pens in their hearts' blood or their livers' bile to write of every conceivable perplexity in moods ranging all the way from saintly resignation to sour despair, frequently shrilling up to shrieking crescendos of spank-worthy hysteria; pardonable, of course, for the times were bad and you couldn't blame the poor things, said the Dean, for blowing the whistle, which was ever so much better than blowing the boiler.

Some, to be sure, were mere cranks with windy verbosities to exploit. They challenged him to substantiate the public statement that had pricked their pet balloon, waxing vehement in defence of fine-spun dogmas and hair-splitting categories. He did not permit such documents to annoy him. When he had read into one of them far enough to see which way it was headed, he would sigh, smile, and pass the letter across the desk to Talbot, who usually helped him with his mail, and Talbot, interpreting the gesture, would file it in the folio assigned to the housing of controversial communications relating to dogmas and categories – the label on which he had absurdly abbreviated to 'Dogs and Cats.'

But Dean Harcourt would have considered himself seriously impoverished without this mounting flood of agony mail. Most people, he believed, were more likely to state their cases honestly and clearly in letters than under the stress of oral confessions in an unfamiliar atmosphere. And it was to these letters, the Dean freely conceded, that he owed much of his intimate knowledge of the various anxieties which bedevil the mind of the average citizen.

Talbot had just left the room with the usual armful of mail bearing pencilled notations for his guidance in replying to fully three-fourths of it. Such letters as the Dean proposed to answer himself lay open on his desk. Stafford's he read again more slowly.

He had almost given up hope of hearing from Stafford. Two months had gone since his mystified receipt of the newspaper clipping and his own prompt reply to it.

An invisible spectator, on that occasion, would have decided that Dean Harcourt had encountered a difficult problem. He had read the clipping through several times with alternating smiles and frowns. Then he had slowly relaxed in his tall chair, tipped back his head, and with half-closed eyes had sat for a long time meditatively tapping his tightly pursed lips with his gold pince-nez.

As for the clipping itself, deduction was simple enough. Paige had evidently fallen in with another gentleman-vagabond who had met with an accident forcing them into the nearest hospital. They had refused to give their names, which seemed unnecessarily imprudent in Paige's case, whatever good – or bad – reasons the other man may have had.

No – the real mystery of this affair concerned this Dr Sidney Stafford's strange action in mailing him the clipping unaccompanied by a note of explanation – sent by air, too, as if he had thought its prompt delivery important. And the return address on the envelope clearly hinted that reply was expected.

'Harcourt' – that was the way it had been sent. Just 'Harcourt' – nothing more – except the street and house number. Not even 'Mr Harcourt.'

It was obvious that Paige had not voluntarily provided the address. What other conclusion could be arrived at but that the name had been found on his person and probably used without his knowledge? The whole affair was very odd. The Dean had pondered deeply for a half hour. Then he had reached for a sheet of stationery.

'Dear Dr Stafford,' he wrote, 'I have received the clipping from the *Chronicle* of San Francisco, the envelope bearing your name, which indicates your hope that I may make some comment, and airmail postage which suggests that your query is urgent.

'The only dog I know named Sylvia belongs to an exceptionally able and trustworthy young man of thirty-one whose decision to conceal his identity is inconvenient and embarrassing to himself and his friends, but reflects no discredit on him.

'If this unidentified young man in your hospital is the person I have in mind, you may be assured of his integrity. If he is in difficulty, please wire me. I shall be obliged to you for further information.'

And now – two months afterward – Dr Stafford had written this unusual letter from Wembelton, Montana. . . . The Dean read it with absorbing interest.

The first page offered a brief apology for the manner in which the clipping had been sent, verified the Dean's guess that Paige's pockets had furnished the blunt address, and explained the writer's special reasons for wanting to identify his patients to the full satisfaction of the Grey Lode Mining Corporation.

On the second page Stafford had explained the nature of his own work in the Research Laboratory in Montana, the circumstances of his brief supervision of the mine hospital, the reasons for his sudden return to take command of the laboratory, and Paige's impulsive decision to go along.

'He has talked so much about you, sir,' continued the letter, 'that I feel acquainted with you. This lonesome and dangerous business has made close friends of Paige and me. I haven't felt like telling him that I had informed you of his being in the hospital. It was an underhand trick – my sending you that clipping – and Paige wouldn't like to know that I had done it. Consequently, he does not know that I had a letter from you, and of course does not know that I am writing this.

'I think you, as his friend, have a right to know that he is usefully employed on a loathsome, thoroughly nasty poorly paid, hazardous job, and apparently happy in it. At present, Paige and I are the only ones here. In the past four years, men have come and gone, three to their graves; a half dozen or so – who either couldn't stand it or saw no hope of its success – returning to more comfortable occupations. We have a three-room shack on the top of Boone Mountain, seven miles from Wembelton, a town of about two thousand, where not more than four men know the nature of our work.

'The reason for this secrecy will be apparent to you. If it were generally known that we are up here handling the makings of spotted fever – they are scared to death of it, and very properly – we should be shunned when obliged to go down for supplies and on other necessary business. The fact is that the only way you can get this fever is from the virus carried by a tick which feeds on . . . we're here to find out what. So we are not "carriers" and are harmless to other people. But it would be difficult to make the public believe that.

'In the opinion of Wembelton – if Wembelton may be said to have any interest in us at all – we are hunters and loafers living a worthless existence as hermits. A couple of years ago, the Government strung a telephone line up here to the shack, but few people know about it and our number is not in the book. When we go down, we dress in rough woodsman's togs. We are shabby, shaggy, untalkative, and, of course, inhospitable. Occasional hikers and hunters are turned from the peephole of our door with a savage curse. This, I think, is the meanest part of our job – damning strangers off the premises. But, you see, we positively cannot let them come in and take the risk of exposure to the stuff we're playing with, and we cannot explain, for they might go away and tell about it.

'The one man in town who knows the most about our affairs is the mayor and superintendent of the most important gold mine in this region. His name is Frank Gibson. If it wasn't for the Gibsons, our life would be pretty bleak. He's not only in full sympathy with what the Government has been trying to do here – his mine operatives have died like flies in some of these midsummer epidemics – but he makes an effort to be cordial to us who are here on this unpleasant errand. Gibson is very well-to-do and has a beautiful home. I have spent many delightful hours in it these past two years. Paige is fond of the Gibsons, too. Goes there quite often to see his dog. These bugs we are studying are just as poisonous to animals as humans. Gibson offered to look after the dog, but she misses Paige. He has a bad time trying to detach himself from her whenever he goes there. It's quite pathetic – the way Sylvia cries when he leaves.

'This letter is far too long, and yet I haven't come to the real reason for my writing it. Of course I wanted you to know about Paige. He's risking his life in an undertaking that may or may not dispose of spotted fever. He is over in the lab. right now, dissecting a fresh batch of blood-swollen ticks that we picked off a sick sheep yesterday. If he accidentally scratches his arm with his tweezers, the chances are he will be as dead as cold mutton by tomorrow morning. But he is contented, and nobody could ask for a more congenial companion.

'Now for the real purpose of this letter. Frank Gibson told me a couple of days ago, when I was in his office, that about a dozen families of the more prosperous sort who have girls approaching college age are thinking seriously of organizing a private school for them and want to find some well-educated socially experienced young woman, recently graduated from a high-grade university – preferably Eastern, Gibson thinks, for the sake of importing a little of that atmosphere – who will come out here and supplement what these girls are getting in the local high school, which seems to be a very frail institution.

'Gibson asked me if I knew of anyone who might be likely to fill the bill, and of course I didn't, for I have lost all contact with such matters. I told him I would write to you and inquire, feeling quite sure – from what Paige has told me of your wide acquaintance – that you might make a suggestion.

'I fear, sir, that it has taken me a long time to arrive at the primary errand of this letter. I apologize for its length. When you reply, please address me in a plain envelope.'

Dean Harcourt put down the letter and sat for some time absently toying with his paper-knife. A happy twinkle began playing about the innumerable pain-chiselled crows' feet at the outer corners of his deep set eyes . . . Phyllis! – why not?

Sonia rattled her keys and opened the mail box.

'One for you, dear,' she called, sorting the letters.

'That would be Pat, I suppose.' Phyllis, who had preceded her up the short flight of steps in the apartment house lobby, waited at the open door, leaning wearily against its stiff tension. They had been invoicing stock all day. And it was as hot as Tophet. She reached for the letter.

'*Wembelton!*' Bracing a foot against the insistent door, Phyllis tore off the envelope with impatient fingers and ran her eyes swiftly down the page, picking up life-saving phrases – dollar signs leading salary figures, the suggested date of her emancipating journey, words of welcome, proffers of hospitality. 'Look – Sonia! I've got it!' She tried to steady her voice. 'It's from that Mr Gibson himself.'

They mounted the stairs, arm in arm, Phyllis quite beside herself with happy excitement. 'Isn't it simply wonderful?' she kept saying. 'I can't believe it! Aren't you glad, Sonia?'

Sonia was glad. No end sorry, of course, but more relieved than she cared to say. It was going to be very hard to give up Phyllis. The radiant girl had been a godsend, coming into her life at a moment when she was desperate for some new interest to divert her mind from the drab little tragedy that had made everything seem so futile.

But business in the shop was bad, with no prospect of early improvement. Small enterprises like Sonia's were collapsing daily. She had not confided to Phyllis the extent of her anxiety, but had kept up a brave front; when queried, she had been reassuring. 'Nonsense!' she would say whenever Phyllis voiced her misgivings. 'I couldn't possibly get along without you. Don't you give it another thought.' The Wembelton offer had come along at the right time. It would be possible now to retrench considerably. She would give up the apartment, pare her expenses to the elementary necessities, and try to weather the gale.

'Glad?' murmured Sonia. 'Why, of course, dear. But I shall miss you frightfully. You know that.' She jangled her keys again and unlocked their door. 'I don't see how I can live here after you're gone.'

'Mr Gibson offers to advance me money for travel,' called Phyllis, from the little hall where she had paused by the pillar light to read her letter more carefully.

'Don't take it,' counselled Sonia, from the bedroom. 'Never let a man accommodate you in money matters. If you haven't enough on hand to see you out to Montana – strictly first class and no skimping – I can let you have it.'

'You're so suspicious,' reproved Phyllis, amused.

'I'm so experienced,' defended Sonia in a muffled tone that sounded as if she was already in the throes of peeling off her natty blue frock.

'The Dean says,' bantered Phyllis, 'that we should be more trustful of our fellow men. There's something about it in the Bible, too.'

'Well – the Dean never was a woman,' came Sonia's reflection from deep in the clothes closet. 'And the Bible was written by men – for men.'

'Dare you say that to the Dean,' Phyllis lounged in, tossed her hat aside, and sat on the edge of her bed.

'About the Bible? It was the Dean who told me. He says there should have been at least one book in the Bible written by a woman – for women.' Sonia turned on the shower. 'Wouldn't mind taking a shot at it myself!' she shouted through the racket. 'I'd call it "Prissy Proverbs" – and the first one would be – "All men are savages; don't trust any of 'em."'

Phyllis laughed; then sobered. A pair of entreating steel-blue eyes invited her to believe that Sonia's declaration of un-faith in men should be qualified. . . . She walked slowly into the living-room and laid the epoch-making letter on the desk. Montana! The wan little hope she had nourished that some-time she might meet him – just long enough to see a bit of relief come into that haggard face – must now be definitely given up. Every mile and every hour of her impending journey west would diminish the likelihood of a chance meeting.

It wasn't, she told herself, that they could ever get together on a basis of friendship. But the feeling had been growing more and more intense that by some means she must rid herself of the torturing haunt – those dazed, hurt, questing eyes. In her dreams they kept following her about. In her mirror she caught painful glimpses of them, reflected in her own. Sometimes she wondered if the hallucination had not become at least mildly obsessive. Whenever their telephone rang, the query involuntarily flung itself into the front of her mind – 'There! – he has come!' A telegram – a special delivery letter – when she met the boy with the cap and the book and the pencil, her heart would pound hard. 'There!' she would whisper to herself. 'He is coming! . . .' Now she was going to put some more distance between them.

But she must be happy! The Wembelton position was setting her free from a situation that would shortly become impossible. The Dean must be notified at once. What a darling he had been to find this place for her! She called him up and after a moment's delay heard his deep voice. Yes, he said, he too had heard from Mr Gibson today. Yes – he was very glad it had turned out that way. Yes – Phyllis must come and see him soon. And Sonia too. Things always came out right – didn't they? – if you weren't too impatient.

'It's almost too much to hope that *everything* will always come out right,' Phyllis was saying into the telephone, wondering why she said it, for surely this was no time to be pensively doubtful.

There was a little pause before the Dean commented on this remark. She reproached herself for having expressed the implied lament in the face of all he had done for her.

'Don't stop hoping, Phyllis,' he said slowly. 'Hope is brimful of vitamins. Better for you than spinach.'

Sonia had not been very favourably impressed with Elise Graham on the evening they spent together at Dean Harcourt's dinner party, and if it had been proposed to her on that occasion that she should share her apartment with the popular contralto from Kentucky the suggestion would have been viewed without interest.

Now that they had been living together for a month, Sonia had quite altered her first judgement. Elise was rather a dear, after all, with a pretty wit, a desire to be companionable, and bubbling with refreshing news of interests to which Sonia had never experienced such direct access. She had found a good position in a well-paid church quartet and was filling club engagements in the surrounding suburbs. Later in the year she would be on tour in the Mid-West under direction of a manager. She was going to marry Eugene – eventually, but why not now?

Dean Harcourt had been responsible for their decision to join forces. It had come about very naturally. Sonia, sickeningly lonesome after Phyllis had left – she had never felt so desolate in her life as when she stood alone on the platform watching the red eye of the tail of the train grow smaller and dimmer – had closed her shop at four, the next afternoon, to seek comfort with the Dean.

'I was rather hopeful of seeing you today,' he had said, when she was seated opposite him. 'In fact, I was so confident you would come that I ordered these violets for you, remembering that you like them.'

She had taken up the little vase on his desk, inhaled deeply of their shy fragrance, and smiled gratefully.

'That's one of the many things about you, Dean Harcourt, that I'll never quite understand.' Sonia's eyes were misty. 'So many people coming to you, leaning on you, and yet you remember all their little likes – and their little hurts.'

'No – not all of them, unfortunately. You see, Sonia, there's a side of my life that would be seriously undernourished if I didn't have a few people in my thoughts whose welfare and happiness mean much to me. I cannot get about. It is too laborious to travel. I have no family life. I tire of reading. The evenings are long. It interests me to think about a few choice spirits and I spend much time wondering how they are – and what they are doing.'

251

'And scheming plans,' added Sonia, with a knowing little pucker of her lips. 'That was awfully sweet – what you did for Phyllis.'

'She got off all right, last night?'

Sonia nodded, and buried her face in the cool violets.

'You'll be lonely without Phyllis. That's why I had hoped I might see you today. You remember Miss Graham? She was in here, yesterday, telling me she was looking for a congenial place to live.'

'With me – you mean?'

'Don't you like her?'

'I hadn't thought much about her. She seemed a bit silly at your dinner when she was trying to hurt Mr Corley. We were amused over her pretence of intimate friendship with that Mr Parker who had done so much for her. I happen to know that it's little enough she knew about him. She didn't even know his real name.'

'Do you?'

'Phyllis told me. He is Dr Paige – the man who made the terrible mistake in her mother's operation. Didn't you know?' Sonia shook her head involuntarily, as she often did when anticipating a negative reply.

The Dean had dropped his pen on the floor and after several efforts to retrieve it was assisted by his guest. Sonia carefully scrubbed off the point with a piece of crumpled paper from the waste basket and returned to her chair.

'Thanks, Sonia. What were we talking about? Oh, yes – Elise.' The Dean's tone was dry – just a bit office-like. It made Sonia grin. What a canny old darling he was! 'Elise is an interesting person and she is looking for an interesting companion. I took the liberty of asking her if she remembered you. She seemed much pleased. I told her I would speak to you about it.'

'Do you want me to take her in with me?' Sonia searched his eyes.

'Why not? She would be pleasant company.'

'Any other reason? . . . Because, if there is, I ought to be let into the secret, don't you think?'

The Dean regarded her reproachfully.

'And after I went to all the trouble to get you the violets, Sonia, you calmly sit there and hint that I'd keep a secret from you.'

'Well – I dare say I'll find out what I'm expected to do,' she countered, pretending a pout.

'Doubtless,' replied the Dean, with the merest suggestion of a smile.

'Will I hear from her?'

'Very soon. I'll drop her a line at once.'

'Shall I go now?' she asked childishly.

'Yes. Want to show the next lady in?'

She pulled off her pretty hat and walked to the door of the little dressing-room, not bothering to close it while she stood toying with her exquisitely coiffured blue-black hair before the mirror in plain sight of the Dean. The spontaneous gesture of unrestraint implied a filial affection that brought a brooding tenderness into his shadowed eyes. Returning, she paused for a moment at his side, detained by his outstretched hand. Sonia took it in both of hers and held it tightly.

'Sonia, my dear,' he said gently, 'you and I have a little job to do. And as I am sworn to secrecy I fear I can't co-operate with you very helpfully. But you will know exactly what your own part is, when the time comes.'

'Is it – something – about—'

'Perhaps you'd better run along now. She will be waiting for you.'

'Thanks! That's all I wanted to know.'

'That's good,' rejoined the Dean, as she slowly released his hand and moved away. 'I wish somebody would tell me all *I* want to know.'

In a week it was arranged, and Elise had moved in. Sonia had been somewhat reserved at first, partly because she felt a bit ill at ease with a comparative stranger in her house after the many months of close comradeship with Phyllis; partly, too, because she had had a letter, that afternoon, brimming with unusual and absorbing interest. It was difficult to think about much else, and Elise found her rather more preoccupied, on the evening of her arrival, than she had expected.

Phyllis had written lengthily of her first impressions. The Gibsons had met her at the train – delightful people, Mr G tall and slim, Mrs G short and fat, young Gerry sweetly pert and pleasantly spoiled. Drove home in a big car. Huge house. Plenty of servants. Almost everything shiny new.

'And what do you think was the first thing I saw when I went in? I'm trying to write about it calmly, but I never was so completely at a loss to know what to do. I tell you, for a minute I was paralysed! Mrs Gibson was leading the way through the wide hall. I saw this red dog lying there, chin on front paws, looking as if it had lost its last friend, and it seemed odd to me that it didn't get up, as any normal dog ought to do, to welcome the family. Well – if you'll believe it – as soon as I passed the dog, it scrambled to its feet and began to jump up on me, and Mr Gibson, following me, shouted, "What do you suppose has got into that dog?" Mrs Gibson seemed terribly embarrassed. Then it occurred to her that I might want to go at once to my room, so we went up, and the dog came too. She tried to drive it downstairs, but it kept right beside me, so close I could hardly keep on my feet. I told her she might as well let the dog stay; that it didn't bother me; and she said it was the oddest thing – for Sylvia didn't pay any attention to anybody. . . . So I closed the door and sat down, a little weak in the knees, and Sylvia came and put her two front feet on my lap and stood there looking into my face, with her mouth wide open and her red tongue lolling out, and her eyes fairly popping with excitement. You would have sworn she was wanting to talk – the way she would close her mouth, and swallow, and then open it again, panting, just as if she was ready now to say it – whatever it was. Well – I don't want you to think I'm a baby. I was tired from the long trip, and about ready to do something silly. And I was lonesome too, dear, away off from everything. . . . I put my arms round Sylvia's neck and held her big soft head against my face and cried until I was completely frazzled. And – I'm half-ashamed to tell you this, though I know you'll understand – I

254

let that crazy dog lick my face and my neck and my hair until I smelled like a spoiled steak and looked like a peeled onion. When I couldn't stand it any more, we went into the bathroom and looked at ourselves, Sylvia standing up beside me with her paws on the basin. Then the whole thing began to seem funny and I laughed until my stomach ached. Really – I wasn't fit to be seen. I don't know what they thought of me. I didn't try to go down for an hour. Sylvia doesn't leave me. It's just a bit embarrassing. Wherever I go – there she is.

'Mrs Gibson explained that the dog had been left in their care by a friend of Mr Gibson's who is up in the mountains hunting. This sounds a bit odd. You'd think a hunter wouldn't park his dog somewhere. They don't seem to want to talk about it. Of course I'm consumed by curiosity.'

Sonia had finished the rest of the letter hastily. Then she went to the telephone and called Dean Harcourt.

'I've heard from Phyllis.'

'Good! Make the trip comfortably?'

'Yes. She is stopping at the Gibsons' until she locates permanent living quarters. Who do you think met her at the door when she arrived?'

'One of the Pharaohs.'

'*Sylvia!*'

'Sylvia *who?*'

'Don't you know?'

'How should I?'

'*Sylvia Paige!*' Sonia's voice rose a little higher than she had intended – almost an impatient shriek. There was a pause.

'Oh?' The Dean's rising inflection hinted that he was mildly interested. 'So he's out in that country, is he?'

'Yes – it's a strange coincidence.' Sonia's tone indicated that there was a great deal more she could say.

'And how are you?' he asked paternally.

'Well – I'm just about the way you'd think I'd be – with a big mystery on my hands – and – and—'

'Yes – I realize that,' said the Dean steadily – though Sonia felt that he was smiling: it seemed somehow to get into his calm enunciation – 'and is Elise living with you yet?'

255

'Comes tonight.'

There was another long pause – so long that Sonia said 'Hello?'

'Perhaps you'd better not confide anything to her about Sylvia – yet awhile. If she has anything to impart, let her do it. I'm told it is customary – anyhow – for the visiting lady to deal first.'

Then Sonia laughed – and murmured something into the telephone that sounded like an endearment that had got itself tangled up with an exasperation. He was an old meanie, she reflected, as she plopped the telephone down, but he was also an old dear.

Elise had returned very late from a rehearsal followed by a party and for a half hour had been luxuriating on the sofa in a pink *negligée*, reading her mail. Suddenly she sat up and perforated the midnight silence with a startling, 'Well – I'll *be*—!'

Sonia, curled up in a big chair on the other side of the lamp, deep in the most exciting episode of a detective story, responded to the clamour with a jerk, and dropped her book on the floor.

'I've found out who Nathan Parker is!' declared Elise, measuring her words dramatically.

'Well – who is he?' asked Sonia, still jumpy. 'Nathan Parker?'

'Come here! I'll tell you a story that will beat the one you're reading.' Elise moved over and made room. 'You've often heard me speak of my pet cousin, Clay Brock. Lately he has been seeing a lot of a young nurse at Parkway Hospital. The other night there was a party – nurses and medicals, mostly – and Clay fell into conversation with the head nurse, Miss Ogilvie.... Listen! ...

' "She wanted to know where I lived and I told her about Leeds. She asked me about my people and I told her about you. She seemed interested in your story, so I told her about Mr Parker and all he had done to give you a push. Then she wanted to know about Mr Parker – most inquisitive woman I ever saw, I think – and I told her a good deal. When I mentioned Sylvia, she shut up like a clam and grew very sober.

' "Later in the evening, as we were leaving, she pulled me aside and said she wanted to talk to me, and would I come to see her, the next afternoon. I did – and she told me that Mr Parker was Dr Newell Paige who had been Dr Endicott's assistant surgeon and had run away after an operation in which the patient died. All that will be interesting enough to you, I imagine, if he never told you himself, but the rest of the story is a knockout! I don't know whether anything can ever be done about it, but Miss Ogilvie says the surgical mistake was made by *old man Endicott*! She saw it with her own eyes! It was this way, if I can explain it so you'll understand. The old boy was doing a kidney excision. The renal artery is well covered with a thick sheath of membranes. He was all shot to pieces, that morning – day of the first big crash on the Stock Exchange, and he had just got word of his heavy losses – so, Miss Ogilvie says, he was in no condition to be operating at all, much less on such a job as that.

' "Well – Endicott failed to dissect out the artery from the fatty sheath and naturally the tie slipped off and the patient died on the table. And here's where Paige comes in. He had applied the ligature. So it's his fault. And why didn't he deny it? Because – says Miss Ogilvie – he had been almost literally brought up by Endicott and was dippy in his devotion to him. She says it's a clear case that Paige decided to take the rap himself, and save the old man's reputation.

' "And there never has been a peep out of Dr Endicott on the subject. He isn't known ever to have inquired what became of Paige. Lately he hasn't been doing very much surgery. He delivered the convocation lecture at the opening of the term. It was the only time I ever saw him, and he seemed to me rather fagged and listless, though maybe I was expecting too much. I saw an article about him, one time, that played up his tremendous energy, etc. When he left the platform, he looked to me as if he was shuffling off to an engagement in the cemetery. Now that I've been thinking over Miss Ogilvie's tale, it occurs to me that he had the appearance of a man who had seen a ghost. (I reckon that's all imagination on my part, for I didn't think of him that way at the time.)

'"I reckon it was impudent, but I couldn't help inquiring why she hadn't informed somebody so that justice could be done Paige, and then she grew sulky and didn't want to talk any more about it. I think she's neurotic and apt to go off at half-cock and then reproach herself for being so chatty. I have a hunch that she is in love with Paige, or has been. Anyway – he's on her mind. I'm sure I don't know why she waits nearly a year – and then tells *me*. Perhaps she had to get it out of her system.

'"Of course I'm not in a position to do anything about it. If it ever came to old Endicott's ears that a measly little first-year medical had bobbed up with a story fit to ruin him, I'd go back to washing dishes at the Mansion. And yet it does seem pretty cold-blooded, after all the kindness we had from Paige, for us to do and say nothing while he rambles about the country with Sylvia. You haven't heard anything more from him, have you?

'"You can't believe everything you hear around a place like this, but there's a persistent rumour that Endicott is tapering off and likely to retire at the end of the year. It would be rather too bad if the old boy passed out before somebody gives him a chance to come clean and save his soul – in case you've not become too sophisticated to believe in hell and all that sort of nonsense."'

Sonia had not been as much amazed over the letter as Elise had expected. She had listened calmly, her eyes moody, meditative.

'Isn't that terrible?' said Elise, prodding Sonia to some appropriate comment. 'Do you realize,' she urged, 'what a frightful thing this is?'

After a long moment, Sonia, stirred from her thoughts, brought her eyes slowly back to the mystified and half-miffed Elise, nodded several times, woodenly, and then, leaning forward with an apologetic expression, she said, rather huskily, 'Sorry, dear . . . What was that you just now said to me?'

Elise drew an audible sigh of carefully disciplined exasperation, reached over the end of the sofa, and picked up the book that had slid out of Sonia's hand.

'I'll have to read this, I think,' she said, with precise irony. 'It must be very absorbing.'

Sonia had very soft, pretty hands, and took such extraordinarily good care of them that Elise had not suspected the sharpness of her claws, or she would – she reflected afterwards – have been a little more tactful in offering her rebuke. There came a sudden hardness into Sonia's eyes.

'You think I've not been listening to that letter, don't you? Well – let me tell you something! I'm a whole lot more stirred up over it than you are, if you want to know. And after all that Dr Paige has done for you, helping you to a career, you haven't the slightest intention of moving a finger to clear things up for him! . . . I never saw him – *but I mean to get into it!*'

'Why – my goodness – Sonia!' Elise swallowed hard and her eyes swam with sudden tears. 'Who would ever have thought that you could pop off like that!'

Sonia laid a hand on her knee.

'Forgive me, won't you?' she entreated contritely. 'I didn't mean to hurt you.' And to prove it, Sonia went out to the refrigerator, returning presently with an avocado – one of Elise's failings – and some sandwiches.

At one o'clock, her feelings quite repaired, Elise yawned off to bed. Sonia sat very still for an hour, on the sofa, her forehead pressed hard against her knees, her arms clasping herself into a compact little bundle of earnest speculation concerning the audacious thing she hoped to do. When the clock struck two, she went to the telephone, dialled a number, and waited, eyes closed. A voice growled response and she came to brisk attention.

'Information? . . . What time do I get a train East tomorrow night on the New York Central?'

Chapter Seventeen

WEMBELTON offered many surprises. Phyllis's conception of a small town had been furnished by straw-munching comedians and bucolic novels besprinkled with tiresome dialect.

The picture she had set up was not altogether incorrect. Her constituency spoke a language distinguished for its homely elisions and grotesque idioms. She had never been fussily meticulous in her speech, but in Wembelton what she had to say sounded – even to herself – amusingly precise.

She was by no means a snob, but the democracy of Wembelton was so pure and undefiled that she could hardly believe her own eyes and ears when Fanny the cook leaned against the highly varnished newel post and yelled up the staircase – 'Chuck Sloat is here about that wood!' – to which Chuck, standing in the hall, bellowingly added, 'Is it fer the fireplace, Frank?' And Frank, upstairs dressing for supper, shouted, 'That's right, Chuck – three foot.' In imagination Phyllis saw them all at ten years old, playing hide and seek – Frank Gibson, Fanny Withers, and Chuck Sloat. Their present relationship probably certified to their good sense, but it was a novelty.

In tow of Geraldine, Phyllis had walked down to the post office on the night of her arrival, astonished to learn that it would be open for business until nine, and was very prettily introduced to Mr Flook, who wore broad braces, a green eye shade attached visor-fashion to the merest skeleton of a white canvas cap, and spectacles on the end of a long slim nose. He lowered his head and grinned at you over the top, for all the world as it was done in vaudeville.

Mr Flook's hands were not very clean, but were moist and warm, and the stamps stuck to his fingers a little. Their palatableness was still further reduced when he laid them sticky side down on the grimy window counter, but his friendliness was genuine. He welcomed the newcomer to Wembelton in phrases more felicitous than one had a right to expect. Phyllis thanked him graciously and bade him goodnight.

Mr Gibson had been thoughtfully prompt in handing her the amount of her travelling expenses and she was here primarily to return what she had borrowed from Sonia. So she stepped to the window labelled 'Money Orders'. There Mr Flook met her cordially and accommodated her. She laughed a little at meeting Mr Flook again after the so recent leave-taking, and Gerry, who had been ready to burst, but had doubted the propriety of letting herself go, released a shrill giggle that bore startling testimony to the cruel compression under which it had been detained. . . . Small town stuff, reflected Phyllis, good-humouredly.

Then they stopped at Himes's Pharmacy, Gerry's thought, and had a maple nut sundae. 'Hello, Buster,' said Gerry to the tall boy who waited on them at the glass-topped table filled with cosmetics on display. 'And don't be holdin' out on the nuts,' she added, blowing up one cheek and closing the other eye impishly. Suspecting, from the involuntary and almost imperceptible lift of Phyllis's shapely eyebrows that her panto-mime was ill-timed, she thought to redeem it somewhat by calling attention to the difficulty of its execution. 'That isn't so easy to do,' she confided, 'as you might think. Look!' She did it again. 'Try it!' Phyllis smiling replied that she would have to experiment in the mirror before attempting it in public. Gerry considered this an adroit parry and thought she would like her new teacher.

'Hello, Goldie,' she replied cordially, to a similar salute from an adjoining table. Phyllis glanced a moment later in that direction. Goldie was what Sonia would have referred to as a nine-minute egg. And unquestionably Gerry knew it. . . . Here they sat, these Wembeltonians, knowing no caste, huddled together, as utterly cut off from the outside world as they might have been on a coral reef in the South Seas.

Next morning when breakfast was all but finished – they were at the bottom of the second cup of coffee served in Cauldron – Mrs Gibson excused herself and, going to the telephone within easy earshot, said: 'That you, Sadie? Oh, I'm well, thanks. Let me have Charley Ritter's meat shop. . . . That you Charley? I want a rib roast for tonight. Bones out – and send 'em along. Yes – about ten pounds net.'

'Welmp' – said Mr Gibson, folding his napkin and squinting one eye against the smoke of his big cigar – 'I got things to do today.'

Phyllis rather pitied the friendly fellow, marooned here for life, moving routinishly from home to office and back again – same programme, day after day. Every morning, doubtless, at eight-twenty, Frank Gibson pushed back his chair, folded his napkin, and drawled, 'Welmp – I got things to do today.' . . . He was at the telephone now.

'Sadie – get me Harvey Aikens, Plymouth Hotel, Seattle.'

After a minute's wait, during which conversation languished at the table, he said: 'That you, Harv? Yeah – Frank Gibson. Goin' to be there all day? Good. Think I'll run over and join you at lunch. I've got some suggestions for that new smelter. Are you fixed so you could go to Pittsburgh again with me tomorrow, in case you like my ideas? . . . OK, Harv.'

Returning to the dining-room, he said, 'Got to go to Seattle, Maudie. Anything you want? . . . Welmp – see you later, Miss Dexter. Don't let them give you any wooden money. 'Bye, Gerry. 'Bye Maudie. Likely Harv Aikens will be here for supper.'

'I didn't know we were that close to Seattle,' said Phyllis, bewilderedly, when the front door had closed.

''Tisn't very far.' Mrs Gibson's grimace scorned the distance. 'Four hundred miles – or such a matter.'

'And Mr Gibson is going to be there for lunch – and back here again this evening?'

'Sure! He goes by plane.' She chuckled. 'You'd never catch Frank Gibson wasting his time on a railway train. I don't believe any of our family has been on one for all of five years. Any place we can't drive, we fly.'

Small town stuff like that, eh? . . . Phyllis, who had never been in an aeroplane, wondered if her picture of a small town was not in need of a little reorganization.

Noting with dismay the width of the chasm between the curriculum of Wembelton High School and the requirements for college entrance, she ventured to hint that it would be a great help if the board could find a Latin teacher to assist, and when they agreed promptly she said they really needed a Mathematics teacher too. 'Welmp,' observed Mr Gibson, 'anything you say, Miss Dexter. We want it to be a success. And, as fer the expense, we might as well throw the tail in with the hide.' She heard herself saying, in reply to some future remark in urbane quarters concerning "small town stuff" – 'Just a minute! I'll tell you something about a small town.'

When she had been there a week, Mrs Gibson asked Phyllis if she'd mind remaining with them as their guest. It would be so good for Gerry. Phyllis was happy to consent, provided she might be permitted to pay for the accommodation.

Frank, sauntering into the room, heard this and remarked, just a bit gruffly, 'Nope! – we're not stuck up, Maudie and me, but this ain't no boardin' house' – after which blunt confirmation of his wife's hospitable offer, he grinned and hoped she would get used to their ways.

'I guess Gerry will have to be rubbed down a little before she'll take a polish,' he observed shrewdly, 'but you'll know how to do it so it won't hurt. The buffer's more tedious than emery, but Gerry'll like it better.'

'You can do anything you want with her, she's that fond of you,' said Mrs Gibson. 'You wouldn't believe what a big change you've made in her already, Miss – Dexter.'

'Will you call me Phyllis, if I stay?'

They beamed – and Frank, puffing billowing clouds from his big cigar, ventured that they would all have a fine time together. Gerry, appearing in the doorway at this point, was informed by her mother of what had happened. A week earlier, she would have received such gratifying news with a boisterous 'Say! – that's swell!'

She crossed the room with so faithful an imitation of Phyllis's graceful walk – confident footsteps put down in a straight line – that her father carefully rubbed a smile from the outer corner of one eye, to the neglect of the other, and her mother tucked in her chin contentedly as if she were saying, 'Just look at that – won't you?'

'I'm awfully happy!' said Gerry, raising her pretty eyebrows slightly and enunciating the p's in 'happy' as if she had something in her mouth that was a little too delicious to swallow just yet. Phyllis looked up at her affectionately and flushed slightly. Then she sobered for a brief instant. It was almost the way her own mother's lips had always looked when she said 'happy'.

It was the last Sunday of October, and the air was already crisp with the feel of winter stealthily slipping down the heavily wooded slopes of Mount Boone into the snug pocket that was Wembelton.

A dinner of festival proportions was always served at one-thirty on Sundays, after which the Gibsons demobilized for naps. About five the family began to revive and reappear. Almost any time after that callers were likely to drift in, for the mayor's big house was a rendezvous for the dozen families who gave Wembelton a reason for carrying on.

Gerry had been invited to the home of a friend for the day and the spacious house had been unusually quiet. When dinner was over and bedroom doors had softly closed, Phyllis – restless and lonesome – decided to take a walk. Sylvia noted with mounting interest the change of costume and could hardly contain herself when the heavy-soled tramping shoes came out of the closet.

One didn't have to walk very far in Wembelton to reach the suburbs and the open country. The easiest way led west and was Phyllis's favourite course, over the gently rising wagon road which, if pursued far enough, was said to terminate some four miles distant in an obsolete logging camp. And from there, at least two well-worn narrow footpaths diverged to straggle circuitously up the increasing rugged flanks of Boone, the highest mountain in that region.

It would be pleasant to feel that one might safely proceed alone here as far as one cared to go, but it seemed rather imprudent. Phyllis had taken this walk several times, continuing only so long as the roofs of Wembelton were well in sight and the wood was comparatively open. This time she was venturing a little farther, made bold by the passing of two lads who overtook her and glanced back over their shoulders to grin admiringly at Sylvia. The pleasant episode allayed her anxiety and she pressed on, feeling it a friendly road.

After another half mile the trees began to close in on her and with slowing steps she decided reluctantly to return. It was deucedly inconvenient to be a girl. Not more than two hundred yards farther on, a huge plateau of rock to the left of the road opened a generous space where, she thought, one might have a good view of the valley in which little Wembelton drowsed. Venturing this added distance, Phyllis walked over the great flat ledge of grey granite until a charming vista broke through the tops of the pines. Retreating to a slightly higher vantage, she sat, arms clasping her knees, feeling very far away from everybody and everything that constituted her natural environment.

Sylvia crouched beside her, so close she felt the dog's warmth through her short tweed skirt. It was a great pity, thought Phyllis for the hundredth time, that Sylvia couldn't talk. Doubtless she would have many interesting things to say. There were important questions Phyllis wanted to ask her. And it was quite possible that Sylvia, too, might like to propound a few queries of her own – as, for instance, 'Where is my master, and why does he neglect me so?'

The dog's predicament, Phyllis suspected, was just one little phase of a mystery that clamoured for a great deal of explaining. On several occasions it had seemed that a bit of light was about to be shed on this secret, but the tentative promise had always failed.

The Gibsons had been much amused over Sylvia's marked attentions to their guest; but, as Mrs Gibson casually observed, there was no accounting for what a dog might do. The Woodruff's Scotty had become so fond of their baby that he wouldn't even let Alice herself touch the child without raising a great hullabaloo.

Gerry, when tactfully asked about Sylvia, had replied disinterestedly that she belonged to a fellow named Paige who lived up in the woods somewhere with an older man, a Mr Stafford, who occasionally came to talk with her father and sometimes stayed for dinner in his big boots and rough clothes – ' a very fidgety man, who can't sit still.'

'I'm sure I don't know what they do up there,' Gerry had remarked indifferently. 'Hunt – maybe. I don't believe they're much good, either of them, though Mr Paige is very handsome. They look like a couple of bums who have seen better times. They may be hiding from somebody. Father won't talk about them and Mother always says it's none of our business. I don't know what they see in this shabby old Stafford, but when he comes here they treat him as if he was somebody, and Mother despises tramps and loafers. Last year she spent a long time knitting a heavy sweater. I thought it was for Father, but when it was done she gave it to Mr Stafford. . . . Don't ask *me!*'

Once Phyllis had had a glimpse of Mr Stafford who was just leaving the house as she was arriving. Mr Gibson had introduced them, telling him that Miss Dexter was their new teacher, but failing to say who or what was Stafford. He was, indeed, a pretty tough-looking specimen of something that had reverted to type. The fact that Newell Paige had not appeared at the Gibson home since her arrival made her believe that Mr Stafford had reported her presence in Wembelton. If so, his continued absence could be easily explained. He didn't want to meet her, naturally.

For a while Phyllis had alternately dreaded and longed to see him, but as the weeks passed, and there was no sign of any intention on his part to revisit the Gibsons – her anxiety on the matter subsided. She was not to see him. He would attend to that.

This afternoon she gave herself to some very realistic daydreaming. With absolute fidelity to the smallest details, she painstakingly reviewed every step, every minute, every word, gesture, smile of that eventful day when she had met him at the Cathedral; his strange behaviour when he first looked into her eyes with something like a startled recognition, her own

266

bewildered emotions when she saw that he thought he knew her and the curious warmth of her immediate response to his tender interest. . . . And the amusing encounter in the park, Sylvia's effort to introduce them, the indecision when a taxi drew up, the ride to the St Lawrence, the earnest, serious way he searched your face and watched your lips when you talked, and you couldn't move a finger without him inspecting your hands almost as if he'd never seen a girl's hands before. It made you so self-conscious that you knew your cheeks were glowing and you talked too fast and too much in an effort to cover your confusion. And then you grew so inquisitive to know what was happening to you that you looked him squarely in the eyes, and saw something that made your heart pound until you were afraid he could hear it.

Suddenly Sylvia raised up, cocked her head on one side attentively and lifted one front paw a little, as if she were signalling for complete silence, though goodness knows the silence was absolute.

'What is it, Sylvia?' whispered Phyllis apprehensively, her heart beating now in a different rhythm.

With a bound and a bark, she was off, over the rocks, through the trees, and had disappeared. Phyllis quickly scrambled to her feet and followed along, trembling a little. At the end of the great ledge near the trees, she paused, preferring to remain in the open until she knew for certain what was up. There she stood, with a dry throat, listening to Sylvia who was barking her head off for joy.

Presently she saw them coming, Sylvia leaping ahead and running back to him in hysterical swoops. He was roughly clad in heavy corduroy trousers thrust into high boots, a leather jacket, and an old, battered, grey felt hat drawn well down over his eyes. His lean face was deeply tanned.

He took off his hat as he neared and ventured a reassuring smile, the sort of smile he would probably wear to hearten any frightened girl he might have met in an unfrequented spot. But he had the same hurt look in his eyes that had haunted her ever since they parted.

A wave of contrition swept over Phyllis. Momentarily

experiencing a recapture of the mood in which she had sat waiting for him that day in the Art Institute, she advanced a few steps to meet him. His eyes quickly responded to the over-ture of conciliation, and when she extended her hand he grasped it tightly. Phyllis lowered her eyes under his pene-trating quest.

'I'm sorry,' she murmured, at length, quite at a loss to know what to say, but anxious to voice her long delayed apology.

'Please!' entreated Paige huskily. 'Anything but *that*.'

Fortunately for both of them at this trying moment, Sylvia, who had been politely demanding attention without success, lost her patience and began bounding up and down before them, pawing at Paige's leather clad arm. They were thankful for the distraction.

'She's happy to see you again,' said Phyllis, her voice steadier.

'Sylvia? . . . Yes, it's a long time. No way to treat a friend, but—' His explanation spun out to an inane 'couldn't very well be helped.' He stopped and quieted the dog with his hand; then, straightening, he faced Phyllis with a troubled look. 'I don't like your being up here,' he said soberly.

'I'll go, then,' she declared quickly.

'You know what I mean.' He defended his remark without a smile, which made her feel about nine years old. 'All sorts of people prowling in these woods. Hasn't anyone told you that?'

'Sylvia wouldn't let me be hurt,' she replied carelessly.

'Well—' His muttered ejaculation was sceptical. 'Sylvia doesn't carry a gun. It wouldn't take much of a marksman to dispose of her. You positively must never do this again, my friend!'

It was queer about words. You thought you knew exactly what some very common word meant, and then – somebody would say it with a peculiar intonation that gave it a brand new value. She had been hearing the word 'friend' all her life. It wasn't much of a word, really; didn't mean anything. 'My friend – how far is it to Gary?' . . . 'May I trouble you for a light – my friend?' . . . It was quite another word now, perhaps because it had been spoken so tenderly, so protectingly. What a lovely word – *friend*.

'Very well, Dr Paige,' she agreed respectfully, 'I shall not do it again. And I should be going now – I was just about to,' she decided to add, for politeness's sake.

'There's no danger now. I'll walk down with you, if I may. But can't we stay and talk for a little while – now we're here? It's early yet.' He did not smile, but his eyes quietly entreated.

Phyllis nodded, after a brief hesitation, and they strolled back to the slight elevation where she had sat musing for so long.

'Lovely!' commented Phyllis, when they were seated facing the valley.

Sylvia snuggled herself in between them and sank down with a contented sigh. Paige approved the scenery with 'Mmm.'

'Likes you – doesn't she?' He ran his long fingers through Sylvia's red coat.

Phyllis, dreamily occupied with the view, nodded absently.

'It's rather strange,' he commented, half to himself.

'Oh?' The rising inflection hinted at a lack of interest, but the fleeting suggestion of a smile made her laconic reply awkward to deal with.

'You know what I mean,' muttered Paige, with a little trace of impatience. 'Sylvia has never cared for women. Look here—'

Phyllis accommodated him literally with wide blue eyes.

'Do you mind my asking you a question?' he ventured seriously, 'just to satisfy my curiosity? Did Sylvia know you – when you came to the Gibsons?'

She pursed her lips in a half reluctant smile and slowly redirected her eyes towards the valley; then laughed a little, in spite of her resolve not to, as the recollection returned with a bound. She reached out and patted Sylvia's head companionably.

'I'm glad,' said Paige. 'It must have been pleasant to be welcomed by an acquaintance when you arrived.'

'It was,' she admitted. 'Sylvia has been very attentive.'

'She sticks close – a little too close, sometimes. She has

often wakened me up in the night,' drawled Paige reminiscently, 'scratching her back against the bed slats.'

'I don't mind,' said Phyllis.

He chuckled good humouredly, but she remained soberly unaware that anything funny had been said.

'She's a great conversationalist.' Paige's somewhat declamatory tone sounded as if he was losing faith in his own ability to promote sprightly talk. 'It's because she's such a good listener,' he explained. 'But I don't suppose you ever chatted to her seriously.'

'Don't you?' Phyllis privately believed this remark to have broken an all-time record for pitching a conversation overboard.

Paige sank back on one elbow, and ran his hand through his own hair, meditatively, Sylvia turning her head to regard him with interest.

'You're a bright dog,' he confided softly, pulling her ears. 'Some day you'll tire of listening – and tell everything you've ever heard anyone say, won't you?'

'She'd better not,' threatened Phyllis, in an aside.

Paige sat up again attentively, and she had a sudden suspicion that he was about to reopen the subject she had been trying so valiantly to avoid. It was quite evident that their futile sparring with each other, talking in cryptics and riddles, had come to an end. He was leaning toward her now, and she knew he was going to discuss it.

'Phyllis—' His voice was very tender.

She slowly shook her head, and turned toward him with eyes half closed and lips parted to ask him not to go on. But the right words would not come. He was waiting for her reply. After a little silence, she closed her lips tightly, and shook her head again. He sighed.

'I can't!' she said decisively. 'Come!' With a quick assumption of lightness, she sprang to her feet. 'It's high time I went back. The Gibsons will be worried about me. Would you like to walk a little way – really? Sure it's no trouble? Were you going up or down?'

He was going up he admitted – but no matter about that.

Up where? – she wanted to know, as they strolled back to the path. Oh – to a shack that he and another fellow had, farther up the mountain – quite on top of it, in fact. . . . Was it fun? . . . Not particularly. . . . Was he hunting?

Yes, that's right – he was hunting. . . . Getting anything? . . . Well, not much yet; nothing to brag about.

The conversation was choppy, inconsequential, unsatisfactory. He gave so poor an account of himself that Phyllis had some difficulty keeping her impatience and disappointment out of her queries. After all – it was none of her business, she reflected, and if he was doing so little that he was ashamed to talk about it, of course it was his own affair.

'I should think,' she did venture to say, rather crisply, 'that one would be frightfully bored – doing – what you seem to be doing. Have you anything up there to read – just to while away the time?'

'Oh, yes,' he answered, as if it didn't matter much.

'And you like it?'

'Well – I've got to live somewhere, haven't I?'

The frowsy outskirts of Wembelton lay in plain sight only five minutes away.

'I mustn't take you any farther, Dr Paige,' said Phyllis, halting. 'I am glad to have seen you because I have felt badly over the rude way I treated you when you tried to be nice to me.'

'Will I see you again – while you're here?' he asked, not very hopefully.

'Perhaps. Of course you know that I'm awfully busy with my school, and you have your – your work up on the mountain.'

He searched her with a peculiar stare. 'How do you mean – my *work*?' he demanded, almost gruffly.

Then she saw that she had offended him. Doubtless he deserved a little prod, if he was loafing his life away. He was humiliated over it, too, it was easy to see, and painfully sensitive on the subject, as he had a right to be. But she wasn't going to hurt him still further and carry the image of his injury back with her.

271

'I'm sorry,' she said softly.

'Are you going to leave me with that – again?' he protested.

She turned and took a step.

'It's true.' Phyllis's tone was gentle but uttered with sincere conviction. 'It's true,' she declared pensively. 'I'm much sorrier than I was – the other time.'

'For *me* – you mean?'

'Yes! . . . Why do you throw yourself away?'

Apparently there was nothing further to be said. Phyllis's 'Goodbye' tried to sound good-natured, as if nothing unpleasant had occurred. He responded, in a tone of discontent, and watched her go. Neither of them had reckoned on Sylvia's dilemma, which now loomed up with dramatic importance. For a moment she stood at Paige's side, giving short barks directed towards the receding Phyllis. Then she bounded down the path and blocked the way, barking another noisy fusillade.

Phyllis turned and waited Paige's approach. They were both reluctantly amused. The disconcerting incident seemed likely to alter the nature of their leave-taking. They had parted with such an air of hopeless finality, and here they were with a common problem on their hands. He drew a not very happy grin.

'Go on – Sylvia!' he commanded, trying to be gruff.

'Why don't you take her with you?' queried Phyllis. 'I should think a hunter might need a dog.'

'You don't understand, Phyllis,' he replied glumly. 'Call her, please . . . Sylvia – Go!' He turned his back on them and with long, swift strides started up the path.

'Come, Sylvia,' she said, suddenly depressed. 'He doesn't need you.' The dog dejectedly moped alongside, occasionally looking back and whining, but resuming the journey down the hill. Phyllis patted her head. 'Maybe he'll come for you, some day.' Her eyes were hot with tears of disappointment. . . . What a mess they had made of everything!

The epochal letter, closely written on both sides, had been folded so that its last sentence was the first to catch Phyllis's attention. 'I am leaving at ten-forty tonight,' she read, mystified, 'to have an interview with Dr Endicott. Here's hoping something comes of it. Love, Sonia.'

The Gibsons were giving a Hallowe'en party that night, and everybody connected with the new school would be there – parents, teachers, and of course the girls themselves. And because it was to be a costume affair, Phyllis had yielded to the clamour for an afternoon off. Sonia's letter lay on the hall table when she came home for lunch. Hurrying to her room, she tore open the unusually bulky script – Sonia's letters had never been more than two pages long – and began to read with widening eyes and racing heart.

'We know now to a certainty that the mistake made in your mother's operation was Dr Endicott's fault! The chief nurse, who saw it all, told young Clay Brock. Here is the full story as he wrote it to Elise.'

Phyllis's breath came faster as she proceeded. Her knees were trembling and she dropped into a chair. Her eyes were shining and her happiness was almost suffocating. She pushed her little hat far back off her forehead, absurdly. As she read, there was an occasional long, 'Oh!' articulated in a gasp of sheer delight. Newell Paige hadn't done it! Newell Paige had taken the blame to protect his senior whom he loved! Sonia was going to see whether Dr Endicott would respond to the situation. She hadn't decided exactly what course to pursue – but she was going to do *something*!

When she had finished reading the letter, Phyllis took off her hat, dragged her chair closer to the window, and read the letter again. . . . Wonderful! . . . Marvellous! . . .

There was a tap on the door and Mrs Gibson entered.

'Ah-*ha*!' she teased. 'Caught you reading a love letter, didn't I?'

Phyllis rose quickly and, slipping an arm through Maudie Gibson's, said in a tone that vibrated with happy excitement: 'It's from Sonia. . . . A friend of ours has been – has come into good fortune! . . . It's too good to believe! . . . I'll tell you about it – when there's time. Long story.'

'Isn't that fine?' Mrs Gibson's felicitation carried just a trace of friendly raillery. '*Friend* of yours! – you ought to see your face! Lovely, dear! And the heavens were opened – and all the little angels were skipping the rope, and singing till their eyes popped out! . . . Don't you try to hold out on your Aunt Maudie!'

Phyllis hugged her warmly and murmured that she was a darling.

'I expect there's something I ought to be doing, down there, isn't there?' she asked, attempting to descend to practical considerations.

'No – it's all done. I came to call you down to lunch. Rather have it up here? Of course you would, seeing the state you're in. I'll tell Ida . . . Does that dog bother you too much?' Sylvia had her forepaws on the west window sill, looking out. In that posture, she seemed to occupy a great deal of space.

'Not at all,' declared Phyllis. 'I like her.'

'Well, just at the moment,' Mrs Gibson observed banteringly, 'you'd probably say you liked a horse in your room if there happened to be one. . . . But this dog would worry me into the jitters if I had her on my hands day and night, the way you do. I wish the man who owns her would come and get her. So does Frank. It's too much of a responsibility. Now that the cold weather has come, there's no reason why Mr Paige shouldn't take her.'

'Cold weather?' Phyllis didn't understand.

Mrs Gibson moved towards the door, replying indifferently: 'He was afraid she would be stung with – with gnats, or something. They should all be in their holes by now – or wherever they go.'

The dainty luncheon came up in a few minutes. Phyllis had no notion what she was eating. Her face was radiant and sometimes she drew a long, ecstatic sigh. Sylvia's head was in her lap, gratefully and noisily wolfing the sandwiches that were passed down to her. They were all gone now, and so was the cake.

'Sylvia – I know something!' Phyllis's voice was serious. 'He left you here so the gnats wouldn't bite you. Now the gnats are all dead, but he won't take you because you like me and I like you, and he's sitting up there, lonely and dismal, waiting

274

for you. Wouldn't you like to see him? Wouldn't he be surprised?'

She rose and walked to the window, Sylvia following. The Gibsons thought Sylvia's owner should take her; couldn't understand why he didn't; wished he would. Newell – she was finding it a beautiful name, and murmured it caressingly – needed Sylvia. . . . The light of a sudden, happy decision shone in her eyes.

'I'm going out for a little tramp,' she explained, meeting Mrs Gibson, ten minutes later, in the hall.

'Don't blame you,' grinned her hostess. 'Go out and walk it off.'

They took the familiar path which Sunday's events had mapped indelibly, Phyllis mounting the increasingly steeper slope with determined steps and a joyful heart. Sylvia grew excited and kept speeding on ahead and stopping to wait with restless impatience. When they came to the spot where the open space in the timber to the left of the road marked the broad ledge of granite, Phyllis paused.

'Sylvia!' she shouted, pointing a straight arm up the path, 'go – find him!'

For a moment Sylvia stood, wagging her tail energetically, her red tongue dripping. Phyllis thought of picking up a stick and brandishing it threateningly, but wasn't capable of putting the act into execution. She walked toward the dog, trying to explain and realizing how silly it was to suppose she would be understood. Dropping to her knees in the rustling leaves, she laid her cheek against Sylvia's long silky ear, and whispered: 'You've simply got to go, you know! I don't want to give you up but he needs you. Hurry up there and find him. And bark "I love you!" . . . and do it a few times for me, too!'

Phyllis's eyes were misty when she scrambled to her feet.

'Go – Sylvia!' she commanded sternly.

Then she turned and walked swiftly, resolutely down the path. Hearing no sound behind her, she slowed, after a while, and glanced back over her shoulder. Sylvia had disappeared.

Chapter Eighteen

Dr Bruce Endicott could not remember the number of times he had commanded men of affairs in their late fifties and early sixties to take it easy. Out of his own abundant vitality he had cheerfully boomed the advice at them, and scurried away to do eighteen holes before sundown. Good joke on them, his manner seemed to say.

'Just two courses open to you now,' he would breezily declare, with a twinkle. 'You must either slow up or slow down. Take your pick,' When, after a week or two of slowing, they fretted under the regulations and invented ingenious devices to dodge the orders he had issued, he always felt they were acting the baby and sometimes went to the length of telling them so.

Now that he was in this predicament himself, Endicott had discovered that it was no fun to be a semi-invalid. A man would be ever so much better off, he growled, if he were put to bed and waited on, hand and foot, sucking his insipid slops through a glass tube. To be up on one's feet, moving about cautiously at reduced speed, watching other people bungle one's work, enjoined to make no unnecessary trips upstairs, to abjure red meat, to retire at ten – Hell! – a man might as well be dead and done with it!

In exasperation he had stood out for a few minor self-indulgences. They had grudgingly winked at his firm determination to smoke one cigar half an hour after dinner. It was about the only luxury he had left now, and there was something both amusing and pathetic in the childish eagerness with which he sat in the evenings, in his sumptuous library, watching a taunting clock whose hands seemed painted on the dial.

Endicott sat here alone. His wife had died, his children had married and were out on their own. The very considerable fortune-on-paper that had demanded so much looking after and fretting over had gone the way of all perishing things. Enough had been salvaged, fortunately, to leave the big house in his possession and permit its maintenance on much the same scale as before the crash. He could be glad of that, he reflected. Penury would have been unbearable.

It was eight-ten now. At a quarter past, he would be free to enjoy the sedative that could be counted on to untwist his fiddle-string nerves. He drew the cigar box toward him, took an expensive Corona, sniffed it appreciatively, and opened his pocket-knife.

Edwards the butler sedately entered the room.

'A young lady, sir; says she has an appointment.'

He had forgotten. But it was a fact. He had been foolish enough to consent to see some newspaper syndicate writer. The office clerk at the hospital had relayed the request to him when he was busy. He had protested that the whole day was occupied. Then she had begged through the Reid girl for an early evening appointment and he had snapped impatiently, 'Very well – eight-fifteen – my house – for a few minutes only.' . . . So here the woman was, and he would have to see her.

'She's early,' he complained gruffly. 'Let her wait a while.' And as Edwards backed himself out, he added, 'What kind of a person is she?'

'Uncommonly handsome, sir, if I may say so.'

'There's no reason why you shouldn't say so if that's your honest conviction.' Dr Endicott expertly cut the end off the Corona. It might not be so troublesome, after all, to have a little chat with a bright young woman on an otherwise empty evening. 'What's so handsome about her, Edwards?'

'Very stylish, sir.'

'Well – go and get her.' He struck a match and sat holding it promisingly. 'I've never seen a stylish newspaper woman.' He applied the light and puffed with benign contentment. 'But – about half past eight, Edwards, you can come back and effect a rescue.'

'You will be wanted immediately at the hospital, sir?' Edwards ventured a conspiratory grin.

277

'Yes – that will do very nicely.' He rose, after the door had closed softly, and pushed the two luxurious red leather chairs facing the grate to a more companionable angle. He hoped this would turn out to be an interesting event. The altered circumstances of his life had made unexpected changes in his state of mind. A year ago, he said to himself, an unknown caller dropping in from nowhere would have had to tell her story in full to someone else before she reached him personally. Now – so lonesome and bored that almost any sort of distraction was welcome – he was preparing to receive a young woman who would probably try to sell him a twenty-six volume set of war memoirs that some alleged 'newspaper syndicate' was trying to float by private subscription. He ardently hoped not. A great many interesting visitors had sat in one of those two comfortable red chairs – eminent doctors, and other celebrities; colleagues, cronies. A little wisp of pain twitched his cheeks at the recollection of the most delightful of them all – the brilliant young fellow who had followed his every gesture with devoted eyes. He backed up to the fireplace and puffed meditatively.

'Miss Duquesne, sir,' said Edwards, visibly impressed.

She entered without hesitation and walked towards him with the confident air of sound social experience, unflustered, self-contained. It was quite evident that she had nothing to sell. Her urbane smile was gracious enough, but it threatened no wheedling or obsequious boot licking. The smile augured well, thought Dr Endicott, as he stepped forward. The hand she gave him was soft, slim, and well-kept, with the firm grip of a business man's. It pleased him to see that she carried her gloves. She had taken them off because she intended to stay until her errand was finished. It was a sign that she was not accustomed to think mousily of her own affairs, whatever they were.

'So you're a newspaper woman,' he said amiably, when she was seated. 'I'm bound to say, if it isn't too personal, that you don't look like one. . . . Cigarette?'

'Thanks.' Her voice was pleasantly soft, and when she lifted her face toward the match he offered, its patrician lines inter-

278

ested him. She was a little older than he had thought at first, now that he was close enough to see the fine tracery in her temples. 'What *do* I look like?' she countered.

'The stage I should say, on a chance guess.' Endicott relaxed comfortably in his chair and surveyed her with undisguised pleasure. 'Wouldn't you like to lay aside your coat? It's warm in here.'

She complied, her host rising to assist, and stood before him momentarily in an expertly tailored black velvet that sculptured her beautifully.

'No,' she replied, 'I am not on the stage. It's queer, though, your thinking so. For you are, I'm sure, accustomed to sizing up strangers and making deductions. It hasn't been so very long since another man of wide experience in reading people asked me if I were not in the theatrical business. Perhaps you would like to know. It was Dean Harcourt, of Trinity Cathedral. Doubtless you have met him. I notice that important men seem to encounter one another in various ways.'

Dr Endicott's amiable lips protruded slightly. Bright young woman, he observed, but moving rather rapidly. However, Dean Harcourt was a safe enough topic of conversation. Besides – he sincerely admired the man and would be glad to talk about him.

'Yes – I'm proud to say that I know the Dean. Very remarkable person. You belong to his flock, perhaps?'

'Unofficially. One of the black sheep. He has been like a father to me. My own died when I was little. Sometimes I've thought that it would work out more happily if an orphan could adopt a father, rather than the other way about. I know of a young man, for instance, whose parents are dead, and a very brilliant older man showed him a lot of attention. And he literally worshipped this big man with a devotion you don't often see even in a flesh-and-blood son.' Sonia's eyes asked for a confirmation of this truism, but Dr Endicott was moodily studying the flame patterns in the grate, and offered no comment. 'They were surgeons,' she added, as if she thought a surgeon might find increased interest in the incident.

'Umm . . . Yes. . . . Well. . . Reverting to Dean Har-

279

court—' Dr Endicott recrossed his legs and carefully deposited a loose fleck of cigar ash in the tray at his elbow. 'I have the profoundest admiration for the man. I suppose no one – except possibly an experienced diagnostician – can even surmise the physical difficulties he has met.'

'But they have made him so great!' Sonia's tone was devout.

'You infer that he might not have been so great if he had not been so unfortunate physically?'

'I fear it would be merely impertinent for me to try to guess what kind of man he might have been but for his illness. Isn't it true, though, Dr Endicott, that a serious disability some-times sharpens the wits and softens the heart?'

'Well,' grumped Endicott, with reservations, 'that all de-pends, I should say, on how much wit and heart one had to start with. And I've known some fairly capable men who went decidedly acid and mean when laid up.' He drew a significantly sour grin which his guest might interpret any way she liked. Sonia noted it and felt that he knew she would.

'You can't possibly be referring to yourself, Dr Endicott,' she objected gently. 'They told me you hadn't been very well. I'm sorry. But I can testify it hasn't made you unkind. Look how you're treating me!'

Endicott stroked his jaw thoughtfully. Perhaps it was time to discover which way they were headed here. Delightful young woman, and all that, but it would be better for her to offer her motion, now, and clear the air of this uncertainty.

'I can't say that I've been doing anything for you, Miss Duquesne, except detaining you from a statement of your errand.' This sounded more brusque than he had intended, so he added, smilingly, 'You're to take your time over it, of course. There's no hurry.'

Edwards appeared at this juncture to say that Dr Endicott was wanted immediately at Parkway Hospital.

The doctor twisted his head around and growled that they'd have to get along the best they could. He wasn't going out any more tonight. Edwards bowed and left with the slightest per-ceptible bulge in his impassive cheek. Sonia regarded her host with wide eyes. She had just ventured a discreet tribute to his kindness and he had thrown it away with a refusal to answer an emergency call to the hospital. He observed her unspoken query and decided to restore himself to her good opinion.

'As a matter of fact,' he confided, 'Edwards is under instruction to come in and say that I'm wanted when he thinks I may be in need of – of—'

'And you aren't – now?' asked Sonia solicitously. 'Sure?'

'Sure!' he said solemnly, burning the last bridge with an amazing recklessness. 'You stay as long as you like.'

Sonia drew a long, happy sigh and smiled delightedly.

'I knew it!' she murmured. 'And I'm very glad. It has helped wonderfully. I did so hope you would be kind to me, Dr Endicott. And now that you've confessed you'd made plans to pitch me out – and aren't going to – it's up to me to tell you that I got access to you with a wee little fib – not a big, solid one like the excuse you had fixed up for me! . . . I'm not a newspaper person at all.'

'I would have sworn you weren't,' he chuckled. 'Excuse me a second. I'm going to have another cigar. . . . Cigarette? . . . There you are. Now! Proceed! And take your time.'

'I'll begin at the beginning, then. For some months I have been sharing my apartment with a young woman who was brought up very tenderly and given every privilege that money could buy. The family fortune was knocked to pieces a year ago, and the family, too, leaving this girl quite adrift. She secured a small position doing something she doesn't care for, and has been living with me. At present, she is in a distressing predicament. I would like to state her case.'

Dr Endicott squirmed a little in his chair and chewed hard on his cigar.

'Well, now, I sincerely hope,' he grumbled, 'that this isn't going to be what I'm pretty damned sure it's going to be.' He shook his head vigorously.

'No,' said Sonia. 'It isn't that – if what I imagine you mean is what you mean, and I'm pretty damned sure it is.'

At that, Endicott laughed. He couldn't remember when he had laughed so uproariously. This young woman was certainly refreshing. She had a very responsive wit. Besides – he was relieved. It wasn't that – she had promised. He laughed again, wheezing a little.

'But it is a distressing predicament, just the same,' affirmed Sonia, when the purple-faced doctor was again ready to listen. 'This girl has fallen hopelessly in love with a chap who has turned out to be quite worthless.'

'That's bad,' said Endicott sympathetically. 'Would you object to telling me just how I get in on it?'

'I'm coming to that. This young fellow is a doctor. I wondered if you might not have some counsel to offer in regard to his rehabilitation. . . . But, first, may I proceed with Phyllis's story? Naturally I'm better posted with that part of it. Phyllis Dexter's mother was a patient of yours about a year ago and died, I believe, here in Parkway Hospital.' Sonia paused a moment, at this point of her narrative, and Endicott, stertorously clearing his throat, said he remembered the incident.

'Her father died, too,' continued Sonia, 'and her sister entered a convent. Phyllis came back home, though in actual fact there was no home to come to, and immediately sought the advice of Dean Harcourt. He had known the family very well. It was there that I met her. I took her to live with me.'

'Supporting her, you mean?' Endicott's eyes were troubled.

'Not at all. Perhaps I should have told you earlier what my business is. I am the proprietor of a dress shop.'

'I can well believe it.' His eyes lighted a little with undisguised admiration.

'Thank you. Everyone likes pretty clothes, I think. . . . So I took Phyllis into the shop, where she has been very useful to me, though I know she despised her job like the devil. A few months ago – she quite often went to Trinity Cathedral to see Dean Harcourt – Phyllis met a very handsome young fellow who was there for a long private conference with the Dean.'

'I'm not surprised,' Endicott interposed reminiscently. 'There's something positively fascinating about the man's philosophy. The last time I met him – it was in his own library;

I happened to be in the city – very shortly after Mrs Dexter's death, by the way – and, knowing of their warm friendship, I wanted to talk to him. There he sat, resting his weight on his elbows, pain-shattered eyes looking at you, and through you, and beyond you, discoursing on what he pleased to call "The Long Parade" – his stock phrase for the human scene. In that atmosphere, one seemed to be curiously hypnotized out of one's participation in contemporary affairs and forced to view the pilgrimage objectively. I remember that while he was calmly pursuing his theme the siren of a swift ambulance screamed, a few streets away, and the thought flashed across my mind – "No matter. A few are hurt, here and there. Some fall down, and have to be gathered up. But nothing can stop the Long Parade. It carries on. . . ." He has a very real and amazingly convincing belief in compensation. You do get what you're looking for. The wages, in the long run, are fair. Things come out right, in the general average. . . . You're almost obliged to believe it – at least while he's talking.' Endicott became suddenly aware that he had interrupted a narrative and apologetically signed to Sonia that she should continue. 'So – Phyllis met her young man—'

'Yes – by mere chance. But it proved to be a case of love at first sight, if there is any such thing. He didn't tell her any details about himself, but she discovered accidentally that he was – or had been – a surgeon.

'Then he suddenly disappeared, leaving no word. My Phyllis became a different girl; lost her appetite, lost her spirits, lost interest in everything and everybody. I grew quite distressed about her. . . . And then, some weeks ago, to our great delight, Dean Harcourt found a splendid position for her, supervising a girls' private school in Montana.'

'Delightful!' exclaimed Endicott.

'That part of it – yes. But she had no more than arrived when she learned that her charming young doctor was rusticating with another older ne'er-do-well in a mountain shack, hunting and loafing, apparently quite indifferent to what any-one might think of his complete collapse into such degrada-tion. It was a shocking disappointment!'

'Most unusual coincidence, I should say, their drifting into the same locality.'

'Yes – if it was a coincidence.' Sonia's tone and brows were sceptical. 'I can't forget that this young fellow had been in a confidential conversation with Dean Harcourt before he left, and it was the Dean who discovered the position for Phyllis.'

'It doesn't sound much like Harcourt,' observed Endicott, perplexed, 'to send this fine young woman out to cultivate acquaintance with a chap of that sort.'

'Now – there you are!' declared Sonia impressively. 'What sort of chap? Evidently the Dean knows more about him than we do. And has confidence in him.'

'He hasn't said?'

'Not a word – except that he was bound to secrecy.'

'It's very odd.' Endicott studied the fire for a moment. 'How did Phyllis happen to learn about this fellow? Run into him accidentally out there?'

Sonia meditated a reply and thought she would like another cigarette. Her experienced host was happy to oblige. He brought her the lacquered box and was hovering over her with a lighted match when she suddenly answered his question.

'He had left his dog at the house where she lives – a fine red setter. She recognized the dog – Sylvia.'

Dr Endicott's hand trembled. He fumbled in the box for another match and had great trouble lighting it. His eyes were averted. Sonia saw that she had given him a serious shock. Muttering an apology for his clumsiness, he returned to his chair and slumped down in it with the supine posture of a very old man.

'So' – concluded Sonia – 'there they are – Phyllis worrying her heart out in little Wembelton—'

'Wembelton?' echoed Endicott, scouring his memory.

'Yes, just a little town. . . . And the young doctor she's in love with is living the life of a tramp and a hermit in a shack on top of Boone Mountain.'

Endicott's eyes suddenly came to attention and his face twitched with excitement. He gave a cry of mingled rage and grief, rose from his chair, and began pacing, staggeringly, back and forth before her, his trembling hands clenched into fists. Sonia sat regarding him with frozen horror.

'*Boone Mountain!*' he was shouting. '*Boone Mountain! By God! – I won't have him up there on Boone Mountain!* I know all about that shack on Boone Mountain! It has cost the lives of the three finest bacteriologists in this country – men who deserved a better death than that of a guinea pig in that damned pest hole! *I won't have him up there, I tell you!*'

Sonia sat stupefied with amazement. If she had come here to give Dr Endicott a hard jolt, he had most assuredly returned it in full. He staggered back to his chair now and sank into it, burying his livid face in his quivering hands. She waited, with mounting anxiety. What if the shock should be too much for him!

'Is there anything I can get for you, Doctor?' she asked, thoroughly frightened now. There was no reply. 'Shall I ring, Dr Endicott?' she insisted, in an agitated voice. 'Do you want me to call the man?' She laid a hand on his sagging shoulder.

He shook his head, without looking up. It was a very difficult moment. Sonia, deeply moved by Endicott's utter breakdown, touched his bowed white head. He straightened a little and, becoming aware of her solicitude, roused to his duty as her host.

'You'll be wanting to go now, my dear,' he muttered huskily. 'Push that button, the one by the door, please. Edwards will let you out.'

Sonia went away bewildered by conflicting emotions, exultant over the clear vindication of Paige and the amazing disclosure that would certainly revolutionize the world for Phyllis, but quite undone by her participation in the scene of an eminent man's collapse.

She had once stood with blanched lips and troubled eyes watching a beautiful and costly building in flames; had seen the fire shatter the large plate glass windows, blacken the finely wrought cornices, and thrust mocking red tongues through the sculptured doorway. But the devastation she had witnessed tonight was infinitely more spectacular. It had completely un-nerved her. The best she had hoped for was an opportunity to inform Dr Endicott how the case stood. She had had no notion of attempting anything so brazenly audacious and unquestion-ably futile as the twisting of a confession out of the sick and unhappy surgeon. It would be enough to leave the thought with him that he might, if he wished, undo at least a little of the damage he had caused; that he had it in his power to bring happiness to the daughter of the woman whose life had been sacrificed to pay for his inexcusable blunder.

It had been her hope to take the eleven-fifteen train home, but she decided that the incredible event must be reported to Phyllis without delay. She went quickly to her room, slipped out of her black velvet and into pink silk, seated herself at the desk and wrote, as calmly as was possible in her state of upheaval, the full minutes of the meeting with Dr Endicott.

The letter was finished at midnight. Affixing airmail postage, she summoned a boy and sent it down. Neurally spent, she tumbled into bed and slept the sleep of utter exhaustion.

Edwards seemed quite mystified by Dr Endicott's request for a whisky and soda. It had been a very rare occurrence for the doctor to indulge in anything more potent than a glass of light wine, and even this innocuous beverage had been denied him for many weeks.

'Pardon me, sir,' hesitated Edwards. 'Did I understand you, sir? Whisky, sir?'

'Yes – you understood me. Go and get it.' Endicott had not stirred from his supine slump in the red leather chair before the grate.

The wretched year passed in review, the humiliating pageant opening with the scene of his standing beside Newell when they were scrubbing up after the fatal operation. He had been too dismayed over what had just happened – on top of the announcement that he had lost a quarter of a million – to venture any conversation. The hour's event had left him speech-less. He had postponed the other operation scheduled for the day and had gone home. Tomorrow he would see Newell and relieve him of the blame he had volunteered to assume for his chief's sake. But Newell did not appear at Parkway the next morning. A rumour had it that he had left town. Doubtless the chap had been so upset over the tragedy that he wanted a day or two for recovery. He would be back presently, and their amicable relations could be resumed. The days became weeks. Nobody seemed to know anything about Newell's whereabouts. Well – he wouldn't stay away indefinitely. One would have to wait until the young fellow returned.

But the worrisome uncertainty had gradually become a torture. One went to bed with it at night and got up with it in the morning. After a while it was not content to be the final blistering thought as the light went out and the first depressing thought when the dawn streamed in. It now resolved to rouse one at three in the morning. It further determined to defer one's sleep until two. It stood before the reader as he sat in his library in the evenings, and sullenly rebuked him at every brief interval when he turned a page.

It had not been Newell's fault, but somehow his name had come to stand for the torture that was now ubiquitous and continuous. Any chance reference to him was painful. Endicott had stopped hoping that he would come back. The sight of him would be unendurable.

But – Boone Mountain had completely reappraised this miserable situation. The young fellow he had admired and loved from childhood, and had counselled as a student, and promoted to a position of distinction, was in danger of losing his life.

Endicott took another generous gulp of his Scotch and soda. So he had confided in Harcourt, had he? Harcourt would probably have contrived to get the whole story out of him. It was unlikely that Newell would go there for that purpose; but, once there, the uncannily prescient Harcourt would make short work of his reticence. He took another large swallow and shuddered – shuddered at the bitter flame of the drink, and shuddered at the thought of Dean Harcourt's disappointment and disgust. For, he remembered, Harcourt had been most comradely in his attitude; had gracefully imputed to him a devotion to tireless duty in the cause of human rehabilitation.

Queer fellow, this Harcourt! — with his other-worldly detachment, as if he were a spectator or a neighbouring star, taking notes on the human scene, viewing it whole, from the dim days of the stone axe to the present clamour of a mechanized era — and yet able to evaluate, with uncanny understanding, the psychology of an endless procession of wretched people who came to him with their difficulties. Endicott recalled that he himself had felt deeply explored when meeting the challenge of those cavernous eyes. The eyes had not directly accused him of anything, but they had diligently inquired how he was getting along — inside.

'The Long Parade' — that was Harcourt's self-coined phrase. It's the integrity of the Long Parade that we're striving for; not the skyrockety conspicuousness of the few who, however high they may contrive to hoist themselves for an hour or two, are quickly forgotten.

Endicott remembered that he had whimsically asked the Dean whether he really believed that humanity was being pushed *en masse* by some irresistible urge, as the strange propulsion that occasionally seizes and drives the uncountable millions of little lemmings across the plains of Sweden, through the towns, over the mountains, and into the sea — and had been suddenly sobered when the man had stoutly declared, 'No! No! We are not driven from behind, but lured from before! Not pushed, but pulled! Magnetized from beyond!'

And Harcourt had been willing to talk to him in this mystical, idealistic fashion because he believed him worthy of opinions about human destiny; considered him, too, an idealist and mystic. Harcourt probably thought of him now as a shameless cad.

Could it be possible, reflected Endicott, that his own moral collapse had been responsible for his physical decline? Was it this catastrophe that had been making an old man of him in his prime, slowing his step, shortening his breath, dulling his eye, deadening his spirit? Could it be true — absurdly paradoxical as it sounded — that whoever tried to save his own life would lose it? . . . He rose, stretched his arms to their full tension, clenched his fists with determination, and walked with something like his old self-confident stride to his desk.

His hand trembled a little as he took up the pen, but it was the agitation of conscious victory. His eyes were misty as he wrote:

'My dear Boy.'

Chapter Nineteen

PAIGE patted the sand and gravel down evenly with the flat of his spade, and walking a little way apart sat rather preoccupied, gazing at the small rectangular mound he had made.

The work had taken him more than an hour to complete, and he had done it bareheaded, saying to himself, as he tossed his battered grey felt hat aside, that he could dig better without it; but now that the task was done, he did not put the hat back on as he sat there dreamily contemplating this little heap of mountain rubble.

He had resolved not to be sentimental about it. Sylvia had been such a meticulously clean person that it was no more than her rightful due, he thought, to be carefully wrapped in heavy burlap, sewn with firm stitches, and nailed securely into the tight pine box, before putting her back into the elements from which she had come.

Stafford had generously volunteered to do it, and had gruffly counselled his associate researchist to 'get the hell out o' here and take a walk' while he disposed of poor Sylvia who last night was a wretched little bundle of hot misery and this morning was cold and stiff.

'Oh, I think I'd better do it, old man. Thanks, just the same,' Paige had replied, feeling that Sylvia really deserved his presence on this occasion. He wasn't going to be silly and soft about it, of course. Dogs, barring accidents, only lived to be a dozen or so years old. Sylvia was nearly seven. He mustn't pretend it was out of the natural course of things, or make any display of his feelings to the disgust of Stafford, who affected a hard contempt toward any sign of emotion.

One thing had troubled Paige more than a little. He should have been more prudent about safeguarding Sylvia. When she had come bounding into the shack, a few days ago, he had been so happy to see her that he hadn't reckoned seriously enough on the dangers of allowing her to remain. After all, the wood ticks had given up the battle for the season, and the chances of Sylvia's being bitten were very remote. Of course, there was all manner of stuff in the laboratory that she mustn't on any account get into, but they could easily keep her out of there. He hadn't counted on Tobias, the sick monkey. Tobias had assisted in the spotted fever research for some weeks and had proved himself to be almost incredibly hardy. Stafford had suggested, after one particularly venomous inoculation of a mess that should have invalided any normal beast, 'Tobias is too damned mean for a germ to live in; that's the trouble. Toxins pumped into his hide simply give up the ghost.' But – even so – Tobias had fallen ill of a fever, and no debate was needed to discover what kind of fever it was. He had made a great deal of noise. Whether it had excited Sylvia's sympathy or merely her curiosity, she had stood in front of the un-pleasant and indisposed Tobias regarding him interestedly with her soft brown eyes. The monkey had suddenly thrust a hot, hairy arm through the cage and scratched one of Sylvia's long, silky ears. They had cauterized the small lesion thoroughly and trusted to luck that they had caught it in time. . . . But that was the way with this dirty stuff; it began operations im-mediately. Germicides seemed to have no value at all.

Well – whoever was to blame, what had happened had hap-pened, and there wasn't anything to be done about it . . . Sylvia probably had been up the mountain road far enough to sense the direction. A day earlier she had seen him climbing the slope. She had strolled out of the Gibson house and pro-ceded on her own, as any bright dog might have done under the circumstances. . . . And as for the poisonous fury of the hell-cat Tobias, such accidents were difficult to foresee. No – it was useless to brood about it. No amount of moping would do Sylvia the least bit of good.

But you could be as unsentimental as you pleased, the fact remained that the death of Sylvia marked the end of an epoch. She had been the one warm, loyal, affectionate link with that other phase of his life. She had sat in his car patiently waiting while he spent the morning in the operating-room back in the days – how remote they seemed, and only a year off in terms of the calendar – when life had been lived to the full.

But – critically examined – was it so full? The work at Parkway had been an unfailing source of challenging interest and the beautiful apartment at the Hermitage had been a luxurious haven after the day's work. But, in sober truth, hadn't the whole routinish round of hospital duties and bachelor-suite diversions resolved itself into a sort of unobjectionable treadmill? Honesty obliged him to confess that he hadn't really lived until the day he met Phyllis.

There had been plenty of time for thinking about her. Sometimes, during his stay at the Grey Lode Mine, after an hour's steady review of her wide blue eyes, her full mobile lips, her ravishingly deep dimples, her exquisitely shaped hands and sinuous form, his censor mind cynically suggested that he had probably idealized the girl out of all proportion to her actual gifts, hinting that if ever he saw her again – which was improbable – he might marvel at the hoax he had perpetrated on himself. But last Sunday Phyllis had not only justified all his day dreaming: she had disclosed some charming little tricks of manner, gesture, inflection, that had made him want her with a longing too deep to be trusted to any words that might attempt to define his feeling.

Sylvia was gone – and with her departure there had gone also his sense of hopeless wishing for a recovery of the monotonous life he had lived as a surgeon at Parkway Hospital. True – surgery was his natural *métier*, and he would never feel entirely at home and happy doing anything else; but he could readjust himself, he thought, to some other type of activity – bacteriology or research perhaps – if only he might have Phyllis.

Of course, he would have a great deal of explaining to do, but he could make out a good case for himself. He grinned a little. Phyllis thought he was a tramp, a shaggy bum. He had allowed her to think so. Indeed, he hadn't much option in this matter, for Stafford had exacted a promise that he would tell no one what they were doing, and Phyllis assuredly was *someone*. She would find out, in due time, and whatever disgust she had felt because of his alleged idleness would vanish. She might even go so far as to be pleased that he had tried to make himself useful in a job that was far from enjoyable.

He heartily wished he might have an hour's chat with Dean Harcourt. He believed he would be able to summon the courage necessary to state the case of his love for Phyllis and ask for counsel. It was odd – her coming out here where he was. Curious coincidence. The thought occurred that he might write a letter to the Dean and tell him how things stood – and did he have a right to tell Phyllis how he felt? Instantly he rejected this idea. You couldn't hope to tell it in a letter.

Well – good old Stafford would be thinking it was about time for him to show up. He gathered a few armfuls of leaves and threw them over Sylvia's grave, shouldered his spade, and strolled toward the shack. There was a note on the table. Stafford had had his lunch and had gone down to Wembelton for the afternoon. 'I suppose you'd be just as well pleased to be alone today,' he had scribbled, as a postscript. 'I'll be back about five.'

Newell poached a couple of eggs, toasted a slice of bread, ate his simple fare standing, lighted his pipe, locked the door, and went out, taking the path down the mountain with the thought that it would be comforting to lounge for an hour on the gray granite ledge where, a week ago, he had found Phyllis.

He had dreamed about her so much and longed for her so passionately, that he was distrustful of his own sight, fearing what he thought and hoped he saw would turn out to be an hallucination. With pounding heart he stood for a long moment wondering if his vision were playing a cruel trick on him.

No – there she was, adorable creature, sitting exactly where they had sat on the slight elevation of the great rock where the full view of the valley burst through the graceful tops of the pines. For some time she was wholly unaware of his coming;

sat with arms clasping her knees, her little hat tossed aside, her coat thrown open and off her shapely shoulders.

He walked slowly towards her from the thick wood and presently she glanced quickly, startled, in his direction. Then – the thing that happened swiftly, incredibly, so astonished him that he stopped in his tracks, unable to fathom it. Phyllis had leaped to her feet and was running towards him with all the abandon of an ecstatic child. She was flourishing an open letter.

'Look!' she shouted. 'Oh – I'm so glad for you! I was *so* in hope you'd come!' She thrust the letter into his hand, and taking his arm, began tugging him along to the place where she had been sitting.

'Read it!' she commanded, curling up so close beside him that her head touched his shoulder. 'It's wonderful!' she whispered. Then, impulsively, she laid a hand over the letter and facing him asked, with an impatience that could wait no longer, 'What is it that's so dangerous on Boone Mountain?'

His promise to Stafford seemed to give way to the prior privilege of this question. She had a right to know.

'Well' – he explained, hesitatingly – 'the Government Research Laboratory for the investigation of spotted fever is up there: is that what you mean?'

'And you are in it?' she asked, laying her hand on his arm, anxiously.

He nodded, and smiled into her apprehensive eyes.

There were two big, hot tears on her cheeks.

'Please forgive me – for what I said to you – the other day.'

Newell patted her hand and said it was all right and that she hadn't any way of knowing what he was up to – out here on the mountain.

'Listen,' she said, when she had recovered her voice a little, 'did Sylvia get there safely? I wanted you to have her, and Mrs Gibson said there wasn't any reason that she knew of why you shouldn't – so I brought her up this far and told her to find you.'

'You're a dear girl, Phyllis,' he said slowly – a little downcast, though, she thought. 'Sylvia arrived – in gay spirits.'

Phyllis studied his face intently when she saw that he was avoiding her eyes.

'Funny she isn't with you. I should have loved to see her.'

'Yes,' he replied mechanically, 'and she would have liked to see you.'

'Newell!' It was the first time she had spoken his name and it stirred him deeply. She caught his arm tightly in both hands. 'Don't tell me that anything has happened to Sylvia!'

There was an extended silence while he tried to think of some gracious way to break the bad news. Interpreting his perplexity, she tugged hard at his arm, and asked in a frightened voice, 'Newell – is Sylvia sick?'

'Yes,' he admitted, adding, 'that is – she *was* sick.'

Phyllis pressed her forehead against his shoulder and wept like a little child. For an instant he was strongly tempted to put his arm about her, but doubted his right to take advantage of a moment when she was giving way to her sorrow and regret over the loss of Sylvia. He laid his hand tenderly on her yellow-gold head.

'You must not blame yourself, dear,' he said consolingly. 'You didn't know there was any danger. And there wasn't really, if I had taken proper precautions. . . . And I believe that Sylvia would have been glad to know that her death had—' He paused for a moment, groping for the right words, and finished with 'She was very fond of us both, you know.'

He felt the yellow-gold head nod an affirmation against his arm.

'She would gladly have died to make friends of us,' said Newell gently.

Presently Phyllis straightened, rubbed the tears out of her eyes with the backs of her wrists, as a very little girl might have done, he reflected, and said, thickly, 'Read that letter!'

To Newell's amazement, she snuggled very close to his side – so close that he could feel her soft contours and the beating of her heart against the arm she held tightly. With her cheeks pressed hard against him as she followed the lines he was reading, it was very difficult for him to concentrate on Sonia's excited scrawl.

295

Phyllis felt him growing more and more tense as the amazing chronicle moved forward toward its dramatic climax. He was almost there now, and his hands were trembling as he shifted the pages.

'*God!*' he shouted. '*The good old duffer's going to come through! He's going to come clean! He's going to set me free!*'

Thoroughly shaken with excitement, he tossed the letter aside, and catching Phyllis in his arms, hugged her so tightly that her cheek touched his. At the contact, they both drew back a little and soberly looked into each other's eyes.

'I didn't mean to be so rough with you,' he stammered apologetically. 'This means so much to me, dear, that I lost my head. I'm sorry.' But he had not released her, and she had made no effort to pull away.

His conciliating smile of penitence for his audacity entreated her to believe that he had been overcome with the joyful news, but Phyllis did not respond to the smile. Looking up at him steadily from under her heavy lashes, she gazed long and earnestly at his face. Her lips were parted, and she seemed about to speak, but she remained silent, letting her amber tinted look of inquiry ramble from his tanned forehead to his tense jaw, and back again, dreamily, confidently, to the questing steel blue eyes that waited and wondered. Her breath was coming fast. His grasp tightened ever so little; and, closing her eyes, Phyllis relaxed contentedly into his arms. Her hand crept up his coat, lingered for an instant on his shoulder, and stole gently around his neck, caressing his hair.

'Oh – my darling!' he whispered. 'Can this wonderful thing be true?'

Sometimes, when half-mad with loneliness and desire for her, he had indulged himself in a fleeting speculation on the ecstasy of having Phyllis in his arms. But his imagination had never pictured the confident and tender response she made to his kiss. After a while he ran his long, strong fingers through her curls. She opened her eyes and smiled.

'It's a lovely head,' he told her softly.

Phyllis sighed.

'It has worried – a lot – about you,' she whispered, regarding him with brooding affection. There was a long pause.

'Tell me something,' said Newell intimately. 'How did you happen to come away out here to Wembelton?'

'Dean Harcourt,' she replied, smiling.

'But you didn't know *I* was here, did you?'

Phyllis shook her head, the smile deepening her dimples, and said, a bit teasingly, 'Now you'll be asking me if I would have come if I had known.'

'So – it was just a marvellous accident – our coming together in this beautiful land.' Newell's enraptured eyes swept the valley and returned to hers.

She laughed softly, and laid her palm against his bronzed cheek.

'I called it beautiful, last Sunday, and you just said, "Mmm" – like that.'

'It was true, last Sunday,' he declared, ' "Mmm" was quite sufficient to describe it.' He drew her very tightly to him again. A great miracle had happened. They weren't quite sure yet that it was real.

On the way down they met Stafford. He seemed to loom up suddenly through the pines like an apparition. Phyllis freed her hand and whispered, 'Now you've some explaining to do, my boy.'

Stafford's eyes widened with interest. The three of them halted and considered each other in an embarrassing silence for a moment, and since it was high time somebody offered an observation, no matter how unimportant, the older man ventured the opinion that it had been a pleasant afternoon.

'You don't know the half of it!' remarked Newell mysteriously.

'Well – I can guess,' grunted Stafford. 'Congratulations!'

'It isn't exactly impromptu, Doctor,' explained Newell. 'We have known each other for some time – long before we were thrown together accidentally out here.'

'How do you mean – accidentally!' Stafford growled. '*I* was responsible for Miss Dexter's coming here. My friend Dean Harcourt—'

'Do you know Dean Harcourt?' Phyllis and Newell shouted in concert.

'Sure!' Stafford's boast was expansive. 'Old buddies. Last time I was out there, we went fishin' together . . .'

Newell grinned.

'When was that?' he asked.

'Oh – five years ago, maybe,' he lied reminiscently. 'By the way, Paige, here's a letter for you I picked up in the post office. Old man Flook opened up for me. . . . Well – I'll trudge along. Good luck to you both.' He touched his shapeless old hat and resumed his tramp up the hill. Newell inspected the handwriting on the envelope, and gathered Phyllis into his arms, his lips close to her ear.

'It's from Dr Endicott!' he whispered.

Chapter Twenty

IT was twenty minutes after four. The carillon was booming historic hymn tunes from the taller of Trinity Cathedral's massive towers. Old Saltus, who played the chimes, was evidently under the influence of this bright and perfumed June afternoon, for his selections were high spirited.

Talbot, who had been expecting him, met Newell at the street door of the Dean's Residence and welcomed him with beaming smiles. The wide hallway brought back stirring memories. There was the thick rug, just inside the door, where Sylvia had waited, and beyond was the reception room where Phyllis had been found gazing moodily out through the window – fourteen months ago.

'I shall take you directly to Dean Harcourt,' said Talbot. 'He will be wanting to see your papers before the others arrive.'

As they passed the door of the reception room, Newell glanced in and saw several women callers waiting. Talbot paused there and made the brief announcement that the Dean would be occupied for a little while, but would see each of them later on if they did not object to a slight delay.

Then they went on until they reached the library door, which Talbot opened and, stepping aside, signed to Newell to enter alone.

The Dean's deep-set eyes smiled affectionately.

'I have been looking forward to this day, my son,' he said warmly, as Newell clasped the outstretched hand.

'And so have I, sir. It was a long winter – and an almost interminable spring.'

'Sit down, Newell. . . . You were wise to wait. It gave Phyllis a chance to keep faith with her people at the girls' school, and you stuck it out bravely with that fine fellow Stafford until he found a good man to replace you.'

Newell grinned reminiscently.

'I have often wondered how Stafford made connexion with you, sir. He speaks of you as his pal; says you went fishing together some five years ago.'

'I wish it might have been true,' said the Dean. 'And when do you begin your work at Parkway Hospital?'

'In September. The Board generously consented that I might have a few weeks before taking charge. It is fortunate for us. We have planned a trip. Doubtless Phyllis told you.'

'Yes – I had a visit from her yesterday. You are attending the Arlen-Norwood wedding in New York on Thursday and you sail on Saturday for England.'

'Phyllis wants to show me some things in London.'

'Saint Olave's Church, for one, I think.'

'She says you can hear the past – at Saint Olave's.'

'And the present and the future. You go there with her, Newell, and listen with Phyllis. If you hear what she hears, you may feel that you are almost worthy of her companionship. . . . May I see your licence now? They will be arriving any minute.'

Newell produced his precious papers and, standing close beside the Dean, laid a hand gently on his shoulder.

'I have been trying, sir, to think of something to say – something that might express at least a little of the—'

Dean Harcourt glanced up and smiled.

'I know what you feel, my boy. It isn't necessary to offer any resolutions of gratitude. I have been abundantly repaid by the happiness that has come to you both. Let's not try to talk about it.'

'You gave me back my life, sir.'

'Well – don't forget that our keen-witted Sonia had a great deal to do with that. Dr Endicott might have been a long time deciding to do his duty if it hadn't been for the – for the encouragement Sonia offered him. . . . Very good stuff in Endicott, after all. He came to see me afterwards. I regard that conversation as one of the most interesting events of my life.'

'I know I shall never live long enough to forget the interview *I* had with you, sir, the day you talked to me about the "Green Light".'

'You believe that now, don't you? You ought to.' The Dean searched Newell's eyes.

'I do, sir!'

'So does Endicott. Don't be afraid to talk with him about it sometime. He's pretty well posted on the subject – now that his health is so much better.'

The door opened and Talbot ushered in Phyllis and Sonia – Phyllis adorable in a silver-grey travelling suit touched with an enlivening bit of cherry, and a smart little hat involved in the same scheme; Sonia stunning in severely tailored black, so admirably expressive of her dashing type.

With affectionate smiles for salutations, they quietly gathered in front of the big mahogany desk and the Dean opened his liturgy. When the *I do*'s had been spoken and the rings exchanged and the impressive blessing had been pronounced, Newell took Phyllis in his arms. Then, reluctantly releasing her, he kissed Sonia tenderly and told her she was a darling.

'Listen to what old Saltus is playing now!' squeaked the excited Talbot, as the melodious measures of 'Oh, Perfect Love' fairly shook the air. Newell and Sonia beamed their recognition of the significant song, but Phyllis was occupied with a private conference she was having with Dean Harcourt, her arm about his neck and her lips close to his ear. She kissed him then, and rejoined Newell, who drew her very close. There was a moment's silence.

'Isn't it ever permissible,' inquired Phyllis roguishly, 'for the officiating clergyman to kiss the bridesmaid?'

Newell and Talbot joined in approving the playful suggestion, fully expecting the Dean and Sonia to accept the challenge without the slightest hesitation or constraint.

A barely perceptible wince of pain fleetingly clouded Dean Harcourt's brooding eyes as he drew a brief smile in response to Phyllis's question. Sonia's face was sober. After an instant of indecision, she went to him, stooped over him, and tenderly kissed him on the forehead. He took both of her pretty hands in his and, holding them for a moment against his deep-lined cheeks, pressed his lips on her fingertips. Not a word was exchanged, or a smile.

301

Talbot noisily cleared his throat and announced boisterously that it was high time to say goodbye if they were to catch their train. Sonia, quite herself again, followed them to the door, where Phyllis and Newell paused, arms tightly linked to wave farewell.

Then they were gone; and Sonia, slowly returning to the desk, responded to the Dean's quiet gesture and sat down opposite him.

Nothing was said for a little while.

'Well' – Dean Harcourt's voice was husky but attempted to be casual – 'it has been a good day's work.'

Sonia nodded, rather pensively, without looking up.

There was another extended pause.

'Well' – said the Dean again, quite obviously with no definite plans for the rest of the sentence – 'I suppose I should be letting you go now.'

Sonia nodded again, and began stroking a glove on to her slim fingers.

'There are some callers still waiting out there, I think,' he said gently, significantly.

She rose, pulled off her exquisite little black hat, and walked to the door of the dressing-room. Standing before the mirror, she toyed for a moment with the blue-black hair at her temples. He reached out his hand as she passed him, and she held it in both of hers, very tightly, her head bowed and her eyes closed. Then she moved away reluctantly.

It was five now, and Trinity's stirring theme song confidently confessed its faith – *O God, our help in ages past; our hope for years to come.*

At the door Sonia paused, her back pressed against it, her hand grasping the knob. The Dean's eyes were dreamily contemplating the Holman Hunt etching on the wall while he listened to the bells.

She stood there, her own eyes following his to the patient face in the picture, until the vibration of the last triumphant measure had begun to die away. Then she turned, and, softly opening the door, as softly closed it behind her.

Lloyd C. Douglas

Monica Dickens

The author of ONE PAIR OF HANDS

THE LANDLORD'S DAUGHTER   35p
Every page of this absorbing novel, which
ranges from the Depression days of the
thirties to the pop stars and 'dropouts' of
today, is richly and compulsively readable . . .
one of today's top selling authors, at the very
top of her form!
'Clever and highly complex murder story.' –
DAILY MAIL

THE ROOM UPSTAIRS   25p
'Here is a grim, relentless story, with touches
of the macabre, about a proud woman hanging grimly on to what is left of her well-
remembered past; a mad woman ready to kill
to preserve her peace of mind.'
                    – MANCHESTER EVENING NEWS

KATE AND EMMA   35p
Set in today's London, the story of two young
women whose friendship is doomed to tradegy
by social forces beyond their control.

THE LISTENERS   35p
This is a story in Monica Dickens' inimitable
style – salted with humour, and inspired with
love. 'A memorable and moving book whose
pathos and humour are expertly combined
. . . an enthralling story.' – WOMAN'S JOURNAL